AN M-Y BOOKS PAPERBACK

© Copyright 2008
Richard Hollands

A CIP catalogue record for this title
is available from the British Library

ISBN 978-1-906658-01-4

Published
by
M-Y Books
www.m-ybooks.co.uk

Cover by David Stockman & Simon Milner
davidstockman.co.uk

The Paradigm Shift

by

Richard Hollands

The paradigm is the way we perceive the world.

The paradigm explains the world to us and helps us predict its behavior.

Adam Smith 1975

A new paradigm puts everyone back to zero, so practitioners of the old paradigm, who may have had great advantage, lose much or all of their leverage.

It is the outsider who usually creates the new paradigm.

Barker 1992

Wednesday, 16th June 2008
Evening - Rub Al Khali, South Yemen

Luke Weaver crouched behind the rock observing the Bedouin camp below him. It was late evening and only the excited crackling of the campfire broke the peaceful tranquillity of the desert. In the darkness, he adjusted the lens on his night vision binoculars and magnified the red silhouettes of the Yemeni royal guards. They were obviously not anticipating any danger; they lay, in various states of repose, around the campsite. The sight did not surprise Luke; he had become accustomed to the poor state of readiness exercised by the Ruler's bodyguards.

Surrounding the campfire, there were six large 'Majilis' tents with their canvas flaps tied open to allow in the breeze. Beyond the camp, about one hundred yards further on, there was a makeshift corral for the camels and horses, which were tethered to palm trees on the edge of the small oasis. Little was happening down below so Luke lifted the binoculars slightly to scan the horizon. The light from the moon helped him make out the wind shaped dunes in the distance but there were no unusual signs of activity.

After he had satisfied himself that everything was as normal, Luke dropped the binoculars to his side and relaxed for a moment. He was positioned about fifty feet up a rocky '*Jebel*' mountain that offered a perfect vantage point to watch the movement in the Ruler's camp below. Turning around, and sitting with his back to the rock, he gazed up at the rising peak in front of him.

Luke Weaver was used to hiding undercover and working alone. Five years ago he had been hand picked from the SAS to work in special ops for the British Secret Service. Now at the age of thirty-seven, he was a veteran of the Gulf War, numerous SAS encounters and several clandestine operations for the British Government. This particular mission was distinctive in that it was more solitary and nomadic than usual.

In stature, Luke was a couple of inches over six feet with broad shoulders, a strong jaw line and classic good looks. His light brown hair, which had been blond as a child, was cut short around his ears in an army style. His strongest features were his piercing, blue eyes, which could be unnerving for those trying to meet his gaze for the first time. Dressed partially in combat uniform and partially in local Arabic attire, he had adapted to cope with the terrain and the weather extremes. His boots and green khakis were standard issue and functional, but above his waist he wore the white, ankle-length Arabic dress of the locals tucked into his fatigues. The evening humidity was high and exaggerated because they were stationed close to an oasis. After taking a drink from his water canteen, he removed the black, Arabic headdress that was wrapped around his head. During the day temperatures soared to over forty degrees, and he was grateful to the headdress for providing some protection against the heat and the sandstorms.

Right now he was miles away from England and he let his mind drift, closing his eyes and pulling the blanket tighter around his shoulders. He contemplated the recent events that had taken him to his present position on the rock face in the Yemeni interior, twenty-five kilometres from the Omani border.

Working for the British Government, on his previous encounter he had been forced to eject from a light aircraft just before it became a ball of flames, crashing into the side of a mountain in the Andes. Reports remitted to MI6 headquarters indicated no survivors and without any eye witnesses, operatives in Whitehall could only presume Luke had died in the crash.

In reality, it took Luke a long time to escape through the Andes and march back to civilization. When, months later, the opportunity finally arose he contacted Sir Thomas Boswell, the Head of MI6 directly.

Sir Thomas saw the opportunity that was presenting itself immediately. Luke was informed that for all intents and purposes he was a dead man, and that was how Sir Thomas wanted it to remain. Only a handful of senior, trusted MI6 executives were to know of his existence and he was requested to remain undercover whilst they established his new identity.

After two months had passed, the department processed his death certificate and carried out the final formalities although these were minimal. There wasn't even a requirement to inform his next of kin. His parents had passed away before he entered Her Majesty's service, and without siblings, his only remaining relatives were distant. Although some had briefly entered his life during his youth, he had lost contact with them a long time ago. A memorial service was held in his honour and all dossiers covering his military and government career were moved to archives.

That was over a year ago, and now he turned his thoughts back to his current mission and its objectives. Below him, inhabiting the six tents or 'Majlis' as they were known, was the ruler of Yemen, Sheikh Obaid bin Faisal Al Salah, accompanied by members of his family, his royal guard and an assemblage of very attentive menservants. The ruler and his entourage were spending a few days in the desert, hunting with their falcons, and enjoying the simple, traditional customs of Arabic Bedouin life that was part of their rich heritage.

The Paradigm Shift

Historically, Yemen had always been a trouble spot in the Middle East even dating back to the cold war, when, in the seventies, the country had been divided into the Russian supported north, and the British-American maintained south. Since the early eighties, the country had become re-united under the wise patronage and leadership of Sheikh Obaid. Acceptance from their wealthy Arab neighbours and the international community was slow in coming but through his perseverance, Yemen's own sovereignty was gradually re-established. Sheikh Obaid was given a seat on the influential Gulf Cooperation Council and further positive relationships were established with the western world.

Unfortunately, and a major cause for world concern, the rulership and continued succession of Sheikh Obaid and his descendants was in jeopardy. The diplomatic progress made by Yemen over the years was at risk. Rebel forces led by the outspoken Jumal Al Suweidi had denounced Obaid's right to rule, and had shown their teeth in bomb attacks on Foreign Embassies and by taking western hostages to publicize their cause.

Their leader, Jumal Al Suweidi, was dubbed the *'desert snake'* by the international media for his ability to vanish into the rocky terrain that characterized the landscape of Yemen's mountainous interior. The 'desert snake' was ruthless and showed no mercy in his quest for power and recognition. Even the international TV networks could not show footage of his more barbaric acts, as they were deemed too shocking for public consumption.

In one incident, he grabbed a ten-year old Swedish girl he was holding hostage and dragged her in front of the TV camera crew. While her captive parents watched screaming in the background, he jerked her head back violently and slowly slit her throat. As the vital fluid of life seeped down the young girl's

dress, he smiled at the camera with his manic, beady eyes and
licked the blood off his curved, Arabic dagger.

Luke had seen the gory recording as part of his MI6 preparation and the haunting look of terror on the girl's face would
never leave him. In disgust, he had sworn privately to avenge the
killing if the opportunity arose.

His assignment from MI6 was to stay concealed and protect Sheikh Obaid from attack by the rebel forces loyal to the
'desert snake'. The British Government knew that the death of
Obaid would knock the region back twenty years. Old border
disputes would re-surface and tension surrounding the access to
religious shrines of Islam would make war a real possibility.

In loud shows of public hostility, the rebels had raised border tension by announcing their commitment to redrafting the
lines of demarcation with Saudi. They wanted their share of the
oil reserves and the wealth that came with it. Unbeknown to
Sheikh Obaid, Luke had been watching over him for months
even residing undiscovered in his palace grounds.

Suddenly, Luke opened his eyes. His acute sense of hearing
was trying to separate the sounds of the night. He had heard a
sound similar to a small shower of shale running down the
mountainside above him. *'An animal could have caused it'*, he
thought to himself. Mountain goats were known to inhabit the
terrain.

For a few seconds he strained to hear it again, but all he
picked up was the groaning of the camels, and the sporadic
murmurs from the campsite below. Seizing his binoculars he
began scanning the rocky *Jebel* above him to his right. Luke saw
their 'glowing red ' images as the thermal imaging equipment
located their heat source and amplified it. The five armed

figures making their way cautiously down the steep rock face towards a small plateau.

Focusing, he could make out that two rebels were carrying weapons over their shoulders that looked like computerized, mini rocket launchers potentially capable of destroying the camp below with one hit. The hi-tech weapon was actually spawned from the US Dragon anti-armour device popular at the turn of the century. Furtively, he picked up his semi-automatic weapon and started to move quickly and silently across the rock face towards a large, jagged boulder that offered some rudimentary cover adjacent to the plateau.

He reached the rock at the same time as the rebels arrived at the plateau and he could hear their frantic whispers as they began setting up the two tripods ready for the composite alloy barrel of the missile launcher.

Although Luke had taken the precaution earlier, he re-checked his ammunition clip, and made a mental note to take out the three rebels standing behind the launchers first. The other two were in the process of squatting down behind the tripods making final preparations to fire the missiles. Unlike the revolutionists standing behind with their rifles at the ready, it would take them longer to react once he was in full view.

Just as he heard the leader give the signal to fire when ready, he took a deep breath and swung around the boulder to face the plateau from the side. With five rebels against him, Luke was relying heavily on the element of surprise.

His semi-automatic gun was fitted with a laser that cast a narrow, red beam directly on to the heads of the three agitators. Luke walked towards them squeezing the trigger as the red dot from the laser jumped to each successive target.

The remaining two holding the launchers stared up at him in horror as their comrades fell to the ground behind them. In front of them, on the tripods, were the very latest in modern weaponry yet around their chests hung the old ammunition belts of yesteryear. Looking up in shock, their long symbolic beards emphasized their fanatical way of life. They had no time to manoeuvre and although one clutched at the pistol in his belt, he was too late. They died instantly as Luke's gun fired twice.

Unfortunately, Luke was powerless to control the next sequence of events. The missile launchers were not actually fired with conventional triggers but by a control button. The control button was located on a miniature computer pad attached by a thin cable to the weapon's barrel.

As the nearest rebel fell against the tripod, knocking the barrel skywards, he landed on the button firing the rocket like a flare into the night sky. As it exploded harmlessly in the air, it lit up Sheikh Obaid's camp and glancing over the edge of the plateau, Luke registered the hive of activity below him. The ruler's guards were running in all directions, waving their rifles and screaming in Arabic as they passed each tent. *'It won't take them long to get organized'*, he thought before turning around to face the rebels he had just killed.

Luke looked down at the dead men as the light began to fade. As he considered his next move he saw something glitter out of the corner of his eye, and he reached down into his pocket for a packet of matches.

He struck it next to the face of the rebel that had caught his attention. It was the 'Desert Snake', his mouth ajar showing his bloodied gold teeth. In that instant, Luke realized his covert operation was complete. He gritted his teeth, the 'desert snake's' death would make some amends towards the ghostly apparition of the young Swedish girl being tragically butchered.

A noise behind him brought him back to his senses. He could hear the first wave of the Sheikh Obaid's royal guard clambering up the mountain behind him. They wouldn't catch him but he didn't want to take any chances. Keeping low, he scuttled back across the rock face to his supply pack. He looked back one last time to check his bearings and then started climbing upwards, over the summit and on towards the Omani border.

Three days later, Luke entered Salalah on the southern coast of Oman. His sand strewn, Arabian dress convinced the inhabitants that he was a Bedouin from out of town and he moved freely through the backstreets of the local 'Souq'.

Several months earlier, he had made escape preparations by hiding a package in the basement of the National Stadium on the highway to Muscat. The stadium was empty, as it was most of the year. Sultan Qaboos, who ruled the country from the capital city in the north, had commissioned its construction in the early 1980's. The building of the stadium was meant to symbolize his control over the Omani families in the south at a time when there were rumblings of a potential coup.

Luke had no difficulty in retracing his steps and breaking into the basement below the stands of the stadium. Once inside, he calmly pulled out a small, flat black case from the hole he had made in the foundations before heading back into Salalah.

That evening he accessed the internet and left an encrypted message on the prearranged page of a web site he had agreed with Sir Thomas Boswell. An additional package attached to the black case also contained currency and passports that he stored in his belt, hidden beneath his Arab dress.

The following day he re-entered the site and looked at his instructions. The sentence would be meaningless to anyone browsing, but to Luke it translated into a new set of geographical coordinates. Two days later he sat on the tarnished deck of a wooden dhow as it headed out of the Port of Salalah on its trading run to India.

Wednesday, 3rd August 2008
Afternoon - The Andaman Islands

The twin-engined Lear jet circled the Islands in the Indian Ocean before commencing its descent. The weather was reliably good at this time of year, and through the clear skies, Balan Krishnamurthy had a picturesque view of the beaches surrounding the Andaman Islands below him. The flight from Orissa on the east coast of India had taken just over an hour and apart from the pilot, he was the only passenger aboard the government owned executive aircraft.

Balan was fifty-five years of age and a long-serving, pillar of the Indian Government. A man of medium height and build, he rejected his country's traditional dress in preference to the well-cut suits he had made for him by from his Piccadilly tailor. His half-moon spectacles rested on his nose and with his full head of greying hair, he gave the appearance of a well-educated, scholarly man who automatically commanded respect among his fellow statesman.

Balan was well known in international circles. Earlier in his career he had been India's representative to the United Nations, and before that he had held the prestigious posting of Indian Ambassador to the United States.

However, over the past eighteen months, his career had changed course at the insistence of the Indian Prime Minister. As a consequence he had taken the difficult decision to forego the luxuries of a western posting and resettle on Indian soil. After spending the previous fifteen years abroad serving the Government loyally as an eminent diplomat, he returned to Delhi as the second most powerful man in India; he was the

Special Envoy and Chief Advisor to Krishna Banerjee, the Prime Minister of India.

Seeing the view outside the window, Balan removed his reading glasses and replaced the papers he had been examining back in the leather wallet on the table in front of him. Across the hillside, he could see the lush green tea plantations from which the Andaman State Government derived most of their income. The intercom buzzed and he heard the pilot announce that they would be down in about five minutes.

Continuing its steady descent, the plane was not landing at the Islands main airport but at an infrequently used landing strip on one of the outer islands. The location had been chosen as a meeting place specifically because of the need for secrecy.

Partially due to neglect, and partially due to the rarity of flight traffic to and from the island; the runway had been allowed to fall into a state of disrepair. Despite this the experienced pilot still negotiated a comfortable landing before taxiing down the runway towards a dilapidated, two-story wooden building. They had arrived on one of the 'Nicobar' islands.

Normally, the area surrounding the runway would be deserted, but that was not the case today as the pilot made the last manoeuvres before bringing the plane to a standstill. Sitting down, close to the runway's grass verge, were two enormous, black military helicopters circled by uniformed soldiers positioned in a defence formation.

The pilot of the Lear jet opened the door and the ladder of five steps dropped to the ground. Balan Krishnamurthy stooped below the door's frame as he made his exit down the steps and crossing the tarmac, entered the derelict building, its door being held open by one of the armed guard. Inside, the room showed its decay, window panes were cracked and there were pieces of broken furniture lying on the floor amongst the dirt and the rubble.

Out of the shadows in the corner, stepped a man wearing the uniform of a high-ranking military officer. The rows of ribbons and the gold braid that lined his jet-black tunic left no doubt about the General's seniority. As he continued forward, his face came into view, and he broke into a smile as he stretched out his hand to greet his old friend.

"It's good to see you again," said the General, as Balan took his hand and they embraced each other warmly.

"My leader has asked me to convey his personal regards to you," continued the General as he stood back.

"Thank you General, please tell him that I look forward to returning his greetings in person one day."

Still smiling, the general motioned towards the door with his outstretched palm.

"This building has decayed more than we thought, and the air in this room is unpleasant, why don't we walk outside?"

"I agree," said Balan making his way back to the door.

Balan had convened the meeting in a hurry, and the information available on the runway had been scant, but at this stage of his Prime Minister's plan, security came before comfort. He was glad to escape the needless darkness and dust of the shack for the afternoon sunshine outside. Passing the armed guard surrounding the helicopters, Balan and the General strolled towards the grassy field that lined the fringe of the runway.

"Balan, we are impressed with the way you have escalated tension along the border without incurring interference from the US and the United Nations. It would seem everything is progressing according to your leader's plan?"

Balan looked across at the General. Since their countries had cemented their pact, they had met regularly over the previous months carrying the instructions of their respective leaders.

"So far, the only problems we have encountered have been with the underground storage reservoirs, but that is behind us now," replied Balan remembering the wrath of his leader at the minor setback.

The engineers and government officials, tasked with the construction of the gigantic reservoirs, had met with an array of unforeseen problems. As a consequence, they had been summoned to a meeting with the Indian Premier, Krishna Banerjee to explain the barriers to the project's completion.

After ten minutes of listening to the self-imposed bureaucratic hurdles, Banerjee's irritation with proceedings exploded and the senior government official on the project was taken away by the Indian Secret Service for questioning.

Ashraf Nawani was the Premier's trusted lieutenant in charge of the notoriously brutal Secret Service known as 'RAW' because they operated from the government department called the 'Research and Analysis Wing'. Everyone in the meeting understood that 'questioning' was a euphemism for torture. This man would probably not see his family again, and the remainder cowered as they were told that failure to meet the deadline would mean life imprisonment in Nawani's custody.

"Everything else has gone according to plan, we're eight weeks away from commencing the final step of our strategy," Balan confirmed, and watched the General nod his head in acknowledgement.

Balan was pleased. He was meticulous in detail to the point of obsession. It was one of the traits Banerjee saw in him early on when he was singled out for high office and promoted above his envious contemporaries.

He glanced sideways at the General. "It is imperative that no links can be established or traced between our countries...later on this won't be so important but the longer we can maintain secrecy the better."

This would be the last time they would meet before the plan was put in action. The General looked back at him; the words were unnecessary but he had become accustomed to Balan's need to make a pronouncement on every aspect of the plan.

"That is clearly understood, remember we too have much at stake," the General responded sharply revealing his mild irritation.

His tone softened as he realized that Balan was seeking further assurances.

"Be assured Balan, my country will remain loyal to our pact.....once the plan commences we'll observe the protocols as agreed."

As the sun began to fade in the late afternoon, they continued walking along the grassy path discussing the finer details for their 'modus operandi' in the coming months ahead.

After two hundred yards they turned and headed back towards their aircraft parked in front of the dilapidated building. Balan noticed that the helicopter blades were already rotating in slow motion as they prepared to leave.

"Have you brought the documentation for me?" Balan asked as they approached the steps to the Lear jet.

The General smiled and snapped his fingers towards one of his subordinate officers who immediately rushed forward carrying a leather case.

"Please go ahead and check it," the General said, pulling out a folder and handing it over to him.

Balan unzipped the side and peered in at the bound document. Quickly he flicked through the papers until he saw the signatures of the General's Prime Minister with the country's seal stamped across the page.

"I am satisfied," he closed the case, and smiling, held out his hand. "This world will be a different place when we next meet General."

"I look forward to meeting you in that *New World*," returned the General.

He had to raise his voice over last few syllables as the noise of the helicopters blades vibrated louder behind him. Releasing his two handed grip on Balan's outstretched hand, the General turned, and dipping slightly, hurried away beneath the helicopter's blades.

Balan watched as the door to the military helicopter was slid open and the General climbed inside. The last two armed soldiers followed him on board. Seconds later, one after the other, the helicopters with the bold red ensign on the side, lifted off the ground, and headed out over the mountainous skyline towards the sea to the north.

'Ten years ago nobody would have given credence to the theory that our nations could ever become allies', mused Balan, as the helicopters disappeared over the line of trees on the hillside.

Holding the folder, he turned and mounted the steps to the Lear jet. Minutes later he was airborne and reading the contents. His next task was to prepare himself for a meeting with his Prime Minister, Krishna Banerjee.

Thursday, 30th September 2008
The Pentagon, Department of Defence, Washington

In the Operations Centre at the Pentagon the red pulse flashing on Officer Davies' computer screen signalled an incoming message. She typed a response from her keyboard and the encrypted message was ready for translation. In spite of the fact that deciphering messages was part of her regular daily routine she was feeling the strain. Her colleagues around the room watched on anxiously as she set about breaking the encryption.

The Pentagon building itself was originally built during the early years of World War II and this room was the nerve centre for monitoring all overseas threats to the national security of the US Government. Under the supervision of the CIA it was also responsible for handling the joint covert activities of the US military intelligence services.

Apart from the occasional surprise training drill, in real life, it was extremely rare that the Operations Centre reached this high state of alert. The panel at the front of the room indicated that they were one step away from putting the United States on full nuclear standby. Officer Davies endeavoured to clear her mind of all extraneous thoughts and focus solely on the task at hand. Behind her stood, Colonel Dan Schwartz, Head of Overseas Intelligence.

"Source, Davies?" Schwartz barked before spinning around to locate his Communications Officer.

"Source Amber confirmed, Sir," Officer Davies replied, continuing to race through the encryption sequences on the terminal in front of her.

"I should have authentication in 90 seconds"

The tension was palpable as the full compliment of Intelligence and Communications Officers, sat at their stations and waited in anticipation. They each controlled military defence functions that could be activated on the command of Colonel Schwartz.

At a glance, the Operations Centre for Overseas Intelligence resembled the theatre used by NASA in controlling the US Space Program. It was similar in size and had rows of computer terminals descending in banks towards the front of the room. At the back of the auditorium was the bridge where Colonel Schwartz was standing issuing orders as he tried to anticipate the next development.

The outstanding feature of the room was the enormous digital computer screen at the front exhibiting an outline of the world map. The projection, built with the very latest technology, was connected to an array of satellites surrounding the globe and could be magnified to pinpoint real images on any given geographical grid reference.

"Ok, hook me up to the Director and the National Security Advisor," Schwartz commanded his Communications Officer.

He issued the directive whilst continuing to stare at the chart on the screen below him.

"I'll take this conference in my office," he finished as the junior officer turned on his heels to establish the connection.

At that moment, the computer screen was not connected to the satellites. Instead the digital display highlighted the troop movements in the disputed Jammu & Kashmir region of northwest India. In different colours, the computer image also identified the key military establishments of the hostile nations along the border with Pakistan.

The Paradigm Shift

The escalating tension in the region had been widely reported in the media over the previous months. Today's headlines confirmed that the third attempt by the United Nations to impose a peacekeeping force had again ended in failure.

'Done it' thought Officer Davies and she hit the print key, ripped the sheet printing the message from the panel to her right and turned to face the bridge.

"Message authenticated, Sir."

Schwartz took the paper and headed down the corridor towards his office, reading the message on the way. In view of the recent events he was not shocked by what he read but the ramifications were menacing. As he closed his office door a voice came through his intercom.

"Colonel Schwartz, I am connecting you to Director Conway and Security Advisor Allen, you are on a secure line"

The line crackled before Michael Conway, Director of the CIA came through loudly on the speaker.

"Are you confirming what we feared, Dan?"

Both the Director and Jim Allen were together at the White House preparing to meet the President.

"I am afraid so Mike, I have an authenticated message from Agent Amber confirming that India have activated their nuclear warheads and are preparing to launch an attack. The Agent states the attack is imminent."

"Ok Dan, myself and Security Advisor Allen understand the message. Maintain full surveillance and I'll speak to you after I've seen the President."

Thursday, 30th September 2008
The White House, Washington

President Whiting was in the third year of his first term in office. His strong Republican and family roots were firmly embedded in his home state of Montana where he was the third generation Whiting to achieve high office. Although state and national politics ran in the family blood, he had disappointed his father in his youth by envisaging a career outside the senate.

In his college days he had been a promising quarterback and was tipped as a potential star of the future before an injury cut his playing days short. The event made him rethink his future and he elected to continue his studies by reading law at Yale University. The young David Whiting was not a natural achiever in the world of academia but he knew how to apply common sense. After his freshman year, he joined the debating society and his political birthright began to show through. His competence was in assessing the demands of people quickly and addressing their individual needs in terms they understood.

He was fifty-two years old now and looking back, he found it difficult to understand why he had ever questioned the decision to enter politics. On reflection, he put it down to the natural rebellious adversity of a son being compelled to take a path against his will.

It was over two years since his election campaign had taken off in the New Hampshire primary when he made his speech supporting strong family values. Gifted as a public speaker, the media intensified their coverage on the Republican candidate from Montana as he swept up the women's vote.

The election's outcome became inevitable when the exit polls confirmed his commanding lead after the series of televised debates against the Democrat front-runner. The media applauded his statesmanlike performances, and with his wife Pam at his side, the country swore in the new President of the United States.

After building his team he contrived to maximize the advantage of his honeymoon period in office; the economy required rebuilding and tough decisions were taken to restore ebbing confidence levels. The initial years at the White House were hard but President Whiting drove himself harder. His popularity with the people remained strong as they watched his enterprise and commitment to some of his grander campaign promises.

As he walked from his Oval Office down the corridor to the meeting room he knew that these domestic issues palled into insignificance compared with the decisions he was about to face now.

"Are we all here?" the President asked as he entered the room. Two security guards held the double doors open for him and swung them shut behind him.

Around the long boardroom table, six men and two women rose to their feet as he ushered them with his hand to remain seated.

"All present, Mr. President," replied his Chief of Staff, Catherine Dennison.

She had served and supported the President well over the twelve years she had known him. Her integrity and ability to handle the pressure had quickly earned his respect. Catherine was a tall woman of about five feet ten inches, and slimly built. She looked every piece the *'media world's'* version of a smart woman executive wearing a dark blue skirt and matching jacket that made the lines of her shoulders appear stronger with the subtle padding. At the age of forty-two, she was attractive and still single.

Catherine had not deliberately avoided marriage. Over the years several admirers had come close to her but in the end, the relationships petered out or turned into friendships as her devotion to the job, and the long hours, took precedence. She looked after herself well and was fortunate in keeping her youthful complexion. Her hazel brown hair was not quite shoulder length and elegantly styled by her regular hairdresser.

Apart from Catherine Dennison, around the table were the members of the Executive Committee of the United States of America. The President took his seat at the head of the table and to his left sat Vice President Martins alongside the US Secretary of State, Margaret Henderson. Next to her was Vance Warner, Defence Secretary and then Jim Allen, National Security Advisor and Michael Conway, Director of the CIA.

On the President's immediate right sat Catherine who was flanked by the three most senior Commanders of the US Military Forces: General Graham, Air Marshal Reiger and Admiral Downey.

"Mike, for the benefit of all, can you repeat our earlier conversation?" the President looked up inquiringly.

All the faces turned to the other end of the table where Director Conway of the CIA was sitting with his hands clasped on the table in front of him.

"Of course, Mr. President," he replied nodding his agreement. "As you are all aware, we have been monitoring the increasing hostilities in Jammu & Kashmir. Until yesterday our satellite surveillance indicated that the escalating tensions were of a conventional nature, something we've seen before and not an issue that marked the situation down as a possible threat outside the region. Indian ground forces were threatening to cross the heights into north Pakistan, air cover was being provided from military bases in the East Punjab…we've monitored similar patterns in the past."

Director Conway paused to emphasize his next point.

"Since then, however, the situation has deteriorated substantially with India provoking a nuclear confrontation. We are now in receipt of intelligence confirming that two mobile nuclear missile launchers have been moved to the mountains of Himachal Pradesh. Our reports indicate that these weapons are being prepared for a direct nuclear attack on the cities of Islamabad and Lahore. If we…."

"We…" the President interrupted him loudly in mid-flow. In the momentary pause that followed the faces switched back towards the head of the table.

President Whiting took off his reading glasses and put down the memo he had been reading on the inlaid mahogany surface.

"We…" he continued, "have a grave situation that could impact on the national security of the United States. I would like to take all your assessments before I decide on our Government's response and initial course of action."

Pausing, he looked pointedly at Director Conway, "Would you like to start by actually sharing your views with us?"

"Mr. President, the hostilities over Jammu & Kashmir have been around for decades. There have been many minor skirmishes in the past that have resulted in a regular flow of casualties and losses on each side; both governments have been vocal with their constant rhetoric over the rights to the disputed territory although neither will tolerate third party arbitration or UN intervention."

Director Conway was aware that the President wanted him to update the others quickly so he made a mental note to summarize matters as succinctly as possible. It was his Agency's views that would form the subject of their debate not the history lesson.

"However, it has been generally accepted by my office and I believe that of the Secretary of State's…" he looked down the table at Margaret Henderson, "…that the war of words has been a political tool used by the Pakistani and the Indian Governments to boost their sagging popularity."

For many years, India and Pakistan had expended huge sums of money supporting the conflict. Repeatedly, lives were lost as the death toll rose due to the mountainous terrain of the highest battlefields ever seen by a military campaign. Troops were stationed on opposing plateau's of the 'Siachen Glacier' which soared over twenty-two thousand feet above sea-level, the freezing temperatures reached minus sixty degrees centigrade in the rarefied atmosphere, adding to the number of fatalities.

Secretary of State Henderson nodded her concurrence as Conway continued to make his point.

"By focusing on the disputed territory and increasing nationalist tension the governments are able to rekindle loyalty amongst their people and their supporters by demonstrating a hard line against the alleged transgressor."

Director Conway hesitated for a second as he collected his thoughts before voicing his own opinion.

"Sir, as I see it, this situation today is different; the current regime is the first non-coalition government since the independence of India in 1947. The Congress Party lead by Prime Minister, Krishna Banerjee is popular by Indian standards and the area of Jammu and Kashmir has no underlying intrinsic or strategic value."

The eyes around the table focused on him intently as he reached his preliminary conclusions.

"I would respectfully suggest, Sir, that the objective behind a nuclear attack on Pakistan must be considered to have wider implications than just recapturing worthless land and superfluous electioneering....it has to be an intentional act meant to destabilize world peace....the problem is right now, we don't know what the ulterior motives are or what Banerjee's future plans could be."

"The Indian Government must know that a nuclear attack would generate a counter nuclear offensive from Pakistan, so something looks seriously out of place?" injected General Graham with a degree of irony in his voice. "We need to know why they feel they have the upper hand this time."

He was not amused at the way this crisis had developed over the past twenty-fours and he partially blamed Director Conway's office. He had been in similar situations to this before and he was still not convinced that the whole situation was any more than filibuster and 'chest-beating' on the part of the Indian Government.

The President took the views of the General seriously. He could be outspoken over sensitive issues but his experience and knowledge of tactical warfare were beyond question. The ribbons on his military dress bore testament to his distinguished career in the field before he was earmarked for high office by the powers that be on Capital Hill.

He was a 'dogged' character, well respected throughout the rank and file. He was considered the army's leading expert and spokesman in the theories of nuclear engagement. As part of his constant brief to educate the officers below him he frequently toured the major military establishments giving lectures covering the latest debates and the well-catalogued arguments supporting the facts.

The driving thrust of modern times was that the bomb's potential for destruction was the main reason that peace, for the most part, had been maintained since the Second World War. However, it was not a theory he subscribed to, and one day he knew it would be extinguished when someone pressed the button.

"You're correct in your assertions General. You must note that the power base of the Indian Government is extremely small." Director Conway continued, turning to address his remarks to the President.

"Krishna Banerjee has been in office for just about a year and, despite his public comments that he is the leader of the largest democracy in the world, he has promoted all his friends and close family members to key cabinet positions."

"Are we dealing with someone rational here, Mike?" The President interjected.

"I am afraid we have an incomplete profile, Sir. We know very little of this man prior to his rise in politics five years ago. His actions in that time suggest a strong autocratic style of leadership, but give no indications of irregular behaviour."

Defence Secretary Vance Warner leaned forward placing his palms on the table. "I think we must assume the following: either they know that Pakistan will retaliate and are prepared for the consequences or they are calling Pakistan's bluff."

"This could be correct, Sir," opined Director Conway. "Although we have monitoring the nuclear testing carried out by

Pakistan, we have reason to believe their detonations may have
been elaborately staged. Our information is patchy on this, but if
we have our suspicions then so could RAW, the Indian Intelligence Service."

"What are you suggesting?" asked the President, incredulous that he was hearing this theory for the first time.

On the table in front of the Chief of Staff, Catherine Dennison, sat the communication server that linked the President to
all the major government installations during times of crisis.
Before Director Conway had a chance to reply the computer
console started flashing. The accompanying buzzing noise sound
signalled that it was holding an incoming call.

Catherine Dennison read the name on the digital display
facing her.

"Sir, I have Colonel Schwartz on line from the Pentagon."

President Whiting nodded at Director Conway to take the
call.

"Go ahead, Dan, you are through to the President."

"Two nuclear missiles have been launched by India, Sir.
Their flight path confirms our information that they are heading
for Islamabad and Lahore. We estimate that they will reach their
destination in fifteen minutes."

The comment was met with stunned silence from all in the
room. After a few seconds it was broken by Catherine Dennison
acknowledging the message and terminating the communication.

The President stood up and looked at the faces around the
table before he fixed on the three senior commanders of the US
Armed Forces.

"Gentleman, take your status to full alert, I would like a full
brief on our armed capabilities and presence in the region at the
earliest possibility."

Turning to his Secretary of State, "Margaret, use your diplomatic channels, I need to know all there is to know about this Prime Minister Banerjee immediately."

The President stood up to leave. As he marched towards the open doors with Dennison and Allen close on his heels, he stopped and abruptly spun around.

"Mike, do you mind waiting, there are some additional matters we need to discuss?"

The laconic tone of the President left no one in any doubt about his displeasure. Director Conway nodded his agreement and President Whiting continued in the direction of his office.

Down the corridor he could be heard barking instructions to Dennison to connect him to the Prime Minister of Pakistan if it was still possible. Turning to Security Advisor Allen, he asked him to prepare an immediate brief on the stance to be taken by the Government.

The President had some calls to make. He knew he would have to deal with the media soon, but it was essential that he took the counsel of their main allies before they combined in their united condemnation of India.

Friday, 1st October 2008
The Prime Minister's Residence – Lahore, Pakistan

The residence of Pakistani Prime Minister, Abdul Wasim Latif, was in reality more akin to a Summer Palace. The main façade of the house was decorated with inlaid marble and the grounds included man-made lakes that had been added as a new feature during the Bhutto dynasty.

In the mid-nineties, under Latif's instructions, the Government had constructed underground facilities within the walls of the residence but away from the main house. In contrast to the decorative opulence of the Summer Palace the bunkers were basic and functional. The facility was constructed to withstand a nuclear attack and maintain the survival of a wartime government for several months. Built on five layers, the self-contained site had its own Communications Centre in addition to its own Engine Room, controlling the generators and water supplies.

New rooms had been bolted on to the original infrastructure over the years. Originally it was designed to support fifty-five lives but with the additions it could cope with an extra ten. As Prime Minister Latif sat, three stories below ground in the Communications Room, he was informed that the head count had just reached ninety-six.

"Impact is imminent, Prime Minister," shouted the anxious voice of one of his leading army officers and a distant family member.

Those that were lucky enough to have gained access to the bunker started to brace themselves for the force that was about to descend. Outside the door, Latif could hear the screaming children and mothers. In their haste to seek refuge in the bunkers some families had become separated, and in the most awful cases, the guards at the entrance had been forced to choose between sons and daughters for the right to gain entry.

The Prime Minister knew the extent of the catastrophe facing his country. He also knew that he had let his people down. Under his guidance, he had deliberately orchestrated a plan to misguide his people and the world, as to their real nuclear capabilities. Latif knew in his own mind that his government was finished and he could expect little assistance from his fellow Islamic neighbours.

The problem had started for Prime Minister Latif in 1999. The Indian government had carried out nuclear tests that had been widely condemned by the civilized world as a threat to stability in the region. At the same time the Indian army had become more vocal about its successes on the heights of Kashmir. The effect had been to whip up the patriotic fervour of India's common people to such an extent that many states witnessed mass demonstrations burning the Pakistani flag and celebrating the 'one-up-man-ship' of owning the bomb.

Against this backdrop of Indian euphoria, Prime Minister Latif had to act quickly to pacify the growing unrest amongst his own people. He needed to demonstrate Pakistan's counter measures and their commitment to retaliate in the face of a real threat. Latif immediately strengthened the forces alongside the disputed border, and gave orders to the military, that no transgression would be tolerated on the ground or in their air space.

The nuclear defence program had been on going in Pakistan for sometime, but like many Government research projects it suffered from constant funding withdrawals. When Latif had first learned through covert operations that India was considering testing, the Prime Minister had requested an internal status report on their own progress. He found to his alarm that his own Military Commanders and Chief Scientists could not confirm a future date for their own nuclear demonstrations.

Apart from condemning the nuclear tests of India, the world media began speculating on whether Pakistan truly had nuclear capability and would produce replica trials of its own.

The Prime Minister was cornered, trapped in a catch-22 situation, under pressure from his own people and the glare of the media spotlight. He had no choice but to go on record and confirm their own nuclear capabilities.

It was at this juncture that Prime Minister Latif had given his approval to a contingency plan that had been prepared by his military for just such an eventuality. The strategy was known to only a handful of top government officials that were loyal to the Prime Minister.

Indeed, it was his Defence Minister sitting across the table from him in the bunker who had been responsible for the initial approach. He had made contact with the 'third party' which was willing to assist them in their hour of need. In confidence, Prime Minister Latif was offered an expensive solution to his mounting problems.

The 'third party' confirmed they could use their own resources and equipment to activate two nuclear tests within *'six weeks'* provided they were granted open access to the existing test sites in the Thar Desert. In return for guaranteed secrecy and anonymity, the price extracted for their expertise was colossal. It was a risk. Even though the finances of the Pakistani Government were not known for their transparency, the Prime Minister knew the size of these payments would be difficult to disguise.

The international media kept the nuclear issues at the top of the world's agenda by constantly asking, *'which nations really had the capability? Would the sanctions now imposed on India be a deterrent to Pakistan testing?'*

The expectations that Pakistan would test drew a highly publicized call from President Whiting's predecessor in the White House. He spoke to Prime Minister Latif personally and suggested that the US would wipe out billions of dollars of Pakistani debt if they refrained from going ahead with the tests.

For reasons unbeknown to the former President, the call was misguided. It served to further magnify the world's focus on the mounting tension between the two countries and ultimately heap further pressure on Latif in the face of his own people.

In the end, the decision was made and the 'third party' carried out the tests on Pakistan's behalf in five weeks instead of six. The aftermath saw Pakistan succumb to the same ritual as India. Internationally, the counter tests were widely condemned by the United Nations, sanctions were imposed and countries united to admonish Pakistan for their inflammatory and immature response.

At home the scene was very different; Prime Minister Latif was praised for restoring his country's pride and the status quo between India. The huge population of Pakistan attached little credence to the trade embargoes and the international rhetoric as the nation witnessed jubilant celebrations across the country.

In the months that followed, Pakistan's existing nuclear program received no additional funding. The burden of meeting the instalments to the 'third party' saw to that.

In the bunker, Latif could hear the voice counting down the final seconds to impact. The explosions shook the world. Both missiles landed within seconds of each other whilst most inhabitants of Lahore and Islamabad were sleeping.

The Paradigm Shift

It was merciful that most of the population near the epicentre did not really have time to question what was going on. Most felt the thunderous shaking before the waves of destruction, gusting with mass radiation, shot out, turning over buildings and leaving death in its wake.

The detonations sent up black clouds in the shape of mushrooms similar to those seen at Hiroshima in the Second World War. The bunker survived the explosion but over ten million Pakistani Muslims did not.

Friday, 1st October 2008
The White House, Washington

"Come on in Mike," said the President holding the door open to his office.

As he returned to his desk he asked his Chief of Staff and National Security Advisor if they could continue their discussions later when their findings were complete. As they stood up to leave, the President flicked the remote controlling the large television screen in the corner. CNN had responded quickly to the calamity by tracking the scenes in a light aircraft. With insufficient regard to their own personal safety, the reporter and his team flew perilously close to the radioactive debris in the pursuit of ground breaking live footage of the bomb's devastation and the carnage that was taking place before their eyes on the ground below them.

The President stared at the screen as the camera zoomed in on the dead and dying, calling out for help. He clicked the remote again and the coverage disappeared. The images, committed to memory, were atrocious, and could never be switched off so easily.

"Mr. President, we have intelligence reports that Indian Armed Forces are amassing along the border with Bangladesh in West Bengal and Assam," said Director Conway.

"I see...no response or retaliation from Pakistan yet?"

"No response at all...we have been monitoring all known nuclear sites and previous testing areas and there has been little or no activity. We know that Prime Minister Latif and key government officials are occupying a nuclear bunker just outside Lahore."

"So it's not a question of no leadership then is it Mike?" the President plainly stated the obvious.

Although outwardly he appeared composed, he was secretly fuming about the earlier revelation that Mike Conway had a notion that Pakistan's tests had been faked. Events were conspiring to support this theory.

"No Sir, if they had retaliatory means then they would have used them by now."

President Whiting trusted Michael Conway implicitly. They had been friends for many years and their wives had also become close. In fact, he himself had been responsible for Conway's elevation to Director at the CIA, not long after he took office. However, right now the President was struggling to remain calm.

"Why wasn't I told that those nuclear tests were bogus? Why did I have to wait to hear it in that meeting?" The President gave up trying to disguise his annoyance.

"It was speculation Mr. President, we had only discovered the possibility ourselves in the last forty-eight hours and we did not have any evidence to support the theory. In hindsight, Sir, we should have made you aware of our suspicions earlier"

"Damn right you should have!" the President shouted irritably.

Standing up, he moved around his desk and sat leaning up against the front. As a semblance of peace was restored he decided it was time to make his position crystal clear.

"Mike I appreciate the information was new and unproven but I need all the facts in front of me, however vague, do you understand? How else can I make the right decisions?"

"Understood, Mr. President. The Agency is doing all we can to uncover who has been assisting Pakistan with her nuclear testing and I will keep you regularly updated with the progress. In this day and age it is not just the major super powers that carry the technology but even some of the larger corporations."

President Whiting nodded; he had made his point and wanted to move on. "Now what plans do we have to deal with this situation?"

Director Conway opened a plastic wallet in front of him and studied the document on the top before continuing.

"The damage has been done, Sir, we cannot undo what has happened…..right now we need to prevent future destruction and remove the threat….we know that all commands in India are given by Krishna Banerjee and if we remove the head then the body will collapse."

"Are you are suggesting that we assassinate the Prime Minister of India?"

"I am Sir, we have one specialist Agent undercover who could complete the task."

The President paused to think through the repercussions. "Where does this leave us with regard to world opinion, how will governments react knowing that we have deliberately killed the Head of a supposed democracy?"

"At the moment, I think the world will be so appalled at the tragic loss of lives caused by this one man that it will be seen as a positive and necessary act. However, I concur that if and when the situation returns to normal, there could be a significant backlash on the US for our unilateral action."

The President frowned, "What are you suggesting?"

"I am suggesting that we carry out this operation in conjunction with one of our NATO allies, in this way any post mortem reveals the decision and subsequent operation was not ours alone."

"Do you have plans for such a contingency?" he asked curiously.

The President's reservations with the proposition began to wane as he imagined a joint initiative.

"I have been in touch with MI6 and subject to receiving approval from Whitehall and the PM, they are willing and in a position to assist us in such a assignment. For your information they have one of their most highly trained special agents in the field now."

The President folded his arms across his chest as he took a minute to contemplate the governing factors of Conway's proposal.

"Ok Mike, I am going to speak to the British PM and give my approval to the mission but I want to be informed of developments this time is that clear?"

"Understood, Mr. President," Director Conway stood up replacing the plastic wallet in his leather case and made towards the door.

"Oh, one last thing Mike, is this man of ours good?"

"It's a *she*, Sir, 'Codename Amber', one of the best, it was her that first alerted us to the missile strike."

The President nodded and reached for the phone as Director Conway left his office, "Get me the British PM."

Friday, 1st October 2008
MI6 Building, Whitehall

The Head of MI6 had a large oak-panelled office on the eighth floor with views stretching over Parliament Square and Downing Street in one direction and Admiralty Arch and Trafalgar Square to the north.

Sir Thomas Boswell was a career spy. He had joined Her Majesty's Government straight from Cambridge University in the early sixties when the enemy was communism and the Cold War was building momentum. As a young recruit, he had worked in the field and his aptitude and talent had been recognized early on by his superiors. On more than one occasion he had put his life at risk for his country.

Since the middle 1980's he had learned to adapt better than most as the role of MI6 underwent significant changes. He took the helm in the autumn of 1989, and through the nineties constructed a highly efficient outfit. This was despite the fact that the number of field officers in service had fallen to below half the level of that when he first joined. The Agents that remained benefited from using the latest technology and the new recruits, as Luke Weaver would testify, underwent rigorous induction and training programs.

The main headquarters of MI6 was situated about a mile away on a large site located on the south bank of the Thames. Sir Thomas maintained offices in both buildings but preferred using the more informal and private surroundings of his Whitehall office when conducting 'face to face' meetings.

The intercom on Sir Thomas's desk buzzed and his secretary came on the line.

"I have Commander Tremett in reception, Sir"

The Paradigm Shift

"Good, please show him in and organize some refreshments for us," he replied. Whereas his vision and concepts of intelligence gathering were firmly set in the present, his mannerisms and speech still very much belonged to the old school.

The secretary opened the door and showed in Commander Mark Tremett.

Sir Thomas paced across the silk carpet to shake his hand.

"Hello Mark, nice to see you," he said affably.

"Why don't we sit over here where it's more comfortable?" and he indicated towards two couches facing each other in front of a large Jacobean fireplace.

"Good to see you too, Sir Thomas."

"Mark, I'll get straight to the point. I am pulling you off your current assignment because the new chain of events has given rise to precedents. I believe your current project can be put on hold until further notice, is that correct?

Commander Tremett was caught off guard with his comments relating to his current operation. An invitation to Sir Thomas's office always meant that the subject matter was important but he had anticipated questions regarding his involvement rather than his retraction from the project.

Frowning, he considered the implications of what was being asked of him. He knew Sir Thomas would also have considered these issues beforehand and in reality the question was construed purely for his voluntary consent.

"Yes Sir, I can delegate sufficient responsibilities if I know how long I am going to be pulled off?"

Without knocking, his secretary entered carrying an ornate handled tray with full silver service. Sir Thomas dismissed her as she began to pour the tea and took over the task himself.

"Indefinitely is the answer I'm afraid…" replied Sir Thomas handing a cup and saucer to Commander Tremett.

"Since the Indian Government has decided to launch its fireworks, I am afraid our priorities have gone out of the window."

Sir Thomas took a sip of tea. It was a brand he had specially imported from an old colleague of the Service who had decided to spend his retirement years on a plantation near Colombo in Sri Lanka.

"Mark, I want you to run point on a special operation we're about to commence. We will be working closely with the Americans and your credentials 'fit the bill' admirably. Your counterpart in US Intelligence will be Dan Schwartz whom I believe you know well and our field agent will be Luke Weaver…whom I believe you also know quite well?"

Sir Thomas smiled as he left his last question hanging. He knew the reaction he could expect from Tremett. Weaver and Tremett had been good friends together in their early days with the Service.

"Luke Weaver – *Christ!*…I thought he was dead," exclaimed Commander Tremett with a look of sheer disbelief on his face.

"He is very much alive although there are only a handful of people who know it. I understand that you were a good friend of his, and with what we have in store for him, he will need all your help and experience over the next few weeks."

"What's the assignment, Sir Thomas?"

Commander Tremett had regained his composure. After some of the deeds he had carried out on behalf of Her Majesty's Government he thought he was shock proof but the latest revelation about Luke had put paid to that.

"Luke is currently undercover at a Hill Station in Maharashtra. He is to meet up with an American Agent and with your help, their joint mission is to terminate the Indian Prime Minister, Krishna Banerjee."

Commander Tremett nodded his head slowly.

"Whose authority?" he questioned.

"Authority is from the PM himself," replied Sir Thomas. "Remember this is a joint operation and I want to be kept in the wheel at all times. I suggest you might like to start by contacting your old friend, Dan Schwartz, and figure out between you, how you're going to get the Agents together."

Commander Tremett replaced his half-finished cup of tea on the saucer and stood up to go. The urgency was implied, any member of Sir Thomas's inner circle would recognize the innuendo in his closing remarks

"I'll get on it right away Sir Thomas."

The Head of MI6 accompanied him to the door.

"Good luck," said Sir Thomas as he shook Tremett's outstretched hand.

"My secretary will give you a folder with all the information you need, remember Mark, keep me posted."

Saturday, 2nd October 2008
The White House, Washington

During a morning appointment, Chief of Staff Dennison and Security Advisor Allen had brought Vice President Larry Martins up to speed on the decisions made in their earlier meeting.

As Catherine Dennison pointed out, the President was keen to have a 'one to one' meeting with his deputy later that day. Since politics remained important even during a crisis time, the President had personally wanted to take a 'time-out' to explain his decision to approve the CIA's covert plan to assassinate the Indian Prime Minister.

The meeting lasted no longer than twenty minutes, and as he hoped, he received the approval of his Vice President. President Whiting was left feeling slightly bemused that the backing of his deputy hadn't been as forthcoming or as whole-hearted as he had anticipated. He himself didn't take the decision to commit his Administration lightly but these circumstances were abnormal.

In the end, he put Vice President Martin's reaction down to political caution. He knew his running mate was ambitious for office himself one day and the stance he had taken would give him a potential 'get out clause' if the mission blew up in the Administration's face.

Larry Martins was forty-seven, five years younger than the President. Their paths had crossed on numerous occasions before he was selected by the Republicans to run alongside the President. Their constant companionship throughout the fiercely fought election campaign had really tightened their bond.

The Paradigm Shift

President Whiting respected his younger understudy as an excellent sounding board and he used him as such during the run up to the live televised debates against the opposition. To the annoyance of his advisors, he frequently by-passed them and presented his thoughts directly to Martins for his initial reflections.

After the Vice President had left his office, President Whiting again contemplated the steps he had taken in approving Conway's proposal. He was totally at ease with his decision to authorize the covert retaliation against India's act of war, particularly so knowing that his chief European Ally fully endorsed the project.

Apart from the joint CIA/MI6 operation, he felt strongly that a vocal condemnation of their action was not enough. There must be a combined display of military unity between America and NATO but *'how big a display?'* The Indian government had shown that they were prepared to use the bomb, so what good were conventional war tactics? If they decided to go down this route, what was in the way of India launching a strike at the US?

One thing President Whiting felt sure of; if this madman Banerjee was prepared to launch a strike killing millions of people, then he had no limits, he was capable of anything. Regardless of any international diplomatic repercussions, he had to be stopped.

In hindsight, it now seemed conclusive that Banerjee had knowledge that his Pakistani enemy couldn't fight back. The President considered this element for a minute. The information must have been supplied to him somehow and this could implicate another supposed nuclear power or ally. In any event, the President made a mental note to be cautious with his trust and watch his allies for any hint of muted condemnation.

He paused to look over the schedule prepared by Dennison detailing his appointments for the rest of the afternoon. Next on the agenda was the meeting with his military commanders who had already been granted entry into his office. The three heads of America's armed forces were huddled in conversation when the President motioned for the meeting to begin. Also present in the Oval office were Jim Allen, Defence Secretary Vance Warner and Vice President Larry Martins.

"First of all I would like to understand our capabilities in the region?" the President began.

Admiral Troy Downey was the first to speak. He was a tall, silver-haired man in his early fifties wearing full naval uniform. As he commenced his dialogue, they all took their seats in the comfortable lounge chairs in the centre of the Oval Office.

"I have diverted our newest sub, the *'Indomitable'*, to the Bay of Bengal. It should be in position the day after tomorrow. As you know, it has full nuclear capability with four warheads all with a range in excess of 1,000 kilometres."

"What else?" responded the President tersely.

"We are moving the Aircraft Carrier *'USS Missouri'* through the Straits of Hormuz towards Maharashtra on the West Coast of India."

Air Marshal Walter Reiger interrupted his colleague.

"Before it reaches this point I have organized a rendezvous off the coast of Sohar in Oman. Five hours ago, a squadron of twelve USAF F16 Phantoms J Class departed from Fort Lauderdale, they are being refuelled in the air and should reach the carrier by early evening. Each Phantom is armed with two nuclear strike weapons."

The Paradigm Shift

General Magnus Graham was an outspoken army man. As those around the table anticipated he would, he seized the opportunity to speak up for the ground forces under his control.

"In terms of total strike capability, Sir, we have one hundred and twenty land based nuclear missiles in our silos that have the range to reach the Indian sub-continent."

"Good, now what about the capabilities of India?" the President said looking across at his National Security Advisor.

In Washington circles, Jim Allen was known as a highly intelligent, articulate man who did not waste words. He had served in the Army Intelligence Corps and the CIA earlier in his career. His networking through the ranks was now paying dividends. He had access to a vast databank of invaluable connections both at home and abroad.

"To the best of our knowledge, India does not have the ability to make a direct strike on the US. They do not have the technology to construct a medium capable of carrying a nuclear war head."

"Well, that's one bit of good news!" No one missed the irony in Vice President Larry Martin's voice.

"I'm afraid that this shouldn't give us false comfort Vice President." Allen continued, "as far as I'm concerned, this attack on Pakistan could have been planned for months. If that's the case and they intend to attack the US then they have had sufficient time to place nuclear weapons in neighbouring territories or even smuggle in the components to make a bomb on our home soil."

"What's their current nuclear strength Jim?" asked the President.

"We believe they have between two and four nuclear warheads remaining with a range of one thousand kilometres. These are only capable of being launched from land based sites and most likely from mobile carriers."

The President sat pensively for a moment before addressing his next point.

"If someone representing another country has passed on information regarding Pakistan's faked nuclear tests to Banerjee, couldn't they also supply him the technology to carry the war heads within range of America? The President asked Jim Allen.

"That could well be the case Sir, but if it is then we need to talk in different terms because I believe India will not be our chief threat….it will be those providing their ammunition!"

"I understand Jim…I want to take no chances and leave no stones unturned. We must satisfy ourselves that no threat exists to our citizens. I want you to speak to the FBI, and organize a full investigation into the possibility that undercover parties working in collusion with the Indian government are already here in our backyard. Use my Office's authority with Immigration and Customs if necessary."

Jim Allen nodded ringing a small note he made on the pad in front of him. President Whiting had his own firm views on the measures the US government should take but now was a time to seek the opinions of his experts.

"Now what is our counter offensive, gentlemen?"

For the military in the room this question had been at the forefront of their minds since the bombs had gone off. The President was aware that whilst he had been engaged in other matters the executives of his Armed Forces had been meeting regularly to discuss nothing else.

"Our advice, and we are in total agreement on this," said Defence Secretary Warner looking around at the serious demeanours of the military men. "Is that we should issue an unequivocal statement to Prime Minister Banerjee and his Government that the United States will not tolerate the future use of nuclear weapons."

Vance Warner had chaired the committee meetings with the military and Jim Allen had also been in attendance. The debate had ranged from instant conventional or nuclear reprisals to sitting back and waiting until Banerjee's true intentions were known.

"In our response, we must make it abundantly clear that we do not hold the common people of India responsible for these atrocities but their leader. We should try and invoke a democratically constituted nation to see the devastation that's been caused and overthrow the mass murderer, Krishna Banerjee."

Vance Warner had the President's undivided attention as he summarized the key conclusions arrived at by the committee earlier in the day.

"We must also make it clear that Banerjee should be in no doubt…" he forcibly emphasized the words *'no doubt'* again. "…That if their government prepares for further nuclear activity, then the full might of America, including all nuclear resources at our disposal, will be used to disarm the Indian threat to world peace."

The President's gaze went towards the Oval Office windows. He was thinking about the anti-nuclear protesters who had already started campaigning outside the White House railings, fearing there would be a nuclear backlash from the US. The thought faded and his focus came back to Vance Warner's statement.

"I am in agreement on this point Vance. I want you to speak to your opposite number in Britain and obtain his Government's formal views on our position. If you are satisfied that they are broadly in line with our own, ask them if they will coordinate the views of their important European neighbours."

President Whiting thought about requesting Vance to discuss sanctions with his counterpart at the same time but then thought better of it. The priority had to be presenting a united front in their potential utilization of a retaliatory nuclear strike. The diplomatic channels of the Foreign Office could take care of the sanctions.

"Ok, I intend to speak to the Nation at midday tomorrow so keep me informed of your progress." The President turned to face Jim Allen. "What is our position if India goes ahead and tries to occupy Pakistan and Bangladesh?"

"As in previous campaigns, we will form an International Alliance with Europe and fight a conventional war to prevent India's military from advancing. At the moment, we are trying to establish who is currently in command of the Pakistani forces and what their capabilities are, if any. Through the Alliance we will support and supply the local resistance but at this point it is not suggested that we will deploy ground troops."

"Ok, let's finish it there for the time being, gentlemen." The President's mind was clouding over with tiredness but a late afterthought came to him.

"Jim, where are we up to on the Space Defence Program?"

The US Space Defence Program was constantly in the headlines with speculation on its progress and whether or not it could actually work. The previous month's copy of Time and Newsweek had both ran the issue on their front cover carrying so-called expert opinions on what the future had in store.

"Shall I go ahead and organize the presentation you wanted, Sir?"

The Paradigm Shift

"Yes, do so, and Catherine…don't let it slip towards the end of my diary, with the developments of the past few days I need to know what we've got." The President cast a tired smile in her direction as they got up to leave.

Sunday, 3rd October 2008
New Delhi, India

In stark contrast to the fear and terror that had descended on the rest of the world, the ordinary people of Delhi and India celebrated the victory over their enemy.

Since early in the morning, the main Indian TV networks and radio stations continually played a pre-recorded announcement by the Indian Prime Minister rejoicing in their hour of triumph. To the outside world that could not imagine the depth of India's hatred towards its neighbour, the sight of jubilation in the streets made a macabre spectacle.

Krishna Banerjee projected an imposing figure unlike some of the frail looking, Indian leaders of the past. He was six foot tall with fair skin except for the dark patches below his eyes. He presented a statesmanlike appearance and looked elegant in his *'churidhar kurta'*, the traditional Indian dress. His white, cotton shirt was loose fitting and worn outside a pair of baggy trousers that were tapered to a tight fit around his ankles. Over the shirt he wore a smart silver tunic that was like a thicker waistcoat with a short stiff, upright collar. On his feet he had a pair of open toed sandals.

In the broadcast to his Nation, the TV showed just his head and shoulders as he sat staring rigidly at the camera in front of him. He had a long, oval shaped face with a high forehead etched with the lines of age, and his thick, grey hair was set in a permanent parting. Prior to the recording, the make-up artists had tried to disguise the fierceness of his glare by toning down the dark skin patches below his eyes.

The TV appearance was brief, lasting no longer than ten minutes. He started off with a small history lesson for his people reminding them of their 'birthright' to the lands under dispute. In the same glorious vein, he then proclaimed that Bangladesh, previously known as East Pakistan, and indeed Pakistan itself, were sub-states of the true India. They had been allowed independence for too long and the fact that they threatened their own mother country was intolerable.

Krishna Banerjee spoke with exuberant passion as the camera panned back to show him sat behind a desk in his residence. The symbolic flag of India was draped in the background for all to see.

With the hostilities and tension rising in Jammu and Kashmir, Banerjee told his people they had been left with no choice. *'What alternative did we have?'* He said waving his arm across the air. *'Pre-emptive action was our only option. It was in the best interests of our people and the future security of our country'*.

He finished by praising the work of the Armed Forces and promised to address the people personally at an open-air meeting in Delhi later that day.

That recording had been made earlier and it was now time for Banerjee to deliver the promised address. At a convenient site in Connaught Place, in the centre of Delhi, a platform was built from where Banerjee could command the attention of his people and the television crews that were invited to the exhibition. A crowd approaching four hundred thousand gathered around the stage and then filtered back over the straight, two-mile stretch of Mathura Road.

The elation and noise from the thronging crowd gathered in intensity.

Krishna Banerjee had carefully planned this moment for months. He knew that this speech would be shown live around the world and repeated several times for the benefit of prime time television.

Banerjee's media organizers had made sure that all the major global TV networks were present. They were given security, VIP treatment and premier positions from which to film their coverage. They were making history, as it was said later, this speech was watched by over four and half billion people.

The huge speaker system was tested and the feedback brought new waves excitement and sound as the crowd began to anticipate the arrival of their leader. The stage was enormous with a red awning and tiered seating at the back for all the senior government officials. In the centre was a large elevated podium.

From the platform you could see the thronging sea of brightly coloured people who filled the square and then beyond down the wide tree-lined avenue. All the buildings in the crescent surrounding the stage and down the main arteries off Connaught Place were full of revellers on the roofs, balconies and leaning out of windows.

Along with the rest of the world, the White House watched the show unfurl as the crowd chanted with the noise reaching fever pitch.

The officials on the rostrum rose from their seats and applauded as Krishna Banerjee walked on from a purpose built entrance at the side. The cacophony of sound that greeted his arrival was deafening. He walked up to his most senior cabinet members and exchanged greetings with them in the traditional Indian manner by putting his palms together as if in prayer and bowing his head simultaneously.

After completing the formalities, he climbed up the stairs of the podium and arranged some papers before looking out at the mass of people in front of him. The crowd's noise was still clamorous when Banerjee raised his hand to ask for silence. Like a wave running into shore, the tone changed as silence rippled from the front of the gathering making its way to those who could hardly see at the back.

"My people…this is a great day for our country and the dawning of a new age. Together we will claim our true rights and unite the lands of India."

His voice boomed out over the speakers that had been stationed at regular intervals.

"My people…the world will try and condemn us for the action we have taken…they will impose sanctions on our country and say that we have brought disharmony to the world."

The crowd's noise abated slightly as they hung on to his every word.

"My people…to those leaders, and to those nations which condemn our actions I say this…"

"Every country has the right to self defence in the face of a threat to its lands and people…did America not launch two nuclear bombs to defend its lands and people against the threat of Japan?"

It was early morning as President Whiting, watching from his White House office, grimaced at the reference to America's nuclear past.

"My people…we are the largest democratic country in the world, we have a population over one billion, we have the strongest growing economy, our advances in technology exceed all other nations…."

Each phrase was marked with the exulted roar of the crowd's excited approval. He paused for effect as the crowd chanted in patriotic fervour.

"…And now our time has come for our people and our country to accept its destiny as the true leaders of our Mother Earth."

The noise filled the TV sets as people around the world reacted in astonishment to his words. Banerjee's face contorted with concentration as he shouted with excitement into the podium's microphone.

"Our people, our Indian countrymen are scattered in communities around the globe…in some quarters they lead industry, in some quarters they number many, and in some quarters, like the states of the Middle East they are slaves suffering at the hands of the ruling few."

Then came the real bombshell as he gazed into the cameras of the world media.

"To our people around the world I say this…now is our time. Arise for your country and throw away the shackles of oppressive dictators and false democracies….Do not accept the condemnation the world puts at our door for defending ourselves in the face of grave danger….but join together, with the support of your nation, and take your rightful place as part of the family that will rule the world."

The gathering screamed their approval. He looked at them, waiting for the crowd's hysteria to abate slightly, before raising his hands to calm the people so he could speak once again.

"My people in New York and America…my people in London and Europe… my people in Africa and Johannesburg…my people in the Middle East, in Riyadh and Dubai…I ask you to support your nation in its time of need and help us fulfil our destiny."

The Paradigm Shift

He waved to the shrieking masses as he took his time leaving the podium and walked across the stage to accept the plaudits of his subservient ministers.

Everything had gone according to plan and as the cameras followed Krishna Banerjee's final wave to the crowd, he knew the next few days would prove vital to his stratagem.

Sunday, 3rd October 2008
Calcutta, West Bengal, India

Codename Amber sat watching the poor reception on her television set. She was staying in a secluded old farmhouse in the Bengal countryside to the southwest of Calcutta. The two-story, brick farmhouse was small and compact with low ceilings. It drew its water supply from a local tributary of the Hooghly Delta that converged with other rivers, into the Bay of Bengal.

In spite of the fuzzy picture, she could still clearly hear the words of Banerjee's speech as he incited the hysterical Delhi crowds to greater levels of excitement.

Her real name was Kirin D'Souza and she was descended from a catholic family that had lived in Portuguese Goa on the West Coast of India. Her grandparent's generation had immigrated to America in the 1930's and notwithstanding her Indian ancestry, this assignment was the first time she had set foot on Indian soil.

Kirin was thirty-three years old and quite tall at five feet nine inches with a slender, graceful figure. Watching the television from a makeshift couch, she wore an all in one jump suit that hid her curves but there was no mistaking her natural beauty. She had a perfect, light-skinned complexion with hazel coloured eyes and a laughing, radiant smile that completed her striking appearance. Her black hair had been long but was now cut to a length just below her ears. She had developed a habit of every now and then, sweeping one side back behind her ear before it would fall again naturally back to the side.

Contemplating what she had just heard, she got up and stretched while walking over to turn the television off. She was tired. She had arrived at the farmhouse that morning after two weeks trailing the mobile missile launchers in Himachal Pradesh. Her training had prepared her for the hardships of camping in the mountains, but she was pleased to be back under solid shelter.

Kirin had been an employee of the CIA for the last eight years, serving in the Special Ops Division for the past three. She had always had a strong sense of adventure and enjoyed the outdoor life. When she was an undergraduate she had won a place on an expedition to the South Pole with a team of scientists and explorers from Canada. The experience reshaped her horizons and to her father's consternation, she made up her mind that she could not settle into an office style career.

After studying Cantonese at St. Louis University in Missouri, she had applied and accepted a position as a translator with the US Government's Foreign Trade Department in Washington DC. The Department ran several overseas trade missions to China, and she would accompany the delegation, assisting them as their interpreter, as and when she was required. On one particular trip she encountered Tom Leiberwitz, who unbeknown to her, worked for the CIA, masquerading as the Trade Commissioner on the US Consul General's team in Beijing.

Leiberwitz recommended to his superiors at Langley, Virginia that she should be considered as a new recruit for her language skills and knowledge of the internal workings of the Chinese government. At the George Bush Centre for Intelligence as it became known after the passing of the 1999 Intelligence Authorization Act, the CIA researched her background and gave her a clean bill of health. She was initially offered a desk job as a researcher at Langley, which she accepted with the promise of advancement if she excelled in her training and handled her job well.

After two years in the position, she gained a level of trust and respect that saw her given small roles in various domestic assignments. Kirin continued to do well and her training record surpassed the regular benchmark set for new recruits.

Consequently her superior officers decided to see how good she really was and they watched quietly from the side, as she was sent undercover to work alongside members of the infamous Triad Gangs in the New York Ghettoes. The slightest suspicion that she was part of a clandestine operation would have resulted in her immediate death. The assignment culminated with the arrest of several notable Chinese warlords and the success took her into Special Operations.

The closing remarks of the speech made by Krishna Banerjee had been aimed at her, and the millions like her around the world who could trace their roots back to India. Her lines of ancestry were slightly more distant than most and she considered herself American through and through. However, Kirin was not typical and she knew it. For most Indians living abroad the links and bonds with their country were far stronger, and having seen the spirit of the Delhi crowds, she wondered whether Banerjee's words could incite them to rise in support of their homeland.

During her earlier years training with Special Operations, she was candidly informed that her background would make her suitable for potential assignments on the Asian continent. Her acknowledgement of the fact was followed by a four-month spell at college where she was taught to read, write and speak Hindi. She quickly became proficient, partially from her strong aptitude for languages, and partially from a basic grounding she had been given by her mother in her formative years.

Her Commanding Officer on this mission was Dan Schwartz, a man she had worked with before and for whom she had a good deal of respect. Kirin's latest instructions informed her that she was to join forces with a British Agent and assist him in infiltrating the security surrounding Banerjee's residence. The message confirmed the objective was to eliminate the Prime Minister and also included a time and map references for her rendezvous with Luke Weaver.

She recognized that the coordinates were close to the farmhouse and she took out a detailed map of the area to pinpoint the actual locality. Spreading the map on the table, she traced a line with her finger down the contours of a hill to a small lake about eight kilometres away. The meeting place was on the north shore of Lake Bala and she carefully began planning the route she would take in two days time.

Sunday, 3rd October 2008
White House Press Room, Washington

It was the US President's turn to make his Government's views known.

The White House pressroom was overflowing with reporters and cameramen eagerly waiting in anticipation of his arrival. Security was tight and their passes were all highly visible, hanging on chains around their necks. The chattering faded as Catherine Dennison, the Chief of Staff, approached the lectern with the American eagle crest on the front, and spoke into the microphone: *"The President of the United States."*

President Whiting was followed onto the platform by Vice President Larry Martins who struck a respectful pose with his hands clasped together behind the podium.

"Citizens of the United States, I come to you at a grave time. In the past few days we have witnessed a nuclear attack that has killed and is still killing millions of innocent lives. We have also seen and heard the Indian Prime Minister account for his decision as an act of self defence."

At this juncture, the President had wanted to inform the people of America and the world that the US Government believed that Banerjee knew all along that Pakistan had no means of nuclear retaliation. However, he had been persuaded not mention it at this stage by Jim Allen. Currently it was only conjecture and the press would pick up on it immediately requesting proof of the President's assertions. President Whiting had backed down quickly when he understood that, if the statements couldn't be substantiated, it could enable India to take the political high ground. The ensuing rhetoric and debate that could follow would work in India's favour, detracting from the real message the President wanted to get home.

"The actions of Prime Minister Banerjee's government have served to create unprecedented levels of tension in the world and destabilize a peace that has existed for over fifty years."

The President appeared calm and composed in front of the cameras, but as he continued reading from the autocue, his natural speech making ability combined with his real sense of injustice, to give a more impassioned performance.

"The United States will not stand by and allow the actions of one nation to pose a threat to world peace. I want to make it clear and go on record to say that if the Indian Government threatens *further nuclear activity* then I will order our military to take whatever steps are necessary to nullify that threat, and that includes the pre-emptive use of our own nuclear capabilities."

Although Vance Warner had cleared the US stance with the majority of their Allies in Europe, he had also returned with feedback for the President that wasn't palatable to their position. Certain Nations were known to be hostile to the United States and could be counted on to be antagonistic whatever the circumstances, but more alarming was the reaction of some countries they had perceived as being on the friendly side of neutral.

These countries were worried by the strong attitude of the US Government feeling a gung-ho, knee-jerk reaction was in the offing that could only serve to escalate the situation further. Other leaders were simply unsure how to interpret India's actions. *'Were they really acting in self-defence? Was Banerjee's incitement to his people a reflection of his fear that India would now be attacked? What further nuclear capabilities did India have and how would Banerjee respond again if threatened by the US?'*

What Defence Secretary Warner found most distressing was the fact that despite the barbaric and inhumane bombing by India, several fringe Nations continued to regard America as a self-appointed, 'trigger-happy' policeman capable of leading them to World War III.

Prior to the press conference, the President had spoken personally to his Russian counterpart in Moscow. Whiting had briefed the Premier on the contents of his speech and the response had been both courteous and supportive. Nevertheless the Russian Leaders level of support had stopped considerably short of outright approval. Concerning the proposed Western Alliance to support a conventional campaign he offered Russia's full backing, but he could not give any assurances for the US position on a "pre-emptive" strike. The pragmatic Russian leader was reserved, he did not want to over commit at such an early stage.

"What constitutes *further nuclear activity*?" asked the Russian leader, "does moving a warhead from the West Coast of India to the East constitute nuclear activity?" The question was meant to go unanswered but the suggestion highlighted the Russian concerns.

In the end, President Whiting told the Russian leader that he felt there was no alternative but to make an unequivocal statement of intent. He reiterated the US view that the strong retaliatory nature of his statement could not be made with such effect at a later date.

However in keeping with the President's desire for improved détente with Russia and as a gesture that he appreciated his counterparts concerns, he suggested two alternative ways forward.

"Either you can send a senior and trusted executive to travel to Washington to accompany our surveillance team at the Pentagon or alternatively, we can agree to keep the phone lines between our Ops Centres open as a constant link."

They both agreed that the former was the preferred option and the Russian Premier agreed that he would nominate a senior intelligence officer in the next couple of days.

In the Press Room, before the full auditorium of reporter's, the President continued his statement. He turned to address the plights of Pakistan and Bangladesh.

"We understand that since the nuclear strike on Pakistan, Banerjee now proclaims this country and Bangladesh as territories belonging to India….the United States, in line with the recent ruling by the Supreme Council of the United Nations, does not, and will not accept this… we, with the our European Allies and friends in the United Nations, will not allow India to subjugate these independent nations….we will combine and coordinate our military forces to prevent this from happening…"

The President approached the end of his address. The speech was designed to be succinct to really drive the main point home. In addition, he wanted to inspire the US citizens watching that his Administration was fully in control of the situation. He approached the end of his efficient performance continuing to give the impression of a confident government at the helm.

"Millions of Pakistani people are suffering the outrageous consequences of this scandalous and shocking act. I am advised that the disease and famine that will follow in the wake of the bombs will account for many more lives before this country's horror comes to an end."

He looked up towards the back of the hall.

"The United States pledges three hundred million dollars in immediate aid, and gives the promise that there will be more to follow…we will do all we can to help alleviate the suffering of these innocent families."

The President took a step backwards and Vice President Martins, nodding sagaciously behind his shoulder, began clapping as he uttered the final words of his speech. The applause spontaneously grew around the rest of the room. Above the clapping, several reporters at the front of the hall tried to shout questions as the President stood back from the lectern.

Catherine Dennison approached the microphone.

"I'm afraid we are taking no questions today ladies and gentlemen, I will of course keep you informed of the President's next statement, thank you," she finished. Behind her, the President left the platform talking to Vice President Martins.

Monday, 4th October 2008
World Response

When the two twenty kiloton bombs landed on Islamabad and Lahore, the first impact of the detonation was a blinding flash, so brilliant that it instantly destroyed the eyesight of those unlucky enough to witness the impact. Any subsequent realization of loss of sight by these unfortunate souls was momentary, as the explosion was followed by a surge of phenomenal heat killing all in its wake. Minutes later came the blast as the shock wave spread from the epicentre, collapsing buildings and throwing up debris miles into the atmosphere. Everything and everyone within ten miles of the epicentre was obliterated. Anyone in the open fifteen miles beyond this radius suffered third degree burns, while properties were demolished for up to thirty miles out.

Across the civilized world, when people heard that India had launched two nuclear weapons against its neighbour there was total disbelief and horror that such an event could actually take place. In the numbing aftermath, constant television transmissions showed the disturbing and gruesome pictures. The cold reality abruptly set in, and earlier incredulity gave way to shock, panic and fear.

In most of the major cities, the populace took to the streets to remonstrate with the barbarian actions of the Indian Government. People were angry and frightened; the decades of peace and stability since the Second World War were now being threatened.

On news channels, the televised scenes of chaos and suffering in Pakistan were intermittently interrupted to show the growing crowds of vociferous, anti-nuclear protesters marching in various corners of the world.

From poignant candlelit ceremonies in Scandinavia, to the sorrowful faces painted with the international sign of peace in New York, the camera crews beamed the distressed and dejected sentiments around the world. Film clips were shown of landmarks such as the Arc De Triomphe standing in a sea of people as they circled the monument with their banners and slogans. In Australia, news headlines showed pictures of Sydney Harbour Bridge crowded with angry young protesters. They set fire to replica nuclear bombs and threw them off into the bay below under the watchful eyes of the police escort.

At the same time as the television stations, the world's tabloid press covered the grief and suffering with unrelenting journalistic license. Some of the photographic imagery used in the papers was too shocking. Newspapers showed pictures of parents cradling their dead children, and 'barely alive' forgotten souls, lying by the roadside dying slowly from radiation poisoning. The suffering was pandemic as families around the world cried for the desperate plight of the Pakistani people. The overriding fear amongst the world's populace was that more nuclear bombs could be launched in the near future. The sensationalism of the press did little to allay their fears.

On the television, seismologists and meteorological experts gave their opinions on whether the explosions would cause a shift in the world's axis. New theories and fears surfaced that the ensuing shifts in temperature could result in the ice caps melting, and the subsequent rising water levels would herald a return to the next Ice Age.

Across Europe the backlash against the Indian communities was severe. In Germany, demonstrators selected the homes of prominent Indian businessmen and set fire to them whilst the occupants were away. In the beginning just one or two cases of premeditated arson were reported but after a few days the misguided retribution spread through the lowlands and into France and Spain. The casualty list began to grow but it still paled into insignificance compared with the rioting taking place throughout Britain. It was no longer safe to walk or travel through the Indian heartlands of England. Sporadic outbreaks of violence towards the Indian communities broke out across the country and they retaliated fiercely. In Bradford, Luton and the Greater London suburbs, nightly rioting became the norm. The police imposed curfews but with little success and the army was called in to the major centres to take and maintain control.

The British Government condemned the racist actions of the organized gangs that terrorized the Indian neighbourhoods. Many of the Indian casualties were themselves second and third generation British passport holders.

The fighting and antagonism had a completely detrimental effect on the way the communities felt about Banerjee's 'call to arms'. Before the attacks from their fellow countrymen, many of the Indians would have wavered and possibly rejected the overtures of Banerjee. The story changed when they witnessed the malicious attacks on their loved ones. It served to polarize their families and communities forcing them to believe that Banerjee was really speaking the truth.

In other parts of the world notably New York and Johannesburg the riots were not as frequent but just as hostile. Camera crews in South Africa transmitted pictures of youths running in waves towards the shield-holding police whilst they hurled petrol bombs into the streets beyond.

Apart from the scenes of violence being shown regularly on the news, a considerable amount of airtime was also devoted to the diplomatic repercussions.

As was to be expected, all international airlines had immediately ceased their flights into Pakistan, and then shortly afterwards, into India itself. Bangladesh was promptly added to the exclusion zones in the aftermath of the speech delivered by Banerjee in Delhi two days earlier.

The planes of India's international airline, 'Air India' gradually returned to the domestic airports having completed the return leg of their outward journeys. No new flights were permitted out of the country and the 'out of service' runways at Bombay, Bangalore and Delhi soon filled up, acting as parking bays for the international fleet.

The only traffic that left Indian airspace was the international evacuation flights carrying foreign residents home. Under the rigid control of the military and the watchful eye of the Indian Secret Service, Embassies were closed, and foreign workers who lived in India, were repatriated. At the same time, the returning Air India fleet brought many of their expelled diplomats home.

In contrast to the overseas flight schedule, the internal service offered by 'Jet Airways' continued without disruption. In fact, Banerjee had been extremely thorough in planning for his countries ostracism from the rest of the world. He had already anticipated the troublesome areas where sanctions could take hold, and had made provisions for that eventuality. As a result, it was business as usual for all the providers of energy and the essential public services. Under his direction, preparations had been thorough, and there was minimum disruption in the daily lives of most his appreciative Indian subjects.

Monday, 4th October 2008
The Prime Minister's Office, New Delhi

The air-conditioned office of Krishna Banerjee was a testament to the British colonial style of the late nineteenth century.
The room was the size of a tennis court with a white, flecked
marble floor, a high ceiling, ornate cornicing and dark wooden
panels climbing from the floor to a wooden ledge just over half
way up the wall. On the walls above the ledge, hung large,
coloured engravings of historical battle scenes and religious
artefacts.

The Gandhi dynasty was well represented amongst the
memorabilia. In the centre of the room stood a large bust of
Ranjiv Gandhi, and on the wall behind Banerjee's desk, was a
collage of framed, black and white photographs. The individual
pictures, and settings with other world leaders, portrayed Indira
Gandhi and more famously, K. Gandhi, before he was bestowed
with the title Mahatma.

On the room's exterior wall, there were four large windows
with wooden shutters pinned to the outside brickwork. The
latticed glass panes provided plenty of natural light. Between the
middle windows was a set of glass double doors that lead out
onto a balcony overlooking the gardens.

The Prime Minister's desk was at the far end of the room
away from the entrance. In the middle was a long, marble
topped, meeting table that had seven St Louis IX carver chairs
positioned along each side.

Krishna Banerjee walked into his office with his trusted
lieutenant, Balan Shirish Krishnamurthy, followed by the ever-
present, attentive 'Indian peon' wearing the black uniform of a
servant, including waistcoat and bow tie.

With a dismissive wave of his hand, he dispatched the peon and marched over to his desk and began flicking through his latest communiqués.

"Well Balan, what did you think of his performance?"

Banerjee made a direct reference to the Press Conference given by President Whiting earlier that day.

"It is as we anticipated, the American President is weak, he will not launch any counter offensive, they are still struggling to understand our motives," he replied.

In stark contrast to the traditional dress worn by Banerjee, Balan removed his suit jacket and hung it over the back of one the Louis IX chairs.

The one uncertainty in their plan had now been resolved without any hitch. They knew that America would take the lead in the aftermath of the bombs, and they had therefore deliberated all the potential outcomes.

One line of thought was that the US would decide to order an immediate nuclear riposte, another was that they might simply commit to a scaled down conventional attack. A nuclear attack was considered extremely unlikely given all the repercussions the United States would then have to face from the international community. Alternatively, a conventional attack, or attacks, would probably be just as unlikely. The US would be too concerned that India's irrational Government may further impair world peace by launching another nuclear warhead.

In the end, an attack failed to materialize and as the President's speech confirmed, India would only be subjected to a nuclear retaliation if they persisted in using their own nuclear capability.

Standing behind his desk, Banerjee hypothesized to himself, that if they did nothing and just claimed self-defence against

Pakistan, then he and his country would probably get away with mass genocide and the obliteration of their Islamic neighbour. Of course his country would be under sanctions for years to come and they would be ostracized from world events and politics, but eventually, they would be forgiven and re-accepted back into society as the German nation had been on two occasions before.

However Banerjee's aspirations were much bigger than the destruction of his neighbour, this was just the sideshow before the main event. He saw a future where India would be the leading superpower of the world and they would control the forums that dictated world policies on foreign affairs and economic policy. In his vision he saw a subservient America reduced to a nation dependent on India for its survival and he, Krishna Banerjee was the leader who would take them there.

"You see how difficult it is for the US President, Balan? Maintaining international protocols and the burden of world opinion makes them a tiger with no bite."

He pressed his intercom system and his private secretary came on the line.

"Please send in General Gupta," he commanded before turning To Balan.

"I am looking forward to hearing about the fruits of your work in the Middle East but let us speak to the General first, it is important we continue the military momentum."

The door opened and General Vijay Gupta entered wearing full military attire with ribbons and braiding suitable for someone who commanded the largest armed force in the world with twenty million personnel.

"Come in General, it is good to see you." And they exchanged greetings and pleasantries before sitting at one end of the marble-topped, conference table.

The General had been promoted on Banerjee's own accession to Prime Ministership, and their personal and professional relationship went back many years before that. Apart from being an extremely competent soldier he was a loyal and trusted friend.

"General, first of all we must secure the territories of Jammu and Kashmir. We should not advance our ground forces further until we have finished observing the effects of the bomb's fall out. Nevertheless, use all the resources at your disposal to knock out any remaining military installations in Pakistan. I don't want to encounter any resistance when the time comes to send our armies in."

The General pulled over a large-scale map of the area that was already spread out on the table. The map showed their positions on the Siachen Glacier and the surrounding Kashmir Heights, coloured pegs highlighted the enemy's location and the forces under his control. Gupta spent the next fifteen minutes running through his strategy for destroying any residual pockets of resistance that may emanate from an army no longer receiving supplies.

The General informed Banerjee that according to his latest intelligence briefs, most of the Pakistan Army and Air force had already deserted. Again Balan noticed that the Prime Minister showed little surprise at this latest detail. His self-assurance that events would unfold according to his original expectations was confidence building.

"Now let's turn to Bangladesh, General. Is there any reason why we should not just go ahead and invade the country now?"

The Paradigm Shift

"The fundamental answer is 'no' Prime Minister but I would request you consider an alternative proposal."

Banerjee looked up sharply and stared at the General, this was not the response he expected and a deviation from the short meeting he had envisioned. He quelled the sudden urge to tell the General that 'his job was not to think, but to fastidiously carry out his instructions.'

"Please go ahead, General." The Prime Minister did little to hide the impatient tone in his voice.

"I believe we are in a position to achieve our goal in Bangladesh without bloodshed," he said factually.

"As you know, the monsoon has been severe in Bangladesh over the past month, and twenty-five per cent of their land is currently under water. Although they are forewarned regarding our intentions to invade, their forces are weak and would put up little resistance. My covert intelligence officers have informed me that their leader would be prepared to avoid unnecessary carnage, and surrender openly, by inviting us into the country."

Banerjee considered his remarks.

"Balan, what do you say?"

"I think if we are invited, as the General puts it, on our terms, then it will be difficult for the US Alliance to justify launching an attack against us. As it is, we know the Alliance do not really have a base in the vicinity to provide aerial support for the Bangladesh Government, and they must know that too."

"I am not so sure," the Prime Minister hesitated.

"This could be a way of trying to stall our advance in order to give more time for the Alliance to arrive in greater numbers. General, am I right in saying that a hostile offensive would be a quicker way to take control, rather than accepting their unconditional surrender?"

"You are correct, Sir, our progress into the country would be slower under this alternative."

As Banerjee contemplated his remarks, he had one ear on Balan who was probing the General in more depth on the issue of timing. *How long before the Alliance would be in a position to defend Bangladesh? How long would it take the Indian military to capture the country under aggressive means or through a willing 'open door'?'*

Balan learnt that a British aircraft carrier, *'HMS Invincible'*, was rounding the Singapore peninsula bound for the Bay of Bengal. In two days time, the Alliance carrier would be in a position to offer aerial defence of Bangladesh. Banerjee listened to the General's considered responses before making his final judgement.

"Then we shall proceed as follows, gentlemen," the Prime Minister stated having roused himself from his thought process.

"I will speak to the Prime Minister of Bangladesh, if your intelligence is correct and he wants to avoid unnecessary bloodshed, I will agree to an unconditional surrender on our terms....I will insist that he publicizes his invitation for our troops to enter his country to the media and the world at large..."

Banerjee redirected his gaze towards Balan, an evil, knowing glint flashed across his face as he proceeded to clarify his instructions.

"In addition, he must meet our troops personally at the border with his family and Government Ministers....they will then ride with our forces into Dacca and Chittagong."

The General listened without comment.

"Their are two important points here, General. Firstly, his surrender and rendezvous on the border must be carried out according to strict deadlines. Any deviations and you should revert to your attack plan."

General Gupta nodded his agreement.

"Secondly, we do not have the luxury of time, so once you have met the Prime Minister and his family at the border, you are to proceed as if no surrender agreement had been reached and it is a full offensive…nothing must be allowed to inhibit your progress."

The General remained motionless. Most men of honour would have been angry and visibly startled to hear such an instruction. In reality, he was being asked to disregard the peaceful surrender and massacre innocent victims who got in the way of their advance.

It was exactly because of such commands that he had selected General Gupta. He knew that the riches and rewards promised to Gupta mattered far more to him than his conscience or personal honour.

"Do you think we can say that we found unexpected resistance beyond the control of the Bangladesh Prime Minister?" Banerjee asked rhetorically, smiling at Balan.

He knew that Balan's loyalty was also beyond question but not because of financial avarice. Balan smiled back wryly.

"Is this a problem for you General Gupta?" inquired Banerjee, in a manner that implied the meeting was over.

"No Sir, with your permission I will set the wheels in motion right away."

They all rose from the table and Banerjee showed him to the door. With his hand on his shoulder, he asked the General to keep him notified of developments as and when they occurred.

Returning into the room, Banerjee opened the double doors that lead onto the stone balcony outside. At this time of year, the weather was very humid and the heavy air created a light haze over the lawns of the attractively landscaped enclosure.

Surrounding the gardens was a brick wall about twenty feet high with a dangerous alignment of metal spikes protruding from the top. The spikes were not regarded as a serious deterrent but were there to warn the trespasser of the menace that lay beyond.

Apart from the regular foot patrols by the Prime Minister's personal bodyguard, the security for the building incorporated the very latest in surveillance technology. Around the wall's perimeter, close circuit cameras were installed that transmitted pictures back to the studio located in the building's basement.

The Prime Minister motioned Balan to join him outside. The balcony had a cloverleaf design with a solid, stone parapet running around the edge. Heading for the left-hand side, they strode across the white limestone tiles that paved the balcony towards a white, canvas gazebo that covered some weathered, wooden furniture.

There were numerous mature trees filling the garden dwarfing the height of the first floor balcony. Apart from the well-manicured lawns, the garden looked tropical with oleander and bougainvillea bushes creeping up the sides of the building and the perimeter walls. Around the bases of the trees were thick clusters of frangipani with their white, perfumed flowers and large, ribbed green leaves.

From this position there was no real fear that they could be overlooked naturally, but it was an event that always gave the watching guards cause for additional anxiety. In their investigations, they had examined all the possibilities. *'Could someone with enough determination and resources find a way to sight the balcony from the government buildings beyond?'* Their subsequent research ruled out the likelihood but there was always the element of doubt.

A peon, an Indian manservant, working for the Prime Minister's household, appeared through the double doors carrying a tray of tea and glasses of water. He placed the tray on the table in the gazebo and poured their drinks.

"So what progress have we made in the Middle East?" asked the Prime Minister.

For the past two months, in his position as Special Envoy for Banerjee (he had been bestowed with the title Deputy Prime Minister for the people), Balan had been collaborating behind the scenes with the Indian Embassies and Consulates in the Middle East. Preparations for their 'master plan' had started shortly after Banerjee had taken power. He had given his government offices permission to commence construction of enormous and secret underground reservoirs. Only one other nation shared these plans, and they themselves worked slavishly to build their own storage depots.

"I am delighted to say that progress has been more rapid than expected. Already we have seen minor skirmishes and demonstrations at public meetings as our people seek to respond to your 'call to arms'."

The number of India expatriates throughout the Gulf States was enormous. Typically employed as manual labour because they were cheap, skilled and plentiful. The total population of the United Arab Emirates was only 2.6 million and of that total, seventy per cent numbered Indian expatriates. This example was representative across the Middle East, in Saudi Arabia, the total population of the country was less than Bombay but sixty-five per cent represented Indian overseas labour.

In the past three years the Arab leaders had tried to regain the initiative and exercise control over the situation. In the long term, they could see that they were losing their culture and heritage as their country's population trend led them to resemble small sub-states of India. In response they had tried many ploys to shift their reliance on those Indian workers, including ceasing new entry visas and government decrees that certain trades could only employ Arab labour. The resultant effect was negligible.

With the discovery of oil in the late 1950's, the Arab families had become accustomed to wealth and the position that went with it. The local laws supported their landlord status and they profited from being sponsors or sleeping partners with the profit-orientated companies of the West. As a consequence, many of the local families grew rich quickly creating an environment where they and their offspring no longer needed to work. The subsequent 'overlord' culture that was created became hard to redress.

The ruling families in the Gulf did try to make changes by bringing material benefits such as the ownership of land to those Arabs who worked for a living. This met with little success and the small section of the population that did work was mainly in the part-time employment of government departments and the state owned utilities. The trend was not going to change as long as the Arab population did not need, or would not lower itself, to carry out the routine and menial jobs in a progressive society.

In contrast, through the industrious machinations of India's Foreign Office, Balan Shirish Krishnamurthy had worked planting the seeds of destabilization in the Gulf. The televised speech by Banerjee had been designed to help germinate these seeds and to incite their people to rise against their Arab oppressors.

Balan continued to inform Banerjee of their progress.

The Paradigm Shift

"In Dubai, the local police surrounded a rally that was organized by our people in one of the local parks. Our Embassy orchestrated an incident that led to one of the Arab police shooting an Indian demonstrator in cold blood."

Banerjee could not hide his callous smile.

"Nothing works better than the martyred death of one of our subjects to stir up tension. His body was wrapped in our flag and paraded through the streets. We have more such events taking place, the Arab Rulers are sitting on a time bomb waiting to explode."

Prime Minister Banerjee was pleased and sipped his tea whilst listening to Balan describe in detail the events that were unfolding in Jeddah, Qatar, Kuwait City, Riyadh and Abu Dhabi. He was left in no doubt that the mistrust that now existed between Arabs and their subservient Indian labour had reached explosive levels.

Balan concluded his brief by summarizing the initial reactions in some of the other world locations where large populations of Indians lived alongside their indigenous neighbours.

Pensively, Krishna Banerjee stood up and walked to the edge of the balcony. The vision he had seen in his mind was now turning into glorious reality. The day would come soon when President Whiting would beg him for his help.

Tuesday, 5th October 2008
West Bengal, India

Luke Weaver trekked towards the coordinates he had been given by Commander Tremett. They had contrived to talk directly over the phone earlier that day. Luke had by-passed the Indian proxy servers and sent an encrypted message through the internet. On receiving the response he dialled up an agreed 'land line' number in Switzerland.

Tremett was delighted to hear he was still alive. There friendship went back to their SAS days when he had served as a Major accompanying Luke on training exercises across the Moors in Devon. Observing Luke in action, he had a tremendous respect for him as a soldier and a model professional. If anyone was capable of carrying out this mission then he could think of no one better.

After Tremett had explained the objective of the mission he then went on to broach the subject of who would be accompanying him. He knew full well that Luke preferred working alone and would take some persuading that he needed assistance. After the initial objections, Luke accepted the political rationale being proffered by Tremett. He could see the logic of a joint initiative with the CIA and knew that someone he could trust, and who could speak Hindi, would be a major benefit on this assignment.

However, Luke's mood changed and he became mildly apprehensive when Tremett told him the name of the CIA Agent. Not because he had any doubts about her ability: she was given glowing references by Dan Schwartz, but essentially because he had never worked undercover at close quarters with a female before.

The Paradigm Shift

Tremett's chief concern had been how to get the necessary supplies, including weaponry, to him at such short notice. After reading the information folder given to him by Sir Thomas, his respect for the MI6 Chief grew further. Whether by foresight or good fortune, Sir Thomas had instructed a cache of supplies to be hidden by one of his field officers earlier that month, prior to his deportation with the other Embassy Officials.

Luke had found the supplies, including weaponry, buried in plastic bags in a forest in Uttar Pradesh. He took everything he considered essential and being careful to leave no signs, re-buried the remaining items.

As Luke's mind continued to play over the prospect of having to work with the CIA, and a female agent, he carried on orienteering his way towards the rendezvous location.

It was dark, and he moved quietly through the undergrowth of the forest surrounding the northern shoreline of Lake Bala. They had arranged to meet at one o'clock under the cover of darkness but there was a full moon reflecting off the lake making it easy to detect any movement out of the ordinary. A grassy ridge ran between the bank of the lake and the line of trees marking the beginning of the forest. Along the ridge was a narrow footpath. Luke followed the trail using the shadows cast by the trees for cover.

He took out the 'GPS' that he had recovered from the cache left behind by Sir Thomas's field officer. The satellite navigation device gave him his exact current location as well as the position of the meeting point about two hundred yards further ahead. Straining his eyes he tried to pinpoint the location. With the help of the moonlight, he could make out an old wooden jetty which was now defunct, with one side of the platform leaning precariously into the water.

Luke took his backpack off and hid it in the undergrowth before making his way down the last stretch of path leading to the jetty. The lake's waters were still and there was barely any noise from the forest as he crouched down and edged closer to the broken-down jetty.

Reaching one of the jetty's crumbling wooden struts, he knelt with his back to it, sitting and listening for any strange sounds emerging from the surrounding darkness. He glanced at his watch and saw it was exactly one o'clock.

"Luke Weaver, I presume."

The voice from behind took him by surprise. Startled, he jumped up and turned around to face the broken jetty. He pulled out his handgun as she walked out from the darkness below the wooden decking of the pier.

The first thing he saw was her engaging smile.

"And you must be Kirin," he replied sternly.

Luke did not return her smile but kept the gun levelled at her chest. He was annoyed for allowing himself to be surprised in such a manner.

"Roll up your left sleeve to the elbow – now," he ordered, pointing the gun with a flick of his wrist towards her arm.

At the same time, he kept a watchful eye on the dark terrain behind her which could afford cover for her potential accomplices. Luke knew that any likelihood of danger would come in the first few minutes of their encounter and he wasn't in the habit of taking chances. He wanted to make damn sure she was the person she said she was.

She pulled up the sleeve of her padded jacket and he grabbed her wrist, turning it clockwise to look at her forearm.

Kirin winced with the sudden sharp pain, irritated because she sensed that Luke's hostility might have had something to do with wounded pride.

Luke saw the birthmark he was looking for and let go of her arm. He didn't apologize but slid his pistol back into its holster at the side of his chest.

"Is this how you treat your friends?" she inquired angrily, rubbing her sore elbow with her free hand.

Ignoring her question, he motioned to her to keep quiet as he continued to take stock of their immediate surroundings.

"My backpack is over there, about two hundred yards." He pointed down the narrow track that he had followed earlier.

"Follow me and then you take the lead."

Luke had a gut feeling they were being watched but nothing he saw or heard could confirm this. Apart from the gentle lapping of the lake, the only discernible sounds came from the animal nightlife that frequented the edge of the wood. Nothing that Luke heard could be classified as uncharacteristic behaviour and he gradually began to accept the possibility that his gut feeling was wrong. The need to be vigilant was more an after-effect of Kirin taking him by surprise earlier.

Keeping low, they quickly reached his pack and she took over the lead. She moved gracefully as they jogged the first seven kilometres back to the farmhouse. Luke's original concerns had been founded on potential sabotage of the rendezvous, but once they had left the vicinity, it was a simply a matter of remaining unnoticed. Being observed, particularly as they got closer to the farmhouse, could lead to unwarranted attention later.

Eventually they slowed down and watched the building for twenty minutes from a suitable observation point. The farm-house had been specially selected because it stood alone on the side of a grass hill with panoramic views in all directions. After Kirin satisfied herself that nothing appeared out of the ordinary, she gave the signal to Luke and they crossed the last few hundred meters to the house.

The brick building was run down and had no electricity supply. The only consideration given to security was the views over the landscape from the windows, apart from this the doors and windows did not have locks and if any passers-by wanted to gain access they could easily do so. For this reason, Kirin kept her supplies hidden about the farmhouse. The only concession to a normal existence was an old, noisy generator that could be used in short bursts if the situation required it.

Once inside, Kirin lit two candles and checked the windows to make sure the covers were properly in place and that none of the light could escape.

On the way from the lake, Luke had been impressed with how she moved. She ran with the casual grace of an athlete and at the same time with an expert precision that knew instinctively which was the best line of cover to hold. As she stood in front of him lifting her protective jumper over her head, he recognized for the first time how beautiful she was. She noticed him looking and smiled.

"Do you like coffee?" she asked. "I have a few comforts next door."

He nodded and his eyes followed her as she bent down slightly to pass through the low archway that led into the adjoining room.

"Why don't you go ahead and make contact?" she called, and he heard her light a small gas stove.

A few minutes later, just as he was closing the lid of his computer, she returned carrying two mugs of coffee. Technological advancements had been dramatic over the past two years with the latest hardware shrinking to palm size and the lithium ion conductors extending the portable life to over six weeks.

"I relayed the message, they know that we have made contact without any problems."

The mode of communication had been agreed in advance and was routed in code through obscure pages on the Internet that could be viewed by Colonel Dan Schwartz and Commander Tremett simultaneously; it was simple and immediate.

"You decided not to mention that you nearly broke my wrist then?" she grinned as she handed him his drink.

For thirty minutes, they swapped stories on how they had arrived in India before being selected for this mission. Luke listened intently and was quietly impressed by her achievement of following the mobile launchers in Rajasthan, but in stark contrast to her openness, his conversation was stifled and to the point. He spoke factually and rarely embellished the answers to her questions more than was absolutely necessary.

Luke fell short of being impolite but steadfastly maintained his reserve despite Kirin's friendliness and disarming beauty. Slightly concerned by his lack of ease, she could sense that he was not entirely happy at the prospect of a partner. Kirin began to wonder how this could affect the next few days, knowing how closely they would have to work together.

Kirin explained the set-up at the farmhouse and they discussed the events of the past few days. Touching briefly on the objective of their mission, they agreed to formulate their initial strategy the next morning after a good night's sleep.

"That's your bed there," she said pointing to a rolled up canvas in the corner. "I'll see you in the morning." And with that she departed up a steep, stone staircase to the only room on the second floor.

Tuesday, 5th October 2008
The White House, Washington

The Director of the CIA, Michael Conway, strode down the corridor towards the President's Office carrying the leather folder that held his classified papers. As always, he looked smart in his dark navy suit and despite being in his late forties, he kept trim by exercising three times a week at the gym he had specially built at home.

Catherine Dennison noticed him approaching, and stopped him by placing her hand on his arm with the folder tucked under it.

"I hope you have some good news for him Mike, the President's not in the best of moods today!"

Mike Conway was a happily married man, and had been for over twenty-five years with three teenage children to show for it, but he was not oblivious to Catherine's sensual good looks. With all the pressure of the long working hours he had decamped to the CIA's Headquarters and it was beginning to take its strain on his home life. He briefly allowed himself to imagine what she would look like without any clothes on.

In the past, he had often felt that she was sending out little signals for him to pick up and return but he could never be quite sure. Whenever her vibes and mannerisms inspired a more confident response something would always hold him back. He would see her being cordial and warm to another visitor and would mentally scold himself for jumping to premature conclusions. Mike sensed that she was flirting with him and enjoyed it, but he could not discount the possibility she was being anything more than friendly.

"Maybe one small item," he said smiling, "but I'm afraid there is precious little going round in the form of good news at the moment Catherine," he then surprised himself by cupping his hand over hers and giving it a squeeze.

"He is still fuming about the fact that we allowed the international media to give Banerjee a free platform to address the world." She smiled at his sudden look of concern.

"Even with the benefit of hindsight it would have been impossible to prevent," he replied as he mentally prepared himself for the President's bad mood.

Turning together towards the double doors at the end of the hall, she held his arm tightly as they crossed the carpet towards the President's office. He could feel her breast against his arm as they walked along and wondered whether she was also aware of the sensation.

"I'm sure you're doing all you can Mike," and she pressed herself closer.

"If there is any way that I can assist then please feel free to ask," and he caught the glint in her eye as she looked at him before letting go. With a smile she turned on her heels returning down the corridor towards her office. *'I can't be mistaken'*, he thought as he knocked and entered the President's office.

"Come in Mike and take a seat."

The President waved towards an empty lounge chair. Already sat opposite the President was his National Security Advisor, Jim Allen, whom he had been grilling on the current feedback from their European Allies.

"What is the latest Mike?"

Mike thought the President looked fresher than when he last saw him. A few new lines had appeared around the eyes, but that was not surprising considering he was surviving on five hours sleep a night.

"Mr. President, I can confirm that Codename Amber has joined forces with the British Agent in West Bengal. They are fully briefed on their assignment and I will keep you informed of their progress."

"How do you rate their chances of success?"

"This is not an ordinary mission, Mr. President. Under normal conditions we would expect to be able to provide them with considerable assistance but in these abnormal circumstances they are literally on their own. " He knew this was not what the President wanted to hear.

"We are asking them to infiltrate the inner circle of probably the most highly guarded man in the world…and in a hostile country. The chances of them succeeding or returning for that matter are not great."

The President wanted to hear an upbeat, high percentage probability but there was nothing to be gained by entertaining false hope, this would only detract from other equally important efforts that were being made on other fronts.

"Regardless of the odds…if you could hand pick your best two people for such a mission then we have them in place now, Sir"

"Ok Mike, I get the message…" the President nodded knowingly. "What's happening in the Middle East? Jim tells me the situation is reaching boiling point!"

"Our information reports are in agreement with those of your National Security Advisor Sir. It would appear that Banerjee's plan to cause unrest in the Middle East had been put in place sometime ago and it is gathering momentum. The seeds have been sown through the Indian Foreign Ministries and controlled by the 'RAW', the Indian Secret Service. With added impetus from Banerjee's speech, they have been inciting their numerically superior communities to take to the streets and overthrow the Arab Rulers."

Jim Allen interrupted Conway's flow. "Local television stations have been banned from showing the demonstrations and I have just had it confirmed that a third Gulf State has imposed Martial Law."

The President nodded and turned back to Director Conway. He had spent a full hour with his Secretary of State Margaret Henderson earlier that morning understanding the US relationships in the Gulf. In previous visits to the region as a Senator, he had witnessed first hand the population discrepancy between the fewer, indigenous Arabs and the mass of imported Indian workers that constituted up to seventy per cent in places. At the time he had wondered how this would affect the Arab's ultimate ability to rule their States when the oil fields finally dried up in twenty years time.

"The anarchy being caused in the region is not just consequential to his speech. My sources have confirmed that this activity has been propagated for the past three months and brought to a head to coincide with the speech."

"In other words this is part of a more elaborate strategy by Banerjee," announced the President concluding his line of reasoning

He raised his voice. "Mike, I want to know what else this madman has cooked up and I want to know now."

"We are giving it our undivided attention Sir, if we had not heard his speech then the easy conclusion to draw would be that he was deflecting attention away from his planned invasion of Pakistan and Bangladesh."

The Paradigm Shift

"Mike, all indicators point to the fact that Banerjee is a schemer and that means his plans stretch beyond his own borders...if we are going to fully assess his threat I need to know what the playing field is for those plans."

The President's expression left Mike Conway in no doubt what was expected.

Director Conway carried on for the next fifteen minutes briefing the President on the disturbances that were stemming from Banerjee's call to arms and the implications of Martial Law in the Gulf States.

Through CIA's intelligence resources, Director Conway produced pictures of the demonstrations taking place across the Middle East. The number of incidents leading to bloodshed was escalating all the time. As the heavy-handed military stepped in at the bequest of the Arab Rulers, trouble would flare up and Indian lives would be lost in the fighting that followed. The demonstrator's stones and makeshift weapons were no match for the modern weaponry of the Arab Armed Forces but with each passing death of an Indian worker their anger against the Arabs grew.

Around the rest of the world, the TV cameras centred on the overseas Indian Communities as new demonstrations broke out around the globe. As for the President, he was alarmed to learn that rallies were planned to take place on his home soil. The large and well-funded Indian community in New York had taken to the streets in Manhattan to voice their support for Banerjee. Faced with hostile on-lookers lining their path, the vocal crowd marched in unison towards Central Park. Carrying their flags and banners, the procession had started peacefully but, as they progressed, violence broke out and the police intervened to prevent them from being attacked by angry citizens.

President Whiting was convinced that there was more to Banerjee's actions than just inciting his people. The loyalty shown towards India was commendable but totally misguided. Jim Allen assured the President that there was absolutely no danger to the US Administration from the incitement of the Indian community. In fact, he summarized the unrest as being transient and non-threatening in North America and Europe.

"It's as if Banerjee is putting up a smokescreen," remarked the President thoughtfully, as he listened to Allen finish his summary.

"There is really only one region that is in political danger from the unrest," concluded Allen, " and that's the Middle East."

The President acknowledged Allen's reasoning and repeated the urgency for the Agency to uncover what was behind Banerjee's thinking. After a small pause, he turned his mind to other related issues.

"Have you uncovered anymore on the origin of Pakistan's tests?" he inquired of Director Conway.

"Our source is very close to Prime Minister Latif and we know that he'd have been on the guest list for the bunker. Our efforts to contact him have failed; we suspect that once the situation stabilizes, the survivors in the bunker will be under threat from the remnants of the army or their own people. In all likelihood they will be killed but we have an agent that is working against time to reach our contact first."

The President was pleased with this development and he pushed Director Conway to obtain third party evidence or documentation that could unlock the secret of Banerjee's plan. The very least they could expect was some light to be shed on who their international co-conspirator might be.

The Paradigm Shift

The conversation turned back to the 'tinderbox' in the Middle East and the recent imposition of Martial Law in Kuwait. All three of them concurred that the right signals would be sent if Margaret Henderson, the Foreign Secretary, was to visit the region.

The President met her later in the evening and asked her to take Air Force One and ascertain what options they had to achieve the return of stability and more importantly, the reactions of the Arab leaders to possible military support from the US.

The intercom sounded and Catherine Dennison's voice announced to the President that his next appointment had arrived with Defence Secretary Vance Warner. They were both waiting to meet him in one of the guest welcoming rooms used specially for overseas dignitaries. The new arrival was General Andrei Karpurov, the Russian Intelligence Commander who would work alongside Colonel Dan Schwartz in Special Operations.

The President wiped the lens of his glasses as he deliberated Catherine Dennison's news.

"You both know him quite well don't you?" the President questioned. "Why don't you come along and help me welcome him?"

Observing their confirmations, he spoke into the intercom and informed Catherine that 'all three of them' would be coming through shortly.

On the way towards the guest meeting room President Whiting brought up the subject of the Space Defence Program.

"The presentations been organized by General Graham, Mike, and I want you there, check with Catherine on the timings."

Thursday, 7th October 2008
Riyadh, Saudi Arabia

The Secretary of State, Margaret Henderson was a career diplomat, and had served in numerous overseas postings, including as Ambassador to Britain before rising to her present position. She was best known for her work in the Israeli-Palestine Peace Accord, and she was a popular choice with Republicans and Democrats alike, when President Whiting announced her appointment. The only negative the President had considered at the time was her age, but having recently turned sixty-three she still demonstrated a strong vitality and enthusiasm to get the job done.

Riyadh was the first stop on her tour. The decision rightly conveyed the importance that America put on Saudi's 'favoured nation' status in the Gulf. Air force One landed in the early evening and members of the ruling Royal Family met her on the concourse. She had been a frequent visitor to Saudi in the past, and was genuinely shocked at the sight she surveyed as the cavalcade swept them from King Khalid airport to the residence of His Highness, King Mohammed bin Abdullah, The Custodian Of The Two Holy Shrines Of Islam.

The Saudi Army was out in force patrolling the whole length of their journey. She knew that Martial Law had been introduced, and her Ambassador had prepared her for the scenes she could expect but the sights were no less shocking. A night-time curfew had been imposed after the constant eruptions of violence that flared up around the city in the evenings. Riyadh itself was a large historic city anchored in the Saudi interior. Unlike Hong Kong or Singapore where the population was concentrated into high-rise developments on a relatively small plot of land, Riyadh's buildings were mainly low level and spread out over a vast area sixty square kilometres in size. As the cavalcade continued its journey at great speed, she could see the overturned cars in the street and the fires caused by petrol bombs lit up the horizon.

His Highness King Mohammed was in his seventies, and she had been met from the plane by one of his younger brothers, Prince Faisal, who himself was in his sixties. Their meeting was scheduled for mid-morning the next day, and that evening she settled into the guest wing of the magnificent royal palace.

As the following day dawned, Margaret Henderson rose early to meet the advisors who were accompanying her on the tour. It was customary in the Middle East for much of the groundwork and negotiations to be carried out behind the scenes ahead of the final meeting with His Highness. The previous evening she had initiated the US thought-process by using her local US Ambassador as a foil for the first round of discussions with the King's closest advisors. During breakfast and afterwards they dissected the guarded, and carefully worded responses that were being passed back through the appropriate channels. It was like a game of 'political fencing or chess' with suggestions being passed back and forth to test the other side's resolution or degree of latitude to fundamental issues. *They're supposed to be our allies'* thought Margaret dryly as another avenue of negotiation was closed by one of the ruler's senior advisors.

The time approached when His Highness King Mohammed had agreed they should meet. As a mark of respect for the King and the Muslim religion, the Secretary of State wore the black, ankle-length abaye over her normal outfit.

In the end, as was customary in this part of the world, the meeting started a little later than originally planned. The setting itself was regal in its splendour. The marble floor was rectangular in shape with short steps leading to an atrium down one side. The white walls stretched up to an enormous domed ceiling whose underside had a lattice design painted in gold leaf. Decorations were relatively few and the perimeter of the room was furnished with wide-armed, lounge chairs. On the wall behind the raised seat of the King was a picture of the 'Kabba' at Mecca where thousands of Muslim pilgrims flock to do the 'Haj' every year.

The King entered and sat next to Margaret Henderson in the middle. Their advisors, who were arranged according to seniority, and Margaret, stood up for his entrance before taking their seats around the perimeter of the room.

Once His Highness had made his own considerable frame comfortable, he leaned over and asked Secretary of State Henderson whether she was being extended all the pleasures she desired on her stay. Courteously, she thanked him for his generosity. After addressing the formalities, he then inquired if she had been appraised of the developments in the Kingdom since the weekend.

Margaret Henderson knew this was a reference to the dialogue that had filtered back to the Secretary's camp during the course of that morning. These conversations were necessary in order that the King was not asked to address anything other than top-line issues or anything else he did not want to arise on the agenda.

During the morning, she learnt that the Saudi economy was under extreme pressure and, if the emergency situation became prolonged, then there was a danger of collapse. The fundamental problem was not containing the demonstrations and outbreaks of violence, although this had worsened, it was restoring the economy's workforce.

Shops, petrol stations, the water and electricity authorities, factories, and building sites were closed because the Indian employees no longer reported for work. The backbone of the economy was crumbling and there was nothing that the Saudi Government could do about it. It was as if the whole country had gone on strike only in this case the employer had more than a simple wage dispute to resolve.

In essence, the Saudi economy was almost entirely dependent on its oil revenue to balance its books. Although government spending had risen dramatically over the past two years it had been matched by the soaring price of crude. OPEC had not felt it necessary to restrict production because the price remained high at over fifty dollars a barrel with no sign of demand slipping. The problem was that production in the Kingdom had already come to a standstill with both onshore and offshore rigs lying unmanned. American and European corporations, including the oil corporations, had taken the decision to evacuate their employees until such time as stability returned.

The Saudi Oil Ministry made stringent efforts to persuade some of the Oil Corporation's technical workers to remain with promises of huge loyalty bonuses but on the whole this met with little success. Most were married expatriates who had their families to think of, but a few stayed behind to form a skeleton team battling against the odds.

In the major population centres, living conditions worsened as the loss of critical services began to take effect and the build up of waste and polluted water harboured the perfect environment for disease. One positive piece of news from the surrounding gloom was that the hospital service was fairing better than could be expected. Mainly because they had their own power supplies, and the doctors and nurses, although predominantly Indian, put saving peoples lives before their countries call to arms.

"Is your Highness open to support from the US? We would be willing to offer financial, medical and military assistance to help you maintain stability in the region?" Secretary of State Henderson inquired.

The King knew that financial and medical support could provide some respite but ultimately, it could not solve their dilemma. Although he, and his government, had been aware of the situation, often considering their over-reliance on Asian labour. They had never acted upon their fears, or ever dreamt that it could grind their country to a halt in such an unrelenting fashion.

The King's options for restoring the status quo were limited. The army and the police were fully occupied keeping law and order. The two earlier 'pleas for help' which he had made to his fellow countrymen had met with some positive response although the net effect was negligible. The Ministry of Labour, grateful for any forthcoming volunteers, assigned them to crucial positions within the utilities sector.

Success was always going to be limited when the posts that really mattered, required either skilled labour or manual labour. The people who operated the country's infrastructure were the drivers, the engineers, the technicians, the enormous manual labour force, the machine operators and the salesmen, and with very few exceptions, they were all Indian.

One of the choices facing the King, and his government, was to take the hard line and deport the Indian expatriates. However this would not help them to resolve their dilemma, and such an evacuation would be costly and difficult to manage. Alternatively they could use everything at their disposal to try and entice the workers back to their positions. They considered every kind of enticement. Better pay, more benefits, improved housing, but the meagre amount of trust that had previously existed between employer and employee was gone.

In giving all the options due consideration, the Saudi Government had concluded that offers of improved living standards or quality of life would fall on deaf ears. The impending meltdown was due to extreme 'nationalistic fervour' on the part of the Indians driven by their feeling of subjugation.

The constant street battles were not just between the Saudi militia and the Indian protesters. Fighting also broke out with the Pakistani workers and despite their Islamic ties with the Saudis; there was no favourable discrimination. They also felt the muscle of the notorious military police as they charged 'en masse' with raised batons into the rioting crowd. In what was little more than a few days, the jails were full to the brim and the death count had now risen to over one hundred.

The final option under consideration was the only one they believed had any chance of success. The Kingdom's ruling committee discussed the proposal from every possible angle before going on to debate the consequences with their Arabic neighbours who were undergoing the same anarchic turmoil in their respective domains.

With the unwritten sanction of their Arab neighbours, the Saudi Government concluded that the only workable solution was to force the skilled and unskilled Indian labour back to work under threat of imprisonment, punishment or even worse.

In arriving at their decision, the ruling committee knew that they would be condoning and imposing conditions of slavery on their workers. They also acknowledged amongst themselves that this would be completely unacceptable to the international community, including the US and United Nations.

All state and private industry would fall under the strict control of the police and the military. They would be licensed to take whatever action was necessary to force the labour back to work and to keep them in line. Without voicing the underlining sentiment in full, the whole executive committee knew that they would be empowering the police to use whatever brutal methods were necessary to get the job done.

In reaching the decision, the proud king, wearing his gold robe of office, had been visibly shaken by the events leading to his country being on the brink of collapse. Internationally, he recognized that they would be denounced as a 'quasi-fascist' state but what choice did they, or his Arab brothers have?

The advisors to His Royal Highness and the Executive Committee had been careful not to confide their decision to the Secretary of State or her delegation.

"Our country appreciates the offer of your President and your people, we would be pleased to receive any financial or medical assistance you can offer us."

"Do you want our military support to assist with you in your control of the country, Your Highness?" replied Secretary Henderson.

This was the burning issue, she knew the response she would receive would be the key to the success of her tour. Before her departure, the President had been adamant that they demonstrate their power in the region by negotiating the deployment of US troops in the Gulf. The positive confirmation from King Mohammed would make her task relatively easy as the smaller Arab states invariably followed the Saudi lead.

"We have always had a close and special friendship with the United States," he spoke slowly considering each word as he spoke.

"My country still owes you a debt of gratitude for your support in repelling the forces of Iraq when they invaded our brothers in Kuwait...but in these circumstance we cannot accept your generous offer of help."

Sitting with his hands firmly gripping the end of his chair rests, he looked an imposing and dignified man. With a black goatee beard and the Saudi red and white chequered headdress, he accompanied his words with a stare that implied this line of debate was closed.

His ruling council had known in advance that such an offer would be made by the Secretary of State and accordingly, had discussed it along with their other options. Under normal circumstances, when the problem was not a domestic one, they would have been pleased to entertain the thought of US troops on their soil. However, once they had taken their decision to suppress, and technically enslave the workforce, it was no longer an option.

Secretary Henderson went on to inquire whether the King would contemplate a UN peacekeeping force in the country. Again she was politely, but firmly, stonewalled. The King and the ruling council knew that no outside forces would stand by idly while they carried out their bloody objective of saving their economy.

After a banquet in the evening hosted by King Mohammed in honour of the Secretary of State, the delegation departed. The mood of the party was low as the convoy set off at high speed for the airport and the onward flight to Kuwait City. Margaret Henderson would report back to the President's office once they were airborne but she was not relishing the prospect of communicating their initial failure. She had not gained the political and military advantage that the President, or his administration, had hoped for.

Unbeknown, but suspected by Secretary Henderson, the government body of Saudi had already spoken and discussed their strategy with their ruling brothers in the other Middle East States. Unanimously, they had all agreed that the Saudi solution was the best way forward. At least by standing united together, they knew there would be some respite from the onslaught of world opinion. As King Mohammed had reasoned, the shoulders of the whole region could bare more weight than any individual country.

Their Arab neighbours in Qatar, Kuwait, Abu Dhabi, Dubai, Bahrain and Sharjah mirrored the Kingdom's plight. They were all suffering the same economic crisis that had been carefully instigated and diligently executed by the manipulative tentacles of Banerjee's administration.

The Arab leaders pledged allegiance to each other as one by one they lavished splendid hospitality on Secretary Henderson and the visiting US delegation, but rejected her political overtures.

Friday, 8th October 2008
West Bengal, India

Kirin was pleased to be taking a refreshing shower out in the backyard even if the water was cold. It was a makeshift arrangement constructed by Luke a few days earlier when he had woken early one morning. Some well placed wooden slats forming a cubicle gave it a semblance of respectability and above Kirin's head, he had fitted an old rusty sprinkler head to a length of hose. The other end was attached to a plastic sack that he had filled with rainwater, caught in one of the animal troughs surrounding the farm.

The air was muggy as the bright morning sunshine lifted the early morning dew from the surrounding fields. The time was approaching seven-thirty as Luke came outside, ducking his head below the top of the doorframe, carrying two cups of coffee.

They had gradually grown accustomed to each other over the past few days as they had deliberated over maps and poured over the architect's plans for the government offices in Delhi.

For Kirin, her initial doubts over Luke's ability to treat her as a partner and equal began to fade. Although his demeanour could not be described as friendly with his reserved and aloof manner, there was something about him which inspired her with confidence. *'Time will make the difference'*, she thought as she considered whether he would ever let his guard down.

For Luke's part, he still felt uneasy at the prospect of relying on someone he barely knew despite her promising credentials. He wondered whether she would really be able to cope with the pressure when it really mattered. *True*, he thought to himself, *'I've never really met anyone quite like Kirin before,'* and he fleetingly allowed himself to recognize how much he had enjoyed her company over the past few days. Apart from her mental agility in etching out a plan to reach Banerjee, he had not been impenetrable to her natural charm and beauty. Luke had been careful to make sure he kept a professional distance and that was how it would remain he thought, as he shut the friendly images from his mind.

"Can you pass me the towel please?" she asked from inside the cubicle.

Luke picked up a white towel lying nearby. It had been her one concession to luxury when she had purchased it on her journey across the north of India from Rajasthan to Bengal. She smiled as he handed it to her over the top of the wooden shutter. Thanking him, she dried her hair before winding the towel around her and stepping out.

"We must destroy all trace that we've ever been here before we leave."

Luke spoke in a cold, 'matter of fact' tone almost to emphasize the distance he wanted between them. For someone normally in total control of his emotions, he felt strangely vulnerable at the sight of Kirin emerging from the shower. It was not a feeling he was comfortable with and it strengthened his resolve that he could perform better without a partner. The assignment would be hard enough without the additional burden of emotional complexities that a relationship could bring. He mentally kicked himself for letting Commander Tremett talk him into accepting a partner

Turning his back on her, he wondered whether she could sense his underlying feelings but quickly dismissed the possibility. In order to combat his desire to be open and friendly with her he had deliberately compensated by giving the appearance of non-interest and keeping the conversation strictly businesslike. Since meeting on the shores of Lake Bala, she had raised questions on his personal life and revealed an insight into her own but with no reciprocation from Luke.

"I've nearly completed upstairs," she replied. "By the way, your tan is coming on very well." He looked up and caught her laughing at him with a mischievous smile.

Over the past few days he had begun to build his disguise by applying a brown skin pigment to all the surfaces of his body. For this assignment he would have to blend in like a native Indian. Right now a person with white skin would attract instant attention, no matter what part of the country they were in. Although he aimed to keep his head covered most of the time, he dyed his hair black and used lenses to change the colour of his blue irises and darken the surrounding white of his eyes.

With his shirt off and his back to her, he allowed himself to quietly smile at her humour. He continued applying the finishing touches to his arms and chest before starting on the harder to reach parts of his back.

"Why don't you let me help?" she said and he allowed her to take the bottle of dye he was holding.

Kirin admired the muscular contours of his back as she gently massaged the liquid gel into his skin. She noticed the scar that ran down one side from his shoulder blade, but refrained from asking him how he got it. The answer, she knew, would be monosyllabic.

She wanted to know much more about him, but could deduce from his abrupt style that questions relating to his background would not be welcome. Her respect for his ability had grown rapidly over the past few days. A competitive edge, albeit a healthy one, had crept into their demonstration of individual skills and knowledge required for the project in hand. No automatic leader had emerged as was sometimes the case in training although Luke's comments could be frequently interpreted as commands. Kirin felt that she had gained his respect even if there seemed to be little in the way of interest in her as a person.

Finishing a second application on the base of his back she tossed the bottle back to him and went to rinse her hands.

"Thanks," he said catching the bottle. "Let's aim to leave in the next hour or so."

She nodded her agreement and went to complete her final preparations in the farmhouse.

They used the time purposefully to erase any indication that they had been present. After packing the supplies that would be travelling with them, Luke performed one last check over the farmhouse. Finally they were ready to depart and Luke emerged to face Kirin for her final touches to his with disguise. She was amazed at the difference his skin colour and clothing gave to his appearance.

Luke wore the traditional dress of a Bengali peasant worker; brown, baggy cloth pants, like pyjama bottoms, tied at the front with some cord, and a loose-fitting shirt with only three buttons descending from the collar. The shirt hung down below his waist and did a good job of hiding his true physique.

Like the majority of women from lower castes in India, Kirin wore a simple and traditional green sari that exposed one shoulder and her midriff. The night before, Luke had broken their weapons down into their constituent parts and fed them into a belt he was wearing, strapped around his waist. Other supplies and clothes were tied in a bundle that he carried on his shoulder.

The Paradigm Shift

Shortly after nine o'clock, they set off on foot over the fields disguised as a Bengali peasant family. The track they had to follow would take them over two valleys to Ranepur where they would begin the first of three train journeys that would deliver them to the outskirts of Delhi.

Friday, 8th October 2008
Bombay, West Coast of India

Balan Krishnamurthy replaced the handset and considered the information that had been relayed to him. He took a moment to acknowledge the genius and foresight of Krishna Banerjee, the decisions and events that marked his strategy were unfolding exactly as he had predicted.

In his private residence at Malabar Hill, he wandered across the chessboard, black and white marble flooring of the hall's atrium. In an overcrowded city like Bombay, apartments were the norm but his family residence at Malabar Hill was an old colonial house set in its own grounds. The house, located in the most prestigious location in Bombay, had been in Balan's family for years and from its high perch, it offered splendid views across the bay and out to sea. Bombay was no more than a narrow peninsula jutting out from the West Coast of India. Its geographical advantages had made the city an ideal port for the blossoming sea trade that it had spawned in the mid-nineteenth century. In more recent times the city had been caught in a downward cycle and was allowed to deteriorate beyond repair. The population had grown to over fifteen million, the bulk of which lived in shantytowns or worse.

Balan reached the hall table and rang a small hand bell. A 'peon,' one of the many servants needed to run such a residence, entered hurriedly to hear his master's bidding, looking suitably subservient. After the peon had taken his order for tea and retraced his steps towards the kitchens, Balan walked into his private study. The room was like an old library. The walls were lined with glass-fronted, dark wood bookcases that stretched up to the ceiling. The cabinets were full of books and artefacts which had been collected over the years.

Sitting down in the leather chair behind his desk he picked up and gazed at his family photograph in its silver frame. The happy, smiling picture showed him, his wife and his daughter looking very proud at their son's graduation in America. His momentary joy at remembering the occasion disappeared as quickly as it had surfaced. The sadness returned as he realized there was nothing he could do to bring his son back.

His son, Ashok Krishnamurthy, had died in a freak accident months after his graduation ceremony from the University of Wisconsin. He had been travelling by motorbike, downtown to his office when the Whiting Presidential election tour was in full swing. The cavalcade procession had included the President, his advisors, the press, security and close supporters.

To Balan the injustice of the travesty still made it seem unreal and difficult to fully comprehend. The press stories that were published later suggested that there had been a real threat to President Whiting's life. The driver of the open top limousine carrying the 'would be' President received an instruction that a possible assassination attempt was in the offing. In line with his orders and training, he veered out of the procession and turned at great speed into a side street. The black limousine did not stop when it hit the boy on his motorbike.

Ashok never regained consciousness and died several hours later in the General Hospital from head wounds. No money could bring him back; Balan loved his son with a vengeance that now materialized as concentrated hatred of the President and all things America. His love for his eldest child was such that he would gladly have traded his own life for his son's.

He despised America for what it had done to his family and it was this trait that the Prime Minister had recognized early on. Banerjee singled out a capable man whose burning, revengeful passion enabled him to confide his plans without fear of disloyalty. The chemistry between them worked and he was soon promoted ahead of others with greater claims to high office.

Balan put the photograph down and turned his mind back to the intelligence reports he had just received. Putting on his half moon glasses, he reread the scribbled notes he had made earlier on. The signs and the intentions were clear; the Arab Rulers had issued instructions to their military to imprison the Indian people and force them back to work in order to save their crumbling fiefdoms. Already he had been recounted numerous stories of police atrocities as they made bloody and brutal examples of anyone who did not tow the line.

These developments were important to the vision of Banerjee but not as important as the consequences. Banerjee's plan was to extinguish the world's supply of oil for a period long enough to effect the 'paradigm shift;' he planned to change the balance of political and economic power that covered the globe. Balan recalled the instant when Banerjee had first spoken and entrusted him with his intentions. He had been amazed. Considering the enormous power and influence wielded by the US, he remembered being staggered at how quickly the projected 'shift' could take place. As Banerjee had so eloquently put it, 'once the oil, the life's blood of their economy is turned off, their heart will stop pumping, and the Governments body will fall.'

For the past year India and their covert ally had been stock piling all available shipments of crude oil. They were the reason why the price of oil never dropped below fifty dollars per barrel despite increased production quotas.

The Paradigm Shift

Massive underground reservoirs had been built to house the tanker loads of crude that was delivered every week. In order to avoid the conspicuous nature of their purchases they had been ingenious in their methods of acquiring the surplus production. Consignment after consignment had been surreptitiously pumped into their newly created storage holds without raising international suspicions. In conversation with their ally, Balan had mockingly given credence to the new term of 'oil laundering'.

In the Middle East, it was normal practice for two or more tankers to bid for the next oil shipment to be dispatched from the refinery on shore. The companies which controlled the tankers had no particular political allegiance, as they were merely carriers, making the purchases on behalf of international governments. Once they were out at sea their cargo was like a stock market commodity that could be bought and sold by the highest bidder.

While the tankers were at sea, the Indian Government, along with their ally, created dummy companies which would then outbid the original buyer and the shippers would automatically re-rout the cargo directly to them. By making the oil accumulation over a long period of time and being careful not to place frequent order quantities with a few shippers they managed not to arouse any undue suspicion.

Balan picked up the phone on his office desk and called the government residence of the Indian Prime Minister to give him the good news. Their initial target had been achieved, all the oil producing facilities of the Gulf States had been shutdown while the Arab Rulers tried to end the chaos that besieged their cities.

The operator at the Government residence put him through to a private secretary who very quickly established the connection to the Prime Minister. Balan, using his notes, meticulously informed Banerjee of the developments across the Gulf.

"Excellent work Balan, now our job is to make sure their oil facilities remain closed for the necessary duration."

Despite the commendation, his stoic voice held no intonation of gratitude or joy at the news. Balan had learned to anticipate this reaction, he surmised that the reason was simply because it was not out of the ordinary for Banerjee. It was no more than he had fully expected.

"What is the level of the American national oil reserve at the moment?" the Prime Minister asked.

"America has emergency reserves that will last for twenty days," Balan replied with a glow of satisfaction.

Saturday, 9th October 2008
Outskirts of Delhi

The wide gauge railway tracks that covered India were a legacy from the colonial days of the British Empire. Passengers exhibited scant respect to the interiors of the carriages and the trains showed their age. On the longer journeys, such as that being travelled by Luke and Kirin, the train offered three different classes of ticket.

They made do with the cramped and unpleasant conditions of the third class compartment at the tail end of the train. While in the densely packed compartment, they rarely spoke to each other and never in earshot of other passengers. Although English was the second language of India, it was still relatively uncommon amongst the peasant classes.

The train rolled into a small station in the northern suburbs of Delhi. They disembarked and made their way through the bustling crowds on the platform towards the exit. Banderi was two stops from the mainline station in Central Delhi and right in the heart of the commuter belt.

Outside the station, the buildings and the sidewalk looked exactly as they did in all the major Indian metropolises. The facades of the buildings were rotten with years of neglect and the roads were full of potholes and lined with rubble. The real contrast from their serene days in the farmhouse was the noise. Yellow 'Padmini' taxis edged forward hooting their horns every ten yards as cows would wander into their path, and out-stretched hands of disfigured beggars tapped on the windows seeking pecuniary alms. On either side of the traffic, the cracked pavements lining the street were alive with squatting vendors and the constant flow of men, women and children travelling in each direction.

It was easy for Luke and Kirin to pass unnoticed, and as planned, they set off towards the shantytown that would be their home for the next few days. Delhi, like Bombay and Calcutta, had an acute shortage of housing. Even if it had been available, unemployment was so severe that relatively few could afford it. Built with corrugated iron, wooden boards and anything else that could be found on building sites or rubbish tips, these black slums provided basic shelter for the masses.

Turning off the main street, they entered the slum by walking down one of the foreboding, narrow alleys that characterized the shantytown. The roofs of the shacks were just a foot or so above head height making it feel like a maze. The alleys were straight and you could only see directly behind you or in front of you. Once you reached a crossroads you could discover that a second alley had been running parallel to you all the time.

After they had been walking towards the centre for about ten minutes, Kirin approached an old woman who was busy sweeping the dirt out of her shelter. When she looked up, Luke noticed the missing teeth and deep creases in her face that reflected years of struggling to survive in a harsh environment.

Kirin spoke to her in Hindi explaining that they were Bengali and had travelled from far away to find work for her husband. She asked if the woman knew of temporary shelter that they could take until they could find permanent lodgings.

The woman pointed to a shack and told Kirin that the old man who had lived there alone for many years had suddenly taken ill and passed away two nights earlier. Kirin politely listened as the old woman took her through the entire story from start to finish. Finally, she was rewarded for her patience.

"He will not be coming back now, so you might as well take some comfort from his shelter," concluded the old woman.

Kirin thanked her and offered Luke's services to fetch her water later that day. There was no water or electricity in the shantytown and it was the daily chore of all the dwellers to go the pumps on the outskirts and collect water for washing and cooking. This was a heavy task for an old woman and she nodded, appreciative of Kirin's offer.

Behind her Luke had interpreted the woman's gesticulating in the direction of the empty shack. He moved closer towards it, partially to avoid any questions the woman might pose of him, and partially to explore the hut's suitability further. He pulled open the shutter and looked inside the shack. Rays of sunshine burst through the gaps in the shelter highlighting the dust in the air. Entering through the door, the roof was not high enough for him to stand upright and except for a few bricks in the corner, the shack was empty. Luke was satisfied with what he saw; he had endured far worse conditions in the past. After Kirin had joined him and confirmed its availability, he set about repairing parts of the hut whilst she cleaned the interior.

As the sun went down in the evening, the noise of shantytown life began to die down. The gangs of little children, many of them barely clothed, stopped playing in the alleyways and returned to their homes lit by candles and small fires.

Later, when Kirin was satisfied she could not be seen, she told Luke to be on his guard and pulled out her small computer to establish contact with headquarters. She quickly informed them of their whereabouts and picked up reciprocal information confirming, as suspected, that Banerjee was currently residing in apartments connected to his government offices in Delhi.

She passed on the information to Luke. He was pleased with the positive news, if they had discovered that Banerjee had switched locations it would have been a set back to their plans. Tomorrow's task would be to undertake a complete reconnaissance of the building and that would involve them working shifts into the night. As part of their preparation, they had to establish the movements and working patterns of everyone who had access to Banerjee's residence.

Luke helped the old woman by filling her water pots and they satisfied their hunger by boiling some rice and vegetables. Settling down for the evening they laid out a canvas mat which would give little respite from the hard, mud-baked floor. Kirin lay looking up at the stars through the gaps in the roof, listening to the sounds of babies crying, and the men, sat in huddles, laughing as they swapped stories out in the alley.

Luke sat in the doorway of the hut watching the alley night-life and thinking to himself. He knew the success of their assignment relied on them working closely together as a team. If they were going to be able to work to best effect then they had to fully understand each other. *'After all, weren't they going to have to sleep, eat, wash and live like a married couple till their job was done?'* he rationalized. Luke decided to lower his guard. Besides he was curious about her.

"When did your family move away from India?" he asked in a lowered tone, so that he couldn't be heard outside the shack.

Surprised, she turned to look at him as he moved into the shelter and sat crossed legged next to her. This was his first real indication of interest in her apart from factual questions inquiring about her professional capabilities.

"My grandfather and mother were forced to flee Goa in the 1930's, the first ship leaving port was destined for the East Coast of America and they took it."

"What was the problem?"

She stared at him again to gauge whether he was genuinely interested. She could tell by his expression that he was sincere.

"It's a long story?" she said rhetorically and smiled.

"Well I don't have any current plans to go out tonight," he said smiling back.

Although she realized that telling the story would bring back some of the hurt from the past, she felt happy that they were at last establishing more friendly lines of conversation.

"My grandfather was a skilled man, and he worked as the Custodian for the Rajah of Udaipur in the state of Rajasthan. In those days the Rajah ruled from a Palace built on a lake and his legendary wealth was known throughout the country. My grandfather had a position of respect, he was entrusted with the safekeeping of the Rajah's wealth....then one day everything went wrong, the Rajah received a visitor, an aristocrat called Lord Blayborne from England. On his last evening as a guest, he asked the Rajah if he could see the treasure before returning on his journey home and leaving for shore. My grandfather was duly summoned to be his guide…"

She paused for a moment as she remembered sitting with her father as a child, listening intently while he passed on the story to her. Luke nodded for her to continue.

"…his treasure was not kept under lock and key but loyal soldiers kept a constant guard on the rooms. The English Lord admired the jewels and artefacts but took a special interest in the 'Neelu necklace' which had a large, flawless sapphire as its centrepiece surrounded by diamonds. After the tour, he bid his farewells and he was escorted to the ferryboat with his wife. They set off for shore and this is when everything went wrong and the action started."

She looked at him and saw that he was intrigued by the story. She carried on speaking in no more than a loud whisper.

"My grandfather returned to the treasure room and discovered the 'Neelu necklace' was missing, knowing this would certainly mean his own execution, he jumped in a boat and set off in pursuit of the Englishman. Catching up, he saw the so-called "Lord' with the necklace and boarded his boat. They fought together and the boat capsized, the rest you can imagine…the English couple and their Punjabi rower drowned and my grandfather managed to swim to shore."

"And the necklace sank with them?"

She nodded.

"His life was as good as over from that moment so he decided to runaway. He escaped the trailing guards and headed back through Maharashtra down the coast to Goa. From there, the first passenger ship to set sail was bound for America. On the journey he met a young girl called Priya, who was also looking to start a new life…she became my grandmother."

"What happened to the Rajah and the palace?"

"He didn't have any children so the dynasty came to an end but the palace is still there, used as a tourist attraction I think."

"Have you seen the palace?" he asked.

"Just pictures." She looked slightly crestfallen after recounting the tale.

Luke smiled at her and took her hand. "Well, here's my promise to you. If we come through this then I will take you to see your palace on the lake."

The Paradigm Shift

In the darkness, he lay down next to her and put his blanket over her.

"Get some sleep we've got an important day tomorrow."

Monday, 11th October 2008
The Pentagon, Washington

Colonel Dan Schwartz sat behind his desk and beckoned General Andrei Karpurov to take the seat opposite him whilst he continued speaking on the phone. It was approaching midnight at the Pentagon but for Commander Tremett on the other end of the line, it was the early hours of the morning in London.

"We are doing all we can to focus our satellite cameras, but the weather's not helping...and before you say it Mark, no there isn't anything I can do about the weather!" Schwartz grunted with irritation.

He and Commander Mark Tremett went back many years. They had worked on several joint CIA/MI6 initiatives in the past. His tone softened as he watched the Russian General taking a seat opposite him.

"Mark, I'm putting you on the speaker, I've got an old friend of yours, Andrei Karpurov sitting in front of me."

"How are you Commander Tremett?" inquired Karpurov.

The General spoke with a thick Russian accent. He was a short, stocky man with wiry black hair and a thick black moustache. His looks gave the impression of brawn over brains but they were deceptive. He had pitted his wits against Schwartz and Tremett in the past and come off better on several occasions.

"I'm fine General, and pleased to hear that you'll be working with us on this one...Dan I'll ring off, speak to me if there are any developments after you've informed Director Conway."

Colonel Schwartz acknowledged his request and clicked off the intercom.

"How was your tour of the facility General?"

The Paradigm Shift

"Excellent, thank you, Colonel. The lay-out is as we had imagined and…" he smiled, "your Sergeant was very hospitable and careful to avoid the more sensitive areas."

General Karpurov spent the next twenty minutes listening to the Colonel explain the monitoring processes they had in place for tracking the warheads in India. The main aggravation to their surveillance was the patchy monsoon weather that prevented the AWACS planes and spy satellites from doing their proper job. When conditions were fine the control room buzzed with live television pictures of almost any part of India depending on the orbiting path of the satellites.

"Here on the East Coast we are ten and a half hours behind India which means a lot of our work is carried out throughout the night. The day has just begun in India and its an important one for us so we're hoping the meteorologists are right for a change and the weather gives us a chance to hone in on certain key installations."

Colonel Schwartz glanced up from his desk and caught the tired look on the General's face.

"It's late General, would you like to be shown your quarters?"

"If it is acceptable, I would like to remain with you here on duty, Colonel."

"Be my guest, I've taken the liberty of organizing your living quarters here at the Pentagon so you are free to retire when you please. The accommodation is quite comfortable….Please bear with me for a moment whilst I update Director Conway."

The administrator put his call straight through, and Schwartz gave his regular update on the status of India's nuclear missiles before moving on to the real reason for the call.

"Codename Amber has collected the information and they are currently located in a shanty town just north of Delhi."

General Karpurov sat motionless staring up at a map on the wall as he listened to the conversation.

Coming to the end of the call, the Colonel briefed the Director on the adverse weather conditions and the possibilities that satellite coverage may improve the next day. He finished the call and stood up from behind his desk.

"Well General you're one of the team now, come, I'll show you to your quarters and you can freshen up for the long night ahead."

Monday, 11th October 2008
Montgomery, Alabama

Director Michael Conway sat in the back of a black limousine as it sped from the airport to the Ritz Carlton Hotel. Due to his earlier commitments that day, he had elected to travel separately from the presidential departure from Washington. Air Force One had landed a few hours earlier, and the party had already settled in to the top two floors of the hotel.

His satellite phone rang again, and he listened for a few minutes before asking his informant to call him as soon as any fresh information became available. The news he had heard was another item on the unpleasant agenda that he was going to have to discuss with the President. Problems were cropping up on too many fronts.

The next morning at ten o'clock he was due to attend the presentation by the US Space Defence Development Program at a military base just outside Alexander City. Arriving at the hotel, he went to the reception and saw that his room was just down the corridor from the President's suite. Catherine Dennison's department had made all the reservations and he called her using the lobby phone to let her know he'd arrived. He also wanted to find out the availability of the President.

"Great, I'm glad you're here Mike, the President's been asking to see you. Just come straight up when you're ready."

He perceived an excitement in her voice that again made him wonder whether she reacted this way to everyone who called or whether she was singling him out.

From the hotel foyer, he stopped briefly in his room to freshen up in the bathroom and store his overnight case before going on to join the President. Jim Allen was already with

President Whiting in one of the comfortably furnished reception rooms which made up the hotel's top suite.

"Good to see you Mike, what can we fix you to drink?" President Whiting was known throughout his administration for his charm and friendly nature. Regardless of his own disposition, he would always make an effort, even to those with the most antagonistic attitudes towards his government's policies.

The butler arrived with a fresh orange juice, just as the President had prescribed. Then with Conway settled in a comfortable chair the President turned to business. In his opening prologue, he made it abundantly clear he wanted to be updated with answers, not more imponderables.

Director Conway decided to begin with the most positive item of news on his agenda.

"Yashwant Puri, the leader of the opposition party in India has defected to France with some of his shadow ministers and aides. His plane touched down in Paris earlier this morning and he has asked for protective asylum from the French government."

"What happened?" the President queried.

"It seems that the opposition leader was outspoken in his criticism of Banerjee. He had gone on public record as voicing his outrage at the launch of the nuclear weapons and has expressed his fears that Banerjee's vision will take them back to the dark ages and certain international ostracism."

"Was he getting any support?"

"Yes, that's why he had to flee in the end. Banerjee ignored his protestations to start off with, but when he began obtaining some support he moved quickly to denounce Puri as a subversive working 'hand in glove' with the West. We monitored his plane taking off and put our phantoms on alert. They reacted quickly when they received a distress call and we identified those on board. An international incident nearly occurred when their fighters arrived just as we were shepherding the plane out of Indian airspace. Air Marshal Reiger confirmed that everything passed without incident and we accepted Puri's decision to go to France."

"This is good news. If this man Yashwant Puri is willing, and it sounds as if he will be, then we should give him all the possible media exposure we can. Maybe he can at least make a few inroads in to the thinking of the overseas Indian communities which are blindly following Banerjee's doctrine."

In America, as in Europe some of the wealthy Indian businessmen sought to fund the resistance. The rioting across the large city suburbs had become worse over the past few days and the Indian communities had wasted little time in forming defensive groups against the bitter, racist attacks that they were regularly subjected to.

In Britain, the scenes were the worst. Apart from the queues and empty roads caused by the beginning of the petrol shortage, the people witnessed running battles in the street as the Indians united against their attackers. At Prime Minister's question time in the Commons, the opposition put the Government under extreme pressure to support law and order and back the military to quell the rioting. Referring to the Indian communities that were trying to defend themselves, one right wing Member of Parliament asked, '*Why aren't we commanding the army to deal with these militia groups once and for all?*'

All the government chambers faced with the problem of dealing with the domestic violence and rioting were encountering the full range of public rhetoric as those with tendencies towards the right became more extreme and those seeking a peaceful solution tried to counter a hard-line approach.

In America, the political chat shows were covering the issues and developments in depth. There was no doubt in the President's mind that an indelible scar was being left on the face of society.

"What do you think Jim?" asked the President.

He turned to get the input from his National Security Advisor. He valued and trusted Jim Allen's views.

"I think that's right Sir. This is a potential media coup for us and I think we should take everything we can get out of it. With your approval I will liaise with Puri and the French Government to coordinate a full media coverage that will last for days."

"You have my approval," instructed President Whiting, "lets try and get a strong wave of support for this man and quickly."

Director Conway opened his folder and looked at his pencilled notes on the next point he had to cover. General Graham had called him earlier and discussed the military activity on India's borders. He had agreed with the General that he would inform the President of the latest military intrusions by India. At this moment, the General had his hands full putting in place the final touches to the next day's presentation.

"I have been working closely with General Graham in monitoring developments on the border of Pakistan and Bangladesh," Conway began.

"The Indian ground forces have moved in to secure the disputed territory of Kashmir and Jammu but have not crossed in to Pakistan. In the aftermath of the bomb explosions and the nuclear fall out, it is probable that they won't invade for a few more weeks."

"And Bangladesh? How did their Prime Minister react?"

"I'm afraid that Bangladesh is now in the hands of India, Mr. President. We argued hard with the Bangladeshi Prime Minister that we, or the British, could get sufficient support to him within a couple of days. But I'm afraid he was correct in his assessment that this wasn't going to be quick enough with the Indian Army lined along his borders. He went on National TV to invite the Indian army to enter without bloodshed and made a plea for peace from his own people."

Director Conway sat back in his seat and clasped his hands together as he relayed the next piece of disturbing news.

"If we weren't sure what kind of person Banerjee was before, we know now…the Bangladeshi Prime Minister met the troops at the border and he was made to sit in the lead vehicles as the Indian Military progressed in full battle formation into the centre of Dacca. The army faced no resistance but still killed thousands of innocent civilians on the way. Even more barbaric is the fact that some vehicles had close members of the Prime Minister's own family, including his daughters strapped to the front of them."

The President shook his head with disgust.

"Jesus! Mike…what kind of animals are we dealing with?"

"And what's more…" Conway continued. "Politically they're trying to paint the bloodshed as a necessary response to quell the local resistance fighters that didn't heed the words of their own Prime Minister."

"Thoughts, Jim?"

Again the President could not put his finger on a straightforward solution to the problem.

"Banerjee's been very clever, by seeming to work with the Bangladeshi Government he has cut out our automatic choices. We cannot go ahead and launch an attack on advancing armed forces when their own Government has condoned their entry!"

"It's not the case though is it Jim?" the President argued.

"You're right of course Mr. President, but we have no demonstrable proof that Banerjee has dishonoured their peace agreement with Bangladesh. To the rest of the world it would be unacceptable if we were to intervene with military action when India had been invited into the country under a peaceful agreement…it would be viewed as an act of war."

The President was struggling to keep his frustrations in check.

"I can't believe this, a country detonates the bomb in anger against one neighbour, and then invades another neighbour…and you're telling me there is nothing I can do about it?"

No one answered the question, they each shared the President's feeling of military impotency, but similarly, each understood the logic that was being put before them. 'Fire' could only be answered with 'fire' when it was carried out under internationally sanctioned rules of play.

One of the President's secretaries entered the room carrying a clipboard and waited patiently before the President turned to face her.

"Yes what is it?" he frowned.

"Just to remind you that you have a dinner function with the Governor and the local business community in fifteen minutes."

The President smiled ruefully and nodded, he knew that the interruption would have been at the behest of the First Lady,

Pamela Whiting. Although it was ten days since India had launched the nuclear attack on Pakistan, the President was determined to keep his engagements wherever possible. He knew it sent a confident message to the people at large.

"We have one more immediate pressing issue that needs to be discussed," said Director Conway. This was the last but most significant and worrying problem on his list.

"We can now see, as can the rest of the world, why Foreign Secretary Henderson's tour of the Middle East failed to preserve our regional interests. The Arab governments have colluded together, military law's been introduced and they have forced their Indian labour back to work."

Over the past few days, the world's media had found a subject that relegated the Indian Prime Minister and the nuclear bomb blasts to the second page. International papers made comparisons with the barbaric treatment being meted out to the Indians by their Arab overlords, and the plight of the Jews during the Second World War. The media attention was a coup for Banerjee, apart from meeting his objectives of closing down the oil wells; it detracted world animosity away from India and even kindled some misguided support.

"The problem is the future supply of oil," Conway stated clearly.

"What's the extent of the problem?" the President asked, knowing already that he would not like the answer.

"The main oil wells in the Gulf are shut down and the Arab Rulers are totally preoccupied with using their forces to restore the status quo. There are no immediate plans on the horizon for the oil fields and refineries to be re-opened."

"I see," murmured the President as he thought through the implications. The magnitude of the economic repercussions slowly began to dawn on him.

"So this is how Banerjee wants to rule the world, he wants to haemorrhage the mature economies by stopping their supply of oil?" The President looked at his advisors incredulously.

"Exactly," said Director Conway. "There is no doubt that this was planned and we are investigating all oil trades made over the past year to find out who's been behind the buying. I can't say for sure Mr. President, but I'd be prepared to lay a lot of money on the fact that it's India which means they're prepared to see out this crisis when it hits."

Jim Allen entered the conversation and explained to President Whiting the ramifications of a shut down in the Middle East. For the US, with slightly under twenty days worth of oil reserves available, the connotations were astounding. Their only source of production, apart from their own, came from South America, which was principally Venezuela. For the rest of the world it was worse, Japan was totally dependent on the Middle East with hardly any reserves and Europe had some pockets of production and reserves, but not enough to out-last the US.

History in Europe provided some indication of the timetable they would now be working to. A few years earlier, French lorry drivers had gone on strike and encouraged other continental neighbours to do the same. They used their trucks to clog the road arteries around Europe and to prevent the distribution of goods in an effort to get a better pay deal from the European Commission.

The strike stopped the production and distribution of oil and petrol from the refineries. In no time at all, the public outcry across the continent from consumers and businesses alike, complaining about the empty petrol pumps was at a fever pitch. Two weeks from the beginning, the Commission and Governments, being held to ransom, caved in and resolved the dispute before the damage to their economies became irreparable.

"How long do we have?" The President stood up and slowly paced towards the window.

Jim Allen peered at Mike Conway, seeking his added approval for the way he was delivering the information to the President.

"We forecast that we have about fifteen to twenty five days to reopen the oil supply. Japan will be in the first wave of countries to suffer, and when the financial markets have their fears confirmed, the Yen will crash and the dollar will not be far behind."

The President stood facing them, listening to the enormity of the issues involved and the revelations that were being presupposed as the consequences were thought through, and the conclusions drawn.

"This is in line with our CIA estimates, Mr. President," acknowledged Director Conway.

"The collapse of world currencies will be to some extent dependent on the markets knowledge. The fact that the oil supplies from the Middle East have ceased will be sufficient to trigger panic in the markets. Countries with a high dependence and requirement for oil, like Japan, will disintegrate surprisingly quickly. Ultimately, the collapse of the dollar and the marketplace will bring financial meltdown to the world economy as a whole. This conclusion is drawn without taking into account the unpredictable and hostile reactions that can be expected from the population."

At that moment, the door opened and Pamela Whiting, apologizing profusely for disturbing them, stepped in wearing a white cocktail dress and matching pearl necklace and earrings.

"We are going to be late, David," she smiled as she gently scolded him.

As she stood there, it was easy to see why the opposition lobbyists for the Democrats struggled to keep up with the momentum of the President's election campaign. The cynics amongst them had accused him of getting all his popularity from the first lady. To a certain extent there was a case to be argued but, in reality, they made a superb team, complementing each other in all departments.

President Whiting told her he would be through in a minute and, seeing their serious expressions, she decided not to put up any resistance and retreated gracefully from the room.

"There is no option gentlemen, those oil fields must commence production immediately, we must take action, no matter how unpalatable it is to world opinion. I will not allow this problem to get away from us…I want you to prepare your teams and instruct the military so that I can hear the options and take the appropriate course of action tomorrow."

Director Conway and the National Security Advisor confirmed that they would begin briefing the necessary personnel immediately. The President, still in a state of shock, stood up and made his farewells before heading off in search of his dinner jacket.

Left alone in the reception room to contemplate how the meeting had gone, Jim Allen turned to his friend, Mike Conway.

"Fancy a drink, Mike?"

Mike Conway felt that sleep was his first choice, but he nodded at the opportunity to relax for a moment and anyway, a drink would help him sleep. They left the Presidential Suite agreeing to meet down in the lobby bar in twenty minutes time.

The 'long bar' as it was known was nearly empty. Security was such that entry in and out of the hotel was only possible for a limited number of carefully screened guests. Most people in the foyer and the lobby bar were either part of the President's team, or in fact security themselves.

The bar's décor was very much in keeping with a five star hotel. The lighting had been dimmed for the evening and the furnishings, like the glass tables and amply cushioned recliners, were low level in style. Jim Allen was already seated as Mike Conway entered and settled into one of the comfortable chairs opposite him. A waiter approached in a white jacket and bow tie to take their orders.

"I'll have a Jack Daniels on the rocks and for you Mike?"

"I'll have beer," he replied. The waiter then ran through his repertoire of house beers before Conway stopped him to select a strong European lager, Stella Artois.

As he disappeared to fetch the drinks, Jim Allen opened the conversation.

"I saw the Chairmen and CEO's of most of the oil companies this morning. They were all prepared to offer whatever assistance is required to rectify the situation in the Gulf. They have committed to building teams from their own resources capable of reopening the refineries and putting the oil fields back into operation should we need them."

"That's good to hear but it's not the critical issue, is it Jim?"

Out of the corner of his eye he noticed Catherine Dennison enter the lobby bar.

"The key to our success has to be diplomacy…can we do this job with the cooperation of Saudi and their Arab neighbours? If they are unwilling partners and we have to take control of the fields by force…well I don't need to tell you, this will open up all kinds of problems."

Mike took the beer from the outstretched arm of the waiter.

"What's more…. We must not make the mistake of under-estimating Banerjee again, I believe he'll have thought this through and he'll still be one step ahead of us…he'll be laying traps ahead to block our next move."

Jim Allen took a sip from his glass before resting it back on the hotel-branded coaster. Rubbing his eyes, he decided this was an opportune time to share his thoughts with the CIA Director.

"I've been thinking about telling the President that we should organize an emergency meeting of the superpowers, maybe at Camp David. We need to inform them of what's around the corner. If we're going to be successful we need to mobilize global support for what we have in mind…what do you think?"

Mike sat deliberating Allen's suggestion. The thoughtful expression changed as he looked up and saw Catherine Denni-son approaching their table. She looked both pretty and profes-sional wearing a beige jacket and matching short skirt that showed off her well-shaped legs. Her hair was neatly brushed back from her face and tied at the back while her make-up was subtly applied, accentuating her lips and eyes.

"Please come and join us Catherine," Conway shouted in her direction as she stopped briefly to have a conversation with one of her team. She smiled and announced she would join them in a minute.

"To answer your question Jim…Camp David is an excellent idea, the only problem is the guest list. Banerjee got that information on Pakistan's nuclear capability from somewhere and who's to say its not one of the other …." He paused for a moment, "…I think our agency investigation into who's been stock piling oil is critical on this one. Whoever is in bed with India will have been building oil reserves of their own."

Allen nodded pensively and swallowed the remaining contents of his glass.

"Then you must get that investigation report quickly," he concluded.

"This sounds important…am I disturbing you?" called Catherine as she approached their table.

"Not at all Catherine," replied Jim Allen looking up, "in fact it's good timing, I was just leaving….I have to make some calls."

He stood up and retrieved the jacket which he'd draped over the armrest of an adjacent chair.

Jim Allen refused Catherine's invitation for another drink and made his farewells. After he had taken a few steps, a thought jogged his memory and he turned round to face Mike Conway.

"Oh Mike, one last thing…why didn't you give the President an update on Codename Amber?"

"I will Jim, it's just that I don't want their assignment to take centre stage at the moment. Let's deal with the issues over which we have a direct control."

"Where are they now?"

"They are in one of the larger shanty towns on the northern outskirts of Delhi."

Jim Allen looked thoughtful, pursing his lips and rubbing his chin before wishing them a second goodnight and heading for the elevator.

"Codename Amber…sounds exciting Mike?" she said smiling playfully at him. Her eyes sparkled wide open, inviting him to explain.

"Not exciting, just business I'm afraid, classified business," he replied. The subject was closed, and he turned the conversation away from the undercover operation by asking her views on the next day's presentation.

The same waiter appeared with the gin and tonic which she'd ordered from the bar.

He enjoyed her company and they carried on talking for far longer than he had intended.

The conversation and her replies stimulated him. *'Was she making signs for him to follow or was this Catherine's normal exuberance?'* he thought. If she was leading him on then he was worried about his own level of self-control.

In the end, he decided it was in his own best interest not to put it to the test, and he announced it was time to beat an honourable retreat back to the room. She agreed and joined him, so they walked through the lobby and stepped into the elevator together.

Mike could smell her 'Christian Dior' perfume pervading the lift as they climbed to the top floor. In that particular moment he wanted to embrace her but they stood apart, smiling at each other's reflection in the lift's mirrors.

Exiting on the same floor, they made small talk as they wandered slowly down the corridor towards his room.

Both fell silent when they got there and he felt the electricity of the moment as he turned to wish her a good night.

"See you in the morning Catherine," he said and bent down to kiss her on both cheeks.

"Good night Mike," she replied looking up at him smiling coyly.

"You'll never guess what Mike, whoever organized the rooms put us next door to each other…can you believe the chances of that happening?"

She gave his hand a knowing squeeze before breaking eye contact and heading the short distance down the corridor to her door. He watched her go in and then searched his own jacket pockets for his room's key card.

Walking into his room, he threw his jacket on the bed and loosened his tie. In front of him was an interconnecting door to Catherine's room. He stared at the door for a moment before walking into the bathroom, leaning against the vanity unit with his palms and stared at himself in the mirror that covered the entire wall. Casual affairs were not his style and he rubbed his chin as he wrestled a losing battle with his conscience.

He stepped back into the room and walked over towards the doors to the balcony. The curtains had already been drawn and he pulled one to the side and looked out. *This time there was no denying the signals'*. He could only think about Catherine and her invitation. His excitement rose further as he imagined her undressing on the other side of the door, he wanted her badly.

He knocked on the door, undoing the catch on his side at the same time. Standing back, he wandered what he was going to say when the door opened.

He heard her footsteps and the catch being pulled loose. His heart pounded with anticipation and excitement. *'How will she look?'* he thought as the door handle turned.

Catherine Dennison pulled it open and looked up smiling at him.

"What kept you?" she asked.

She was wearing nothing but a large white towel wrapped around her. She had just stepped out of the shower and she glistened in the light with her hair falling into wet ringlets around her face.

He stepped forward and lifted her face to his. Holding her, he looked into her eyes before their mouths met and they finally shared the passionate embrace he had been longing for. He gently pulled her to him by the waist and her towel slipped to the floor as she lifted her arms around his neck.

They lay together on her double bed in silence. The excitement and intensity of the lovemaking had drained them both. He gazed at the ceiling while stroking her face. It was the first time he had been unfaithful, and he tried to analyze his feelings. Years of married sex had removed the fire and passion from his home life. The whole spontaneous adventure with Catherine had rekindled the old feeling of excitement in a new courtship. He had surprised himself with his appetite for sex and he lay there wondering why he wasn't feeling more racked with guilt.

As if Catherine could sense what he was thinking, she kissed his face and jumped up pulling the sheet across her chest as she did so.

"Don't shoot yourself Mike, we both needed the attention and it's our secret."

He watched her naked back as she walked across the floor into the bathroom. She stepped into the shower and the steam began to escape under the door.

'I'm not feeling guilty,' he thought as he got up and followed her into the bathroom.

The Paradigm Shift

He pulled open the shower door and, smiling, she held out her hand as he stepped in to join her.

Tuesday, 12th October 2008
Bombay, India

The houseboy walked into the garden looking for his master, Balan Krishnamurthy. The grounds of his residence were extensive but Balan was a creature of habit and the smartly dressed 'peon' knew where to find him. After his son had died he'd planted three magnolia trees in a pretty corner of the garden where his ashes were spread. He would often spend some of his leisure time tending the plants and remembering.

He stood up brushing his hands clean of the dirt, alerted by the bleeping phone that was being carried by the houseboy. Balan admired his handiwork while he waited for him to arrive. As the boy approached, he could see that the phone he was carrying was not the usual portable.

Only one person would call on the satellite phone, and they had agreed that contact would not be made at this stage. The incoming reception would be scrambled but there was still a small chance that it could be intercepted. Whatever the probability was it didn't matter, it was an unnecessary risk and the fastidious Balan was annoyed at the broken protocol.

He answered the phone curtly and after the initial distortion, he heard the General speak.

"Balan, I will be brief. Our intelligence source has confirmed that there are two western agents in a shantytown on the northern outskirts of Delhi. They have instructions to assassinate Banerjee."

"Can you tell me anything else?"

The brief statement from his General friend had dispelled any remaining feelings of annoyance. The importance of the message warranted the call and Balan's irritation was replaced by concern.

"It is believed that one is British and the other is American, that's all we have."

"I understand, your call is appreciated General," and he clicked off the handset and marched towards the house.

Inside, he gave instructions for his case to be packed, and informed his secretary to make sure his private plane was on standby. Satisfied his preparations were being taken care of, he went into his study and asked to be connected urgently to the Indian Prime Minister.

The call was placed quickly and Banerjee came on the line.

"Balan, can it wait? I am in the middle of discovering which idiotic fool let that traitor Yashwant Puri escape," irritated, his voice was short and to the point.

"No it can't wait," Balan replied firmly. "I have some important news that is too sensitive to discuss over the phone. I want your confirmation that you will not leave your apartment or the government offices until I get there, I am travelling immediately."

"Balan, you have stimulated my curiosity, I will be waiting for you when you arrive."

The chauffeur driven car was already packed as he climbed in the back. They sped off in the direction of Bombay airport, slowing down briefly to pick up the police escort that was waiting at the bottom of his drive.

Balan looked at his watch and estimated that he should be with Krishna Banerjee in about two and half-hours time. He still had some preparations to make before that meeting and he reached over for the car phone. His next call was to Ashraf Nawani, Head of India's notorious secret service.

Tuesday, 12th October 2008
Alexander City, Alabama

The President looked immaculate in his dark suit and yellow tie. The tie had been a birthday gift from his daughter. He walked through the hall and entered the auditorium for the presentation. Catherine Dennison walked at his side looking composed and in charge.

Most of his advisors were already in place and, similar to a teacher entering a noisy classroom, the talking subsided as he walked in. The auditorium was like a small cinema; the lights were low and there was a bank of seats facing a stage with a large digital screen in the background.

On the stage behind the lectern were two chairs reserved for the presenters and having seen the President enter, they duly climbed up some steps at the side and took their seats.

First to approach the lectern was General Magnus Graham who was the linchpin of the presentation and the Space Defence Project itself.

He began by welcoming the President and then gave a brief series of introductions to the main government officials who would assist with the presentation. He started with Dr Ramsey, who was the Director of the US Space Defence Program sitting alongside him on the stage. He then introduced some of the key members of his team who sat in the audience.

Once the introductions were completed, he began giving an in depth history of the origins and early developments of the Space Defence Program.

"The original charter of the Space Defence Program was to examine and turn some of those wild ideas, which people regarded as belonging in Hollywood, into reality." His strong army voice boomed out through the hall's speakers.

General Graham then ran through a sequence of some of the crazier theories which had been propounded by the experts before being putting them to one side as completely unworkable.

One such notion had been the nuclear defence shield. This had received a lot of hype and media attention. The scheme involved putting up an impenetrable light or sound shield in the shape of a dome above the United States. The theory was that any nuclear weapon or missile aimed at the US would explode on impact with the shield. During the months of research, the Defence Program would leak the occasional positive development and raise the hope of success in the eyes of the public. In reality, the raised hopes were a ploy to put pressure on the administration for further funding. Unfortunately after years of testing it was dismissed as beyond current capabilities and the failure gave the Defence Program a bad name.

As the General ran through his well-rehearsed speech, the digital screen behind him filled with pictures of the projects and the locations used for testing by the Space Defence Program. The funds expended on the various programs over the years ran into billions.

"And now I'd like to bring you up to date before handing over to Doctor Ramsey."

General Graham commenced his introduction of Project Sabre.

This project had ninety per cent of the Space Defence Program's personnel resources allocated at its disposal and took up an even higher percentage of their annual funding.

"Project Sabre is the most successful strategic development program so far, and has the highest probability of becoming reality," concluded the General before handing over to Doctor Ramsey.

The entire audience was made up of top ranking officials who had been cleared for the top-secret briefing that was about to follow.

"Thank you General," began Dr Ramsey. "Project Sabre is the most sophisticated global missile tracking system ever developed."

"We are currently in the advanced stages of combining the tracking system with counter attack measures. Putting it simply, with the success of this project we will not only have the ability to follow the exact flight path of an incoming ballistic missile, but we will also have the technology to lock on the target and destroy it."

A large demographic was introduced on the screen depicting several satellites connected in a ring orbiting the earth's circumference.

"As you can see, the satellites interconnect to track the flight of the missile and pass the data to our new creation."

Using a pointer, he raised it towards the screen, indicating a regular telecommunications satellite that was floating freely in space with its readily identifiable corporate logos on either side.

"It was launched in February this year. As you can see it looks like an ordinary communications satellite…now observe," he commanded.

Several outside panels began moving as the oval shape of the satellite began to transform before their eyes. From inside the cone, a protrusion like the barrel of a canon began to extend, and around the edge appeared an elaborate matrix of metal antennae. The audience was later informed that these were to dissipate the excess electro-magnetic energy produced at the time of activation.

"This gentlemen, is the fruits of Project Sabre. If you look here…" he used the long baton to point to the relevant place on the screen. "You can see that it has rocket boosters enabling it to take up any position around the globe."

He moved the baton up the screen.

"The protrusion you see here is capable of delivering what we have termed a nuclear electric jolt."

He put the baton down and returned to the lectern.

"The array of satellites can track the target and feed the positioning data into Sabre. To complete the process the tracking connection must be established with the target for three minutes. During this time, Sabre processes the tracking data and activates a controlled nuclear fusion. This fusion produces a nuclear electric surge that is the equivalent of a week's output from a standard reactor."

The President leaned back in his seat, his attention was fully focused on the riveting performance in front of him. *The latest developments sounded very positive indeed'*, he thought. According to what the Doctor was saying, the scientists appeared to have accomplished far more than he could have hoped for.

"I would now like to give you a demonstration of Sabre's power," said Doctor Ramsey again turning to the screen behind him.

The audience watched as the short pre-recorded film was shown. It began with an old tank alone on the flat, deserted saltpans of Utah. The camera panned in and out from the vehicle showing the distance at which the army and scientific spectators were standing. Judging from the image, their observation position must have been about half a mile away from the stationary tank.

Finally, the camera steadied on a close up shot of the tank. In the right hand corner a digital countdown continued to mark the time till Project Sabre would be activated. The room watched in silence as the clock reached zero and what could only be described as an enormous thunderbolt hit the tank making it jump into the air. The camera picture shook for a few seconds as the recorder tried to hold it steady amidst the noise and vibrations.

Below, the main screen was a smaller television picture replaying the same footage only from a greater distance. The 'nuclear jolt' as Doctor Ramsey called it, flashed like fork lightening through the sky hitting the ground where the tank was sitting.

The cameraman then zoomed in to show a close up of the tank. The outer shell was still gleaming white hot from where the thunderbolt had pierced straight through the metal casing.

"That is a stationary target gentlemen," Dr Ramsey went on. He was left in no doubt from their faces that they were impressed with the demonstration.

"Our problem is that we have not completed successful trials on moving targets."

The screen then showed new footage of a series of attempts by Sabre to lock on and shoot down a dummy ballistic missile. The best attempt managed to flash close enough to divert the course of the missile but not to impede its progress.

As the film came to an end, the lights in the auditorium were turned up and General Graham came back to the lectern. He thanked the Doctor for his presentation and faced the audience to summarize proceedings.

"It is our conclusion that we should be able to get Project Sabre operational with a high degree of reliability in the next three to six months…this is only if we continue to place full resources at the disposal of the Defence Program." He thanked them for their attention and acknowledged the applause with a nod as he picked up his papers from the lectern.

The President leaned towards Jim Allen and Director Conway who were sitting to his right. He had been greatly impressed with what he had seen and heard.

"Unfortunately three to six months doesn't do it for us, does it Jim?"

"No, Mr. President," he whispered back. "I'll look into all the possibilities of accelerating the program."

"Do that, we needed Project Sabre working thirteen days ago."

Tuesday, 12th October 2008
Government Offices, Delhi

The media crews were packing up their cameras and loading them into the back of their vans as Balan's cavalcade arrived from the airport. They swept around the front of the government offices and into the gravel drive, taking him up to the main entrance.

His driver held the door open for him and he hurriedly set off to confront Banerjee with his news. Balan recognized the face coming towards him; it was the lady reporter from CNN. As she passed, he paused, turning around to look at her for a second. Pensively, he then climbed the steps and strode through the pillared entrance of the imposing government building. Unbeknown to him he was being watched himself by Codename Amber.

Despite the heavy security, Balan by-passed the checkpoints and walked straight up the stairs and into the Prime Minister's office. Apart from the Head of Indian Secret Service itself, he was the only close aide within Banerjee's team who was allowed to dispense with the usual formalities.

"Balan, you made good time," exclaimed Banerjee looking up from behind his desk as he entered.

"You have just missed my heartfelt appeal for democracy and common sense to prevail," he said, laughing at his own irony.

His subservient advisors smiled sycophantically at their leader's reference to his recent press conference. Standing in a semi-circle around him he dispatched them all with an impatient wave of his hand.

"I saw the CNN woman leaving," Balan remarked

The Paradigm Shift

The Prime Minister then explained the purpose of his exclusive interview with CNN which would be broadcast around the world later that day.

"We must keep two steps ahead of the Americans, my friend," Banerjee answered, looking pleased with himself.

"By now the Americans will be doing somersaults about the impending oil crisis...they will have done their calculations, they know they haven't got long."

He paused for a moment contemplating his interview. For clarity, he wanted to repeat the language he had used in front of the camera to his trusted deputy, Balan.

"I expressed in no uncertain terms our disgust and outrage as a nation at the atrocities that were being carried out on our people by the Arab Rulers in the Middle East...I made it clear that these military dictatorships in the Gulf could not be allowed to enslave our citizens. I beseeched the United Nations and civilized democratic governments of the world to unite in their international condemnation of the Arab Rulers."

Balan decided the purpose of his own trip could wait; the Prime Minister was enjoying demonstrating his own genius. Listening intently with his hands clasped behind his back, he wandered towards the windows and looked out across the lawns.

"And then came the masterstroke," Banerjee confidently announced.

"I told the nations of the world that if this situation could not be resolved by united, peaceful means, then India could not, and would not, stand by watching the inhuman treatment of our brothers...if necessary we shall use whatever military means are at our disposal to secure their rights and passage to freedom."

Balan's mouth was twisted in a wry smile as he calculated the global ramifications of Banerjee's speech. His genius was unmistakable.

"The world will not know which way to turn?" he said out loud with his back to the Prime Minister. Balan stared out through the lead-lined panes imagining the international turbulence that would be caused by Banerjee's interview.

"That's right Balan, we just have to keep up the confusion for fifteen to twenty-five days more and then we're home and dry."

There was nothing that Balan Krishnamurthy wanted more in the world that to bring the President of the United States to his knees. His anger ran deep. Suddenly he flinched and broke out of his trance remembering the purpose for his visit.

"We have visitors, Prime Minister!"

"Aah...the reason for your journey, I take it these are not welcome visitors."

"There are two undercover agents, one British and one American, and we believe they are currently located in one of the slums north of the city and..." Balan looked into the eyes of the Prime Minister, "...their mission is to assassinate you."

There was no flicker of emotion, no look of terror on his face; to the contrary a thoughtful expression crossed his face.

"This could be very useful Balan, very useful indeed."

"Ashraf Nawani is taking control of our counter measures personally. His secret police have identified two slum dwellings that fit the bill. They are going to supervise the operation with the military at their full disposal. He has assured me that they will take no chances. They will surround the entire area and block off all exits to the alleyways before conducting a house to house search leaving no stone unturned."

"I want them alive," said Banerjee.

"It's not possible to…" but Balan was not given a chance to finish.

"I understand Balan," he repeated forcefully. "But I want them alive if possible." He stared at Balan implying further discussion was meaningless.

"If we can capture these agents and expose them to the world as the international assassins of the so called superpowers, then do you not think it will add further to the confusion of who's in the right and the wrong?" asked Banerjee.

"It will further discredit world opinion of the US and bring disunity to their Alliance."

Balan could see the logic of his suggestion; he would need to make adjustments.

So far that day, his discussions with Nawani had been conducted over the telephone but this situation was urgent. Balan decided a personal meeting was in order especially now that Banerjee had indicated a change of priorities. He stood up to leave.

"I will instruct our Secret Police accordingly, but until we have completed the capture I think it is advisable that you keep your movements and public engagements to a minimum."

"Don't worry Balan, I have complete faith in your capabilities."

Tuesday, 12th October 2008
Government Offices, Delhi

The sun was not yet up when Kirin woke Luke at five o'clock that morning. They drank boiled water and ate some fruit and leftover food from the night before. The 'slept in' clothes they were wearing blended in well with those of the other slum dwellers. At this moment Kirin sorely missed the makeshift shower back at the farmhouse.

Outside in the alley, close to where Luke fetched the water, a hose was attached to a bent rusty tap sticking out of the ground. Youngsters and adults alike used the hose to wash themselves and the few clothes they were wearing. Around the tap, they would think nothing of stripping off and standing naked, as one member of the family would turn the hose on another.

The journey to the Government Offices in Central Delhi was an easy one. Outside the slum, Luke had flagged down one of the small, yellow taxis; once it had stopped, he made way for Kirin to do the talking. She asked the driver to take them to a fruit and vegetable market located close to the Indian Parliament Building. Nearby, across the road from the Parliament were the offices and private residential apartment of Krishna Banerjee.

When they started in the early hours of the morning, the streets were relatively clear and they sped quickly down the bumpy roads. As they approached the centre of town with the sun rising, the streets soon began teaming with life. Against the background noise of hooting scooters, the driver slowed down and dropped them off.

"Shukriya," said Kirin thanking him in Hindi and handing over a few rupee coins.

The Paradigm Shift

Together, they entered the covered market and Luke followed Kirin to a colourful stall selling all types of tropical fruit. She bought a mixture of mangos, melons and coconuts, giving Luke the wooden trays to carry. At another stall outside the market, they purchased some additional items including knives and other utensils for the project in hand. With the shopping complete, Kirin led the way on the short journey to the Government Offices and Banerjee's private residence.

Across the road from the main entrance they laid out the plastic wicker matting they had just acquired. Kneeling down they spread it on the ground in front of them like a marker to others that this was now their pitch. On either side of them, all the way down the pavement were street vendors squatting on their mats. As a rule you needed to start early if you wanted a prominent position. The vendors sold a wide variety of cheap goods from tobacco and food snacks to presents, such as silks, imitation jewellery and ivory statues. Sitting on the mat, Kirin cleaned the fruit in a bowl they filled from a nearby tap and then carved them into fresh slices. As the morning temperature rose, she neatly laid out the pieces of fruit on the wooden board in front of her and prepared to sell her wares to the passers by.

Several weeks earlier this promenade had been one of the main tourist attractions in Delhi for visiting foreigners, ranking only behind the Red Fort in terms of popularity. However the tourist trade was a thing of the past, the tips and bonuses gratefully received from the westerners was over for the foreseeable future. Nowadays, the vendors survived because the high density of office and government workers in the area sustained them.

Once settled, Kirin sat watching the front gates of the government building, keeping track of all the comings and goings whilst occasionally selling a piece of fruit to a passer-by. As she watched, her thoughts drifted to Luke for a moment. She recalled the compliment he had paid her earlier that morning. As they were walking from the market, he had remarked that she was a very pretty woman and that she better cover up her face otherwise she may attract attention from individuals interested in more than just purchasing fruit.

Luke had gone off alone as agreed. He was walking the entire outer perimeter of the building to ascertain any weak links and scrutinize the security systems in place. The route was busy and he found it easy to amble along the path without being conspicuous.

From her position, Kirin saw the arrival and departure of the camera crew, and not long after, the stretched black Mercedes with the dark windows. The limousine was accompanied by police on motorbikes and at the rear, a jeep with a mounted machine gun. She wanted to know the identity of the passenger and crossed the road leaving her stall unmanned. She timed passing the closing gates to coincide with the Mercedes door opening. As Kirin glanced up the drive, she saw the dignitary pause for a moment and turn around as a western lady passed him. Kirin recognized him instantly, it was Balan Krishnamurthy, the deputy Prime Minister of India. She could sense from his expression that he was agitated about something.

Contemplating the importance of the new arrival, she crossed the road and thanked her neighbour for looking after her stall in her absence. *With the camera crew departing and Balan's arrival it definitely confirms Banerjee's presence in the Government residence,'* she thought.

Several hours later, Luke returned from his scouting mission around the wall's perimeter. He reported his findings and announced his intention to sleep in one of the street's doorways that night like so many of the city's vagrants.

With the light fading, Luke and Kirin collected their belongings and began the return journey to the slum dwelling. They had agreed that they would spend an hour together back at their shelter discussing the days findings before Luke would return to the city centre for the long night ahead.

Tuesday, 12th October 2008
On board Air Force One

The President, Jim Allen, Catherine Dennison and Mike Conway were in the middle of their discussions on the oil crisis as Air Force One flew over the state of Virginia. They were flying at thirty-two thousand feet on the return route back to Washington. The cabin of Air Force One offered the height of travelling luxury with its spacious and tastefully decorated presidential lounge. The plane was also responsible for keeping the President in touch with the rest of the world and housed below the flight deck was it's own international communications centre

CNN had informed the US Administration of their interview with Banerjee but without giving them an opportunity to pre-screen it or to prevent it being shown on the grounds that it was against the public's interest. Nevertheless the President was angry with this development and Banerjee's ability to manipulate the media.

Their conversation on what Banerjee could be planning was interrupted when Jim Allen pointed at the flat screen on the cabin wall. CNN proudly announced that its world exclusive with Krishna Banerjee would be coming up next after the break. They moved their seats to get a more comfortable view of the picture.

The American anchorwoman began by asking the Prime Minister's views on developments in the Middle East. It quickly became clear to the expert eye that she was feeding him with prearranged questions, which was probably the price CNN had to pay to obtain the exclusive interview rights.

The Paradigm Shift

The face of Banerjee, with the dark skin colouring under his eyes, feigned sadness and despair as he slowly talked of the inhumane conditions and terrible suffering of his people across the Middle East. His posture and narration was designed to extract maximum sympathy from the worldwide audience.

As the interview progressed, his mood changed, he became more animated and impassioned as he tried to invoke the support of the 'civilized democracies of the world against the evil Arab dictators'. In response to one orchestrated question he banged his fist on the desk and again reiterated the word 'we' when referring to the world's leading democracies.

"We, the true democracies of the world, must stand against any such unlawful suppression and enslavement," he repeated.

The final scene was a tribute to his acting ability as again his mood reverted to the pacified persona he had started with. Banerjee became calm and controlled, speaking in a slow, deliberate manner to deliver his final ultimatum to the millions of watching viewers.

"If the civilized world will not stand by our side in our time of need, then we cannot and will not stand idly by whilst our people suffer such inhumane and barbaric treatment...if necessary we shall use whatever military means are at our disposal to secure their rights and passage to freedom."

"That confirms it for me, Sir."

Jim Allen swung round in his chair to face the President.

"I am now of the firm opinion that we need to organize a summit of the superpowers at Camp David in the next few days."

The CNN reporter was just announcing that they would be returning shortly with their usual post interview analysis to be carried out by a carefully selected panel of experts. The President signalled to one of the cabin staff and the monitor was turned off.

"Banerjee is trying to fragment the Alliance and disrupt world opinions, time is not on our side Mr. President, we need a united international front against India if we are going to avoid this oil crisis," continued Allen.

"I agree with the National Security Advisor," said Conway. "We should keep entry to a minimum and my suggestions are: Britain, China, Russia and France only."

The President stood up and wandered across the cabin deep in thought. There was no doubt in his mind that Banerjee posed a greater threat than the world had ever known. None of the notorious dictators of the twentieth century had so much power. Certainly none had the ability to change the course of history in such a short period of time.

"Let me see if I have got this correct." The President stopped and began to recount their earlier recommendations.

"You are suggesting that the United States must do everything in its power over the next two days to reason with King Mohammed and the other Gulf leaders...including me calling them personally."

Apart from Jim Allen nodding his head, they remained quiet allowing the President to express his thoughts.

"We must convince them to open their doors willingly to our military units in order that our teams of oil industry technicians can enter the oil field facilities and restore production."

He carried on pacing the floor as he continued.

"If by day three, we are unsuccessful then we have no choice but to take control of the oil fields by force, am I correct?"

'That's correct," interrupted Jim Allen. "The only change that I suggest is that we delay the use of force until after the Summit."

"Ok, and the headline contents of the Summit?" The President posed the question to Jim Allen.

"Director Conway should present India's true game plan, and provide hard evidence of their strategy by sharing our intelligence with the other superpowers. The objective is simply to get their full support and commitment to our using force in the Gulf."

"Good, it makes sense but with one change."

They looked at the President awaiting his suggestion.

"We should invite Japan, in the event we are struggling for agreement I would like to have allies around that table. I suspect that we can anticipate the support of France and Britain but the others are in the balance. The Japanese know they will be the first country to suffer in the oil crisis and this will make them proactive to our cause. Margaret can sound them out through our diplomatic channels but I am sure we can count on their total support."

The President addressed them all.

"Does anyone have any reservations?"

"It's a good idea, Mr. President and maybe..."

Conway was cut off as the President interrupted to speak to Catherine Dennison.

"Speak to Margaret, and ask her to get onto it right away."

She jumped up and made her way towards the onboard telephone passing close to the seat of Director Conway. As she passed she noticed his warm smile but her face remained blank and devoid of emotion. *'Strange,'* thought Conway before turning back to President Whiting.

"Mike?" the President queried.

He stumbled for a second as the point slipped from his mind. *'Why the cold look from Catherine?'*

"Go on Mike?" the President repeated.

He quickly came back to his senses.

"Mr. President, our concern has to be that a third party is in tandem with India. The Agency is making every effort to determine who this party is…we believe the investigation into the countries which have been stock piling oil will give a clear indication, as well as our research into who was behind the dummy Pakistani testing."

"I share your concern, for all we know it could be one of our proposed guests!"

"That's right Mr. President, the sensitivity and timing is such that we may be inviting a hostile nation into our own camp."

"Then we need the answers from the Agency quickly, don't we Mike?"

Thursday, 14th October 2008
Shantytown, Outskirts of Delhi

They reached their shelter at about six o'clock, and the old woman they'd met the day before was again sweeping her floor. Seeing them approach she stopped and asked Kirin if her man could fill her water pots again. Luke listened to her cackling voice and waited patiently for an interpretation.

As she finished Kirin turned around laughing and told him he was back on water duty.

He grabbed the pots and headed off in the direction of the taps, he wanted to get the chore done so that they could get down to the real business of analyzing the days findings.

As he stood filling the pots, he saw a military truck parked across the road that bordered the shantytown. The canvas flaps were down at the rear, but when a light gust of breeze blew the covers apart he could see that the back was full of armed soldiers. Initially, he didn't sense any danger as you often saw trucks carrying the military around Delhi, but he wondered what reason they could have to be parked there?

Ten minutes later, Luke returned balancing the heavy water pots on either end of a yoke slung across his neck. He smiled as he saw Kirin and the old lady still talking. Placing the pots in her shelter he nodded at the old lady, accepting her gratitude.

Kirin finally managed to disengage from her conversation and joined Luke in the shelter.

"The old lady was saying that people have noticed a few soldiers on either side of the shantytown this evening."

"Where?" asked Luke. The alarm bells were ringing now.

Experience had taught him not to trust coincidences. If there were soldiers on either side of the slum it could be for only one reason, they wanted to surround it.

"Over by one of the south alley exits." Kirin replied sensing his anxiety.

The answer confirmed his fears.

"We've got to leave now, if we get split up, we'll meet at the market we visited this morning ok?"

"Ok, but how could they…." She started but Luke cut her dead.

"Later Kirin, we must move quickly."

She tossed the few items they had in a bag as Luke lifted his shirt to check his belt. He removed a flat silver object the size of a cigarette packet and started scraping the dirt in the corner of the shelter.

Outside, the light was starting to fade in the early evening. They had not seen anything unusual on their approach into the slum from the West, so that was the direction Luke took them in. As they approached the last hundred yards to the alley before it reached the main highway, they saw the soldiers blocking the exit. Some of them were slowly walking into the alley and Kirin could hear them asking the children if they knew of any new arrivals.

Kirin tugged Luke's sleeve and they stopped. They were shielded from the soldier's line of vision by the corner of a shelter.

"Listen Kirin, I want you to make your way to the exits in the north, they'll be guarded as well but be ready for I have planned…now go," he ordered in a low voice.

Kirin looked at him and touched his cheek. She didn't like the idea of separating but had no alternatives to offer.

"Go!" he repeated in a loud whisper and this time she turned and set off up the alley towards the north without looking back.

Luke checked his watch and then glanced back to check on the position of the army sentries who had entered the alley. They were gradually working their way closer.

Although the soldier's presence had removed some of the usual crowds that inhabited the alleys, there was still sufficient cover for him to avoid detection. Leaving the corner of the shelter, he stepped out into the alley and walked back the way he had come.

Coming towards him was a man selling mangoes. He was pushing a wheelbarrow cart laden high with the green and red fruit. Luke, thinking quickly, pretended to have dropped something and stooped down in front of the cart. As the man shouted at him to get out of the way he attached one of his silver devices to the bottom of the cart. Clicking a button, a digital screen on the side started counting down from five minutes.

The man's Hindi shouting got louder. He was in real danger of attracting the attention of the soldiers unless he hurried.

Luke finished and rolled to one side to get out the way of the cart. He jumped up clutching a rupee coin pretending that it had fallen in the man's path. Luke put his hands together as if praying for an apology and the salesman continued on his way, muttering angrily

Luke checked his watch again and set off at a fast walk towards the exits in the East. The soldiers had advanced further into the labyrinth on this side. The leader of this patrol had clearly decided there was no longer a need for secrecy now. He was shouting instructions into his walkie-talkie whilst his soldiers kicked open shelter doors. Other supporting troops stood back with their guns raised for what might emerge from inside.

Luke punched the button on his last silver device and slammed it to the under side of a shelter roof. Keeping one eye on the progression of the soldiers he turned and retreated thirty yards back down the alley.

The soldiers had taken to their task with relish. They dragged the cowering slum dwellers out of their shelters shouting and waving their rifles. A mother screamed as one of the soldiers threw her naked little girl across the alley. As she raised her hands to protest, a rifle butt struck her across the face and she fell bleeding and unconscious to the ground.

The noise escalated around the slum as the soldiers moved on to repeat their next act of savagery. The little girl, sobbing, picked herself up and ran towards her mother throwing herself on her motionless body.

Only the leader stayed aloof from the brutality of his men. He talked into his radio whilst arrogantly pointing out the next shelter to be ransacked. The troops continued to show no mercy and the leader shouted at his men, goading them on to be more virulent in their duty.

Luke knelt down; the soldiers had now reached the shelter where he had attached the flat silver case. He took one last look at his watch and then walked into the centre of the alley, thirty yards back from where the soldier was kicking down the door to the shelter.

Amidst the noise, he stood watching them standing perfectly still in plain sight of everyone. His feet were apart and his hands rested on his hips as stared at the soldiers. The leader carried on talking with his head to one side into his radio until he noticed Luke watching him. *Who was this insolent man standing arrogantly in front of them?'* and then the realization slowly dawned across his face.

The leader stopped talking into his radio and his mouth fell slightly ajar as behind him the soldiers carried on beating another hapless victim. Luke was the last thing he saw, seconds later he was dead.

The explosion had the equivalent power of five hand grenades. The noise was deafening and the force of the blast demolished everything in a radius of twenty yards sending pieces of the shelters and rubble high into the air.

Kirin was watching the soldiers proceeding down from the northern exits when she jumped at the noise of the explosion. As she turned to see where it had come from, another explosion detonated to the West.

The panic and screaming came next. The alleys were overflowing with India's poverty stricken classes running for their lives. As the crowd engulfed all in its wake, Kirin saw a baby clinging to the chest of her sister. The older girl herself could be no more than four years in age.

Kirin forgot about her own safety and ran towards them, scooping them to one side before they were caught by the stampeding herd. She put the baby under her arm and held the little girl's hand tightly. The force of the crowd heading for the streets beyond the slum was too strong, and clinging to the children, she got sucked into the flow. The selfless act completely contradicted the CIA rules for undercover agents but that is what separated her from the mainstream. Behind her, she could hear the results of Luke's diversionary tactics.

The third explosion went off, briefly drowning the screams of the crowd before they returned, louder than before. The soldiers did their best to hold the exits, but the chaos and the throng's momentum gave them little chance of success. They were brushed aside like flies. Kirin broke through into the street still clinging on to the sobbing children.

She wanted to get them as far away as possible but the little girl shrieked, pulling free of her grip. She raced in and out of the masses and into the arms of her grateful mother. As Kirin caught up with her, she handed over the baby. The woman's eyes were full of tears.

"I thought I'd lost them," she wailed and clutched her babies closer. The surrounding noise made her joy barely audible.

Kirin looked over the wailing woman's shoulder. Across the road, standing at the back of one of the army trucks was a high-ranking military officer. Next to him was someone she recognized instantly. It was Ashraf Nawani, the infamous chief of the Indian Secret Service. He was responsible for turning the old information bureau, known as the 'Research and Analysis Wing', into the feared government department that used brutal procedures to get what it wanted.

Nawani and the Army Officer were engaged in a hopeless task. They were trying to scrutinize every fleeing victim out of the slum's alleyway as they appeared onto the street.

Kirin gripped the woman's shoulder, wishing her luck and then pushed outwards through the crowds and made her way into the back streets. She felt elated to be heading towards safety, but her mood changed with every step as she wondered what had happened to Luke.

Thursday, 14th October 2008
Presidents Office, The White House

The connection was already established. Catherine Dennison looking smart and in control as usual, strode into the President's office.

"Mr. President, His Highness King Mohammed has taken his place."

President Whiting looked up from his reading and pulled off his glasses.

"Ok, let's go Catherine," and he got up to accompany her. They walked back past her office and into an adjoining room that was constructed specifically for the purpose in hand.

The studio was quite small in White House terms, and housed just one desk in front of a large US flag. In front, was a camera pointing at the desk and to one side was a wide screen monitor for the incoming transmission.

As the President took his seat behind the desk he looked at the monitor and saw that King Mohammed was already present. He was sitting in the same seat he had occupied for the visit of Secretary Henderson a few days earlier. The time was mid afternoon in Saudi and the King looked calm, watching the President's arrival on his own monitor.

"Good afternoon your Highness," began the President.

Also present in the room, but outside the range of the camera, were Jim Allen, Catherine Dennison, Defence Secretary Warner, Foreign Secretary Henderson and Vice President Martins.

King Mohammed returned the pleasantry and then fell silent. It had taken huge diplomatic efforts to get the Saudi leader to appear for this conference. His own advisor's had counselled strongly against it but the King had insisted. He felt beholden to America for its assistance in the past and although this would not change his stance, he felt honour bound to be civil with the President.

For his part, the President knew the onus to talk throughout the conversation would be on him and he had a speech prepared that succinctly covered the main topics of conversation.

Getting straight to the point, he asked the King if he would accept a US military presence on their soil. The King replied this could be considered in the future. The President asked if he could send in specialist teams to reopen the oil fields, and the King responded that they would consider his suggestion further.

The answers the President was looking for were not forthcoming and he decided to raise the temperature by being blunt with his demands.

"I have to make it clear to your Highness that *'time'* is something we do not have. I repeat, are you prepared to accept a US military presence? Are you prepared to allow in US teams to control and operate your oil fields?"

The King with his red and white checked headdress did not respond immediately but when he did, he spoke calmly and assuredly.

"Mr. President, we are in control of the situation. Please be convinced that restoring oil production is our top priority. I am advised that we will be able to reopen the wells shortly."

The President's advisors had made it clear to him that in the current conditions there was no chance of the Saudis completing the job themselves.

"I must make it clear your Highness that our information indicates that your country is not in a position to re-establish the oil fields in the time frame required. Do you understand our position?"

The President looked at the monitor as it crackled before going dead.

He leaned back and looked at his team standing in the wings.

"I guess we know where this takes us!"

Thursday, 14th October 2008
The Pentagon, Washington

Colonel Dan Schwartz picked up the transcript sitting on the desk in front of him. He read it again and then slammed it back on his desk. The contents of the message were difficult to believe. If it was true, then there was a mole in the joint CIA/MI6 operation that had tried to blow the cover, and ultimately terminate their agents in India. *'But how many people know of their mission for christsakes?'* One thing was for sure, Director Conway was not going to be happy.

There was absolutely no reason to doubt the authenticity of the message from Luke Weaver. It came through the correct channels and revealed the details of the ambush attempt in northern Delhi. In no uncertain terms, it made it clear that the attack was premeditated. Ashraf Nawani and the Indian Secret Service had been told where to find them.

The phone rang in front of him. He was expecting to be connected on a secure line to the UK so he could get the reaction of his British counterpart.

"I have Commander Tremett on the line."

"Put him through," growled Schwartz.

They dispensed with the usual formalities.

"This leak has come from your end," the Commander's tone was sharp.

"What makes you so sure?" he replied defensively.

"Dan, we've known each other a long time, I think you suspect the same."

Commander Tremett had seen Sir Thomas Boswell before making the call. Normally a calm and controlled person in times of crisis, Tremett had been shocked by the ferocity of his rage. He was instructed to leave the Americans under no illusion about the source of the leak.

"At our end access is restricted to six people who have knowledge that the project exists, they are the PM, his deputy and two other members of the cabinet. As you know the other two are myself and Sir Thomas."

"What are you talking about Commander?" said Schwartz indignantly. "That sounds like plenty of potential for a leak."

Commander Tremett let him finish and came to the punch-line.

"Dan, we didn't tell the PM and the Cabinet Ministers about their location in India. Are you understanding what I'm saying?"

Schwartz fell silent at the other end. Tired, he rubbed his eyes as he thought about Director Conway's reaction.

"Ok, Mark you've made your point. What about someone being able to break into our communication system?"

It was a last gasp effort. He knew their systems were fool proof, he was clutching at straws before the inevitable conclusions were drawn.

Commander Tremett didn't feel the question warranted an answer and abruptly jumped to the next line of discussion.

"We want to know exactly who was party to the information on the location at your end?"

"Subject to confirmation..." The Colonel began thoughtfully: "Director Conway, National Security Advisor Allen, Vice President Martins, Andrei Karpurov and, of course, the President...but there could be more."

"One name stands out Dan," Tremett said caustically.

"Ok, I don't think we can jump to conclusions...Karpurov's under surveillance and off the information list for now."

Colonel Schwartz felt frustrated as they concluded the call. It was time to face the music with Director Conway but he had nothing to add beyond the simple transcript sent by Luke Weaver.

When the message had first arrived in the Communication Centre, Schwartz had alerted Conway to the news over his car phone while he was on the way to another appointment at the White House. Schwartz was uncomfortable with going into details over an insecure telephone line so Conway immediately turned his Range Rover around and headed back at full speed towards the office.

'He *should have arrived by now,*' thought Schwartz, and started walking up the metal staircase towards the Executive Floor.

His knocking on the door was met with a curt response and he entered, sitting at one of the chairs in front of the Director's desk.

"What the hell is this all about Dan?" he asked leaning back in his chair.

Colonel Schwartz showed him the transcript and briefed him on his call with Commander Tremett. Conway shook his head in disbelief.

"There is something strange here, Dan, it just doesn't make sense for Karpurov to come here and pass on the information, its too obvious, he must know that any such leak would expose him and his country..."

"The alternative is unthinkable, if we believe the British, then the choice is Karpurov or we have a mole living at the very top of our US Administration with access to every move we make."

"Christ it doesn't make sense....do you think that Russia could be India's backers?"

Puzzled, Conway stared at the ceiling trying to answer the question himself. His gut feeling was 'no' but it was more palatable to entertain than a spy in their own camp.

"Ok, who was informed about the location in northern Delhi?" asked Conway.

Schwartz ran through the names he had confided to Commander Tremett as being party to the agent's whereabouts.

"Are there any more names?"

The Director thought for a minute about who might have been party to his conversations on the India infiltration issue over the past few days. He remembered the events in Montgomery and the drink with Jim Allen in the lobby bar. *'How much had he told Catherine?'* he wondered trying to recall their conversation. Conway slowly shook his head.

"No, I think that's everyone, Dan."

He sat there in a trance for a couple of minutes, imagining how Jim Allen and the President would react to the news. *'It has to be the Russians,'* he thought with a trace of guilt.

"Is everything ok Mike?" Schwartz face showed his concern.

"Yes, yes, fine," replied Director Conway breaking out of his trance.

"We have to get some positive news and we have to get it quickly!" he exclaimed.

"I must be able to tell the President that we will have that Investigation Report completed on whose been building oil supplies before the summit takes place."

'This should crucify or vindicate Karpurov,' he thought.

"We are working on it round the clock, the problem is partially getting hold of the sales records with all the Middle East States being incommunicado and also pinning down the final shipping destinations. Many of the carriers are Liberian based tankers held under 'bearer share' companies."

"We need the answers now Dan," Conway said forcibly.

Schwartz confirmed he was ninety per cent sure the Report would be in his hands before the summit started.

"What about our Pakistani connection Dan? Can we get that link established fast?" he inquired.

Colonel Schwartz promised to do all he could to follow up with their undercover agent and his contact in the Pakistani Government. They both realized, there was every chance that their man would lose his life in the pursuit of this information.

"The answer should be the same in both cases," commented Schwartz.

They finished by discussing how they would proceed with General Karpurov.

"I want you to treat him like normal," ordered Conway. "Don't confront him, monitor his calls and just make sure he stays away from any sensitive information from here on."

As Schwartz closed the door, the Director was again stung with the guilt of his stay in Montgomery. He hadn't been wholly truthful with Schwartz and he was his most trusted friend. Why had Catherine been so cold towards him on the return flight? Was she hiding her own guilt?

The questions flashed through his mind before he brought them to an abrupt stop.

'What am I thinking? It's ridiculous, she's been with the President for decades,' he thought.

Thursday, 14th October 2008
Delhi Market

The time was fast approaching midnight as Kirin sat in a dark corner of the market place waiting for Luke's arrival. It was deserted, and she was surrounded by the bare frames of the stalls and the empty wooden palettes used for storage. In this case the goods were fruit and vegetables and the air was suffocating with the smell of rotting produce.

Despite the pungent aroma she was not entirely alone, the market offered shelter from the street and vagrants took full advantage. The market itself was like an elongated shed with a roof, albeit a flimsy one, made out of ply-board. She wasn't tired; she still felt the adrenaline from the evening's earlier incidents and sat observing the movements from the dark.

Four hours had passed since she first arrived and she began to despair for Luke's safe arrival. If he had escaped unharmed he should have arrived by now. All the possibilities ran through her mind. Could he have been captured by the secret police? Had he been caught in his own explosions?

Normally her single-mindedness to complete the mission would have kept her mind focused on her own safety and the next stage of the job but this was not the case. At this moment she realized her own feelings towards him were stronger than she imagined. The thought of him dead seemed unbearable. Luke had saved her in the slum, he had put her life before his own by pushing her towards the safety of the north, knowing that his detonations would drive the people in that direction.

Surrounded by darkness she sat hunched on the dirt floor, she hugged her raised knees with both arms and slowly rocked back and forth.

"Come on Luke…" she whispered to herself under her breath.

She stopped and strained her eyes as she saw a man's silhouette moving across the street.

Her hopes had been raised on a few occasions already. Characters had appeared out of nowhere approaching the market only to disappear in another direction at the last minute.

As the person moved closer she could see that his profile matched with Luke's. She stood up to get a better view.

In the darkness, the man's figure paused, deciding which way to go and Kirin picked up a piece of rubble and threw it against the side of a stall. It clanged as it hit a piece of metal piping. The figure turned and headed in the direction of the noise.

She stayed hidden in the corner until she could recognize the face. It was Luke and she sprang forward to embrace him unable to control her relief.

"I'm pleased to see you too," he whispered softly, smiling at her reaction he hugged her back.

She was about to launch into her questions when she saw Luke holding his finger up to his lips for her to keep quiet. He took her hand and led her deeper under the covers of the market. When he was satisfied that they could speak without being detected, he found a place for them to sit down. Kirin, still full of excitement at his return, was first to speak.

"I saw Ashraf Nawani outside the slum. It was his operation." She kept her voice low.

"I know," said Luke, "That's where I've been, I followed him after the last explosion in case he'd planned a rendezvous with Banerjee, it could have given me the opening I was looking for, but no luck I'm afraid."

The Paradigm Shift

There was no hint of self-acclaim in Luke's voice. Already, she knew him well enough to know that he played his exploits down. Dispassionately, he told her everything as it happened and Kirin still marvelled at his ability under such pressure. It gave her added confidence that between them they could get the job done.

She listened to Luke's logic regarding the mole that had deliberately leaked their whereabouts to Nawani's henchman. They agreed to keep the channels of communication open for the time being and Luke confirmed he had already sent a message to their mentors. They trusted Schwartz and Tremett but the problem was who knew beyond them?

"What now?" Kirin whispered.

"I think we need a new place to stay," Luke said, smiling and stretching out his hand.

Thursday, 14th October 2008
The White House, Washington

Mike Conway and Jim Allen walked into the President's office and sat down in the less formal chairs surrounding the rectangular coffee table. They waited patiently while he finished his business. Catherine Dennison was sitting in front of him with a note pad, running through the list of points she had to discuss.

"The summit has been organized for Saturday, the first session will be at two o'clock in the afternoon after the opening ceremony for the media…" she paused, checking her notes.

"We have confirmations that the British PM, the French President and the Japanese PM will be attending in person," she said, not looking up from her pad.

"As regards the Russian Premier and the Chinese President, they have both confirmed their Deputies will attend. In case it proves to be necessary, both have agreed that they'll be available via live television links throughout the Summit."

"I guess that was to be expected since we're hosting it on American soil…have all the arrangements been made for their arrival?" The President knew he didn't really need to ask the question. Catherine Dennison had excelled in the years she had worked for him, and if she had failed in any arrangements in the past, he certainly couldn't remember it.

She produced a folder and passed it across the table to the President. Opening it he scanned the index and saw that it covered every aspect of the Summit preparations right down to the individual food preferences of the Heads of State.

"Ok," he smiled, "it looks like we're all set for Saturday. Any other points?"

Catherine could tell he was becoming agitated to move on. She knew Conway and Allen were sitting behind her and they had much more important matters to discuss.

"Two closing points, firstly Foreign Secretary Henderson tried again with King Mohammed but with little success. Her conversations with other Gulf States confirmed that they are following the Saudi lead."

"Tell her to keep trying, I want the efforts we made for a peaceful solution with the Saudis to be a matter of record," he replied promptly.

"And finally the British PM is flying in early with his wife and I have provisionally organized a dinner engagement for tomorrow evening, shall I go ahead and confirm?" She raised her eyebrows seeking his approval.

"Good, go ahead Catherine and please make sure Pam's fully aware."

The President stood up from behind his desk signifying the meeting was over. He thanked Catherine for her work and walked over to join Allen and Conway in the lounge chairs while she made her exit.

Mike watched her as she departed looking for a friendly sign, but nothing was forthcoming. She seemed oblivious to his presence. He wondered what the problem could be. *'It must be something to do with our night at the Ritz Carlton,'* he thought. Maybe she was expecting more attention from him.

The President leaned back on the sofa opposite them. He looked tired but that was hardly surprising given his current workload and schedule. During normal times the Presidency of the United States was widely accepted as the most stressful job in the world so given the current dilemmas, it needed an outstanding figurehead. Whiting was a fighter who possessed the stamina and energy levels to remain on top of his game. Director Conway, who had his own strenuous regime to cope with, marvelled at the way the President took the unfolding developments in his stride. They were in the midst of the gravest crisis ever to be faced by the civilized world and he was determined to rise to the task.

"Ok Mike, your body language is telling me you have bad news."

'Christ, was it really that bloody obvious,' he thought. The offhand comment of the President made him realize his shoulders were slumped and he automatically sat upright to compensate.

Conway began his brief by giving the President the full lowdown on developments with Codename Amber and the British Agent. Whiting was shocked and dismayed to learn that there could be a mole inside his administration, but he listened intently until he was finished.

"At this stage, the most likely source of the leak points towards Karpurov and the Russians," Director Conway concluded.

"This is crazy Mike, we are just over twenty-four hours away from one of the most important Summit's of all time and you are telling me that we may have a spy in our Administration and that one of the countries we've invited is in collusion with India!"

His cynical tone could not disguise his disappointment. Whether they were friends or not, Conway could sense that he was getting perilously close to losing the President's confidence. Certainly his enthusiasm for the agent's assignment seemed to have waned. The President's expectation of success had tumbled on the back of the news.

Conway decided it was time to steer the conversation away from the leak towards areas where he could be relatively more upbeat. At this stage, it would not serve their purposes to turn it into a 'witch-hunt'. He needed more time to turn up leads and information that could help identify the leak's source.

He switched the subject to the CIA investigation into the oil stockpiling that was being carried out over the past year. He saw Allen's surprised expression as he went out on a limb, and guaranteed the President that he would have the conclusions of the investigation before the Summit started. President Whiting's irritation appeared to have eased slightly.

Allen asked about the investigation into Pakistan's testing and this gave Conway a further opportunity to appease the President. Although he stopped short of any guarantees, he gave hope that the information would be available shortly. Conway described the hurdles that Colonel Schwartz's Agent could be expected to encounter in Pakistan.

President Whiting nodded, his mind still on the fact that Russia could be a hostile threat to the United States. He had heard Conway list the names in his Administration who knew of the Agent's whereabouts in North Delhi and immediately discounted them. *'How could Allen, Conway, Schwartz or Martins possibly be working for the other side?'*

"Should I confront the Russian Premier?" the President asked Jim Allen.

"No, in my opinion it's too early Mr. President...I don't think we should rule it out but now's not the time. If we are wrong in our assertion, they will be upset and refuse to attend the Summit; if that happens the force of our Alliance is weakened."

The President nodded his agreement.

"Besides," said Jim Allen smiling at Conway, "our CIA Director has committed to delivering the information we need on time."

"Once we establish who is behind India how are we going to deal with this at the Summit?"

The President's question was to be expected. Jim Allen's mind worked quickly as he ran through all the likely scenarios.

"Evidence..." he replied.

"We need demonstrable evidence. If Russia is in concert with India then we have to prove it. The other nations at the Summit must be under no illusions about the truth."

The comments heaped further pressure on Conway to deliver the answers. If evidence was required then CIA material would not be good enough, they would need to find authentic third party documentation.

President Whiting listened to Allen's comments and weighed up his priorities. The crux of the matter was getting the results of the CIA investigations in time. He knew that he was relying heavily on Mike Conway, and given the recent developments, he wondered whether he was up to the job. He hoped so for all their sakes.

Jim Allen concluded his argument.

"If we can do this with independent evidence, then we can turn the Russian presence at the summit from a negative to a positive...the resulting publicity will gain the world's support for the Alliance and we can proceed thereafter on a united front." Jim Allen could picture the exposé in his mind.

"Ok, then get us the proof, Mike," the President commanded.

Director Conway acknowledged the President and then went on to discuss the format of the presentation that he would deliver at the Summit. The presentation highlighted how the Indian Government, under Banerjee's ministrations, had been behind the turbulence in the Middle East.

The President and Jim Allen recognized that Conway had done a good job here. The documentation he produced and the links he made, were clearly established. An independent observer would be left in no doubt about the conclusions. Banerjee had deliberately conspired to close the oil production in the Middle East and he was responsible for creating the suffering of his own people.

The intercom buzzed and his secretary came on the line.

"Sir, General Magnus Graham and his colleagues have assembled in the meeting room."

"Ok. I'll be through shortly," he replied. A new thought struck him suddenly.

"Aah…that reminds me Jim, what did you discover about accelerating Sabre?"

"It's good and bad Mr. President, we can get the project finished quickly but Sabre will be untested and they estimate the chances of bringing down a missile at around thirty per cent."

"Not great odds but get it done…let's hope we don't need it."

Jim Allen wanted to emphasize the fact that he had squeezed his contacts to get the President's bidding done. President Whiting should be aware of that when the favours were recalled.

"Defence Secretary Warner had to bypass the Senate to get the funding sanctioned and Vice President Martins has signed the release."

Mike Conway knew the strings Jim Allen had pulled to get the job done and was impressed with his powers of persuasion.

Difficult times required difficult decisions and the consequences of Allen's actions would ultimately be judged on the success of the project. In the face-saving world of politics, his friends would soon disappear if the strategy behind 'Sabre' failed.

The President concluded the briefing. It was time to move on to the next stage of his concentrated schedule before the Summit opened. In a meeting room down the corridor, the key military officials of the US Armed Forces were waiting to determine how they should recapture the Gulf oil fields by force.

Thursday, 14th October 2008
Prime Minister's Residence, Delhi

Ashraf Nawani stood in the middle of the hand-woven, silk carpet that typified the lavish décor of the room. A few paces behind him stood General Gupta who had recently returned from his conquest of Bangladesh. He had been present at the shantytown, helping Nawani spearhead the search for the two enemy agents. Apart from Banerjee himself, the only other person in the room was Balan.

The private quarters of the Prime Minister were magnificent and a tribute to the great heritage and natural beauty of the country. Many world leaders who had graced the apartments with official visits, had remarked on the splendour of the interior. The penthouse apartment extended over the whole wing of the Government Offices. Banerjee appreciated the residence for its style and its convenience. He had no requirement for relaxing pastimes, or pursuits outside his role as Prime Minister. To him, the apartment's principal advantage was that it allowed him quick access to the Government Chambers, with a minimum amount of fuss.

Krishna Banerjee was sitting behind a lavish, gold coloured desk with a brown and white marble surface. The antique was French in origin. He continued to look out of the window shaking his head as Nawani narrated the events from the shantytown. Banerjee had heard the bomb blasts himself from the balcony of his office. The noise had startled his own bodyguards into believing an attempt was being made on their leader's life.

"We have missed a great opportunity here through the incompetence of your soldiers, General."

Banerjee spun around in his chair to face General Vijay Gupta who was standing a few feet behind Nawani's shoulder.

"My men are…" but Banerjee held up a hand to silence him.

"I don't want excuses – I want results, what do you propose to do now?" he barked, addressing the question to Nawani.

Ashraf Nawani had considered nothing else since their failed ambush.

Most members of the government were scared of Nawani; he was a fanatic and used his power and control of the Secret Service to instil fear into those who stood in his way. He was ruthlessly loyal to Banerjee who was the only man to whom he showed any degree of respect. The stories constantly circulated about how the 'Service' tortured and killed those who posed a threat to Banerjee's political party. The past year had seen the disappearance of several members of the government's opposition party under shady circumstances.

"How do you propose to capture them now?" asked Balan, repeating the point forcefully.

"We will have to wait," Nawani replied. "We know what their mission is, and they'll still try to complete it. When they come we will be ready."

"You'll have to cancel your public engagements until this is settled," said Balan turning to Banerjee.

"I suggest that you remain here where you are fully protected for the foreseeable future."

He knew this would be a major irritant to his leader but the whole operation could not be jeopardized by lapses in security around the Prime Minister.

"This time I will have my men running the operation!" said Nawani, and he shot a look of total contempt at General Gupta standing behind him.

The General's temper rose and he took a step towards him; he, like many others, despised Nawani for his cowardly activities and the tactics employed by his henchmen.

"Stop!" Banerjee shouted holding up his hand.

"General, please take a seat, we do not have time for this."

The General looked contemptuously at Nawani before obeying the Prime Minister and taking his seat. Nawani had not altered his pose in the face of the angry General and he watched him take his seat with a snide, paper-thin smile on his face.

Nawani resumed his explanation of how his intelligence officers were both better placed to catch the agents and to provide additional protection for the Prime Minister in his office and residence.

"I have increased security in the building, I have put officers on the inside, and some on the outside of this building, the ones on the outside will be patrolling undercover, watching for suspicious activity from the streets."

Nawani looked at Balan for a sign of approval as he finished his speech.

"They will show themselves again, and when they do my men will be ready."

The General looked pained as Nawani referred to the sadistic corps of the Secret Service as '_my men._'

"Ok, I want both of them and I want them alive...do you understand?"

Banerjee raised his voice, shouting the question directly at Nawani. The Head of his Secret Service looked at the ground.

"Do you understand?" shouted Banerjee even louder than before.

Nawani respectfully bowed his head.

"Good, now leave us,"

He bowed his head again in deference to the Prime Minister, and taking two steps backwards, turned and exited the room.

Banerjee waited till the door was closed before speaking.

"General, the time has come," he said sharply.

Both Balan and the General knew straight away what Banerjee was referring to. They had spent hours together discussing this part of their strategy. The oil fields in the Gulf had to remain closed for a few days more and this part of the plan fulfilled that objective.

"Now is the time for us to send our troops and our mobile missile launchers into Pakistan!"

The General held the Prime Minister's gaze. The timing of this part of their plan had always been critical. To dispatch the troops in too early would result in sending many of the young men to their deaths. Although those moving towards the epicentres of the explosions would be given protective clothing and headgear, it was impossible to escape the radiation clouds and uranium depletion which had not yet fully dispersed.

"It's still too early," the General counselled.

Balan could see that the General was hesitant to commit. He was concerned that an early invasion would result in too many soldiers' lives being expended.

"I understand your concerns General but above all, the timing is crucial and it is politically and strategically right to make the move now…we always knew there would be lives lost in this decision."

The Paradigm Shift

Taking control of Pakistan, like capturing Jammu and Kashmir was a means to an end. It was an irrelevant part of the grand master plan to bring America and the Western World down to its knees. Soon India would be the new superpower controlling world affairs and he, Banerjee, would be its architect.

"Do you personally have any problems with the timing General?"

Balan wanted to hear the General's wholehearted support for the mission.

"No problem at all, my units are ready to move the minute I give the instructions," he responded instantly without hesitation. Balan felt more comfortable with the General's attitude.

"And the missile launchers?" Banerjee inquired.

"Everything has been taken care of Sir," replied the General. He looked more confident and rejuvenated after his heated exchange with Nawani.

The repositioning of their two mobile launchers and their nuclear warheads was *the* principal reason for the invasion of Pakistan. It was necessary because of the range of the ballistic missiles carrying the warheads. If they were to reach the targets that Banerjee had in mind, then the warheads had to be transported to Kiwar in the westernmost point of Pakistan. From here they could reach their destinations; the missiles were to be aimed into the heart of the Middle East.

The invasion of Pakistan was central to Banerjee's plan. By sending in the ground forces in a multi pronged formation it carried out two of his fundamental strategies.

Firstly, it provided the intricate camouflage for the two mobile missile launchers to be escorted in convoy along the coastline of Pakistan. They knew the spy satellites and planes would be screening every movement of the invasion, and they'd created an elaborate series of manoeuvres to draw attention away from the convoy.

Secondly, and the most important reason for Banerjee's insistence that now was the right time to proceed, was what he termed the *'defocusing factor'*. By launching an invasion of Pakistan, he sought to divert the attention of the superpowers away from the impending oil crisis.

Banerjee had revised his timings after Balan had informed him of the steps being taken by the US Administration. The mole had passed the information to the cloaked allies of India, and in turn they had passed it into the hands of Balan.

The information gave the inside story on the proposed international convention that was being orchestrated by the US to bind the world's superpowers against India. Banerjee knew that the meeting would be used as a platform to take control of the oil fields. He was under no illusion that the Alliance, once it was formed, would not hesitate to use force if it considered it necessary.

The decision reflected Banerjee's evil ingenuity. The invasion of Pakistan was timed to coincide with the first day of the Summit. The objective was to 'muddy the waters' and blur the Summit's first day objectives. Instead of talking about oil, he wanted them concentrating on a military strategy to oppose his forces entering Pakistan.

Over the next few days, the bulk of the US 5th Fleet would be entering the Straits of Hormuz and taking up their positions in the Arabian Gulf. Banerjee's intention was to fuel confusion in the minds of the Alliance Navy. They would be forced into decisions that would eat into the precious time they had left available. *'Should they deploy military resources in an attempt to combat the advancing forces of India or should they spread themselves across the oil locations of the Gulf?'*

Banerjee allowed himself a small smile of satisfaction at the way events were unfolding.

Information was power and he had a total insight into the affairs of the Summit because his clandestine Allies had a seat at the table.

"I will give the orders to advance at daylight tomorrow," General Gupta informed them.

He added that he would be travelling north immediately to personally take control of the convoy carrying the nuclear warheads to Kiwar in West Pakistan.

The General stood up and straightened his uniform.

"The overall success of our plan is in your hands General," Banerjee reminded him.

"I will not let you down," he replied and turned on his heels, and marched briskly towards the door.

Thursday, 14th October 2008
The Pentagon, Washington

'Jesus Christ what's going on?' thought Colonel Schwartz sitting behind his desk at the Pentagon.

He stared at the top-secret intelligence report in front of him. The information in the folder had ultimately cost the life of his agent in Pakistan. It was under his orders that the brave agent had disregarded his personal safety and obtained the documentation necessary for Director Conway.

Colonel Schwartz felt ridden with guilt for relaying the final instructions that would send one of their best agents to his death. He took solace from knowing that the man had not died in vain, the results of his work would change the course of history and the events of the next few days.

As Director Conway had impressed upon him, it wasn't sufficient to have verbal confirmation of the deal with the third party which carried out the dummy nuclear explosions on behalf of Pakistan. They needed hard documentary evidence if the political will of the Governments attending the Summit were to be fully convinced.

Colonel Schwartz flicked towards the back of the folder; the contract that opened up before him clearly identified the seal and signature of the Prime Minister of Pakistan. His Intelligence Officers had already confirmed that Abdul Wasim Latif was the signatory and further down the page, the crest of the third party stood out like a beacon. There was no mistaking the national identity and for added confirmation, the highest authority in the land had signed the agreement on behalf of the secretive facilitators.

The Paradigm Shift

In the end, his Agent ignored the peril of radiation poisoning that would be responsible for his death. He had been present when the Government bunker was opened and extracted the documentary evidence from the Pakistani Defence Minister. The circumstances surrounding the opening were violent and chaotic. Those inside tried to keep the hatches secure but the vengeful anger of the people would not go away. He was well positioned when the 'drawbridge was finally lowered' by the angry and dying crowds. Ultimately, most of the government executives and their families were killed in the bunker. A few children escaped to suffer a more painful and slower death outside.

Amidst the mayhem that ensued the Agent realized his objectives. Slipping into the bunker whilst the Prime Minister was the focus of attention, the agent had got the information he needed. The Defence Minister had offered no resistance; he actually felt some redemption for his acts, as if he was putting the record straight. The verbal information came quickly, but he had to open a sealed vault to obtain the contract. The Prime Minister himself endured a torturous death for his lies. The act of getting the document transported back to Colonel Schwartz was the last act the Agent carried out.

Once this nightmare was over, Schwartz was determined to do all he could to ensure that his Agent and his family received the plaudits they deserved.

If further confirmation was needed to identify the third party and the country working in collusion with India, it sat in another folder to his right. The investigation into the oil sales over the past year had revealed alarming results. When combined with the Pakistani evidence there was no doubt about the identity of India's sleeping partner. The problem was that they were invited to the Summit. *They are probably getting settled in to their guest quarters at Camp David as I sit here,'* thought Schwartz.

The President, his advisors and Director Conway had already made the trip to Camp David. Schwartz's administrator had made plans for him to use the Agency's jet for the short journey down to West Maryland.

Schwartz sat there contemplating the enormity of this discovery when the door was pushed open and the stocky figure of Andrei Karpurov entered.

"Yes, General?" Schwartz said curtly.

Karpurov was taken back by the tone of his voice. The friendliness which he had become accustomed to was missing.

"There's something going on out here I think you should see," he replied flatly. His initial enthusiasm to inform Schwartz of the news was tempered by his terse response.

"Ok, I'll be right out," he said dismissively, and dropped his head as if he was reading the papers on his desk.

Puzzled, Karpurov closed the door behind him. As soon as it shut, Schwartz pulled out a metallic coloured briefcase from under his desk. He carefully put the two folders in before pressing the locking system and watching the digits confirm that it was electronically sealed.

Pressing the intercom he barked some instructions to the Head of Security before locking the case in his desk draw.

As he stood up, a knock at the door signalled the arrival of the military guard he just had ordered. He gave them strict instructions that under no circumstances was anyone allowed to enter the room.

Satisfied, he made his way down the corridor towards the noise. As he reached the Operations Room he saw the lights flashing all over the large-scale, digital map of the Pakistani border with Jammu and Kashmir.

"They're moving," said Karpurov as he saw the Colonel approaching.

Something was wrong. He had noticed that the Colonel looked pale and agitated when he had called at his office.

'So they've taken the decision to enter Pakistan on the eve of the Summit,' thought Schwartz. *'This invasion together with the contents of the briefcase could throw the whole occasion into jeopardy.'*

Schwartz looked vexed. He continued to stare at the screen, something about the emerging pattern of lights didn't make sense.

"What is it Colonel?" Karpurov asked. He was unsure why his friend had chosen to distance himself.

"It's probably nothing…" replied Schwartz.

"I think you know more than you are prepared to say."

"It's probably nothing, General…" Schwartz replied a little more forcefully. He realized that he was being overly curt with the General and remembered Conway's orders. Reveal nothing but maintain a semblance of goodwill.

"It's the attack formation they're employing, we conducted many simulations with the help of the military on how their land based invasion would roll out and well…"

Schwartz shrugged his shoulders.

"Go on…." Karpurov pushed him to finish the thought.

'That's enough' thought Schwartz, *'I've got more important news to deliver.'* Suddenly he straightened and walked over to one of the Intelligence Officers handling the inflow of data from their satellites.

"I am leaving in ten minutes and I want to know exactly what forces are on the move and where they're going, do you understand?" he ordered sharply.

Schwartz marched back past the bemused looking Karpurov.

"May I ask where you are going in such a hurry?"

Schwartz stopped and turned around.

"I am going to update the President and Director Conway on the latest events...can I tell them that you will be joining your country's delegation in the near future?"

Karpurov stared at him. He knew that Schwartz was holding back on something.

"You can, I'm going to call the Russian Premier now," he said coldly.

As Schwartz recommenced his journey to his office, he heard Karpurov call after him.

"If my trust is a problem, maybe you can pass on any further information of importance to my countries Deputy Prime Minister when you see him at Camp David, Colonel!"

He made one last call to notify the CIA Director of his imminent departure. Ten minutes later, with the report carefully stowed in his metallic case, he jumped into the back of the limousine and set off towards the airport. When the car came to a halt on the runway, he discovered that he had two Air Force fighters assigned to him as an escort.

Friday, 15th October 2008
Outskirts of Delhi

After their failed ambush in the shantytown, both Luke and Kirin knew that Nawani and his minions would become more vigorous in their pursuit. Already, instructions had been sent out to all the hotels and guesthouses in the area to be on special alert for any new arrivals.

In their favour, the reception staff were told to watch out for two people travelling together, probably male. It was unlikely that the reception staff would be particularly sensitive to a man and a woman travelling together looking like a married couple. However, the staff was also told to insist on speaking to all new arrivals. Anyone that could not converse in Hindu or spoke with an unusual dialect was to be reported immediately.

It was past midnight when Luke put his suggestion to Kirin. She agreed immediately. They would seek a cheap guesthouse far away enough to be safe. Luke felt that if Kirin carried out any negotiations alone then the risks of taking a room were acceptable.

After walking in the shadows for two hours they finally chose a guesthouse that would attract little attention. They observed the building from the outside before agreeing on its suitability. Kirin entered the dark hallway and walked towards the counter lit up by a dim night light. A young boy was looking after the reception. He looked surprised as she walked in; he was not used to any activity in the early hours of the morning. After briefly haggling over the rate, he showed Kirin to a room out the back. She requested a room on the ground floor if it was available. Their earlier observations had confirmed that such a vacant room existed, and Luke checked around the back to make sure it had another means of entry.

Giving the boy two days rent in advance, she closed the door and turned to survey her new accommodation. In the centre of the room was an iron bed slightly wider than a single, with a thin, dirty mattress and no sheets. Apart from the bed, there were two wooden seats and a small chest of drawers. A door, hanging from its hinges, led into the bathroom.

She looked in with disgust. The brown stained tiles on the floor dipped towards a hole in the corner. On the left were a cracked mirror and a hand basin covered in scale and the hairs of previous guests. Several plastic buckets stood in a line beside the toilet that was no more than a hole in the ground. Kirin thought the smell was worse than anything she had encountered in the slum. She opened the window next to the mirror and twenty seconds later Luke climbed through, careful not to be seen.

In a couple of hour's time the sun would be rising. Luke locked and then barricaded the main room door with the chest of drawers. The staff would have the key to the door and Luke knew was always a chance they could be disturbed. The chest of drawers would ensure that it couldn't be pushed open from the outside without their knowledge. They were exhausted and both slept soundly and uninterrupted on the mattress until the early afternoon.

Kirin woke first, and Luke opened his eyes to the sound of water from the shower splashing against the plastic buckets in the bathroom. She had not had a shower for days and, despite the stench of the bathroom, she was delighted to be able to wash away some of the grime. Before sleeping, they had both taken the opportunity to wash their clothes in the hand basin. They hung out to dry on a temporary clothesline across the bathroom.

The door to the bathroom was slightly ajar and he could see Kirin's back as she looked up at the nozzle rinsing her hair. They both knew that privacy would be at a premium while they were in Delhi and neither of them made a fuss. Nevertheless Luke made whatever effort he could, and he stretched out his arm pushing the door closer to its frame.

After they'd both finished dressing, Kirin disappeared out into the street to find them some food. She met the mother of the boy on the way out. She was naturally curious about a single female guest and Kirin repeated the story she had told the night before. She explained that she would be staying a couple of days while her sister was recovering from an operation in the nearby hospital. The boy's mother was sympathetic and fully understood why Kirin wanted to stay at her sister's bedside until so late in the night.

After thirty minutes Kirin returned to the room with some cooked vegetable dishes, bread and some fruit. Luke pulled the chest of drawers back to let her enter and they ate the food on the bed.

"Have you thought of any ways into the Government Buildings?" she asked.

"I'm afraid it's going to be much harder for us now."

When he had first completed a circuit of the buildings' grounds, he had been pragmatic about their chances of entry. With the expectations of a break-in attempt it would take an extraordinary plan to bypass the current level of security.

"They know we're here and they'll be expecting us. Nawani will have put the fear of God into those soldiers guarding the Government Offices."

"Ok, so we'll have to wait until Banerjee shows himself?"

"Not possible, we don't have the time, and anyway he's not likely to show himself in public knowing we're here."

"So what's the answer then?"

The situation seemed impossible from whatever angle she chose to look at it.

"I don't know yet......I'd originally been thinking that I would break into the building by myself and locate Banerjee, but that's exactly what they'll be expecting right now. I'm considering a method that will take us both in."

He looked at her face to gauge her reaction.

This was not a solution that he felt happy with but it was the only way he could see them succeeding. He was distinctly unhappy at the suggestion of putting Kirin's life in danger and it was not solely because he preferred working alone. _She was a highly trained undercover agent in her own right,_ he thought, but it still didn't make it easy to separate his personal feelings.

Luke determined that he would try and focus on alternatives without Kirin. Maybe if they had a bit longer, he could come up with a satisfactory solution.

"Fine, I don't want it any other way," she said firmly, looking straight back at him with a look of indignation.

She held his gaze for a few seconds.

"Ok, I'm going back to the government building," he said, and started packing a few items into a bag.

Luke wanted to observe the guards firsthand and understand the timings of when the staff's change of shift took place. If an opportunity was going to arise, then the best time was normally towards the end of the night's watch when attentiveness to details could slip.

"We'll need to change locations again tomorrow."

"I'll make reservations at the Sheraton." she said with a hint of irony. Luke smiled at her.

"I'll have a look around tonight and see if I can identify something else suitable." Kirin continued. "After all, the staff here will expect me to be visiting the hospital."

She was still exhausted from the previous night's encounters and gratefully accepted the opportunity to catch up on some more rest.

Luke pulled open the bathroom window to make his escape.

"I will be back at eight-thirty tomorrow morning."

Friday, 15th October 2008
Camp David, West Maryland

Camp David originally became a government property under the Presidency of General Eisenhower. He changed the name from 'Shangri-La' to 'Camp David' after his own grandson, David Eisenhower. The Presidential Retreat had first come to prominence during the Israeli-Palestine peace accords during Jimmy Carter's reign at the White House. The meetings had been successful, and Camp David had become a symbolic venue associated with establishing international reconciliation. President Whiting accepted Jim Allen's recommendation for Camp David without question. He wanted to capitalize on the positive atmosphere created by the earlier successes.

The buildings were spread out over the picturesque Catoctin Hills that characterized the Maryland countryside. Out of sight from the accommodation, US soldiers guarded the entire perimeter. The security services were taking no chances and closed down all the connecting roads for a further five-mile radius.

The Summit had attracted the world's media attention. Around the globe, people watched the news headlines to find out how the major powers were going to handle the escalating tension with India.

Each 'superpower' leader brought a substantial delegation with them, and, having landed at the airport, they were chauffeured by helicopter to their allotted buildings in the confines of Camp David. The accommodation and furnishings could not be described as luxurious or hotel like, but were more simple and homely in nature.

The Paradigm Shift

Whenever the visitor's landing times had permitted, the President had wanted to greet each leader in person but, with so many duties to perform it, had been almost impossible. On such occasions his deputy, Vice President Martins ably stood in for him.

The main forum for the meeting was at the centre of Camp David; the conference hall had been especially organized with each country having its own table. The tables faced each other in a hexagonal formation and were all overlaid with white linen cloths. The name plaques of the country's representatives were arranged at the front with decorative miniature flags identifying their nationality. Behind the main tables were further tiers of chairs for the junior government officials and the advisors.

Although the spotlight was on the meeting between the world leaders, there were in fact two Summits taking place at Camp David. The second ancillary meeting was due to take place in parallel at another conference hall nearby. After certain fundamental agreements were reached at the main Summit, the second Summit was to devise the strategy to support those agreements. It was attended by the delegations military advisors and Jim Allen, supported by General Magnus Graham, was handling the show for the US.

The agenda for the main meeting had already been drafted and agreed amongst the nations prior to commencing the afternoon discussions. In the event that certain fundamentals could be agreed early, the leaders had determined that they would give their go-ahead for their military advisors to commence strategic and operational planning in the second conference hall.

The historic occasion was to commence with a large press gathering outside the main conference hall. The six leaders would meet initially in a face-to-face session lasting about forty

- 202 -

minutes, before the Summit was due to start in the main hallway. To satisfy the demands of the international media companies and promote the Summit around the world, they would then move outside to shake hands and pose for photographs under the colonnade at the top of the building's steps.

At breakfast time, the accommodation blocks of each of the six delegations had been sent into a commotion with the appalling news that India had started its advance into Pakistan. The President and his wife had first received the news the night before when they'd been hosting the dinner engagement with the British PM. He had been handed a note which had served to dampen what had otherwise been a very enjoyable evening entertaining their British counterparts.

President Whiting realized immediately how clever Banerjee had been with the timing of his invasion. The purpose of the Summit was to resolve the danger to the world from the oil famine. At the top of the agenda must be the resurrection of oil supplies. India and the conspiracy of its megalomaniac leader featured strongly in the subject matter, but this latest tactic of Banerjee was a masterstroke.

The breaking news meant that the leaders and their advisors would be drawn into a debate on India's invasion of Pakistan, detracting them from the core issue. The media questions would focus on the member countries response to the invasion, and advisors would become embroiled in writing their leaders' press releases. The natural result would be the loss of time, concentration and attention to the matter that really needed solving; the oil crisis.

The President sat discussing the ramifications late into the night with General Graham. In the end, he was more determined than ever to come out of his corner fighting. He had to try and turn the negative impact into a positive one. As Jim Allen had pointed out, it was vital that the President steer the direction of the Summit and take the lead.

One decision the President had taken the day before was to send the civilian teams down into the Gulf. They numbered over six hundred in total, covering the entire range of skills and technical abilities necessary to restart the oil fields. Most worked for the large American oil corporations. They had volunteered to make the journey, fully briefed on the risks they could expect to face. The Aircraft Carrier USS Missouri had moved back into the Gulf, and they were scheduled to join the Commander of the 5th Fleet later that day.

The military exercise of capturing the oil fields by force was extremely complicated. A normal campaign is typically based on one, two or sometimes three prongs of attack, making sure that lines of communication and supply keep up with the speed of the advance. The situation here was completely different; the logistical exercise of attempting to take so many locations simultaneously was unprecedented in modern warfare.

In case the level of difficulty wasn't already sufficient, the Generals and Admirals also had to take into account that many of the oil rigs were at sea. Beyond that, there was the potential hostility of the Arab Nations themselves to consider.

The President hoped that the Summit would convince the Arab leaders of world opinion and the urgency of the situation. If King Mohammed was prepared to cooperate and let the Alliance assume control of the oil facilities, there was still a chance that ultimately, the Alliance would return the gesture and agree to a smooth transition back to Arab supervision. In reality, it was unlikely that total control of oil production would return without being policed by the United Nations or a newly formed representative body of the superpowers. The unfolding events had shown how quickly oil-starved economies could disintegrate once the natural energy source was taken away.

Japan's dependency upon the Middle East for oil was now clear for all to see. Even the most pessimistic views on how long the economy would hold up had been wrong. The Government tried hard but had been unable to give confidence to the market despite tough oil rationing measures. The pressure took its toll, and the Yen tumbled in the world financial markets regardless of Japan's huge dollar reserves.

President Whiting had sat with the Prime Minister of Japan earlier that morning. It was as he'd suspected; the Japanese were desperate, they would support any military action necessary to restore production. The Prime Minister made a plea to the President that Japan be the beneficiary of the first shipments out of the Gulf. News that this might be on the cards would give his economy some much-needed confidence. President Whiting politely responded, without commitment, that he would do his best to assist Japan's interests.

After the meeting was over, the slight elation he felt at Japan's strong vote of support was tempered by a phone call from Director Conway. Colonel Schwartz had met with Jim Allen and the Director whilst the President had been with the Japanese PM, and it was imperative they meet right away.

"Does this relate to what I think it does?" he asked and Conway confirmed his fears.

They both filed past the secretaries and security guards lining the wall outside the President's temporary office. Walking straight in, the President saw their strained faces and loudly dismissed the aides standing around him. After the last one had closed the door he ushered them to take a seat.

"Ok what have you got?" he looked at Mike Conway.

"We have independent evidence that confirms one of the countries attending this Summit is in collusion with India and supports its plan to cut off the world's oil supplies!"

The President grimaced, it was the news they had all suspected but it still didn't prepare him for the moment of truth.

"Mike, I'm meeting and shaking hands with the five leaders on the conference hall steps in thirty minutes."

The President's anxiety crept through but he quickly regained his composure.

"You'd better give me the news then?"

Nevertheless, he couldn't hide his irritation. The news of the invasion followed by the late revelation of an enemy in the camp were conspiring to sabotage the Summit.

"Are we going back to the days of the Cold War as you suspected?"

"Its not Russia, sir." Director Conway paused before dropping the bombshell.

"It's China!"

"Sonofabitch!" replied the President sharply. The surprise lit up across his face.

"The investigation into oil purchases leaves us in no doubt that China has been accumulating oil reserves well in excess of its normal quota. The investigation wasn't easy, the Chinese and Indians have gone to extreme lengths in their efforts to keep the final destination of the tankers a secret."

"China…" he said slowly, "this means they have been planning these events for quite sometime?"

Director Conway delivered the final part of the jigsaw.

"We also have third party evidence that China carried out the nuclear tests on behalf of Pakistan."

"What was their incentive for helping Pakistan?"

"Money," interrupted Jim Allen. "Pakistan paid them a fortune to carry out the tests."

"...Incredible...and they gave the information to Banerjee so he could use it to destroy the Pakistanis without fear of reprisal..."

'The scandalous deceit of the Chinese almost denies comprehension,' thought President Whiting.

"Incredible...Just incredible," he repeated to himself.

"What are your suggestions?" he asked eventually looking at his watch and then crossing the room towards the window.

He still couldn't believe the audacity of the Chinese. Deputy Prime Minister Chen was now preparing to shake his hand on the steps of the conference hall, in the full glare of the world's press knowing that his country was behind the plot.

"In the light of this information we have no alternative Sir." Jim Allen was anxious to brief the President on the one course of action that he felt was open to them.

"The media show cannot proceed at this point, it must be delayed indefinitely until you meet with Deputy PM Chen..."

"...Meet him before I speak to the other leaders?" the President broke in.

"Yes, there is no time to speak to them all individually, there will be time afterwards to explain your decision to expel China from the Summit."

The comment focused the President's mind on the imminent confrontation he was about to undertake with one of the world's superpowers.

"I have made plans for the entire Chinese delegation to be escorted directly to the airport once you've finished," Allen informed the President.

The Paradigm Shift

"And what about the repercussions once the news is out that China is a partner with India?" He tried to visualize the events that lay ahead.

"Apart from dealing with the oil crisis, it is now vital that the Summit sends an unequivocal statement to China that any military intervention by them in the Middle East or otherwise, will result in war with the Alliance." Jim Allen stared at the President to gauge his reaction.

The President considered Allen's statement and the rhetoric he was recommending. *'Is this the way that we're going?'* He thought to himself. *The stakes were too high in this nuclear age for the world to survive such a catastrophe. He'd seen the deceit that China was capable of, but what if they couldn't see reason and felt a tactical war was possible?'*

President Whiting switched back to the present: *'one step at a time'*, he thought.

"Ok Jim, let's go and see what Deputy Prime Minister Chen has got to say for himself."

He looked into a mirror and checked that his tie was straight. As he made a few adjustments he focused on Director Conway standing behind him, waiting expectantly.

"I'd like you to be there as well Mike," he added.

Director Conway, meanwhile, was contemplating whether to raise the one remaining, unanswered question.

'If the enemy wasn't Russia and the mole wasn't Karpurov, then who the hell was it?'

He decided the question could wait for the time being and he stood in behind the President as he led the way out of his office.

Friday, 15th October 2008
Manama, Bahrain

At the same time that the Summit was taking place in Camp David, the Arab leaders, under the patronage of His Highness Sheik Faisal, the Emir of Bahrain, were attending their own engagement. Since the meeting was summoned at short notice at the bequest of King Mohammed, the Emir's sumptuous palace on the Island of Bahrain was chosen as the most convenient location.

The ruling families of Abu Dhabi and Dubai flew in on their private jets as did the Kuwaiti's and the Sultan of Oman. The ruler of Qatar travelled the short journey from Doha in a helicopter and King Mohammed also flew in, but most of his entourage drove across the five-mile causeway that joined the island to the Saudi coastline.

Relationships between the Arab Rulers, and the way they governed their countries, was different from the norm expected in the democratic world. In the Middle East, the ruling families were also the Government. They could commit their countries according to their own judgment and desires without recourse to an elected parliament. The Saudi King, the Emirs and the Sheiks were well acquainted from an early age. They were tied together by the geography of the region and their mutual bond to the Islamic religion. As they were taught by their fathers, the Rulers placed an enormous respect on their fraternal relationships with their Muslim neighbours.

The British Empire still exerted a lot of influence in the Middle East when the abundance of oil was first discovered in the late 1950's. In the following decade, the British Foreign Office helped to shape the region. The Trucial States, which

ultimately laid claim to a substantial portion of the Gulf's oil
wealth, were at that time under British rule. The Foreign Office
helped the Arab families establish their own charter and the six
territories that constituted the Trucial States became the United
Arab Emirates (seven when Umm Al Quwain joined). Kuwait,
Qatar and Bahrain participated in the original negotiations to be
united under the United Arab Emirates umbrella but ultimately
elected to maintain their independence.

Compared with the history of democracy in the West, the
government and constitutions in the Middle East were embry-
onic. The ties between the States grew as the families became
accustomed to their newfound status. They attended each
other's royal weddings when occasional cross border marriages
strengthened their bond further. In addition, the ruling families
graciously assigned large plots of land to each other. These plots
of land were given in order that they could build their impressive
palaces on their neighbour's soil.

The Emir's palace in Bahrain regularly played host to such
conventions as this one called by King Mohammed. The palace
was kept in a constant state of readiness, providing the very
highest level of luxurious hospitality to the descending dignitaries.

A domed hall was used for the exchange of greetings and
friendship which always preceded the rulers' meetings. Once
they had assembled and the welcomes had been concluded, they
took their seats in the adjacent boardroom.

The advisors and peripheral members of the delegation
were obliged to remain in the hall as the large double doors were
closed. Only the leaders of the Gulf States were allowed inside
and they sat facing each other across a large circular table.

The size and wealth of Saudi meant that King Mohammed was always considered the unofficial Chairman of such meetings. He opened the discussion by suggesting it would be wise for all present to reveal the extent of their political and economical problems. Going around the table, they took it in turns to tell the forum of the latest developments in their bid to restore normality.

King Mohammed went first. Speaking slowly and deliberately, he informed them of the progress they had made under martial law. The manual workforce were housed in labour camps and policed by the military. Previously they had lived in these camps but had been given a degree of freedom outside their usual working hours. Under the new regime they were effectively under a twenty-four hour guard. If they stepped out of line or showed any signs of resistance then the military response would be swift and frequently violent. A curfew was imposed on the skilled labour. They were left under no misapprehension about their fate if any of the workers broke the rules, or failed to check in and out at the correct times.

In the beginning, the ruling families felt a strong degree of guilt at their actions towards the Indian workforce. They fully expected the massive wave of rebuke that came from the rest of the world. Then as time went on the US informed the Saudi government of the organized incitement being carried out by the Indian Foreign Office to provoke the public disturbances. The Whiting Administration told the Saudis hoping the information would make them more amenable to authorizing US troops on Saudi soil.

The result was that the mindset of the ruling families changed quickly. No longer were they the persecutors, in their minds they became the persecuted. Very quickly they turned the blame on India for their predicament and justified their actions as a legitimate measure to protect their interests. When they first imposed Martial Law they had not suspected any underhand activities from India and they had allowed most of their Foreign Embassy Officials to leave the country. In retrospect, if they had known of India's duplicity then they would have placed them under lock and key.

The Arab Rulers listened intently as one by one they told their stories about how they had managed to restore control through subjugating the numerically superior Indians. When the last dignitary had finished King Mohammed announced there were two immediate issues that needed to be addressed by the forum. Firstly, they had to achieve a consensus on how they were to proceed with regard to the resumption of oil production, and secondly, whether they would invite military assistance from the Alliance.

They were all aware of the Summit at Camp David and realized that one potential outcome was an Alliance decision to take control of the oil fields by force.

Their own efforts to restore production had not met with success. The fundamental problem was the absence of technical expertise and skilled manpower capable of running the refineries and oil rigs.

The compounding problem for the Gulf States was monetary. They thought that they could cope without the revenues of oil whilst they addressed their own internal problems, but the financial crisis had now grown to similar proportions. The UN had issued a directive imposing sanctions on the Gulf States in response to their inhumane treatment towards the Indian population. Saudi itself was running on the brink of financial collapse;

its budget deficit exceeded six billion dollars with no income on the horizon to bridge the gap.

After a lengthy debate, they agreed that for the sake of survival the only way ahead would be to accept the offer of assistance from the Western Alliance. The alternative of trying to defend their oil interests by force was not even contended as a serious option.

The Arab leaders concurred that if they allowed the Alliance into their territories on a friendly basis, then there was a greater likelihood that they could negotiate favourable terms for their ultimate withdrawal and the handing back of oil production.

The lengthy meeting turned to address the issues which would surface if they granted the Alliance access to their facilities: *'Would the Alliance compromise the Gulf's own right to financial and economic stability? Would it impact on their abilities to govern and rule their own countries?'* Regardless of the feeling of vindication that stemmed from the exposure of the Indian Government's underhand activities, the Arab leaders were still cautious about the West condemning their actions, and stopping them from maintaining Martial Law.

In the end, lead by King Mohammed's argument, they accepted the fact that it was better to be in control through negotiation, rather than face the belligerent threat of attack from the US and Alliance Forces that were already rapidly accumulating in the Gulf's waters.

The Council agreed that these sensitive negotiations should be conducted through one voice. His Highness King Mohammed was unanimously elected and empowered to speak on their behalf. In return he promised to keep them informed of developments as they unfolded.

The Paradigm Shift

They rose from their seats pleased with the decisions they had reached. In turn, they wished King Mohammed the support and guidance of Allah in his discussions with the Alliance, before thanking their host for his generous hospitality.

Friday, 15th October 2008
Camp David, West Maryland

As Jim Allen accompanied the President and Mike Conway towards the guest accommodation of the Chinese delegation, he gave instructions to the guard that the occupants should be restrained from leaving. They were to be placed under house arrest.

The security that joined the President's convoy as it sped down the interconnecting lanes of Camp David was impressive. In the air, two military helicopters trailed the procession and landed in the field adjacent to the building.

The President was pleased with the fast response of their military as they responded to an entirely new set of circumstances outside of those normally rehearsed. His limousine door was opened and the soldiers lined the way to the main entrance of the guesthouse. Jim Allen and Mike Conway followed two paces behind as he strode purposefully past the security and through the double doors into the main foyer.

Inside the President paused giving Jim Allen sufficient time to finish a conversation with the military officer responsible for security on the premises. There were no signs of life in the lobby, just guards with their guns drawn standing next to several closed doors.

Jim Allen stepped towards the President.

"Deputy Prime Minister Chen has been escorted to the library over there," he said pointing to a door down the corridor. Two guards in full military uniform were posted on either side.

"Is anyone else with him?" the President asked, walking towards the door.

"Just Ambassador Ling."

The Paradigm Shift

They had agreed on the way there that it would be best if a second representative of China was present to hear what the President had to say firsthand. Ambassador Ling was China's representative based in Washington. The President agreed that his testimony could be important when the story of their encounter was repeated for the benefit of Prime Minister Ziang in Beijing. Any emphasis or slant that was given to their words by Deputy Chen could be corroborated by the Ambassador.

The guards who had taken charge of security at the guesthouse were part of a specialist unit and the brainchild of Jim Allen on his appointment as the head of the National Security Agency. They were an elite band of soldiers recruited from the ranks of the regular army to form a first line response force in the affairs of national security. They were dressed in black combat uniforms and there was no mistaking their single-minded professionalism for the job in hand.

Seeing the President approach and the signal from Jim Allen, the guards opened the door to the library. The two military guards entered first and then close on the heels of the President followed his National Security Advisor and the Director of the CIA. Inside, the two guards resumed their positions on either side of the doorway taking the total number of security officers present to four.

The guesthouse library had a high ceiling, with bookshelves covering the walls from top to bottom. Just over half way up was a metal balcony that ran all the way round the room with sliding ladders attached, enabling readers to fetch the books down from the top shelf. The balcony offered the perfect observation platform for the two additional members of the elite squad who were already present guarding the Chinese deputy.

As the President walked into the room, Deputy Prime Minister Chen jumped to his feet, not as a mark of respect but in a fit of pique.

"How dare you imprison me!" he screamed in outrage, and continued for some time in the same vein with a tirade of vitriolic abuse against the treatment he had suffered before being deposited in the library under an armed guard. His face burned with colour at the exertion of his rapid outburst.

The President registered the uncontrolled ferocity of the man's character and felt an instant dislike for him. After a few seconds the President raised his hand.

"Enough…that's enough!" he snapped forcefully at the Chinese deputy leader.

The protestations from Deputy Chen ceased and he looked quizzically at the President in the sudden silence that followed. Ambassador Ling looking shocked, stood silently behind his leader.

"Your country will not be participating in the Summit," the President said sternly, glaring straight into the eyes of Deputy Chen. They stared at each other as Chen tried to assimilate the implications behind his statement.

"I have a message and I want you to take it back to your leader, Prime Minister Ziang."

Deputy Chen's puzzled expression slowly began to dissolve giving way to a thin, arrogant smile. Chen had played his part in developing the 'master plan' alongside Prime Minister Ziang in Beijing. He realized that the Americans must have uncovered something that linked China to the activities of India but had no idea whether the President was basing his remarks on conjecture. Either way he was not going to make his departure easy for him.

"I have no idea what you're talking about," he responded indignantly.

His feigned innocence made no impression on the President.

"Then let me enlighten you, Deputy Chen."

The President knew the importance of making it transparently clear that the US Government would not tolerate China's scandalous behaviour. He kept his expression and voice firm, dealing succinctly with the facts.

"My Government has knowledge that your country has been acting in concert with India to cause the events which are currently threatening world stability."

"This is outrageous, you have no proof of such assertions, where is your evidence?" he replied in defiance.

"What are you talking about?" asked Ling, his face screwed up in astonishment.

Ling turned away from the President.

"Deputy Chen, what is this about?" he repeated incredulously.

"Quiet," snapped Chen.

"We have independent evidence that your government has been accumulating oil reserves in readiness for this oil crisis."

The President turned to Jim Allen and ushered him to come forward. He handed the President a copy of the contract bearing the red crest of China over Prime Minister Ziang's signature.

"We have evidence that your country was responsible for the unlawful murder of millions of innocent Pakistanis when you carried out the dummy tests on their behalf and then fed the information to your co-conspirators, India."

He held the contract in the air before handing it across to Deputy Chen.

Deputy Chen stared down at the paper scrutinizing it for a few moments. He recognized the signature and seal of Prime Minister Ziang. It was the same document he had seen months earlier.

When he finally looked up, his will to carry on fighting had gone. Further protestations of innocence would be futile in the face of such damning evidence.

The sombre look of acceptance was quickly replaced by his surging arrogance as again, he sought to establish the upper hand.

"My Country will not allow you, or your Alliance, to re-open the oil fields," he said coldly.

This was what the President had hoped for. There could be no better confirmation of China's intentions than the acceptance of truth by Deputy Chen. Under the instructions of Jim Allen, the whole encounter, including the statement by Chen, was being filmed by one of the guards standing above them on the metal balcony. His arrogance was a weakness. His outburst was a confessional statement which could help them win the confidence of the Alliance and provide concrete evidence of China's involvement.

The President was angered and amazed at the man's audacity while he was standing on American soil. How dare he smile at him and threaten the United States in such a fashion.

"Take this message to Ziang," the President said, dropping the requirement for diplomatic niceties.

"Our Government will tolerate no interference from China of any kind. If your country makes any manoeuvres towards military aggression, or if your country shows military support for

India of any kind…then be under no illusion that I will command all the forces at my disposal to destroy that threat to humanity."

Deputy Chen heard the words and continued to stare at the President with his thin, facetious smile. The President didn't give him a chance to respond.

"The meeting is over Chen, you and your delegation will be escorted out of US air space immediately."

With that pronouncement, he turned and left the room with Conway following a short distance behind. Jim Allen stayed behind to give instructions to the security guard.

As he stepped out of the library and the door closed behind him, President Whiting's rage escaped and he banged his fist into the wall opposite. It had taken all his self-control to remain calm.

He turned around to face Director Conway.

"You said what had to be said, Mr. President,"

The President's nodded, his expression didn't change.

Friday, 15th October 2008
Outside the Government Building, Delhi

Luke had found a comfortable point from which to watch the arrivals and departures from the Government Offices across the street. From his observation point, he could see the entrance more clearly than during the day when his view was obscured by the myriad of roving Hindu pedestrians. He could see the sentry box to one side of a large wooden gate which swung open whenever transportation needed to get in or out. On the other side of the sentry box was a walkway which allowed access for those seeking entry by foot.

Luke felt tired, he had been watching the proceedings for the past four-and-a-half hours with little comfort. In the darkness, he was positioned below the large overhanging porch that led to the building's main doorway. The porch belonged to another government building of far less importance than the one on the opposite side of the street. Luke shared the shelter with several homeless vagrants and pretended to be asleep so as not to attract undue attention.

Despite it being the middle of the night it wasn't particularly cold. Opposite him, three vagrants lay huddled together against the wall. They slept whilst Luke sat with his back to the wall pretending to doze.

Luke raised his head as he saw the bright glare of headlights appear at the end of the street as a small minibus drove towards him, navigating the potholes in the road. The bus stopped abruptly in front of the sentry box and the driver jumped out, walking around the side to open a sliding door and let his passengers out.

The Paradigm Shift

Surreptitiously, Luke checked the time and then watched with interest as the Prime Minister's personal household staff changed shift. Out of the alley alongside the sentry box appeared the departing crew. They promptly climbed on board the bus resting their heads against the window in an effort to get some sleep. In all they numbered about sixteen, the majority of which were male. Those who served the Prime Minister personally were easily identifiable in their smartly tailored uniforms.

As Luke watched the changeover something caught his eye. The driver opened up one of the flaps at the back of the minibus and proceeded to take out two large wicker baskets which looked like laundry hampers. A metallic-looking frame, specially designed with rollers, was pulled out of the shadows and used to transport the hampers. The contents weren't checked and with the assistance of two helpers, one of the new shift proceeded to push the baskets up the drive towards the tradesman's entrance.

Once the old laundry baskets had been loaded, the driver shut the passenger door and drove away. The whole process took approximately eight minutes. Luke began playing back the change of staff in his mind. He wanted to assess whether he had seen any opportunities to gain access. Nothing had caught his attention as being of special interest. Switching places with the staff or the driver wouldn't be possible and access via concealment in the laundry hampers was taking too many risks. The mission wouldn't be achieved by taking chances with such long odds.

Suddenly, the murmuring of one of the sleeping vagrants against the opposite wall got louder. He heard the man get to his feet and edge towards him out of the darkness.

As he got closer, he noticed that he had the face of an old man, with twisted yellow front teeth, matted hair and a long beard. The vagrant stumbled towards Luke babbling incoherently to himself. Staring wide-eyed at Luke, he continued rambling as Luke wondered how he should play the situation.

Luke did not want to attract the attention of the guards across the street but the vagrant's mutterings were getting louder and they would soon feel the need to investigate. He decided the best option would be to carry on pretending to be asleep and ignore the man's advances. Hopefully the vagrant would pass in front of him and continue on to wherever he was going.

As he came alongside, the old man suddenly turned to face the sleeping Luke and started prodding him with his finger. *'Kaise ho, kaise ho'* he kept repeating the Hindu greeting. His voice was nothing more than a harsh whisper to begin with but when he saw Luke open his eyes, he started raising his voice and poking harder.

Luke realized that at any moment the guards across the road could get suspicious and wander towards them to see what was going on. In that split second he decided that his only option was to kill the vagrant. He could do it quickly with his bare hands if necessary and he quickly assessed whether leaving a murdered vagrant under the porch was going to damage their chance of entry. It was sure to ring alarm bells for the Secret Service in the morning and alert them to the time he had been watching.

The words in Hindi kept repeating as Luke manoeuvred himself to strike. Suddenly the old man stopped. He turned, hobbled down the steps of the porch, and set off shuffling along the pavement. Luke felt relieved at his sudden good fortune. He resumed his sleeping posture and turned his attention back to the building and the guards across the street.

The Paradigm Shift

Ten uneventful minutes passed before Luke cursed as he spied the old man returning down the street. The hunched tramp was barely visible behind the iron railings that ran around the outside of the building. As he reached the porch steps, he stared up at Luke before moving on.

Something was wrong. Luke's senses telling him to be on his guard. Suddenly his body froze as saw the unmistakable shape of a gun below the Hindu cassock of the departing tramp.

'Christ, it's a set up,' he thought and he looked furtively down the street for further signs of life. The old man must be working for Nawani and he must have been watching me all the time from the shadows across the porch. Whether he'd caught a glimpse of Luke looking at his watch or whether it was his failure to respond in Hindi earlier no longer mattered. Luke was sure the informer had seen enough to alert others.

In the background, Luke could hear the noise of racing engines and that was the only signal he needed. He jumped down the steps and ran towards the tramp. Hearing the footsteps behind him the tramp swivelled around holding a knife, he looked somewhat younger and taller now the need for pretence had gone.

Luke was on him before he had a chance to respond. In seconds, he swung him around and put his arms around his head ready to snap his neck. Just before he jerked the agent's head violently to the side he felt a searing pain in his forearm where the knife entered.

It was too late to save the agent. His body slumped in Luke's hands with an audible crack as the top of his spine was disconnected from the base of his skull. Luke lay the body on the ground and reached up to the source of pain. He felt for the metal head of the knife still sticking out of his arm.

He looked up sharply as the lights of several armoured vehicles came hurtling around the corner. Wincing in pain, he pulled the dagger out and flung it to one side. There was no time to think he had to act quickly.

Luke's training for such eventualities had been comprehensive. The importance of maintaining escape plans when keeping a vigil in hostile territory had been drilled into him. In the heat of the moment, he was thankful for the time he'd spent earlier, casting his eye around the available options in the quieter moments of observing the government building.

Behind him was a wall with railings along the top. He turned and clambered up the wall, pulling himself to the top by gripping hold of the metal poles. At the top of the wall, he jumped up, swinging his leg over the top. He grimaced at the shooting pain in his arm.

The heads railings were blunt, and although the rolling movement hurt it was lot less painful than it could have been. The armoured carrier headlights shone directly on him as he fell to the ground on the other side. He could hear the excited shouting as he got to his feet and ran down the alley between the old government buildings.

The armed guard running towards the wall from the two armoured vehicles were members of Nawani's Secret Service. On the instructions of the patrol leader, one of the armoured car drivers dropped the gears, revved the engine, and drove at full speed towards the section where Luke had crossed. With the sound of tearing metal, the vehicle crashed into the wall, rearing up over the collapsing brickwork. As the driver reversed, it became clear that the armoured vehicle had been successful. It had done sufficient damage to create a way through the rubble and twisted metal railings. The watching guards wasted no time;

they climbed through the gap and set off down the alley in pursuit of their prey. It was dark as Luke reached a T-junction at the end of the alley. He looked over his shoulder and saw the searchlights of the chasing pack. In an instant he chose to take the left-hand lane.

He sprinted down the alley at full speed clutching his arm to his chest. The pain from the wound was excruciating. Luke tried to recall the map of the area. He knew what he was looking for but was he heading in the right direction?

The shouting behind him got louder. He tried to keep his speed up but it was harder for him in the darkness. There was a strong smell of decay on either side of him that he didn't stop to explore. Despite his haste he had to be careful, the ground was dangerously uneven in the pitch black, high-walled alley.

After no more than a couple of minutes, the alley finally opened up as he came to some stone steps descending at a sharp angle towards a bridge below.

The Iron Bridge over the powerful river Yamana was deserted at this time of night. Luke paused for breath; he knew that if he could get across the bridge there was a chance he could lose the chasing pack.

The noise behind was closing in as he looked at the way ahead. The pain from his arm hurt with every step. Worried about being out in the open, he mustered all his energy and made a dash down the steps and out onto the bridge. The bridge's causeway was about a hundred yards long rising towards the middle before descending to the far side.

He got half way across the bridge before the powerful headlights of an army convoy came out of a side street and stopped at the opposite end of the bridge. Luke stopped, breathing heavily and glistening in sweat from the exertion. Looking at the convoy, he saw the gloating face of the commanding officer as he dismounted from his jeep. He looked back the way he had come and saw the first patrol guards descending the steps, he was cut off.

He looked down at the swirling river over one hundred feet below him. There was no choice. He straddled the stone parapet cradling his injured arm and stood on the ledge. The commanding officer's face changed as he hurriedly gave the order to fire. A shot ricocheted off the wall behind Luke as he leapt out into the darkness. In seconds, he fell through the air, plunging downwards into the cold, murky waters below.

The current was strong and when he surfaced he looked up at the bridge, he could see the armed guard peering over the wall where he had jumped.

In the icy waters, he paddled himself faster down the current with his good arm. The torches lit up the water around him and the occasional shot rang out as the guards fired at floating pieces of deadwood they mistook for his body. In seconds the current washed him out of range.

'Unless they followed me into the water it would be impossible for them to catch up with me now,' he thought. He strained to hear the splash of any oncoming pursuers prepared to risk their lives from the fall and the dirty river, but there weren't any. On either side there were huge storage warehouses with their loading jetty's sticking out into the river so there was no chance that vehicles could follow along the bank.

Five minutes later, he steered himself through the swirling water towards a steep concrete incline. It had metal rungs running up the slope that could assist his climb. He felt sick with the effort and pain from his arm, but he knew that he could not stop now. They would be back to hunt him down shortly, possibly by boat, and he needed the hour or so of darkness that remained in order to move unseen.

He picked himself up at the top of the bank and using all the cover available made his way in the direction of their guest-house.

Friday, 15th October 2008
Camp David, West Maryland

President Whiting arrived at the main Camp David conference centre. The leaders of the other member Nations were already inside the Great Hall talking amongst themselves prior to their planned introduction to the world's media. As was to be expected, the hot topic of discussion was the breaking news surrounding India's invasion of Pakistan. The delegations, eager to assess each other's views, were vocal in their condemnation of India to such an extent, that China's non-arrival at the Great Hall completely escaped the attention of most of them. Those who did briefly consider China's lack of presence assumed they were late. The British, French, Russian and Japanese leaders informally discussed the strategic options at their disposal for defending Pakistan's sovereignty, oblivious to the oncoming bombshell about to be delivered by the Summit's host. In the President's absence the Secretary of State, Margaret Henderson, politely ushered them through to a more comfortable reception room.

Outside the Conference Centre, the fact that the Chinese delegation had not yet arrived had not escaped the attention of the inquiring media. As President Whiting stepped out of his limousine, the reporters shouted questions from behind the police cordon. He ignored the calls and headed up the steps amidst the flashing camera bulbs behind him. Climbing the steps, he heard questions from the shrewder journalists through the general backdrop of noise. *'Where are the Chinese delegation Mr. President? Is there a problem in the Alliance with Deputy Chen?'* Although most journalist's concentrated on his reaction to India, he was slightly taken back by the China questioning given that none would be aware of the recent conversations.

Inside the building, the President made his way through the Great Hall to the reception room beyond. Without wasting anytime, he passed through the security guards on the entrance and into the room's foyer. The world leaders turned to face him. The pleasure at seeing the President's arrival hid the underlying seriousness of the news about India's invasion. President Whiting walked slowly down the line to greet each leader in turn. He shook their hands warmly, expressing his country's welcome to the Summit.

At the end of the line was his friend, the British Prime Minister whom he greeted in a slightly less formal manner. Concluding the welcome, he dropped his friendly smile and replaced it with a more serious expression as he turned to address them. What he had to say was not part of the original agenda, events that morning had superseded any adherence to the old schedule. The President, in his opening remarks, was about to set the tone for the Summit's success. His words were unprepared and unrehearsed except for a few minutes thought on the way in the limousine.

"As we all know, India has sent its armies into Pakistani territory this morning."

He paused so that each line would carry great effect. Fortunately all the leaders had an excellent grasp of English. A requirement for translation would have upset the delivery and slowed the speech further.

"During the course of this morning, disturbing information has come to light that threatens to ruin the chances of our success at this Summit…the news has greater ramifications for our countries beyond this Summit, it ultimately affects the future stability of world peace."

The leaders stared at him in amazement. They wondered what could have transpired to drive the President of the United States into making such an alarming statement.

"Not long ago I expelled Deputy Chen, and his delegation, from the Summit. They are currently on their way back to China."

The faces of the world leaders stared in surprise. Since the President's entry, they had all realized that Deputy Chen and his delegation had not arrived at the conference centre but various reasons had surfaced to explain their delay.

"It is essential that I justify the position of the United States to you and make you aware of the true dangers that we face…I have changed the order of events so that my team can make a full presentation to you, they will explain the chain of events that gave us no other option than to take the course of action we did. The meeting with the media that was originally scheduled to take place next has been provisionally postponed until we know how we want to proceed."

The leaders shared the President's grave expression as they listened intently, determined to understand the root of his fears.

"In order that everything can be fully explained to you, I have organized the presentation for you and your delegation in the lecture theatre down the corridor on the other side of the Great Hall," and he indicated with a outstretched arm the direction of the room.

"If you would all care to join me, we can start the briefing right away."

The President led the way. After a moment's deliberation, the leaders followed him out of the room and across the marble floor. The delegations buzzed with excitement as they jostled to advise their leaders on the best way to handle the situation.

Catherine Dennison, looking as elegant as usual, was applying the finishing touches in the lecture theatre. She had been informed of the change in procedure by Mike Conway and had taken charge of setting up the arrangements personally.

The lecture theatre began filling with the political and military advisors to the superpowers. They were ushered to their seats by members of Dennison's team according to a plan she had devised earlier. The layout of the lecture room was exactly the same as that which you would find at any University Campus on the East Coast, only twice the size. Apart from the scale, the other point of differentiation was the degree of comfort it offered. There were no hard wooden seats, but each row had a long cushioned bench that ran in parallel with a desktop to the opposite wall. The rows descended in a gentle arc formation from their lofty view at the back towards the more intimate ground level benches in front of the Presenter's desk.

About half way up the bank of desks was a walkway to the other side and Catherine Dennison had used this platform to assemble five chairs for the world leaders. The President had emphasized the importance of sitting them next to each other and not next to their first line of advisors. He felt the need to present a united front at the start outweighed the requirement for internal deliberation with their advisors. After all, at this stage they were being asked no more than to watch and listen to the contents of the presentation.

The leaders were the last to take their seats and the presentation began with Director Conway taking the role of lecturer. He slowly began working through the material they had accumulated on China's subterfuge. Unequivocally, he presented the trail of events that confirmed China's alliance with India and their involvement in Banerjee's plans. For every statement he made, using an overhead projector, he produced documentary evidence and extracts of reports which supported his case. He fully justified the rationale for China's expulsion.

Although the US position was substantiated, Director Conway asked for the lights to be dimmed while he produced the final piece of damning evidence. He showed the reel of film taken earlier when the President confronted Deputy Chen. The auditorium gasped in astonishment as they saw the arrogant sneer and retaliatory threat from Chen. Deputy Chen was clearly seen and heard to be stating that China would not allow the oil fields to be re-opened.

The film was replayed once again at the request of the British Prime Minister before the lights were raised. Director Conway summarized the current position and justified their decision to allow Chen's return to China. He concluded by informing the delegations of the message that Chen had been told to relay to Prime Minister Ziang.

Silence followed Mike Conway's closing remarks. The audience had been riveted to his every word and was aghast by the dilemma that now faced them. In the urgency to organize the delivery itself, the next steps had not been scripted. The President knew this was the case, and broke the silence, by rising from his seat and making his way down the aisle towards the front.

He thanked his CIA Director for his clear and concise presentation, and walked over towards the microphone. Leaning on the lectern in front of him he looked up to address the room.

"Gentlemen, you are now up to date…you have been presented with exactly the same information that is currently available to the United States…"

The President was a confident speaker and took his time to give ample consideration to the points he wanted to make.

"We will make all the papers presented today, open for your inspection and independent confirmation should you require to establish beyond any doubt, the evidence behind our assertions…"

He noticed the nods of approval coming from certain quarters of the room. As he tailed off, he realized the future of the Summit hung in the balance. The President decided to go for one last push.

"We accept that we are faced with how to respond to India's invasion of Pakistan, but this is not the biggest crisis threatening our countries survival…"

He paused and looked up towards the back of the lecture room.

"…The biggest threat before us, is the conspiracy between India and China to bring down our countries and destroy our economies…"

The anger in his voice reverberated around the room.

"They are cutting off the worlds major supply of oil and waiting for us collapse in the impending chaos that follows…their aim is to orchestrate the downfall of our economies and elevate themselves into a position to dominate our countries and world politics…I have no doubt whatsoever, that once they have achieved that position of strength, they will seek to impose their will on us…"

The President paused, feeling his grip tightening on the lectern

"…Unless we can join hands and make this Summit a success, I believe their plan has a chance of success, we must not get waylaid by the invasion of Pakistan, that is their desire, we have to re-start the supply of oil from the Middle East….or ultimately they will succeed."

He looked at the Prime Ministers and the Deputy leader from Russia sitting either side of the seat he had just vacated. They listened intently to his heartfelt appeal.

The keynotes of his speech had been covered, it was time to make one last impassioned plea before succumbing to their reaction.

"Our priority has to be the oil fields…we must join together and deal with the barriers that India and China have, and will, put in our path…time is not on our side…I ask you to think wisely and quickly over what I have said…"

As the President pronounced his final words he looked up and fixed his gaze on the Summit leaders. He looked for clues in their troubled faces. *'That's it,'* he thought, *'how are they going to react now?'*

The atmosphere was electric in the stunned silence that followed. President Whiting collected himself to leave, he assumed they would need time to think over his words. As he stepped back from the lectern, the Russian deputy leader rose to his feet and began slowly clapping his hands in the direction of the President.

The slow, steady handclap was the only sound emanating from the silence. The Russian Deputy stood alone, applauding for several seconds before the Japanese Prime Minister also rose from his seat and joined the Russian's slow handclap.

The president looked up and amidst the initial looks of surprise, one by one the leaders stood up along with their delegations to applaud the President's speech. As they clapped in unison the President felt a shiver run down his spine at the spontaneous reaction of the assembly.

Still standing back from the lectern, he felt elated. There was along way to go but he had made the best possible beginning.

With the respectful, slow handclap still echoing around the room, he walked up the aisle to the row where the world leaders were standing. He stretched out his arm in the direction of the exit, indicating that they should take their leave ahead of him. The leaders accepted the offer and the President followed them through the door.

Friday, 15th October 2008
Government Building, Delhi

Balan paced the floor of the Prime Minister's office, considering the information he'd received from General Vu, the head of China's military and the leading advisor to Prime Minister Ziang. The news of their pact was in the open now, and there was no longer a need for hosting clandestine meetings. So many developments had passed since their rendezvous, months earlier, on the Andamman Islands.

Sitting in a chair next to a porcelain statue of a prowling Bengal tiger was Ashraf Nawani smoking a cigarette. He sat there contemplating Balan's presence in front of the balcony windows, while coolly watching his tobacco exhalations spiral towards the ceiling.

"Relax Balan, the Prime Minister will join us in a minute or so." He exaggerated his own calmness by adopting a laid back posture.

Balan didn't need to look up to see the expression of glee at his discomfort. It was no secret that Nawani revelled in other people's discomfort.

"Don't you think you should start worrying about how you let the agent slip through your hands again?" Balan retorted angrily.

He disliked Nawani intensely and only put up with the disrespect shown to him because of Banerjee's support for the loathsome individual. In the past he had often tried to steer the conversation with the Prime Minister onto the subject of Nawani and the 'goings-on' in the Secret Service. Unfortunately, the discussions never shed any light or revealed any reasons for why Banerjee should display such loyalty towards the man.

"No one could have survived that fall into the Yamana," Nawani replied sharply.

Balan stopped pacing and stared at him.

"Have you pulled out a body then?" his mouth twisted with the intensity of the sarcastic jab at Nawani's performance. *'His own inflated views of his self-importance know no bounds,'* thought Balan.

"Don't you tell…"

But Nawani's voice tapered off as he saw the stony expression on Banerjee's face. Unbeknown to both of them he'd surreptitiously entered the room and was standing at the door watching them.

"I'm sorry Sir, I didn't see you…" Nawani lowered his head, he was alarmed by his sudden arrival. His disrespectful tone to Balan had gotten him into trouble and he knew it. The Prime Minister had counselled him in the past on his aggression to those in authority; such an outright display of arrogance could not go unpunished.

Frowning, he walked towards them holding up the palm of his hand for Nawani to stop his pleading whilst Balan secretly smiled at the timing of his entrance.

"So no dead body has been found yet?" the Prime Minister questioned rhetorically.

"It's just a matter of time your Excellency, my men are combing the river but the body could have been washed away outside the city itself." His slumped shoulders emphasized the apologetic nature of his lame excuse.

In a low key, understated dialogue, he repeated his assertion that there was little chance anyone could survive the fall let alone the conditions of the river itself.

"Nawani..." the Banerjee spoke firmly, standing with his back to him admiring a woven tapestry depicting an elephant-hunting scene of a bygone age.

"Even if one's dead there is still a second – am I right?" Without waiting for a reply, he span around, the dark patches below his eyes giving a satanic streak to his already dark countenance.

"Get me their bodies dead or live," he shrieked at Nawani.

He could no longer contain his rage over the man's failings. His earlier show of arrogance towards Balan had tipped the scales. Outside in the corridors and in the adjacent rooms, his cry of displeasure was heard by the guards and members of his household staff.

His temper was legendary and extraordinary for its ferocity. As Nawani knew to his cost, it was not reserved for just the subservient minions and even the most senior advisor could not escape the humiliation. He himself had witnessed high-ranking army officials crumple in the face of Banerjee's protracted ravings. His mood swings were characterized by his extraordinary and irrational behaviour; sometimes the torrent of abuse could last seconds, sometimes hours.

The outbursts were shocking and even Balan felt uncomfortable when Banerjee appeared to lose control. He often wondered how it was possible that such an intelligent, charming man could have such a foreboding, darker side. *Does it just surface or is he deliberately cultivating an irrational persona for our benefit?*' he thought as he continued watching Nawani shudder at the screaming.

"If I don't have them in the next five days then you'll pay – am I expressing myself?" he ranted hoarsely, almost losing his voice with exertion.

"Am I expressing myself?" he bellowed again looking straight at Nawani.

Nawani nodded his face lowered looking at the ground like a chided schoolboy.

"Now get out!" Banerjee commanded his voice coated with disgust.

Nawani left the room. He realized now, that finding the agents was a matter of life and death for him. In Banerjee's own astute way, he wanted more industry from the rank and file below Nawani. The thinly veiled threat to the Head of his Secret Service would manifest itself again. Organizations like the Secret Service survived on fear and Banerjee could play the game well. He knew he could expect results if their lives depended on it and Nawani would make sure that was understood.

Banerjee was momentarily drained, but his composure returned and he turned to face Balan.

"We are on the threshold of achieving our dreams, we cannot afford to make silly mistakes, like our friend."

Earlier that day, Balan had revealed that China had been expelled from the Camp David Summit. The news was not well received by Banerjee who had hoped to secure further time with China on the inside before the pact was discovered.

In the beginning, Banerjee had first conceived the unholy Alliance with China when they'd come to him with information that Pakistan was impotent. The Chinese had listened to his plans and readily agreed to his proposal to be a sleeping ally, ready to rise as the oil crisis brought down the western superpowers. They had no love of America and the ways of the West and this opened a window of opportunity to them. For over ten years, the current men in office, the senior hierarchy of China, had schemed to recapture the rebellious island of Taiwan. The embarrassment caused by the renegade State over the years, with its democratic elections, had bruised their national pride but soon this would be in the past.

The other predominant threat to China lay along its northern border. The men in power smiled as they debated the opportunities that would surface to neutralize Russia, as their already fragile economy crumbled before them.

"How is the convoy progressing?" he looked up at Balan referring to the warheads under General Gupta's control.

"According to plan," he replied sharply. He wasn't keen to see Banerjee lapse into his earlier mood.

"….it is still travelling undetected to Jiwar on the western tip of Pakistan….barring any unforeseen circumstances, it should be in place by the day after tomorrow."

"Taking control of the oilfields is not going to be as simple as the Alliance thinks, is it Balan?" he said, satisfied with the news. His mind was already jumping ahead to anticipate their next move and his ploy to counter any resistance.

He stood up and felt the fabric of the ornamental rug that he'd been admiring earlier as he rationalized his thoughts.

"Balan, I think it is time that you travelled to meet with our Chinese friends."

Saturday, 16th October 2008
Outskirts of Delhi

Kirin heard the window opening and rushed towards the bathroom door. Luke was trying to pull himself in by his good arm, she saw the state he was in and grabbed him under his good arm, hauling him through.

"What happened?" she kept repeating, but the words weren't registering.

He fell in a heap on the floor and grimaced at the pain shooting through his arm. She helped him sit up with his back against the wall and rushed to fetch some water. His clothes were dirty and torn, his head and arm were coated in blood and he looked physically exhausted.

Drinking the water gratefully he looked up at her for a few seconds with a weak smile before his vision clouded and he fell to one side unconscious.

When he awoke, he was staring at the large fan that hung from the ceiling slowly rotating. He felt the breeze hitting him as he tried to remember where he was and how he'd got there. Kirin stepped in through the door and everything began flooding back. She moved towards him and sat down on the side of the bed.

"How long have I been out?" he asked in a hoarse whisper.

"About six hours," she replied softly.

Luke tried to sit up and winced with pain caused by the exertion. He could sense a lemony, soap smell and realized he'd been washed from head to toe. Above him, he saw his clothes hanging from a temporary clothesline. A sheet was pulled up to his waist protecting his modesty, whilst his bandaged arm was strapped to his chest by a makeshift sling.

"The belt!" he exclaimed suddenly.

"Don't worry it's safe," she said pointing to the bag in the corner.

With her help he drank some water and began narrating the story from the night before.

She put her hand on his arm as she sat listening to him recount the lucky escape from Nawani's clutches.

"You're fortunate the knife missed the bone," she said, leaning over and adjusting the bandage slightly.

"Did you have any luck finding new accommodation?" he asked. "We've got to move out of here soon, it's possible someone will have seen me returning."

"I've found somewhere much closer to the government building, but don't you think it's sensible to get out of town for a few days until you've recovered properly?" she questioned logically.

He lay there and turned his head towards the window considering her question for a few minutes. His strength wouldn't return as fast as he'd like it to and he still had the ringing in his ears caused by the pressure of the cold river water.

"You're right. There's nothing to be gained by staying in town at the moment, we'll return in a couple of days when my arm's healed and the attention's died down."

"There's a coach station nearby that takes the main highway to the south of Delhi, we'll travel from there." She didn't try to hide her delight at his decision to lay low for a few days.

"Ok" he smiled, "There's no time like the present," and he swung his feet off the bed and onto the ground, trying to lever himself up.

The Paradigm Shift

Thirty minutes later Kirin had checked out, and they were walking towards the coach station for the next bus travelling south.

Saturday, 16ᵗʰ October 2008
Camp David, West Maryland

Jim Allen sat across the breakfast table from Mike Conway as they discussed the events of the past two days and the agenda at the Summit in the afternoon.

Catherine Dennison's department had worked most of the night organizing the framework for today's discussions which were scheduled to begin early that afternoon. It had been decided that the best way to stop all the issues from over-running would be to set up preliminary forums with the political and military advisors. These committees had commenced work a couple of hours earlier at six o'clock in the morning and were there to debate and conclude a coherent strategic plan. The decisions made in these committees together with any unresolved issues were then to be the focus of the leader's meeting in the afternoon.

The waiter approached the table and refilled Mike Conway's cup with black coffee.

"There are a couple of issues we need to discuss," he said looking up at Jim Allen.

They'd been through most of the material concerning the Summit, but not matters closer to home.

"Ok, what's on your mind?"

"The leak," Mike said simply.

"Has there been any further progress at all?" Allen quizzed.

"Where do we start?" said Conway shrugging his soldiers.

Everything had pointed towards Karpurov and the Russians earlier, but now that the news of China's treachery had surfaced, this no longer seemed plausible.

"The source of this information came from the top," Conway hesitated, "do you suggest that I carry out an investigation on the top officials of the United States including the President and Vice President?"

Jim Allen wiped his napkin across his mouth thinking for a second.

"This your area Mike, that information came from somewhere, you're going to have to solve the leak yourself."

Director Mike Conway held his look for a moment then shook his head. He'd anticipated a non-committal reply from Allen, but given the circumstances surrounding them, had thought he maybe willing to give his added authority to such an investigation.

"What's the other issue?" Allen wanted to move away from this subject.

As the President's National Security Advisor, the last issue he wanted to debate with the Director of CIA was an investigation into his boss.

"I had a call from Dan Schwartz this morning."

Colonel Dan Schwartz had gone straight back to the operations centre at the Pentagon after his meeting with Mike Conway to hand over the contents of his metal brief case.

"And?" Allen inquired.

"A combination of the bad weather and employing our satellites to monitor the progress of India's ground forces has meant we've lost track of India's warheads."

"Jesus Christ Mike!" Allen sat back in his chair.

"I know, I know…it's just what we need right now," he felt personally responsible that this had been allowed to happen. He continued, his words tinged with a feeling of guilt.

"I've fed the information to the military committee of the Alliance and they're alerting all satellite stations to search for the mobile missile launchers."

"Pick them up quickly Mike, God knows what they could be planning."

Mike nodded.

"...And you'd better let the President know." Allen added.

Right now Mike Conway didn't want to create any more waves with the President. The events of the past twenty fours had gone a long way to restoring his credibility with President Whiting. The last thing he needed now was to feed him more bad news, especially when he could have done something about it.

"By the way what is the latest with our friends in India?" Allen took a sip from his third cup of coffee.

"No news, but I wasn't expecting any for a few days yet," he answered.

"The last message made it clear that they would be keeping contact to a minimum and you can't really blame them considering they know there is a leak out here, can we Jim?"

He raised his eyebrows at Allen, adding emphasis to the question.

He wanted to turn the subject back to the investigation of the leak. Frankly, he could do with Allen's support if he was going to undertake a full investigation into the White House. Intuitively, they both knew that authorization sanctioning an investigation could, and probably would, come back to haunt them later on. Rarely were such probes commissioned by the CIA and when they were, they were normally justified by scandals or cover-ups, like Nixon in the sixties and Clinton in the nineties.

"Well let's hope they are successful, otherwise our problems are going to be around for a long time, aren't they Mike?"

Jim Allen's reply signalled his intention on the subject. He had no inclination to reopen the debate.

With breakfast finished, they stood up together and made their way to the first of several committee engagements they were due to attend prior to the main Summit meeting that afternoon.

Throwing his napkin on the table, Director Conway considered his priorities. He had a long day ahead of him with the final event being the rescheduled press conference. *'I must get back to Washington,'* he thought as he left the dining hall.

Saturday, 16th October 2008
Camp David, West Maryland

Without the need for any debate the world leaders knew that time was not on their side.

The presentation made by Director Conway the day before had included a visual extrapolation of the oil crisis. It showed the events that would unfold to cause their countries economic meltdown on a day-by-day basis. The speed of decline was staggering as the global impact of the oil crisis brought the transportation systems and the production of vital energy resources to a standstill.

The Prime Ministers of Britain, France, Japan and the Deputy leader of Russia all agreed on the over-riding need for a simple approach. They decided to restrict the attendance numbers to the afternoons meeting to an absolute minimum. Each leader was to sit with their two key aides who had chaired the earlier committee meetings in the morning. If any additional advice or information was required then that particular aide could be called in at short notice.

Catherine Dennison, a model of efficiency, had responded quickly to their request for a less formal surrounding. She changed the venue from the conference hall, built to hold a large capacity and requiring the use of microphones for communication, to a more informal and friendly environment. The room selected had a decorative, relaxed lounge at one end and an antique, circular meeting table at the other.

The four leaders were served tea or coffee as they sat in the comfortable sofas of the lounge awaiting the arrival of the President.

The Paradigm Shift

In a small office down the corridor normally used by the conference administrators, the President had paused briefly 'en route' to take an international call. It had to be an important call for him to deviate from the scheduled start of the Summit Meeting. On the other end of the line was His Highness, King Mohammed of Saudi Arabia.

They had spoken several hours earlier when His Highness had first called to discuss the possibility of their stepping aside and offering the Alliance any assistance it needed to control and operate the oil fields and refineries.

President Whiting listened intently to the King's approach for letting the Alliance assist with their problems and understood immediately the need for diplomacy. The King implied that with the help of the Alliance they could speed up the process of getting the oil fields back on line. He claimed they were already a long way to re-establishing the supply but the President knew this was not true, just a tactical ploy. It was obvious reading between the lines, that political assurances and future guarantees surrounding ownership of the fields were the real issue.

The President leapt at the chance to take control of the oil fields without a struggle. He agreed with the King that the oil-fields would be restored back to their control in a phased manner over the next two years providing this was agreeable to all the Arab rulers in the Gulf not just Saudi. The King agreed in principle and committed that he'd speak to his Arab brothers and give him their decision prior to the afternoon meeting of the Summit.

For his part, the President informed each leader of the latest development. They were all pleased with the news and fully supported the President's stance of a two-year moratorium before the oil fields were passed back into Arab hands. In the case of Russia, the President had made special efforts to converse with the Premier over the past twenty-four hours. His counterpart appreciated his diplomacy and reciprocated with his full approval.

After the presentation by Director Conway yesterday, he'd invited the Russian deputy leader to join him in a live television conference meeting with his counterpart in Moscow. He'd meant to use the platform to summarize proceedings but in practice they'd gone into the same level of depth as at the presentation. The benefit of this effort was immediately clear. The Premier denigrated the behaviour of China and promised his country's total support to the Summit and its conclusions.

In the hallway prior to entering the lounge, Jim Allen stood in the doorway with Mike Conway as they watched the President negotiating over the phone with King Mohammed. It sounded from the bits of dialogue they overheard that the President was achieving the confirmation they urgently needed.

"Thank you your highness, I will speak to the other leaders right away," and he replaced the handset.

"I think we have a deal but the King has made a specific request."

The President strode past his two advisors and entered the meeting room where the leaders were assembled around the fine mahogany table.

Following on behind, Jim Allen and Mike Conway took their seats on the side of the President as he commenced the afternoon session.

"I have good news…the Saudi King has confirmed that the Gulf States will accept our terms for taking control of the oil fields."

The Paradigm Shift

The leaders nodded, acknowledging the positive break-through.

"The king has requested that we jointly sign a document at this table confirming our respective nations agreement to the terms….in return he will arrange for the Gulf leaders to counter-sign their agreement. Do I have your approval?"

The President turned and whispered something to Jim Allen who promptly got up to supervise the preparation of the official manuscript.

One hour later it had been signed by all present, and delivered to a local US air force base from where duplicate hard copies would be flown direct to Riyadh. For their part, the Arab leaders had agreed to convene in Saudi for its imminent arrival. Once the agreement was in their hands, they had committed themselves to opening up new lines of communication with the ships of the US 5th Fleet stationed in the Arabian Gulf.

With the Agreement taken care of, President Whiting turned the focus back towards the Alliance Treaty, and the formal statements drafted earlier that day in the meetings held by their chief advisors.

The document covered the boundaries and framework in which they would work together in the face of the threat posed by India and China. The leaders had not read the document and all its appendices, but had been briefed on the key points by their aides. Sections of the agreement covered the individual responsibilities of each member nation. It was comprehensive in content considering the short time that they had to pull the relevant sections together.

Responsibilities included the monetary contributions to be made, the military resources to be deployed, the political connections to be established, and the main communication centres to be shared throughout the campaign to coordinate their unified strategy.

The President chaired the meeting efficiently and pushed ahead when a contentious issue threatened to slow down proceedings.

One such point came on the subject of Israel's assistance. Although the Saudi King had agreed to keep the issue out of their agreement, the Arabs had made it abundantly clear that they would not tolerate any Israeli troops on their soil, even if they were part of a UN peacekeeping force.

On the other hand the Alliance knew the benefit of Israel's involvement. They had a well-trained army with the very latest weaponry, and they were willing to assist the Alliance in pushing back the Indian ground forces from Pakistan. In the end, the Summit leaders agreed that their help could not be taken, the concept of Israeli forces fighting in an Islamic centre of the Middle East, would not be tolerated.

It was early evening when they eventually stood up around the table to sign the final copy of the Treaty. The tension of the lengthy discussions was over, and the mood became more convivial as the President invited them into an adjacent room for a photo-shoot. The President's wife, Pamela joined them for the photographs. *How would time remember the Summit?* She wondered. *Would the framed picture hang on the walls of the White House for posterity or would future generations pour scorn on their efforts?* She squeezed the President's hand as the camera flashed. Right now the pictures were required for distribution to the waiting journalists at the Press conference.

Catherine Dennison, amid the tightest security, had coordinated the media briefing in the same Press Hall that had been used many years earlier for the successful release to the world of the Israeli-Arab Peace Accord.

The five leaders walked onto the stage at the front of the Hall, smiling and shaking hands for the benefit of the camera crews who were beaming the occasion around the world.

As the noise in the room began to abate after the initial euphoria caused by their arrival, President Whiting approached the lectern. He felt exhausted from the day's tribulations and more than a little concerned about his own appearance. His brief visit to his personal make-up lady on the way to the Press Hall had at least covered up some of the new stress lines appearing around his eyes.

Standing bolt upright, he informed the world of the historic agreement that had been signed minutes earlier, but professed an apology that he could not go in to the details at present, due to the sensitivity of the international issues which the Alliance Country's were combining together to oppose.

The press conference fell quiet when President Whiting began running through the series of events that led to China's initial expulsion from the Summit. He carefully articulated the reasons for the united stand taken by the Alliance, and the need to restore Middle East oil production at the earliest opportunity.

His stance was uncompromising, he wanted the watching public to take heart from this Agreement. Sensitivity in his responses was applied where necessary, and he explained the dangers of the oil crisis in a manner that would not cause undue panic, but left no one in any doubt about the severity of the issue.

The normally vociferous reporters remained unusually quiet throughout. At the end of his speech he reiterated an apology that none of the Alliance leaders would be taking further questions at this stage, but reassured them that they would keep their combined channels of communication open twenty-four hours a day.

As he finished his last remark and turned to stand with the other leaders the Press Hall burst into life as journalists stood up in unison to shout their questions. The noise was deafening and Catherine Dennison returned to the lectern to repeat the apology and make a plea for them to calm down. For a few final minutes, the Alliance leaders continued smiling and posing for the cameras before filing out of the hall.

Sunday, 17th October 2008
USS Missouri, Gulf of Arabia

Admiral Troy Downey sat across the table from Admiral John Stone, the commander of the US Fifth Fleet. Having joined the academy for naval officers a couple of years apart they had known each other for over twenty years.

Also sitting in the operations room of the aircraft carrier, US Missouri, were Air Marshal Walter Reiger and Conrad Dexter.

Conrad Dexter was an employee of Exxon, one of the largest US Oil Corporations. He'd worked in the industry for over thirty years and was identified by the CIA as the ideal candidate to run the civilian teams being deployed in the Gulf.

Before moving back to Houston as the Vice President in charge of Global Technology and Production Services, he'd been stationed in the Middle East for eight years running Exxon's oil interests. His experience of the region and his long contact list featuring most of the eminent Arab dignitaries, made his local knowledge invaluable to the complex logistical exercise they were undertaking.

Across the wall behind the table was a large-scale map of the Gulf region pinpointing all the oil fields at sea and on land. Different coloured pins then graded the wells in terms of importance according to varying levels of crude output and of vital importance, the map highlighted the sites of all the on-shore refineries. Coloured arrows distinguished the sea channels which needed aerial protection for the constant flow of super tankers in and out of the Gulf.

Admiral Troy Downey, as the highest ranking officer present, chaired the meeting and began his address by informing them that the Alliance Agreement had been put in place with the Saudi's enabling them to work together.

Earlier that morning, Jim Allen's draughtsmanship had been reviewed by the ruling families in Riyadh. Once they were agreed that the terms met the principles they had expressed to King Mohammed, they quickly added their signatures and stamped the Agreement with their royal seals.

Since approving the document, their eagerness to help was instantaneous. Conrad Dexter had spent most of his time on the telephone. He was updated by authorized personnel working for the Gulf States on the status of their oil fields including accessibility and any likely problems to be encountered.

The operation to send in the expert teams was scheduled to begin in three hours, and was expected to take twelve hours to complete. The Chinook helicopters aboard the US Missouri would be expected to work around the clock to deliver the teams to and from the various destinations. Furthermore, in view of the technical expertise of certain groups, they would be expected to perform at several locations, repeating their function until their job was done.

Earlier that day, Conrad Dexter had used the aircraft bay below deck to brief the teams on how and when they were to be dispatched.

Admiral Downey, Admiral Stone and Air Marshal Reiger were not unduly concerned about the likely success of delivering the experts to their destinations; their worry was protecting them once they were safely installed.

"What's the latest on the Chinese fleet, Troy?" Admiral Stone asked.

"It's as we suspected, the bulk of the fleet have put to sea now, with the main body moving towards the Taiwanese Straits."

The Government of Taiwan had contacted the US Military and Presidential Office as soon as they identified the build up taking place off their shores. Although the economic success of Taiwan had enabled them to invest heavily in the latest and most technologically advanced, military hardware, they knew they couldn't match any direct offensive from China alone. Unfortunately for them, their persistent requests for help from the United States met with little success. They were promised support as soon as it was available.

The reason was simply a question of resources. The US Military and President Whiting took the Chinese threat very seriously, but they just didn't have the naval reserves on hand to deploy immediately. Most of the 5th Fleet was now stationed on full alert in the Gulf or off the shores of West India.

In the end, President Whiting knew he had to seek alternatives for the Taiwanese cries for help and he voiced the dilemma to his Treaty partners through Jim Allen. With the potential provocations of China, he left them under no illusion as to the urgency of the situation. The up shot of the communication with the Alliance was that Russia agreed to send its east coast patrol of two destroyers from Vladivostok, whilst NATO and America combined to send three nuclear submarines.

"The bad news for us is the route of the Chinese carrier, it's rounded Sri Lanka, and is bearing on a direct course for the Straits of Hormuz!" Downey added.

"Christ…this place is getting too crowded," Admiral Stone voiced their thoughts.

Apart from the 5th Fleet and several allied subs, over forty empty super tankers had dropped anchor along the Gulf's coastline.

The two Admirals and Air Marshal Reiger spent the next hour debating the areas that could threaten their mission. Apart from the imminent arrival of the Chinese carrier they viewed the Indian Air Force as the most likely source of danger.

Air superiority in the region was massively weighted in favour of the US and the Alliance partners. However, as a consequence of the number of locations they had to protect, and the limited number of bases from which their planes could be fully serviced, there was a high probability that hit and run attacks by the enemy could meet with some success.

They decided the best deterrent to such attacks was to run constant sorties. Sitting down with the squadron leaders they created an elaborate matrix of flight patterns based on the oil fields they were seeking to protect. The fighter pilots followed the routes across the Gulf serving to confuse would be observers and predators with the randomness of their patrols.

At four o'clock the operation commenced, and the first helicopters took off from the US Missouri, on their mission, to ferry the civilian teams to the oil fields and refineries. With the help of Admiral John Stone, Conrad Dexter controlled and monitored progress from the communication bridge of the giant aircraft carrier.

Throughout the evening and night, the map gradually registered their success as the colour of the markers changed to reflect the oil wells under the Alliance control.

Monday, 18th October 2008
Manipur, On the border of India and China

Balan climbed out of the helicopter wearing a thick bear-skin hat pulled down over his ears and a thick overcoat to protect him from the sleet and biting cold wind. They had landed along the northern most border of India close to Nepal at the foot of the Himalayas. With two armed guards following closely in attendance, he jumped briskly into the grey darkness below the rotating blades. Looking up briefly into the face of the howling wind, he saw the blurred vision of a train carriage standing forty yards ahead of him. Memorizing his course, he put his head down into the collar of his overcoat and trudged forward.

It was an old-fashioned, wide gauge train and wiping his eyes with his gloves, he climbed up the metal plates at the end of the carriage. His Chinese host had been observing the helicopter landing and the door was instantly pulled open for him as he arrived at the top of the steps.

Inside it was warm and light. Despite it being late afternoon, darkness descended quite early at this time of year in the remote northern hills.

As Balan pulled off his hat, handing it to one of his guards, General Vu walked up the aisle in his trademark black uniform. They greeted each other like long lost friends before the General escorted him back down the corridor. At the end of the carriage they suddenly emerged into splendid reception room. Balan stood for a moment, surprised, admiring the interior décor of the train. The lavish, patterned fabrics around the windows and the luxurious, dark wood furniture, with its fine gold braid trimming, had been assembled many decades ago for the Chinese royal family, prior to the onset of Communism in the East.

"Would you care for a drink?" General Vu asked, clicking his fingers in the direction of one of the carriage attendants.

"Tea would be fine," Balan replied and the boy was dismissed with the order.

Although Balan had the broad outline of events at Camp David, the General began their conversation by taking him through some of the finer details. Both Balan, and the General were right-hand men, key advisors, and the tone of their voice and the manner of their speech, reflected their reverence for the real men in charge.

The message from Banerjee was simple: *'The oil fields must remain closed whatever the cost.'*

They had gone too far down the road to watch their plans fail as the Alliance sought to reactivate oil production. They were close to success; in fact they could count the days remaining before the oil crisis would reach such a propensity, that the western economies would be beyond redemption. As they stood by, watching the disintegration happen right before their eyes, the power and control would shift from the crumbling edifice of the West, leaving them the victors in the political aftermath.

Sitting opposite each other, in two high-backed, well-cushioned chairs, they evaluated every development of the campaign so far. As usual, Balan was thorough, refusing to cut corners and the General shared his meticulous nature. They compared notes on their original strategy with the actual events that had unfolded.

For most of their appraisal they were very self-congratulatory as the events transpired according to their master plan. The only area that gave rise for concern was the timing of the Alliance entry into the Gulf. It had been the hardest part of the plan to predict. How long could they stop the Alliance from entering the Gulf and taking control of the oil fields? Balan had shared General Vu's faith that China's underhand role in Washington's political scene would remain undetected for a bit longer. In addition to the uncovering of China's cooperation, it was mildly irritating that the ruling Arab families had not put up greater resistance to the Alliance, before caving in to their demands.

As Banerjee had repeated to Balan many times over the past few months, the key to their success was *'time'*. The oil fields must be kept closed for a few days longer.

Throughout their dialogue one question played on Balan's mind. He listened politely as Vu expanded on the options to stall the progress of the Alliance before stepping in when his opportunity arose to interject.

"Is your inside source still live, General?"

The General gave a wry smile. He was extremely protective whenever the conversation turned to his inside source, but he couldn't hide his feeling of smugness that his intelligence services had embedded a mole at the very top of the US Government.

"Our source, as you put it, is still very much alive," he replied, the smile remained along with his gloating demeanour.

Balan nodded his head in understanding and then proceeded to take the General through the next step in Krishna Banerjee's plan.

It was Balan's turn to lead the conversation and General Vu listened, totally absorbed, as he heard the genius of Banerjee's strategy. His intent expression finally broke into a tight-lipped smile as Balan reached the conclusion.

"Your Prime Minister's suggestions are brilliant," the General pronounced.

Despite his patriotic love for everything Chinese and his own inflated self-importance; he was prepared to acknowledge the wisdom of Banerjee's words. *This is the solution to our timing problems,*' he thought to himself.

"And what should we do for our part?" He had understood the role of India but how did his beloved China feature in Banerjee's plans. He looked quizzically at Balan.

"You must continue to raise distractions, major distractions, so that the Alliance won't know which way to turn," he responded thoughtfully. His mind kept reverting to the General's mole in the Washington administration. *'How high in the administration? Capable of killing the President himself?'* he wondered.

Ultimately, the plan really relied on India for its success, but Balan and Banerjee knew that with China's help, they could deflect unwanted attention from themselves and possibly away from the Gulf. Any diversion taking up valuable, decision-making time of the Alliance would work in their favour.

"Maybe you could consider launching an attack on Taiwan ahead of schedule, or take your nuclear missiles along the border with Russia to a full state of alert!"

The General understood, nodding his head slowly deep in thought, he asked one of the highly-trained officers standing by the door to connect him to Prime Minister Ziang.

"To what lengths would your man on the inside be prepared to go for our cause?" Balan asked as they waited for the call to be put through. *'Surely the possibilities had not escaped the General?'* he thought, and then his mind cast itself back to the tragic and needless death of his only son. The bitterness and resentment flooded back until the phone ringing broke the spell.

The Paradigm Shift

General Vu was considering Balan's question as the phone rang. Unclasping his hands, he stretched for the receiver on the table in front of him. The Government operator in Beijing wasted no time in connecting him to Prime Minister Ziang who listened carefully as Vu explained the conversation with Balan.

Balan knew the call would take a while and stood up to stretch his legs. He appreciated art and wandered around the carriage, admiring some of the exquisitely framed scenes of Chinese life with the Cantonese writing painted in black, broad brushstrokes alongside.

After about twenty-five minutes, he turned round to face General Vu as he finished the conversation with his Premier. Although he did not understand the language he could sense the deference being shown in his closing remarks.

"My leader has asked that you convey his greetings to Prime Minister Banerjee."

Balan stood eager to get a feeling for China's commitment. Despite there being no signs to the contrary, he would still feel a sense of relief at the General's words.

"He has also instructed me to convey our whole hearted support for his ingenious plan," the General smiled up at him. He too was pleased with the outcome.

"He wishes him success and promises to ensure that the Alliance have plenty to think about in other corners of the world."

The General laughed and offered Balan a drink to toast their future success.

He joined the General drinking a large scotch before taking his time to put on his hat and coat. The weather outside was the same and after a lengthy goodbye, he climbed down from the carriage and made his way back through the ice-cold wind.

'Banerjee will be pleased with the news,' he thought as the helicopter lifted off the ground and commenced the journey back to Delhi.

Monday, 18th October 2008
The Pentagon, Washington

It was the first time Mike Conway had been back to his office in several days. He frowned as he looked at the pile of correspondence sitting in the in-tray; there was a lot of catching up to be done.

With the evening rapidly approaching, he finally sat back in his chair and reviewed the outstanding workload. Much to her pleasure, he decided that he could afford to dismiss his secretary an hour earlier than intended. After all it was a question of priorities, and he was keen to start his scheduled appointment with Dan Schwartz and General Karpurov. Her last act before departing for the day was to call Colonel Schwartz and pull the meeting forward.

The atmosphere of the meeting was friendly. Since returning from Camp David, Colonel Schwartz had cleared the air with Karpurov who had, fortunately, fully understood the requirement for secrecy. The information in Colonel Schwartz's metal briefcase was extremely sensitive and when General Karpurov finally learnt the truth, he appeared quite shaken for a man normally in control of his emotions. *'Their southern border must be an enormous concern,'* thought Schwartz, observing his reaction to China's underhand dealings.

Their meeting concentrated on the effort that was being made to locate the nuclear missile launchers which had disappeared in the turmoil of recent events. Once they were satisfied that every possible route was being explored by their satellite monitoring system to locate the missiles, they turned to the overall issue of the Indian invasion. With the aide of detailed schematics from the spy satellites they analyzed the various prongs of attack being used by the ground forces advancing into Pakistan.

Colonel Schwartz again reiterated his observation that there was something unusual about the pattern being developed by the Indian army. Director Conway tended to agree and registered his concern. Looking at the detailed schematic in front of him, it certainly didn't follow conventional strategies.

"Banerjee's a bastard, he isn't concerned about the lives of his own troops," Karpurov's thick Russian accent was filled with disgust.

Russian intelligence sources had informed him that only some of their frontline troops approaching Lahore had been lucky enough to have protective clothing. The fall-out had still not fully dispersed, and whilst the suits were not likely to save them from radiation poisoning in the long run, those without, were condemned to die quickly.

"It's almost as if they're trying to disguise something?" Schwartz murmured to himself as he stood up and stared at the enlarged map in the Operations Control room.

Conway's office had the benefit of a wide, observation window which looked down on the Control Centre below, similar to the rooms above operating theatres used by trainee doctors to watch the surgeon at work.

Karpurov's thickset frame sat hunched, deep in thought as he listened to Colonel Schwartz's concentrated efforts at deduction. Slowly Karpurov wheeled in his chair, turning to face Director Conway as the realization dawned on him:

"They're taking them into Pakistan."

Conway and Schwartz looked up at each other in the same instant. *'Did this make sense?'*

The Paradigm Shift

'*Why had he not considered this possibility earlier?*' Director Conway kicked himself for not having thought of the idea himself.

"It's logical," Schwartz nodded towards his superior.

"Those missiles are limited in range, if they want to threaten the Gulf they would have to move them into Pakistan," he continued, rationalizing the suggestion.

"Good, let's brief the teams to work on it," Conway said.

His deputy jumped up, he was eager to get back to the Operations Room and re-examine the data against their new revelation.

"Not bad, General," Conway said smiling at Karpurov.

The General stood up to follow Colonel Schwartz out of the room. Before leaving he graciously acknowledged the Director's backhanded compliment by bowing slightly and returning his smile.

Colonel Schwartz asked his team to replay the advance of the Indian Army on the huge screen at the front of the Operations Centre. The model, controlled by a timer, was based on recorded information digitally processed and stored by their satellite system. The screen showed the overall outline of Pakistan but could be magnified several times to show individual streets or buildings. The imprint of the advance was relayed to the map and like any visual recording, the process could be slowed down or put into fast-forward, highlighting the progressing troop and convoy movements.

Once they adopted the assumption that the missile launchers were part of this pattern, it quickly became evident that what was emerging on screen was a deliberate strategy to put observers off the scent.

He briefed the team to study the satellite recordings and look for any clues which might highlight the possible route being taken by the convoy. The satellite surveillance systems that were programmed to watch the advancing Indian forces were recalibrated with new coordinates.

Colonel Schwartz updated his Director, by reporting back through the intercom system that the surveillance sweep of Pakistan had now been altered to take into account Karpurov's deduction.

Mike Conway loosened his tie as he heard the news and asked, rather than ordered, if he would join him in his office when he was free. The clock on his office wall showed the time approaching quarter past nine as Dan Schwartz knocked on the door before entering.

He gratefully accepted Director Conway's offer of a drink before asking him: "What's on your mind?"

On several occasions during the events of the past few days they'd shared a drink under similar circumstances. Mike Conway trusted his number two implicitly and often used him as a sounding board to clarify his own thoughts and judgements.

After pouring two glasses of scotch from a cabinet behind his desk and, handing one over to his friend, he began elaborating on his problem, a full-blown CIA investigation into the US administration at the White House. The intelligence passed to Banerjee's Government on the whereabouts of Codename Amber and the British agent had nearly cost them their lives.

Schwartz sat sipping his drink as he listened to Conway outline the options, the unanswered questions and the politics of such an inquiry. He wasn't at all surprised to hear how Jim Allen had deflected the issue over their breakfast meeting.

"So what do you think? Any recommendations?" Conway asked knowing it wasn't really a fair question.

Dan shrugged. "Why not obtain the President's views? Or even ask him for authority to carry out an investigation?"

"Non starter, do you really think at a time like this there can be any doubts or allegations cast on the present administration?"

At the side of Director Conway's desk was a computer system. He had selected details on the President himself, followed by Vice President Martins, while sipping his scotch and idly scrolling down the information on the screen looking for inspiration. The CIA had transferred all their records on to a secure mainframe computer many years earlier and had a vast database at their disposal.

Access to the data he was perusing was restricted to only the most senior executives in the Agency. Some of the more sensitive information could bring down foreign governments.

"Something's strange about all this..." Schwartz was staring across the desk at the screen.

"Yes, go on Dan," Conway interjected, as Schwartz train of thought seemed to tail away.

Conway sipped his drink and continued toying with the computer as he waited for him to speak again. His curiosity was aroused at any new thoughts or light that could be shed on the situation.

"If we take ourselves out and accept that Karpurov's Russian through and through, then that only leaves the President, the Vice President and National Security Advisor..."

The intercom sounded. The Operation Centre wanted a second opinion from Colonel Schwartz on an early satellite picture that they had unearthed.

"Better check this out, could be the one," said Schwartz hopefully and seeing Conway's wave of approval got up to leave the room.

Director Conway leant back in his seat looking at the ceiling remembering his tryst with Catherine Dennison in the hotel at Montgomery. Had she been present in the lounge when he discussed matters with Jim Allen? He tried to remember the point at which she'd entered and then suddenly dismissed the notion; after all she'd been with President Whiting for decades and he was sure they had not discussed the agent's location in public.

'Then again', he thought, considering all the candidates, 'whoever it is they have been working alongside the President for years.'

The image of Catherine Dennison kept playing on his mind.

'Dammit!' he thought and banged his tumbler on his desk spilling some of the contents in his exasperation: 'I've got to satisfy myself.'

He picked up the phone and rang the internal number. The surprised male voice at the other end confirmed he would sit tight, and await his arrival. Logging out of his computer, he left his jacket over the chair, and headed towards the lift.

The interior of the Pentagon was like a maze although its innovative design in the 1940's made it still one of the most efficient office buildings in the world. Corridors ran through all the levels with doors requiring finger print authorization before access could be obtained. The lift took him down three levels into the basement where the documentary records and files, compiled over decades, were stored in secure compartments.

The CIA had taken the decision to keep the hand written files even though the information had been stored on computer.

The Paradigm Shift

Mike Conway decided to follow his hunch and personally review the information filed in archives that would have been processed all those years ago.

At this time of the evening the employees who worked underground in the Pentagon had gone home. It was unprecedented that the Director of the CIA himself would be carrying out his own search in the archives. The surprise was registered on the attendant's face when he saw Mike Conway enter through the final fire proof, security door.

The attendant had been with the CIA for over twenty years and it was the first time he'd met with the Director in person. He was still startled from the earlier call arranging his visit to the basement.

"Have you identified the sections I requested?" Conway asked sharply.

"I have…I'll take you right to them," he replied and scurried towards a large metal gate which marked the entrance to the enormous underground warehouse. The storage compartments were housed in shelf racking that stretched from the floor to the ceiling.

The attendant's cabin door was open, and Director Conway could see that the room was like a library with pull out draws providing the indexing system. He could see some of the draws open where the attendant had been working, and remembered their decision not to employ computers in the warehouse to guard against the threat of hackers.

On the ledge of the cabin was a signing in book and he quickly flicked through the pages of who'd been present in the past few months. His fingers stopped when he reached an entry made two weeks earlier. *'Christ that's strange!'* he thought, *'what on earth was Jim Allen doing down here?'* Puzzled, Conway turned the register around back into its place and went over to join the attendant who was rattling his keys while trying to open the lock.

After the gate was opened, he followed the warehouse attendant to all the locations in the basement which had been identified as housing the records he wanted to see. Once he was satisfied that he'd been given the necessary information to carry out his search, he dismissed him.

Mike Conway sat in the warehouse going through the archived files on the President, the Vice President, the National Security Advisor and, reluctantly, the Chief of Staff, Catherine Dennison.

The files were thick with accumulated information over the years and contained early pictures, transcripts of telephone calls and personal information that would have shocked anybody under investigation.

Oblivious to time, he waded through the piles of documents for over three hours. Sitting on the cold floor, tired from reading, he rubbed his eyes as he reached for a thick, brown folder close to the bottom of the pile in front of him.

Opening the file an old black and white picture fell out. Lifting it off the floor he went rigid as he saw the faces posing for the camera. His tired senses alerted; he started leafing his way quickly through the folder in front of him. *'Jesus Christ no! this can't be true'* he thought, as page after page the story began to emerge.

After awhile, he sat back struggling to take in what he'd read, he still found it difficult to believe.

Sighing deeply he called to the attendant who responded immediately despite the late hour and the length of time he had been working.

The Paradigm Shift

"Return these files to their original location, this one is coming with me," he said, patting the folder in front of him.

"No one must know I've been here tonight, do you understand?" he commanded staring at the beleaguered attendant.

He nodded, it was not his place to question the authority of the Head of the CIA.

Tuesday, 19th October 2008
Outskirts of Agra, Andra Pradesh

The bus they had caught from the coach station in Delhi had taken them to Agra. The journey had been as unpleasant as it had been difficult. They both tried to blend in with the mass of Hindi peasants surrounding them without giving too much attention to Luke's injury.

The old Tata coach travelling south, occasionally stopped at the roadside to increase the discomfort by taking on board more passengers into their already cramped confines. Before departing from Delhi, the driver had stood beside the coach slinging the worldly possessions of his fare-payers on to the roof. By the second stop, the roof was the only space for new passengers, and Kirin watched them embarking through the window. They climbed up a ladder at the back before scrambling across the metal ceiling above her.

Fortunately for Luke and Kirin they managed to get a seat together half-way down the carriage but the scant padding left in the seats still couldn't protect them from the constant shuddering. The suspension of the bus had broken years earlier and they felt every bump and jarring pothole on the four-hour journey.

The road south was a straight one and not so long ago, it would have been used by many of the tourists seeking to explore India's treasures. Agra was home to such a treasure, the Taj Mahal, a beautiful ornate temple built with inlaid marble. In bygone times, the masterpiece was commissioned as a shrine to the loving memory of a beautiful woman who had tragically died too young. Her distraught husband lived out the remainder of his days in the Taj Mahal's gardens gazing at his creation, honouring the love of his dead wife.

The Paradigm Shift

Luke had chosen the destination deliberately because of the anonymity it could offer. Even though Agra no longer attracted the tours and streams of descending foreign tourists, it was still frequented by many Indian travellers. They came from all corners of the sub-continent to marvel at the monument's beauty, and feel the romance and dedication that went into building one of the wonders of the world.

Kirin shared his views, India's village communities were typically close-knit, kindred societies that watched out for newcomers but Agra was a transient town. Their presence as 'out of town' strangers would not seem out of the ordinary in a place used to the regular flow of sightseers on their pilgrimage to see the Taj Mahal.

Stepping off the bus, they made their way through the centre of town. They noticed the divide that separated the local inhabitants from their visitors. On one side, there were the relatively clean streets and the large western style hotels which had been built to cater for the booming tourist trade. On the other side, passing through the divide, they emerged from the modern buildings and commercial developments into a diseased, poverty-ridden slum.

No tourists would ever venture through these parts, the filth and dirt that lined the semi-dark alleys was enough to deter most from entering these foreboding parts. If more persuasion was needed, the menacing looks and unease caused by the slum dwellers gave rise to instant thoughts of self-protection.

From Luke's point of view the shantytown suited their purposes well and walking along together, they continued their search for somewhere to stay.

Eventually, they came across a doorway in one the seedy alleys with a half-broken neon sign above it advertising rooms.

Ignoring the stares cast in her direction from a huddle of Hindu men drinking tea at a table opposite, Kirin went in and negotiated a room rate.

Although the cost was negligible she spent a few minutes haggling for the sake of authenticity, before they were shown upstairs. As in Delhi, the room was barely adequate with basic amenities, but with the knowledge that Nawani's Secret Service was out there trying to find them, living standards were unimportant.

As they sat drinking hot tea out of disposable plastic mugs, Luke decided now was as good a time as any to discuss their future strategy.

"My arm's feeling much better, just a little stiff, but by tomorrow it should be ok," he announced, rubbing the side of his forearm.

"Good," she looked up, "and then we return to Delhi?" she watched Luke nod his head. "I suppose taking the first boat out of here to Hawaii is out of the question?" she laughed.

He laughed with her. Her spontaneous sense of humour had kept both of them sane through some of the darker moments.

"We've got some shopping to do first," he said still grinning at her.

Luke then proceeded to take Kirin through his elaborate scheme for entering the Government Offices in Delhi. After giving detailed descriptions of some of the purchases she would have to make, and then explaining how they fitted into his plan, he reached the part where he described his own dramatic entry into Banerjee's safe house. She listened aghast.

"Have you done this before?" she looked up at him incredulously.

"Once or twice," he replied smiling, "but I must admit the circumstances were a bit different on those occasions!"

She let the subject pass; he clearly didn't share the same concern for his life that she felt.

"And what about me?" she sounded slightly offended that his plan had not taken her into account yet.

Her expression soon changed as he went into graphic detail of the role she would have to play. Contrary to her original thoughts, her self-esteem and importance grew as he made it abundantly clear she wasn't a passenger on this project. Piece by piece he outlined his strategy, breaking down the constituent parts into time-sensitive actions, and key responsibilities.

When he'd finished explaining, he asked her to repeat everything back to him and then criticize the plan for any weaknesses that may have escaped him. They both acknowledged that the randomness of certain variables, like the movement of guards they may encounter, would be out of their control. Luck, as always, played a major part in the success of such operations.

As they continued discussing the finer points, Luke made a list of the items they needed to purchase. When he finished, he handed it over to Kirin and they discussed all the possible alternatives that could be acquired if the exact article couldn't be found.

She looked at her watch, it was getting late, and they were both exhausted by the lack of sleep over the past few days. Kirin changed the dressing on his arm before they made themselves as comfortable as possible and fell asleep.

The following morning, they woke early and after washing, Kirin set off to purchase the items on the list. Before she left, Luke pointed out that if she could get the top three items first, and bring them back, he could get to work in the room, while she went out to locate the rest of the list.

After two hours, she returned carrying a folded, rectangular piece of cloth, some rope and various instruments as he'd requested. Luke studied her purchases approvingly, and congratulated her on being able to find them, he knew it couldn't have been easy. Pleased with her own ingenuity, and bolstered by his comments, she returned to the market to find the rest of the list.

Later that afternoon, Kirin cut up some fruit she had bought on her last shopping expedition, and handed a piece to Luke. Oblivious to her outstretched hand, he stood up to admire his own handiwork. During her outings, Luke had been working hard with the items she'd acquired and now was the moment of truth. He spread the material with its attachments across the bed and checked the various measurements for accuracy.

Kirin gazed at his creation.

"I can't believe your going to do this!" she said shaking her head.

Ignoring her comment, still deep in thought, he wandered over to his rucksack sitting in the corner. He pulled out the small pocket size computer that was their communication lifeline. Throughout their ordeal, he'd managed to save it from being left behind.

"I think we're ready, don't you?" he announced.

He then dialled in and connected to the internet, sending an encrypted message to his friend and mentor, Commander Tremett. Luke and Kirin had discussed the communication position at length after the leak that lead to their narrow escape in the Delhi slum. In the end, Kirin reluctantly agreed that the source of the leak must have come from the American side. With her approval he began sending the message.

The Paradigm Shift

Addressed to Tremett's alias, he typed out the succinct phrases which would convey their plan to return to Delhi and complete their mission the following day. In the end, he left it up to the discretion of his MI6 friend as to how, and who, he should inform on the American side.

Tuesday, 19th October 2008
USS Missouri, Gulf of Arabia

Admiral Troy Downey looked up; the symbolic, coloured markers on the map hanging above him highlighted the success of their mission. Without exception, all the oil fields, refineries and 'platforms-at-sea' were now under the control of the Alliance.

"You've done a great job…one that the American people will want to thank you for," he said, praising the individual efforts of Conrad Dexter.

It had been a difficult night and his eyes were sore from lack of sleep but the Admiral's commendation made him realize the results they had achieved. During the operation, he had become so engrossed in the individual problems encountered by the teams around the Gulf that he'd not really had time to sit back and contemplate the whole picture.

"It's been a team effort," he replied, feeling proud of the expert volunteers and the way they'd gone about their job.

"How soon do you think they can get things working again?" the Admiral asked.

He was due to call Washington shortly and apart from passing on the news of the operation's success, it would be an added bonus if he could discuss the resumption of oil production.

"Too early to say for sure at the moment, Admiral, but the initial indications are very good." He was fairly confident of the position from the technical feedback received from his teams, but he didn't want to cause undue optimism until the facts were established.

"I will be in a position to give you confirmation in three to four hours," he added.

The Admiral nodded, _'at least I can give a preliminary indication on timing back to Washington,'_ he thought, and turned to leave the room. Conrad Dexter remained deep in thought, he was tired and exhausted but there was still a lot to consider.

Apart from the task of manning the oil facilities around the Gulf, he also had two teams under his supervision in separate operation rooms down the ship's corridor. Their task was to concentrate solely on the logistical problem of allocating the super tankers to their correct loading sites. The second team also had to deal with the flow of crude oil through the offshore pipelines which ran along the seabed to the refineries.

In this modern age, loading unrefined oil directly into the storage bays of the supertankers was simplicity itself. The larger offshore fields had flexible, steel cord pipes that ran into the seabed oil reservoir at one end, while at the nozzle end, they were hooked up to buoys floating on the surface. The tanker would then screw the super-sized hose to the tap in the hold, and with the pumping equipment activated, would suck the oil directly on board.

The two teams working for Conrad Dexter were in constant touch with Washington for instructions on oil priorities. During the course of the Summit at Camp David, the oil sector advisors to the delegations had quickly sensed that the allocation of resources from the Gulf was going to be a major problem.

Each participating member put their case for why they should be supplied with the first outgoing shipments of oil. After taking into account they're own requirements they then had to work through the official pleas for help received from numerous countries not invited to attend the Summit. The delegations from Britain and France had pledged their support to assisting other members of the European Union. They bartered on their behalf as best they could, whilst their EU neighbours watched from the fringe, eager to learn their future oil entitlement.

In the end, allocation had been decided in the fairest manner possible. The emphasis was put on getting as many shipments out in the shortest possible time, supplying the neediest first. This solution certainly met with the approval of the Japanese Prime Minister. He was delighted with the outcome and made his feelings known. Before leaving the Summit, he personally expressed his gratitude to President Whiting for upholding his promise, 'to do what he could for Japan.'

Capturing the oil fields and re-commencing production was vital and important, but the mission didn't end there. Everyone involved in the operation, from the senior officers to the civilian teams on the ground, knew that taking control of the oil fields was one thing but protecting them from subsequent attack was another.

Admiral Stone was a 'straight talker', well respected by his officer's and the crew. With carefully edited news reports, he kept the Fifth Fleet abreast of any new developments. Previous experience had taught him the importance of maintaining morale by circulating up to date information.

The excitement caused by the unveiling of the pact between China and Indian had descended on every communication outlet for the world's media. The papers and the television devoted all their space and airtime to the incredible revelation that rocked the world. Headlines in the papers, and questions on the lips of expert commentators, were full of histrionic speculation about where this unholy alliance would lead. The atmosphere aboard the US Missouri was somewhat different. The crew of the Fifth

The Paradigm Shift

Fleet were highly trained professionals and they went about their drill in a calm and orderly fashion.

For his part, Admiral John Stone sat eating his supper from the bowls in front of him. He enjoyed the surroundings of the officer's mess and found it a good place to relax. He also wanted to be conspicuous amongst his fellow officers, the ship was cruising at one rating below full alert, and his composed presence would inspire confidence.

He sat alone at the end of the officer's dining table finishing his meal tray as Admiral Downey and Air Marshal Reiger walked over to join him. They had no problem locating Admiral Stone, at such states of readiness, it was standard policy to be kept informed of senior officers' movements and whereabouts.

"The Chinese carrier is about three hundred miles away, on a heading for the island of Abu Moosa," Stone informed them as they sat down next to him.

The Arabian Sea, separating the landmass of the Gulf States, was a closed cul-de-sac. It could only be navigated through the Straits of Hormuz, and the strategic island of Abu Moosa was situated right in the middle of this narrow gateway. The Straits themselves were forty miles wide at the narrowest point dividing the southern tip of Iran, and Mussandam, the northern most territory of Oman.

Protection by the Alliance Fleet didn't just stop at the refineries and oil fields. The super tankers themselves were easy targets for the enemy's submarines or air force. Each loaded tanker departing the Gulf would require its own naval and airborne escort.

"That carrier is going to sit at the exit and block the traffic out," said Reiger.

"I tend to agree," Stone paused as he patted his lips with his napkin.

"I think it's time we issued instructions to the Chinese Commander not to approach any further don't you Admiral Troy?"

He looked up for confirmation from his superiors. He was in charge of the Fifth Fleet and the decision was his, but out of respect he solicited their approval.

"Yes, get it out right away, that's my view," said Troy immediately, and Reiger added his support with a nod of the head.

Admiral Stone called over one of the ship's communication officers, and briefed them on the short, resolute message to be transmitted to the Chinese ship of war.

It stated unequivocally that any progression in to the Straits of Hormuz, beyond a specified latitude, would result in its intentions being deemed hostile. If the carrier persisted on its course, they would reserve their rights to take whatever steps were necessary to prevent its continued advance.

"In case its commander decides to ignore our directive, I've instructed two cruisers to set a course to meet the carrier head on," Stone informed them.

"Good," Air Marshal Reiger agreed before inquiring about their official state of readiness.

It was essential that all three of them were kept abreast of their status. Although none of them anticipated instructions for their use, the Fifth Fleet had its own nuclear capability in the Gulf if it was required.

They both turned to Admiral Downey for guidance.

"It's as before gentlemen...I spoke to Washington five minutes ago, we're on nuclear stand down and we're to retaliate only when fired upon, not otherwise."

Tuesday, 19th October 2008
The White House, Washington

Mike Conway drove himself towards the White House in his black, four-wheel drive Range Rover. He had called the President earlier and left him under no illusion that he needed to see him right away. He had information in his possession which was of vital importance to the Country's national security, and it could not wait, even if it highlighted the failings of himself and the CIA to a degree. The President, curious to the nature of the sudden meeting, confirmed his availability without wasting too many words.

As he drove down the freeway, he pressed the keyboard buttons on the dashboard computer which controlled his in-car telephone system. The crystal display screen showed the computer dialling a memorized number that would connect him to the British Secret Service in London.

Connection was established, and through the Range Rover's loud speakers, he heard the voice of Sir Thomas Boswell's secretary inquire who was calling.

"It's Mike Conway here, can you put me through to Sir Thomas," he shouted towards the microphone. The noise from the outside traffic was only partially offset by the reinforced glass on the customized vehicle.

"Go ahead Sir, I'm putting you through," she replied promptly.

"Sir Thomas?"

"Hello Mike, to what do I owe this privilege?" he greeted his US counterpart with usual, abrasive style of English politeness.

"I'll keep it brief....I'm on the way to see the President now."

"Ok," he responded simply, recognizing Conway's appeal for brevity.

"I believe I've uncovered the source of the leak Sir Thomas, it's at our end."

"I see," Sir Thomas's voice was deadpan as he considered the startling announcement.

Although fascinated by the news, Sir Thomas was not about to embarrass Director Conway by being so crass as to ask the identity of the traitor. However, given the circle of suspects who had access to the information, it was clear that the culprit worked at the very top of the US administration. *'The intelligence he or she could access was frightening,'* he thought to himself.

"In which case I believe I have some news for you." Sir Thomas resumed after a brief pause.

In an instant, Sir Thomas had weighed up the position. As far as he was concerned the call from Mike Conway added confirmation that he could be trusted. They had worked together on several occasions, and although he didn't take the past for granted, he felt he knew him well enough.

Just before his call came through, he had been locked in debate with Commander Tremett on whether or not they should pass on the message they had received from India. The communication from Luke Weaver had been coded for their attention only, and they questioned the logic of informing the CIA until they knew the source of the leak.

However, they both recognized the importance of this intelligence. This news would have a serious impact on the political and military decisions currently being considered by the US administration. One alternative they had seriously considered, was to pass the information directly from the British PM to the President in person. The call from Director Conway changed matters, Sir Thomas felt sufficiently confident to trust him with the latest developments from India.

"Mike, we have had a communiqué from India, our agents are preparing to strike in two days time."

It was Director Conway's turn to act surprised. He mentally acknowledged the thought process that Sir Thomas must have undertook before revealing the latest information.

"Thank you Sir Thomas, I appreciate your trust."

As Mike Conway turned into the driveway towards security at the back of the White House, he promised to call Sir Thomas back later that day.

He realized the revelation of the informant's identity would cause anguish to the President as he considered his options for breaking the news. '*How would the President react?*' he thought, after all they'd known each other for years. Under his arm he carried the folder he had discovered in the basement of the CIA building together with supporting evidence he had established the previous night.

'*At least the news from Sir Thomas offered a glimmer of hope,*' he thought as he passed the security checks and made his way up the stairs to the President's office.

Passing the final checkpoint, he focused his attention on the large double doors to the Oval Office as he made his way briskly down the corridor. The President had told him 'just to come straight in' when he got there. As he marched down the final few yards passed the waiting room, he failed to see Catherine Dennison step out. One second she was smiling, about to say hello, the next, they had collided as she moved unwittingly into his unerring path. He was momentarily startled. The impact knocked his folder from under his arm and its contents tumbled to the floor.

"Oh Mike, I'm so sorry," she said slightly shaken and putting her hand across her mouth. She looked down at the papers spread around the carpet.

His face reddened angrily, as he bent down, scrambling to put the papers back in the folder.

"I'm really sorry," she repeated apologetically.

"I didn't realize you were moving so fast," she added, and kneeled down to help him pick up the documents.

"I'd like to see you again," she said softly lifting her face to look at him while he was crouching on bended-knees. Ignoring her, he pushed the last papers into the wallet. He had more important matters on his mind and she was in the way. The smell of her expensive perfume returned but it was his turn to act distant.

"We'll have to see," he responded coldly without emotion.

For a moment he returned her stare, before standing up and walking the last few paces to the President's office. *'Damn! How unlucky can you get?'* he thought as he turned the handle to the door. *'Had she seen any papers?'* He convinced himself there hadn't been time to take into account the contents of the folder.

Visibly upset, she stood up, looking after him as he entered the office.

The President was engrossed in a phone call. Smiling, he waved Mike Conway towards one of the chairs in front of his desk with his free hand.

"Well Mike, what is it that's so urgent?" he said as he finally replaced the receiver.

The President's friendly demeanour changed as he registered the seriousness of Director Conway's expression.

The Paradigm Shift

He started by showing the President the black and white photo that had fallen on the floor in the archives. Although the photo had become creased with age, the President could make out the faces in the Group starting with Chairman Li, the predecessor to Prime Minister Ziang. He had ruled China with an iron fist for over thirty years.

He looked up in surprise as he recognized the other faces.

"I need your undivided attention for the next half an hour Sir," Conway requested.

He could see the President was shaken as the realization dawned of what he was about to tell him. He hit the intercom calling his secretary and informed her that he was not to be disturbed under any circumstances.

Director Conway placed the folder on President Whiting's desk and took him through the story piece by piece. Every now and then he would produce documents or refer to telephone transcripts that corroborated his findings. The facts as presented were conclusive.

The President sat in silence listening intently the whole way through. He took into account every nuance as Director Conway brought him up to the present day.

"It just doesn't seem possible," he starred down blankly. He wasn't really focusing on the array of photographic evidence confronting him.

Mike Conway remained quiet; he knew how close they were.

The President stood up and walked towards the window looking out over the White House lawns. He put his palms up to his face and rubbed his tired eyes.

"What now?" he said. He felt drained and despondent at the disclosure put before him.

"We are the only people who know the truth, Sir."

The President turned around to face him, a puzzled expression on his face.

"What are you suggesting?"

"If we go public on this Sir, with all due respect, you know it will jeopardize the Alliance and probably halt our program in the Middle East…is that in the best interest of the United States?"

Conway had to get the President to see the whole picture if America's best interests were to be served.

"Agreed," he paused. "The American people will want answers without delay, there is every chance that I'd have to go; isn't that right Mike?"

Director Conway knew that President Whiting was an honourable man and came prepared for this reaction. For the next twenty minutes he outlined the main reasons why the President should not consider stepping down.

At one point he touched on the legal and constitutional angle of his position. It quickly became apparent that he had done his homework. The argument was compelling, given the current status of the worlds oil crisis and the threat of India and China's pact, what choice did they have? Only a strong leader could uphold the best interests of the Country.

Any step down by the President would throw the administration into chaos.

"Now is not the time for divisive in-fighting," concluded Conway. Any step down by the President would throw the administration into chaos.

He could sense he was winning the President over and they agreed to keep the disclosure of the informant to themselves.

The President accepted Director Conway's logic on the subject. No further damage could be done now they knew who it was and anyway, behind the scenes there would be a classified surveillance team reporting only to the Director.

"You've done a good job," he said, patting Conway on the shoulder. He still had an over-riding feeling of sadness but the efforts put in by the Director of the CIA were clear to see.

"I'd like to cover one last point?" he asked the President, "it's to do with the Agent's progress in India."

He saw some of the colour return to the President Whiting's face as he briefed him on the progress being made in their mission to assassinate Banerjee.

"Two days...let's hope they can do it!" he said optimistically.

The voice of his apologetic secretary burst into the room through the intercom. They had lost track of time and she could not leave the President alone any longer.

"I'm very sorry to disturb you Mr. President, it's Jim Allen and he wants to talk to you about Project Sabre...he says it can't wait."

"That's ok, we're through here now," said the President flicking the button.

"Thanks Mike, I appreciate it can't have been easy," he said nodding gratefully at Mike Conway.

Mike Conway picked up the documents that were spread on his desk.

"Put him through," the President commanded to his secretary, and then he stood up and walked around to the front of his desk. He stretched out his hand towards Director Conway.

Holding each other's gaze, they shook hands firmly. He left as the President picked up the receiver to take Jim Allen's incoming call. He was pleased with the way the meeting had gone.

Wednesday, 20th October 2008
Government Offices, Delhi

Prime Minister Banerjee stood with his hands behind his back looking out over the picturesque gardens below him. The weather was hot and hazy meaning another downpour was on its way. At this time of the year, the autumnal months saw the onset of monsoons and the sporadic thunderstorms which erupted to clear the air. Banerjee enjoyed the tropical climate and took the opportunity for early morning walks around the grounds and relaxing on his office balcony whenever he could.

Balan sat in one of the ornate wooden chairs and continued his dialogue on the meeting he'd held with General Vu. Occasionally, Banerjee would interrupt to predict the reaction, or to describe the next event that had occurred before Balan had a chance to arrive at the conclusion. His speed of thought and intuitiveness never ceased to amaze Balan, it sometimes seemed as if Banerjee had Delphic powers, like the great Oracle of Ancient Greek mythology.

"And the phone call with Ziang?" Banerjee interrupted.

Balan stared up at him, *'How had Banerjee known that?'*

It was typical of his foresight but he was still not accustomed to its alarming regularity. In conversation, he had made no reference to any call, or indeed even hinted that one was likely to happen but Banerjee had jumped straight to the conclusion of his meeting with General Vu.

Bringing his earlier monologue and train of thought to an abrupt halt, he moved on to the part where General Vu had sought the instructions of his leader Prime Minister Ziang.

"Excellent, excellent," he muttered to himself quietly as he listened to Balan summarizing the final platitudes and assurances given at their meeting in the cold, mountainous wilderness of the north.

"They will attack Taiwan you know?" he said with disdain as if it was obvious.

Balan's faith in Banerjee's predictions was such that he registered the outbreak of hostilities in the East as a fact.

With Banerjee continuing to enjoy the fresh air, Balan began to update him with the latest military brief.

They had taken far more casualties than expected in their invasion of Pakistan. Pockets of resistance had somehow managed to organize themselves, and they were fighting stubbornly against the advancing Indian formations. Amidst the background devastation and chaos caused by the nuclear attack, Balan found it amazing to see how a people's resolve could not be broken during such a crisis.

The radiation residue also accounted for larger numbers of casualties than those originally estimated, but the information fed to the Indian people told a different story. The local television and the news headlines exulted in the successes of their loyal army fighting in the frontline. No casualties were reported and film clips of the troops advancing were carefully stage-managed.

Banerjee showed no signs of concern over the faltering attack. After all it was just a subterfuge, an elaborate sideshow, devised so that they could steal the nuclear missile launchers into position. There would be plenty of time in the future to make the Pakistani rebel forces pay for their futile aggression.

"Both launchers are securely in place, we are satisfied that the convoy has reached its destination without being traced." Balan had reached the point that justified the deaths of thousands of innocent Indian conscripts.

Banerjee rubbed his eyes, pinching the bridge of his nose as he thoughtfully considered Balan's remark. He accepted his conclusions. If the Alliance had any notion of the cargo being transported across the length of Pakistan they would have taken action by now. This was proof enough that his plan was still enshrined in secrecy.

"What are your thoughts on their defence program? Do we have much intelligence in this field?" Banerjee asked.

He listened as his deputy summarized their latest reports on the subject of America's defence program. *'You're not telling me anything I couldn't read in Time magazine,'* he thought.

It didn't take him long to perceive that this was one area in which they had insufficient information. The lack of knowledge made him feel very uncomfortable and he considered ways of addressing the acute shortage of facts.

"I want you to speak to General Vu and ask him to get all the information from his source in the US administration as soon as possible," he ordered.

Balan nodded, sensing that there was something troubling him. This reaction puzzled him slightly because Banerjee was not in the habit of making such outbursts. Why should the developments of the US Space Defence Program worry them? After all their activities were written off as Hollywood dreams by most of the western world.

Banerjee was annoyed with himself for not thinking about this earlier. He should have taken this avenue to recover information on the subject, days, if not weeks ago. Even if the mole in the US administration fed back the latest intelligence now, there was probably very little he could do about it. It was too late to change their plans now.

Balan put his leaders uncharacteristic behaviour to one side and asked him if he would like to view a documentary they had compiled on the global effects of the oil crisis. This met with his approval, and they accompanied each other out of the bright sunshine of the balcony towards the presentation suite down the corridor from his office. Reaching a small flight of stairs, they stepped down through two swing doors into a small theatre capable of seating around twenty at any given time.

As Banerjee took his seat in the centre, Balan remained standing in the aisle next to the door. As the lights dimmed, the production engineer waited patiently for the instruction to begin. Balan swivelled round, and with a wave of his arm, motioned him to start the screening.

The film was an edited collection of all the newsreels taken around the world. The global suffering had reached epidemic proportions. The program started in America, showing clips of the enormous queues of irate lorry drivers mixed with regular consumers waiting for petrol outside the gas stations. The Indian film editor had overwritten each clip with the name of the location, and Banerjee managed a wry smile as he watched the fleeting scenes of chaos spreading across the United States.

The film rolled on to take account of the rest of the world. After the pictures of the petrol stations came the airports. It soon became apparent that the countries deadlocked in gas station queues were the lucky ones. The eerie sight of Tokyo airport, as well as others, lying dormant was shocking. It was a strange sight seeing a centre normally so vibrant with activity twenty-fours a day, standing empty like a ghost town. The planes of their national carrier, Japanese Airlines, sat in darkness lining the length of the runway.

The Paradigm Shift

All around the world the pictures were the same, empty roads, idle factories, queues and then the ugly scenes. The short film concluded with footage crystallizing the fate that was in store for all the civilized societies in the world. The screen in front of him jumped from shots of peaceful demonstrations and protest marches to outbreaks of violence and looting. Very quickly, the Governments lost control of law and order, and the projected pandemic and political 'in-fighting' which ensued, caused country after country, to grind to a halt.

'*We're nearly there,*' thought Banerjee, as the lights in the mini theatre were turned up, marking the end of the production.

Getting up, he congratulated the team at the back of the room for putting together the review. In deference to their leader, they stood huddled together with lowered heads as Banerjee passed them on the way back to his office.

Accompanied by Balan, he switched the topic of conversation to the progress being made by the Alliance to take control of the oil fields in the Gulf. They had anticipated the response of America and their Allies over the past two days but now it was time for the next public overture behind their menacing strategy.

"I think it's time that we distributed the message, what do you say Balan?" he said smiling to himself as he led the way down the corridor.

"It's time…I have the studio set up ready for your arrival," he said, casting a glance ahead of him for his leader's approval.

"Do it – and speak to your friend in China as well," Banerjee called pointedly over his shoulder as he disappeared into his office.

"I'll carry out the final checks," Balan replied, and immediately strode off in the opposite direction to inspect the final preparations in the studio.

Wednesday, 20th October 2008
The Pentagon, Washington

Hearing the alarm, Director Conway rushed to his observation post above the Operations centre. He stood there looking at the flashing lights on the screen as the intermittent wails from the siren continued in the background. Watching proceedings through his elongated office window, the rows of computer consoles below him were a hive of activity as the personnel rushed to their stations. Intelligence officers already manning their consoles were shouting into their microphones trying to be heard over the reverberating noise surrounding them. Following instructions, they were anxious to obtain independent confirmation of the events unfolding on the screen ahead of them.

Colonel Schwartz looked up and saw Director Conway standing at his office window watching the furore below him. Exchanging knowing glances, Director Conway disappeared from view and seconds later he'd descended the stairs to join his deputy, General Magnus Graham and General Karpurov.

"The Chinese have launched two missiles at Taipei," Schwartz informed the approaching Director.

The screen had been magnified to show the coastline of China, the Island of Taiwan and the Straits that separated them. Lit up across the geographical backdrop were two concave lines marking the flight path of the Chinese missiles.

"They are testing us," Karpurov said calmly with his thick Russian accent.

Director Conway listened intently as Schwartz briefed him on the information they had managed to obtain so far. Despite the early danger signs, they agreed with Karpurov's suggestion, the situation could be a lot worse than it actually was. The missiles launched by the Chinese had relatively small explosive capacity compared with some of the weaponry in their arsenal.

"If they wanted to, they could launch fifty missiles and do the job properly, I think they are looking to get us involved," Karpurov paused, looking up at the screen again.

The map also highlighted the position of the Alliance warships and submarines, while inset around the edge were magnified satellite images of other key Chinese military installations being observed for threatening behaviour.

"What's that in the corner?" Colonel Schwartz shouted, pointing at one of the inset images.

He barked out a series of orders to one of his intelligence officers. The operator moved his hands quickly across his controls sending instructions to the spy satellite orbiting China.

As the picture intensified on the screen, Director Conway could make out the shape of a crescent gradually diminishing in size.

The instant the focus was fine-tuned the image was unmistakable.

'*Sonofabitch,*' mouthed Schwartz as the picture cleared to show the circular door of an underground nuclear silo opening before them.

"Get the President immediately," Conway shouted above the noise.

In the background, he heard General Graham relaying the orders: "Move to DEFCON One immediately."

'*We've actually reached the final state of alert before we start launching our own weapons,*' thought Conway. He imagined the anxiety in the faces of those specially trained officers whose job it was to turn the launch key.

The sight of the satellite camera honing in on more silos going through the same chilling motion was frightening. The communication officer returned and handed a headset to Director Conway which he fitted over his ear before pulling the mike down across his mouth.

The President and Jim Allen were already on the line as Director Conway began explaining what he was looking at and why General Graham had taken the US defence system to a state of full alert.

"Views, Mike? How is this going to play out?"

"We need to hold tight Sir, our view is that they're testing our reaction; they will not launch, they want our attention away from the central issue," Conway responded rapidly while looking at Karpurov, Schwartz and Graham. They all gave approving nods confirming their agreement with his assessment.

"Ok that's what I'm telling the Alliance, keep your eye on the ball down there and make sure you let China know that we have taken our own position to a full state of alert."

'You have to admire the man,' thought Conway. It didn't get any worse than this and yet the President's voice remained calm and in full control. He was in command of the situation and the American people knew it. He felt a wave of self-satisfaction as he remembered his earlier conversations persuading him to stay in office.

"Mike," the President added, "I have been advised that I will be receiving a communication from Banerjee in the next hour or so, I would like you to be here when it arrives."

As the President signed off to speak to his Alliance counterparts, Karpurov pointed at another screen showing the Russian silos engaging a similar state of readiness.

The Paradigm Shift

"Keep the satellites looking for the Indian missile launchers," Conway instructed.

Wednesday, 20th October 2008
The Government Officers, Delhi

Balan had personally supervised the presentation of the studio ready for the Prime Minister's address. The television link had been established to all the world leaders selected by Banerjee for their importance to his plan's success. Apart from the Alliance leaders they also contacted the ruling families in the Middle East since their views would play a big part in how events would unfold.

The broadcast had been scheduled for ten o'clock in the evening Indian time, and advance notification had been given to all the leaders concerned, advising them of the transmission timing and that it would be fed directly to their offices. They had given sufficient advance warning to the Gulf rulers that they had time to congregate together at each other's palaces. The timing was the worst for those in the Far East, with Japan receiving the transmission in the middle of the night, but most Governments were now getting accustomed to working around the clock.

The stage set was kept simple. The studio was located in the east wing of the government building and the set had been dressed up to resemble the formal study surroundings of the Prime Minister. Approximately five minutes before the scheduled start, the production office in the studio established communication links across the world. Television monitors in the offices of Alliance leaders around the world tuned in to see the background stage set specially created for Banerjee's announcement. The screen showed that the camera operator had focused on the empty chair sitting behind the mahogany desk with the Indian tricolour draped behind it. The flag was considered very symbolic. At the time of their Independence in July 1947 when it was incorporated into their constitution, the coloured segments were specially chosen to represent the four virtuous '*p's* on which they wished to build their future. The top band of saffron or orange signified *patriotism*, the middle band of white stood for *peace* and the bottom band of green meant *prosperity*. The final '*p*' was depicted by a blue wheel or 'chakra' in the centre of the flag represented *progress*. As the cameraman narrowed his focus, the world sat and waited for the Indian Prime Minister to take centre stage and explain his version of 'progress' for the future.

Mike Conway had made it to the White House on time and sat with the President and Jim Allen in the front row of the President's Oval Office. They discussed the latest efforts being made by China to distract their attention and the response of Taiwan to the latest developments. In the second row sat Vance Warner and Margaret Henderson, the Defence Secretary sitting next to the Secretary of State. Beyond them sat Catherine Dennison, Vice President Martins and General Magnus Graham who had travelled to the White House with Director Conway.

The large screen in front of them was focused on the desk and a clock in the top left corner had a counter running showing the minutes and seconds to the live broadcast. The situation was duplicated in the offices of other world leaders as they contemplated what Banerjee had in store for them now. Even Chinese Prime Minister Ziang was awake in Beijing waiting for Banerjee's speech to begin, although he was already briefed on its content. Standing behind Ziang, in a resolute pose, was General Vu. He had already initiated the elaborate communication procedure they had for establishing contact with their Chinese informant. Vu smiled to himself as he imagined the scenario, their insider would be sitting alongside the President of the United States watching Banerjee's spectacle.

In the studio itself, the technicians waited anxiously for their leader to appear. The room had inadequate air-conditioning and was hot and stuffy from the bright lights being beamed towards the desk. At the back of the studio, behind the pointing cameras, was the production office. Balan took out a handkerchief and rubbed it across his forehead. He was feeling the tension as he watched the sound engineers going about their last minute checks.

In Riyadh, King Mohammed sat watching the screen with several close members of his family. He had been joined by the Amir of Kuwait who had flown in at short notice on the special invitation of the King.

Around the world, aides watching the broadcast pointed out that the digital clock had reached the appointed time of transmission. The assembled audiences finished what they were doing, and in an air of apprehension, concentrated on the screen in front of them.

In the studio, the door was held open and in walked Khrishna Banerjee looking totally composed. Balan approached and informed him that everything was in place; the broadcast could begin whenever he was ready. Banerjee nodded his approval and walked into the spotlight to take his seat behind the desk.

His calmness was exaggerated by the length of time it took him to arrange himself comfortably. Only when he was satisfied did he focus on the camera pointing directly towards him. When he did look up, Mike Conway, like all the others in the room, immediately noticed how menacing his apparition really was. His masked smile could not veil the evil that radiated from his expression. The black shadows below his eyes made his demonic stare more pronounced.

Whilst Banerjee had been settling himself, Balan had walked into the sound proofed, production office at the back of the studio. His calmness was restored as the technicians quickly handed him confirmation that every transmission link was functioning normally.

"Fellow leaders," Banerjee began, "I appreciate your making yourselves available at such short notice to hear what I have to say."

No one missed the insincerity in his voice; what choice did they have but to listen?

"My people are still being imprisoned and treated like worthless slaves throughout the Middle East," he paused, "you know that I have made pleas for the intervention of help from your countries in the past."

His voice rose and fell in a crescendo.

'Ok, he's going down that track,' thought Conway.

"He must be looking to bring the Arab rulers back into the situation somehow," Conway whispered into the President's ear.

"Instead you, the Alliance…have come to their aid…with your battleships in the Gulf you are protecting the oppressors of our people."

He paused emphasizing each word as he sat leaning with his arms on the desk while his hands were pressed firmly together in front of him.

"In the name of God, why do you protect these dictators that persecute our people?" he spread open his palms in a gesture designed to add surprise to his compassionate plea.

President Whiting, his anger rising, watched, incredulous at his effrontery. *'There was no other possible answer',* he thought. *'This*

*is a mad, egotistical maniac capable of outrageous acts of human suffering.
How could he sit there talking about his own people's imprisonment when he
had been responsible for the horrendous deaths of millions of Pakistanis?
This man, invoking the name of God, has sacrificed his own soldiers in his
desire to bring global chaos through the oil shortage.'*

Jim Allen leaned over to the President. He had noticed the
growing signs of irritation etched on his face.

"This is for the benefit of his own people Sir," Allen commented.

"If you are not prepared to assist us….if you seek to uphold the regimes oppressing my people then what choice do we
have?" He paused, and feigned a look of desperation towards
the camera.

"…No choice! – No choice but to take action of our own."

Balan watched from the side admiring his leaders cameo
performance as he reached the punch line.

"As I speak to you, we have two nuclear warheads pointing
at the Middle East..…"

'Christ! he's threatening a nuclear attack,' thought Conway.

"If the forces of the Alliance do not leave the
Gulf….within the next twenty-four hours…..and allow us free
access to our people so that we can return them home, then…."

He looked up into the eye of the camera, "…then we will
launch both nuclear warheads at two targets in the Gulf."

The President along with his chief aides stared at the screen
in shocked silence.

"Am I expressing myself?" he said, fixing his gaze on the
faces he knew were watching him behind the camera lens.

The Paradigm Shift

Across the world, the chilling realization of the implication of his words descended on the viewers. The consequences of Banerjee's threat were unimaginable.

"Any remaining presence will be considered a threat, you have exactly twenty-four hours to leave the Gulf."

Suddenly, the picture of Banerjee behind the desk vanished leaving just a row of white numbers counting down from twenty-four hours. The column showing the hundredths of a second was spinning like a wheel.

"Switch it off," the President barked.

"Why haven't we found those damn warheads yet?" The President expressed his annoyance to no one in particular.

Director Conway shifted uncomfortably, he knew the underlying sentiment of the President's displeasure was pointed in his direction.

The intercom sounded and Chief of Staff, Catherine Dennison, jumped up to take the call; it would be the first of a deluge to descend on the White House switchboard.

"We need time to think Catherine," the President said as she passed him.

"Tell them we'll organize a conference call of the Alliance members in five hours from now and then pass them through to Margaret."

The President knew the switchboard would shortly become overloaded with the leaders and advisors of foreign governments eager to express their views, and take those of the White House.

"Margaret, do you mind?" he inquired turning to face his Secretary of State.

She got straight to her feet. Diplomacy and handling the relationships of friendly and unfriendly nations towards the United States was her area of expertise.

"Please make a brief of their concerns, and note any recommendations they may have….we'll meet again later," the President concluded.

"What indication shall I give them of our current stance?" she questioned.

During the pause that followed, she finished pushing some papers into her briefcase whilst the President thought through the issues. During her time in office she had developed a tremendous respect for the hardworking President and she was anxious to help him in anyway she could.

"Nothing at the moment Margaret…just tell them the Fifth Fleet will remain present until we've had a chance to think this one through properly."

He disliked indecision. He often felt that it was better to make a bad judgement than to sit on the fence and not make one at all. Decisive leadership was critical. Its importance could not be overstated, particularly when the rest of the world would probably follow the US lead. However, there was a big difference between being decisive and being rash.

The President turned to Conway, Allen and General Graham as his Secretary of State followed Catherine Dennison out of the door.

"Will Banerjee pull the trigger if it comes to it?"

"Yes, he will," said Director Conway without hesitation. Both the General and Jim Allen nodded their heads in agreement.

"In fact, I suspect they may launch regardless of whether we comply with his demands or not," added Jim Allen.

"We have to find those missiles gentlemen, and we have to find them now…please do whatever is necessary."

The Paradigm Shift

In Delhi, Balan congratulated Khrishna Banerjee on his performance.

Wednesday, 20ᵗʰ October 2008
Outskirts of Delhi

Luke and Kirin travelled back to south Delhi by train late that evening. His arm felt much better, thanks largely to her efforts.

The return journey had been considerably more comfortable than their previous one in the dilapidated, old bus. The carriage of the train was nearly empty due to the time of night they were travelling. *'This was good planning,'* thought Kirin, they needed the extra space with the additional luggage they had picked up in Agra.

On the train, he spent a brief passage of time hidden in the closet that barely passed as a toilet on the old locomotive. The safety catch had been removed a long time ago but he managed to wedge the door shut with the help of a piece of wood. The closet was never cleaned and the base smell, combined with the putrid stench of ammonia, would make even the hardiest feel nauseous.

Inside he pulled out the computer which was attached to the belt under his Hindi clothes, and made the internet connection, looking for messages which may have been left for him. He scrolled down the site and found two messages that any normal person looking at the page would simply pass off as regular email conversation. The ordinary looking statements had key words that only Luke would recognize.

The process of deduction was time consuming. The security was such that the real message was fragmented on different parts of the web and the context could only be fully understood by accessing several different portals. It was time consuming but he followed the trail of key words until he could put the messages together in their entirety.

There was a knock on the toilet door and Luke stopped what he was doing. It sounded like an irate passenger waiting to use the closet but he wasn't prepared to take any chances. He was about to save the data and exit, when he heard Kirin's voice. She was shouting something at the man in Hindi and Luke heard the man's gruff response before it went quiet again. About thirty seconds later, there were two knocks on the door and he heard Kirin whisper it was all clear.

Later on he learned that she had stood up to complain about the man pushing in. He laughed as she mimicked his expression when she told him to get to the back of the queue.

In the closet once the noise subsided, he returned to the palm size computer, and continued downloading the streams of data needed to assist with the deciphering. After thirty minutes of straining his eyes in the poor light he finally retrieved the message from Commander Tremett.

Sitting down in the seat next to Kirin, he looked across and saw her handing him a piece of fruit. They had chosen seats at the back of the compartment where they wouldn't be heard but kept their voices low to be on the safe side. It was pitch black outside the train, and with barely adequate lighting inside, most of the passengers were trying to sleep.

"Well?" she said, prompting him for the details of his search.

"Two messages," he replied.

"The first confirms our suspicions, apparently the leak definitely came from your side and they know who it is now."

"Who is it then?" she asked, concentrating on cutting another piece off the mango in front of her.

"Don't know, the message doesn't give the identity but, I guess it must go right to the very the top!"

"What was the second?"

"It's deadline time, Banerjee has issued an ultimatum that unless the Alliance pulls out of the Gulf by ten fifteen our time tomorrow, he's going to launch two nuclear warheads into the Middle East."

Her face winced with the news as she considered the impact on their plans.

"That means we've got to bring our entry forward by two hours, how's that going to change things?" she asked.

"If there was an element of surprise its gone now, the guards will be primed for action during the next twenty-four hours."

Originally, Luke had planned to make his entry whilst the changeover of the guards took place in the middle of the night. However with the latest news, the timing was no longer possible.

He saw the worried look on Kirin's face.

"Look, as long as it's dark it's not going to change things."

They had grown so accustomed to each other's company in such a short space of time that they could almost sense each other's thoughts. His confidence and bravery in the face of such overwhelming odds amazed her. *'He has never entertained a thought about the possible failure of the mission,'* she thought looking up at him.

For his part, Luke had never come across a woman with so much feminine beauty who was prepared to put her country ahead of her own life. He smiled as he recalled his first thoughts when he had been told he was to work with a female agent. How wrong he had been.

"Just make sure you're where you should be at ten," he said smiling at her, "I don't want to end up walking home."

"I'll be there don't you worry," she said and pinched his arm.

As the train rolled into the station, it was the early hours of the morning and collecting their bags they set off for the hotel. On their previous stay in Delhi, Kirin had taken the telephone numbers of a few of the hotels around the station when they had passed through on the way to the government building.

Before they had set off from Agra she had called making reservations for them as a married couple. She apologized profusely to the receptionist for the inconvenient timing of their arrival but the hotel did not see it as a problem. After all, without the tourist trade most hotels were struggling for business.

The Head of the Indian Secret Service, Ashraf Nawani, also made it difficult for their peaceful existence. During the course of their investigation to find Kirin and Luke, he had frightened the hoteliers into passing on information about all new arrivals. They were all issued with potential descriptions of the Agents. However, Kirin had circumvented the potential details they were to keep an eye open for by sending a fax confirming their stay whilst in Agra. The fact that they were coming from out of town took the spotlight off them.

Kirin was pleased with the new hotel. Initially, Luke had taken some persuasion, but in the end he had agreed that it would make no difference to their safety. For the one night they planned to stay in Delhi they may as well be comfortable. Even so, the accommodation wasn't particularly special but it was a definite upgrade from what they were used to.

Whilst in Agra, Kirin had gone out to buy new clothes for them both. The appearance helped and when they arrived at the hotel, they had little difficulty convincing the girl behind the counter that they were a respectable married couple.

One of Nawani's instructions given to all the hotels in Delhi by his notorious enforcement officers was to question new male arrivals in Hindi. Luke had anticipated this problem.

Listening to conversations and practicing with Kirin, he had learnt some basic Hindu conversation. When they entered the reception hall, they went through some well-rehearsed lines for the girl's benefit before he disappeared upstairs carrying the bags.

Joining him inside the room, her face lit up when she saw how clean it was. In the previous places it didn't matter how many times she tried washing, she still felt dirty afterwards.

She bathed and changed into a nightshirt she had purchased and jumped into bed looking forward to a proper night's sleep.

Luke, busy unpacking, looked at his watch and decided it was better if he got some rest as well. After washing, he wiped his face with a towel and switched the overhead light off.

She was fast asleep and looked prettier than ever in the clean white sheets. *'I hope I see you again after tomorrow night,'* he thought, and without disturbing her he went to sleep on the other side of the bed.

Wednesday, 20th October 2008
Meeting Room, The White House

President Whiting sat at the end of the long, boardroom table. He had convened the meeting with his top advisors to hear their views, and finalize the US response to Banerjee's proclamation. He had Jim Allen and General Magnus Graham alongside him on his left and Director Mike Conway to his right.

"Ok Mike, let's start with the tough one…have we found their warheads? Are we likely to find them?" the President asked firmly. He placed the glass of water he was holding back on the coaster.

Since they had sat together watching Banerjee's ultimatum in the Oval Office, Conway and General Graham had worked on nothing else. They both realized, as did the President, that if they could locate the launchers there was every chance they could neutralize their threat in time. Unfortunately, even with the help of the Alliance, their investigations had led to nothing.

"If we had a chance of tracking them sir, then it was whilst they were in convoy…now they've reached their destination they'll have dug themselves in," Mike responded with a degree of pessimism.

General Graham sat in full military uniform with his arms folded across his chest. He was normally an unflappable character, but the look of abject frustration on his face was plain to see. He was aggrieved that they were letting the President down in his hour of need. *'How could they not uncover any trace with all the resources at their command?'* he asked himself.

"We thought we'd located them a couple of times when some of our fighters did some low level runs, but they've disguised several convoys to look as if they're carrying the warheads." General Graham wanted to go on and tell the President some of the difficulties and problems they'd encountered but knew it wasn't the time or the place.

"So what you're saying is that there is little chance, if any, of finding those rockets before the deadline is up, is that correct?"

"There's always a chance Sir," Director Conway interjected. "Colonel Schwartz and his team are doing all they can, and there is still time."

Conway had always sensed the President held him personally responsible for allowing the Operations Centre to lose track of India's remaining warheads. In reality, President Whiting was extremely disappointed that the CIA had lost the trail. *'After all, Codename Amber had held the warheads under ground surveillance when they were first launched against Pakistan?'* He did not try to apportion blame at this time; they had to focus on the information and the facts that were real, and under their control. Despite this he still felt a touch of annoyance. Maybe the mistake was taking Codename Amber off her assignment to track the warheads. Maybe it was his mistake. *'Why had he let Mike Conway convince him so easily that she should carry out an impossible mission?'*

The President stared at Director Conway.

"Do you think we can leave this to chance, Mike?" the President didn't disguise his irritation. He was in no mood to hear the empty plaudits for the efforts being made. He needed results, he needed options and he needed them now. He didn't wait for a reply.

"What are the likely targets?" he asked turning to the General.

General Graham picked up a plastic wallet in front of him and pulled out the top sheets of paper. He had only received the intelligence reports moments before the meeting began, and as such had only managed to scan the contents.

"We can only 'best guess' Sir, but if we assume that he wants to cause the maximum damage to our efforts to restore oil production then…." He tailed off as he looked at the report.

"…Then that suggests he'll aim for Riyadh or Abu Dhabi, they have the highest density and proliferation of oil terminals," he paused, continuing to inspect the document.

"Alternatively, they could decide that destroying the oil routes themselves would end our efforts in which case they may target the Straits of Hormuz itself."

Nodding for him to carry on, the President leaned over and pressed the intercom button connecting him to his ever-present secretary.

"Please ask Margaret to join us," he asked.

Director Conway decided to throw his own thoughts on the subject into the ring.

"My view is that Banerjee will not only target the oil installations, he will also fire on densely populated civilian centres," he paused before justifying his remarks.

"I think we know that he won't be concerned about the deaths of his own people, and the name of the game here isn't just damaging the oil fields, is it?" he asked.

They looked at Director Conway, waiting for him to answer his own question.

"It's about causing total chaos in the Gulf to an extent where it becomes impossible to restore order and the oil supply."

"I tend to agree with you Mike…What about you, Jim?" the President said, looking past General Graham.

"Yes, it makes sense to me, I don't believe he has anything to gain by targeting our airbases or by direct hits on our own or Alliance forces…no, I think he'll opt to cause maximum damage and disruption."

"I see…do we have any defence capabilities?" the President asked.

General Graham pounced on the opportunity to bring the advancements they had made at Montgomery to the President's attention. The government scientists had been working around the clock to complete the project.

"If we knew where they were hiding the missiles then conventional methods would be an option, but as we've agreed that it's unlikely we'll locate them at this stage…" he paused to see if Conway or Allen were going to pull him up on this point but neither did.

"…Then we still have the option of utilizing project Sabre."

Jim Allen had kept the President in touch with the latest developments on a daily basis since their flight down to the southern states.

"The latest tests show that – " was all the General could manage on the subject before the President held up his hand, interrupting his flow.

President Whiting was genuinely impressed with what he had seen and heard at the presentation in Montgomery. The General and Dr. Ramsey had put forward a strong case but how could he place any reliance on the project when the chances of success were only fifty-fifty? There was no doubt in his mind that it was a fall back option. However it was a last resort, and not an option upon which to become overly reliant at a time when critical decisions were being made.

"Look General, let me ask you one important question."

The Paradigm Shift

The General was irritated by the President's abrasive manner. As the most senior military commander in the United States he was not used to being cut off so abruptly in front of others. Nevertheless, he held back from confrontation, he had a strong respect for President Whiting and now wasn't the time to get upset by injury to his ego.

"Can I take it that the system is now foolproof?" the President looked at him with his eyebrows raised.

The General backed down, putting discretion before valour; he shook his head confirming that Project Sabre still had its shortcomings.

"Then it's a last resort, Magnus, it's not a choice!" the President's use of the General's first name had the desired effect. This was not a time for them to be at loggerheads and some of the defiant stiffness in his body language eased with the recognition of the President's gesture.

In the brief silence that followed, there was a knock on the door and Margaret Henderson, the Secretary of State entered taking a seat next to Mike Conway on the President's right.

"What's the feedback Margaret?"

She took out a sheaf of papers from a transparent plastic folder she'd carried in. On the sheets were the transcripts of all the calls she'd made and received over the past few hours. Everyone in the room knew her reputation for meticulous attention to detail. The pages were annotated with comments she had made after the calls and specific phrases had been highlighted with a marker pen.

"I'll start with Middle East because I think you need to know their position straightaway."

Listening intently, the President took off his reading glasses and placed the message he had been handed by his secretary on the table in front of him. As she was leaving he asked her to organize some refreshments.

A few minutes later, a waiter appeared with a tray of drinks followed by Catherine Dennison. She knew their preferred requirements and helped distribute the drinks whilst the Secretary of State carried on talking. The President shot a quizzical look in the direction of his CIA Director. *'There was more to that big smile that Catherine gave Conway,'* he thought.

"King Mohammed speaking on behalf of all the Gulf States has made it clear he wants the US Government and the Alliance to remove their forces immediately."

"I suppose that was to be expected?" the President responded.

"They feel that if the armed forces move out of the Gulf within the deadline then they will be able to negotiate a deal for their own safety along the lines of oil for labour."

Jim Allen understood the thought processes that the ruling Arab families must have undergone. His office, responsible for America's national security, was constantly faced with complex decisions based on 'what-if' scenarios.

His department responded by performing simulated exercises, like the one faced by the Arabs, in all the world's trouble spots. The theory was that by placing themselves in difficult situations they sought to improve their reaction time. If they could predict the outcome then the President could respond that much quicker.

"They will have drawn the same conclusions as us about India launching the nuclear warheads," Allen commented factually. "Once they have thought through the destruction and consequences of such an act, then they'll choose to be subservient to Banerjee before losing everything."

The Paradigm Shift

Director Conway added his agreement to Jim Allen's comments.

"They clearly don't think we, or the Alliance can protect them, and they've seen what's happened to Pakistan."

The Secretary of State, Margaret Henderson had one last word on the subject.

"As far as King Mohammed is concerned the agreement he countersigned at the end of the Summit is now null and void, he wants to know if we are going to leave peacefully...they have already made contact with Banerjee's Government seeking to extend the deadline."

"General, what's the military position in the Gulf?" the President swivelled to face him.

"As you know, Sir, the operation to take the refineries and oil fields was a success, I believe we have sufficient resources in the Gulf to be able to protect those sites from conventional attack whether it comes from Saudi or India."

They fell quiet round the table for a moment with all eyes on the President. It was his decision on how the US should react to Banerjee's threat and his decision alone. The course of action that he would take would surely be endorsed and followed by the other members of the Alliance.

"What is the feedback from our friends, Margaret? Are there any new ideas or options they've put forward?"

"No new solutions to report, I have spoken to all the Alliance leaders and their thinking is very much in line with our own."

She stared down at her notes before continuing. The president was sat deep in thought.

"The Alliance share the view that it's really a catch 22 situation, retreating from the Gulf will result in victory for Banerjee.

The subsequent oil crisis will bring meltdown to the political and economic systems of the western world. Alternatively, he will fire the missiles, which we can do nothing about. Once launched we can't stop them, and out of the resulting destruction and chaos comes the oil crisis."

The President put his hands behind his head and stretched. He was feeling the strain and there were no new avenues opening up to him. In sharing the thoughts of the Alliance, she had put the case very succinctly. *'What choice did he have?'* he thought, listening to her finishing off.

"All Alliance members agree that any direct assault on India will simply advance the decision of Banerjee to launch the missiles…they are waiting to hear what we have to say," she concluded.

"Thank you Margaret," the President knew the constant efforts she put in and genuinely appreciated her shrewd diplomatic skills.

"Is it still your conclusion that the activities of China are being carried out as a distraction or is there something larger afoot here?" The President aimed the question at all his senior advisors.

"All three of us are in total agreement on this point Mr. President, it's a decoy," said General Graham. "We have copied their nuclear state of readiness step by step."

"Furthermore," he continued, "we've communicated with the Chinese Government, and they know that if we get so much as a puff of smoke coming out of one of those silos they will have fifty inbound nuclear warheads from us and the Alliance before they know it!"

"What about Taiwan?" said the President, he held an anguished smile after the General's animated outburst. *That's about all we have got,'* he thought to himself. *'The ability to threaten massive retaliation.'*

"They're screaming for our help," Jim Allen replied, "but again, that's exactly what the Chinese want."

"We've got to leave that situation for the moment," Director Conway interrupted, "in my view China will launch an all out strike on Taiwan as soon as they see ourselves and Europe buckle from the oil crisis."

"I think we all share that sentiment," said President Whiting, and the faces around the table expressed their agreement.

"Ok, let's just keep the surveillance on China turned up to the maximum at the moment, agreed?"

They all nodded their concurrence; after all there was nothing really further to add to the President's comments. To engage in further debate would really be playing into China's hands by allowing them to get distracted.

"What about our own ultimatum, General? Can't we threaten India with retaliation, the likes of which have never been seen before unless they draw a halt to this nonsense?"

"Yes we can, and I believe we should," the General started before Conway broke in to stop him.

This was a contentious area. All three of them with General Karpurov and Colonel Schwartz had discussed this issue until it was threadbare. At the end of the debate, there was no consensus; they had all reached different opinions.

"If we issue an ultimatum to Banerjee now, he will launch the rockets now, and that means that we as a country, are finished," he paused looking at the General. "We have all seen the scenes outside, we have all played the tape forward, and seen what happens without oil."

"So what are you suggesting Mike?" the President snapped.

He felt the widespread threat of retaliation should be considered seriously and was irritated at the thought of another option being closed down.

"It's no good blasting India to hell and back after they've launched the missiles is it Mike?" The President continued, enforcing his support for General Graham's line of reasoning.

"No, I appreciate that, Sir," replied Director Conway, remaining composed.

"What then?" he asked again.

"As Margaret said earlier, it's a 'Catch 22' situation, there are no easy options or answers here, Banerjee is not expecting us to leave," Director Conway paused to register the expressions around the table. He looked at Jim Allen for support but his face was blank.

"He intends to fire those rockets and he's only giving us time so there is justification for his decision in the history books, and to his people back at home," he continued.

Mike Conway knew he didn't have all the answers, but accelerating Banerjee's program was not one of them. Issuing their own ultimatum would simply add justification to Banerjee's preemptive strike.

"At the moment we have time," he said looking directly at the President. "We have seen the support building up for the opposition leader, Yaswant Puri, around the world, if we can take out Banerjee himself then the situation changes immediately."

It was true, the American and European administrations had put Yashwant Puri in the spotlight on a program designed to build up his support, and it was working. The manner in which he had escaped from the clutches of Banerjee when his plane left India added to his growing appeal.

The Paradigm Shift

The Alliance was pleased with Puri's progress having checked his credentials in full before embarking on their strategy of building his popularity. Before the road show began, the US Administration and Governments across Europe, had interviewed him in depth. He came across as a genuine candidate who really had the interests of his people at heart. As a result, they had decided to endorse his campaign by allowing him to hold his own press conferences at the Summit. They were tightly monitored but this was not really necessary. His views on Banerjee and what was really happening in India reflected those of the Alliance.

"I don't understand what your saying, Mike?" the President looked at him confused.

"I am simply saying Sir, that at the moment we have time, we also have two of the best, most highly trained, secret agents in the US and British Services ready to strike before the deadline takes effect," he stopped to look at the reactions around the table.

"It's Banerjee's plot to stop the oil, not the Indian people's…if he's killed then there's no longer a reason, or a person with authority, to hit the fire button for those missiles!"

The President stared at him in the momentary pause that followed. For a second, he thought he had over stepped the mark with his aggressive stance.

"Do you really think they can do it?" the President said. It was not something he had given any serious thought to despite his initial enthusiasm early in the project.

"You want options Sir, this is the best you've got!" and he held the President's gaze waiting for his response.

President Whiting rubbed his chin slowly as he contemplated the option Director Conway had just put forward.

He finally broke the silence turning to Jim Allen and the General on his left.

"I'm inclined to agree General, the third world war will have to wait until after the deadline, I want our armed forces to stay exactly where they are and carry on protecting our positions…and that includes any offences that maybe taken by the Arab Rulers."

He turned to face his Secretary of State. The President had arrived at his decisions.

"Margaret, please inform all those who need to know of our decision." She acknowledged her instructions and started gathering her papers. She had a lot of work to do in the next few hours.

"Jim, please make sure everything is in place for Yashwant Puri, should the occasion arise, and General, inform the Gulf of our decision."

The President recognized the hope in Mike Conway's appeal. They could not retreat now.

He saw the look on General Graham's face. The General's position was understandable but there would be no winners, only losers when World War III breaks out. *'No, Armageddon could wait bit a longer,'* he thought.

"Well Mike," the President conjured up all the optimism he could muster, "I hope those agents are as good as you say, because now they are carrying all the hopes of the United States and the Alliance on their shoulders!"

Thursday, 21ˢᵗ October 2008
Jiwar, West Pakistan

General Gupta lifted the binoculars that hung around his neck, and again surveyed the rocky peaks that made up their immediate surroundings. The journey through Pakistan had been arduous, but now they were safely camouflaged in the mountainous terrain which characterized the Jiwar peninsula, near the Iranian border. From his ridge halfway up the mountainside he had an excellent view of the valley running down to the coast.

In the beginning, the whole convoy, stretching over one mile in length, had departed from the army base in Rajasthan. The procession of tanks and army trucks drove in single file down the wide gravel tracks that lead across the border into Pakistan. Every time the convoy reached a major junction, part of the convoy would be dispatched on the new trail as a decoy. The main section carrying the mobile nuclear missile launchers continued on its path as the convoy in front and behind, gradually reduced in length.

The General was well trained, he had attended Sandhurst in England during his early years as an officer, before steadily rising through the ranks. Accompanying the main section, he had followed conventional tactics and sent out an advance party to make sure the way ahead was clear. His chief concern was the terrain rather than the likelihood of random attacks by bands of local rebels.

The huge military transporters were slow and cumbersome, any serious problems with the road could hinder their progress. The advance party cleared the path of any debris, levelling potholes, as well as guiding the way ahead during nightfall. On two occasions, the well-armed team encountered Pakistani rebel forces but they were no contest for the well-drilled elite of India's top battalion.

Standing on a ridge he could see the shapes of the two mobile launchers below him covered in camouflage netting which matched the colour of the grey rock. The vehicles were not out in the open; they'd managed to find a narrow pass through an empty riverbed that could conceal the enormous transporters.

He knew the only way they could be detected was from above and they hid themselves well. Apart from the low flying reconnaissance planes, the spy satellites would be trying to pick up their location, so movement on the ground was kept to an absolute minimum.

General Gupta lowered his binoculars, and turned to face the young Major standing alongside him. He ordered him to take some soldiers and carry out another ground sweep of the valley to the north. They had travelled a long way to get here and he was not going to jeopardize the operation now by being careless.

Behind him the Captain responsible for their secure communication link with Delhi approached him. General Gupta had kept Balan informed of their steady progress with regular updates since leaving Rajasthan.

"I have a call for you sir," the officer handed him the satellite communicator.

"Hello General, is everything set?"

"Everything is set and under control, Balan," he replied. "We're ready for your instructions and will prepare the launchers in two hours time when nightfall descends."

The time was approaching fast and Balan wanted to make sure that there were no last minute hitches. His confidence levels in General Gupta had risen sharply over the past few days as he had listened to the way he had dealt with unforeseen problems.

The Paradigm Shift

"We've programmed in the coordinates for Riyadh and Abu Dhabi as agreed and will continue operating under those instructions unless we are informed otherwise," said General Gupta in his commanding and confident military voice.

"Very good General, you can next expect to hear from me just before it's time to launch the missiles at ten o'clock Indian time, nine-thirty your time, is that understood?"

The General responded affirmatively and handed the receiver back to his Captain as the line went dead. Balan was delighted the General's performance, *'I will make a point of mentioning this to Banerjee,'* he thought. If Banerjee heard such praise from Balan, he would surely see that the General and his family were well rewarded.

As the Indian Prime Minister had predicted, the US and Alliance armed forces were making no attempts to leave the Gulf. Enough time had passed for them to make serious inroads into an organized departure but it was clear they intended to stay.

Balan called Banerjee and informed him of the favourable status report on the missiles' state of readiness. He was pleased with the news but told Balan to send another communiqué to the US Administration and the Alliance.

"They are making no efforts to leave," said Banerjee, "let it be a matter of record that we have observed this, and issue the ultimatum a second time."

Thursday, 21st October 2008
Delhi

It was nearing seven o'clock as Luke and Kirin disposed of any items not required for their mission and left their guesthouse for the last time. Outside in the street, Kirin stopped a yellow and black 'padmini' taxi, and asked the driver to take them to a shopping district close to the Government Offices. The backseat of the small taxi was cramped and Luke sat with his knees pressed into the back of the drivers seat, and his head tilted against the roof at an angle. The journey took about twenty minutes as they sped down Mathura Road past Connaught Place, and on towards the Government offices where Banerjee was staying.

As they drove through the hustle and bustle of 'downtown' Delhi, the last remains of daylight disappeared. They stopped a few blocks from their final destination and completed the rest of the journey on foot.

Getting out of the cab, Luke swung the small rucksack over one shoulder and took Kirin's hand with the other.

"Are you ok?" he said squeezing it gently.

"I'm fine," she smiled back.

For the first time in days she no longer wore the traditional Hindu sari that she had become accustomed to, but instead, jeans and a shirt. Her part in the plan required speed and agility, their was no way she could remain flexible and move quickly in the long cloth of the sari. Luke wore the same traditional, baggy Indian peasant clothes but this time the loose-fitting nature of his outfit suited his purposes. Underneath he was dressed in his combat fatigues.

The Paradigm Shift

When they first arrived in Delhi, Luke had hidden a water-proof, canvas bag with their additional outfits in the black water of a man-made reservoir. Attached by a length of cord to a hook below the surface, he had retraced his steps early that morning to retrieve the bundle.

The road was busy with shoppers, as it was every evening. They walked through the crowds holding hands, their adrenaline rising as they thought about the mission ahead and the fact that they were about to part. As Luke's original plan dictated, they were due to separate when they reached the corner of this block.

"Check your watch," he said as they slowed reaching the corner, the plan called for split second timing.

The precision watches had been hidden in the canvas bag along with the clothes. Both had been calibrated by Luke and were showing the identical time.

The Government Offices where Banerjee was staying, and where Luke had spent the night trying to gather as much information as possible, lay three hundred yards further down the road.

At the corner, Luke pulled Kirin into a doorway next to a restaurant. The pavements were full of evening walkers and shoppers enjoying the Delhi nightlife.

"It's time Kirin, good luck," Luke whispered, leaning down to speak in her ear.

She looked up at him with tears in her eyes. *'How could he be so damn impersonal at a time like this.'* She wanted to say so many things at that moment but they would have to wait. *'God, get a grip of yourself, this is making it harder for him,'* she thought, and quickly brushed her eyes.

"Yes, good luck," she whispered back. She was churning up inside as she looked up. The sadness of the moment was in his eyes as well, but he smiled and turned to move away into the crowd of people.

"Luke!" she tried to keep her voice down.

He heard her call and turned round looking at her beautiful face. Her usual air of confidence had gone. She was desperately upset but doing her best to be brave. He walked back to her through the throng of people and she jumped forward clutching him.

"There is something I have to tell you Luke," and her mind raced with the words she wanted to say.

"Don't," Luke said forcefully and tightened his embrace. "We'll have plenty of time later. Don't you remember? I promised to take you to that lake one day."

He saw the smile come to her face at the recollection. Telling Luke the story of her grandfather's escape to America seemed so long ago.

"Well, I keep my promises," he said, slowly releasing his grip.

She stood back smiling at him, her eyes told him everything he could possibly want to know.

He took one step backwards, before turning and disappearing into the crowd. As she watched him go, she silently mouthed the words that had been running through her mind. Stepping out of the doorway, she set off past the café in the opposite direction.

Luke made his was back to the alley where he had been chased with such vigour by Nawani's loyal servicemen. The experience had helped him conceive his plan. It was when he had clambered over the railing and made his escape, that he had spotted the alternative entrances. These doorways were the tradesman's entrances to the Government buildings across the street from the Prime Minister's main office.

He retraced his steps down the alley until he came to a doorway which was partially covered with cardboard boxes and broken, old crates used by the wandering vagrants as places to sleep. Although there was barely any light, except for the weak glow from the street-lamps, a quick scan of the area couldn't detect anyone else present.

In the darkness, he pulled some of the debris and rubbish to one side, leaving the path clear down a small flight of stone stairs to a wooden door that led into the basement.

He shone the torchlight on the door. The wood was rotten with age, and it did not take him long to prize the hinges free with some of the tools he carried with him. As the door came loose he pointed the torch inside, it looked like a rarely used storeroom. Pushing past the door as quietly as he could, he replaced it in its original position by propping a filing cabinet up against it.

Inside it was pitch black and he turned on the flashlight to get acquainted with his new surroundings. Running the light around the basement, he could see it was used for storing old government records. This building belonging to the Ministry of Education and as a result the security was reasonably relaxed compared with the Prime Minister's residence across the road. Only two security guards worked in the building on the night-shift.

Placing the torch on a shelf so he could see, Luke stripped off his Hindu dress to reveal his black, combat fatigues. Throwing the clothing in one of the empty boxes he made his way slowly up the interior staircase. He could see the dim light from the reception hall where the two guards took it in turn to patrol the ground floor.

He looked at his watch and saw it was approaching eight-thirty. Timing was crucial to their plan; he needed to get past them immediately and started weighing up his options.

Standing on the staircase leading up to the ground floor, he peered around the corner at the two guards. The colonial style, reception hall had a large, high ceiling and in the middle was a central bureau. It had four, 'chest-height' wooden counters connected together in the shape of a square. Anybody who entered the building had to present themselves at the counter facing the front. The two guards sat in the middle of the bureau with their feet up, talking and occasionally laughing at some passing comment. Although Luke couldn't see it from his position it sounded as if they had wired up a TV below the level of the counter.

The building did have a lift, but it was one of the very old fashioned varieties with a sliding metal grill that pulled across the front before it would move. As he considered his options, he had a stroke of good fortune when one of the guards decided to leave the bureau. He stood up laughing, clapped his friend on the back, and marched off towards a door leading away from the hallway. The remaining guard, chuckling, carried on watching the television with his back to Luke. Only the top of his head was visible above the counter.

Downstairs, Luke had replaced his sandals with training shoes. If the guard stayed in his present position, he knew he could get past unseen so it was a question of doing it quietly. Any sound on the tiled floor could be enough to alert him. Quickly, he hopped up the flight of stairs to the reception level and then slid past the front of the lift and up the next staircase.

The Paradigm Shift

He stopped to look back and check he had not been seen. From his new elevated view, he could see the guard suspected nothing and he continued up the flight of stairs until he reached the tenth and final floor.

It was still very dark inside the building. A thick, glass sky-light ran the length of the corridor above him and as he made his way to the middle, the moonlight cast grey shadows across his path. Keeping his hand over the end of the torch to dim the beam, he quickly found what he was looking for. He pushed the rucksack further back across his shoulders and climbed up the metal spiral staircase which led out to the roof.

Once out onto the flat roof, he crouched down, and started to unpack his rucksack. He stuffed a few small items into the pockets of his trousers. This was the time when he would find out whether his handiwork in Agra would live up to his expectations. Putting the rucksack back on, he secured it tightly under his arms and across his chest.

In his right hand, he held up a piece of cotton cloth the size of four large napkins sewn together. At the corners, it had strong fibre cords attached to it that ran over his shoulder and under the flap to his rucksack. Continuing to hold the cloth above his head, he ran over to the edge of the roof. Looking out across the street, he could see the building housing the Prime Minister's offices, surrounded by the wall and the gardens. Checking the road below him was clear; he climbed onto the wall running around the roof's parapet.

In the same motion as throwing the black, cotton cloth into the air, he launched himself out from the building. Immediately, the cloth flew open forming a miniature parachute that pulled the main chute out of his rucksack. In the next second, the main chute flew open and using two handles; he controlled the rapid descent as he passed over the wall and into the gardens beyond.

In his early days with the SAS, Luke had trained specially for such exercises. The television media called it 'base jumping'. It was a very dangerous sport, and it gained notoriety when thrill seekers were filmed, jumping from famous landmarks such as the Eiffel Tower, or the Leaning Tower of Pisa.

Hitting the lawn feet first he rolled over grabbing the parachute as he did so. He took cover behind one of the thick, tropical bushes on the garden's perimeter, kneeling so he could not be seen. He stayed there motionless for a minute taking stock of his new surroundings. If he had been detected there would have been a surge of activity and the chances of him completing his mission would be over.

The calm remained; all he could hear was the distant voices of some guards talking together at the front gate. *'He was in,'* he thought, and looking up, he strained his eyes trying to find the location of the close circuit TV's.

As he surveyed the garden from behind the bush, he realized how dark it was. When he had been camped across the street doing his surveillance he had got a different impression but this worked in his favour. *'By keeping one eye on the cameras and moving through the intermittent patches of darkness, I should be able to work my way to the building,'* he thought.

He checked his watch again. Time was passing quickly. He gave a brief thought to the progress of Kirin, before he started weaving his approach towards the main house, keeping as low as he could.

For her part, Kirin was several blocks away in a district known for its car and lorry showrooms. In India, the gap between the rich and the poor was enormous, and only the wealthiest individuals could afford new cars. Although a few sold new vehicles, the bulk of the showrooms catered for the thriving second hand market where most cars sold were over ten years old.

She walked past the front of the 'brightly-lit', Suzuki showrooms. The Japanese firm had been one of the first international manufacturers to enter the country, when it started local production in a joint venture with the Indian Government. The window display of cars and motorbikes showed off some of the latest models. Turning into the side street, Kirin walked along by the brick wall that separated her from the Suzuki service centre at the back of the building. The wall itself was only a few feet taller than her.

The main road was busy but it was a bit quieter in the side street. For fifteen minutes, she watched the flow of traffic and the people coming and going. The usual entrance to the service centre was a large swing gate that you could drive in through, but this was chained and padlocked shut.

The height of the wall didn't present a problem to her even though broken glass had been cemented into the top to prevent would be trespassers. It was finding a moment when the traffic died down to a level where she could gain access without being seen.

She checked her watch; she had plenty of time remaining and was sufficiently composed not to rush the moment. Every now and then she noticed opportunities arising as the traffic lights on the main road changed. Watching carefully until the right time presented itself, she moved across the street as the flow of cars stopped.

Looking both ways, there was no one immediately visible. She pulled on a pair of black gloves and seized the chance to scale the wall. Below her loose fitting shirt, she was wearing a compacted fabric, body suit that allowed her to put her midriff across the broken glass. The padded suit could easily take her full weight on the glass shards and in the same movement, she smoothly swung her legs over the wall landing safely on the other side.

It had taken no longer than a couple of seconds to complete the manoeuvre and she felt confident she had made it without being seen.

She checked her watch. *'Luke should be inside by now,'* she thought.

The thought pleased her. She was only a few blocks away from the Government Buildings, close enough to hear the uproar that would follow if he had been discovered.

Thursday, 21st October 2008
USS Missouri, Gulf of Arabia

It was approaching seven o'clock in the meeting room of the USS Missouri, the largest aircraft carrier in the Fifth Fleet. The missiles carrying the nuclear warheads were due to be launched in the next thirty minutes. Admiral Stone, Admiral Downey and Air Marshal Reiger sat with Conrad Dexter, watching the time tick away on the wall clock. Conrad Dexter drummed his fingers on the table repeatedly, the noise served to heighten the tension that had already gone off the scale. They looked at each other in silence, powerless to change the course of events. Fate was out of their hands.

They had received their final orders from headquarters and it was now too late to propose any alternatives. In the time they had available, they themselves had debated the ultimatum from Banerjee long and hard. They arrived at the same conclusion as Washington regarding whether or not to remain in the Gulf.

"Would anyone care for a drink?" asked Admiral John Stone breaking the silence.

Getting up, he walked over to a steel cabinet firmly screwed to the wall. They all nodded and he poured a large whisky from a decanter into four crystal glass tumblers.

"I normally use this decanter when we're celebrating an occasion," he said, handing out the drinks, "but in this case I think we should drink to hope and good fortune."

"To hope and good fortune," said Admiral Troy Downey raising his glass in the air, and they all simultaneously joined him in the toast.

That morning had seen the first action of the campaign since they had taken control of the oil installations. The attacks hadn't come from India or China but from the Saudi Air Force. Ironically, it was Margaret Henderson who had brokered the deal selling the planes to the Saudi Government.

The conflict was fairly tame, no actual shots were fired but the Saudi pilots did engage in low-level attack runs aimed at the aircraft carrier. The fighter pilots were followed all the way by a squadron of Phantom's with instructions to kill if necessary. Their on-board computers systems told them if the Saudi pilots were engaging their weapon systems but, fortunately, Air Marshal Reiger's interpretation of the situation proved correct; the fighter's pulled away without discharging any of their armoury.

The exercise was a futile attempt by the Arab rulers borne out of desperation. They desperately wanted to persuade the Fifth Fleet and the Alliance it was in their best interests to leave Gulf waters. At the same time, the mock demonstration was also put on to show Banerjee where their real allegiance lay.

By attacking the US and Alliance ships they hoped to convince Banerjee that they could still come to some arrangement. In the end, the Saudi pilots were cautioned over the radio and shepherded back to their airbase on the coastline, near Al Khobar. The firepower and air superiority of the Alliance forces in the Gulf was not to be matched, and the Saudi's knew it was not a time to lose some of their expensive weaponry.

The events had served to make the time pass more quickly but now everything fell into slow motion. Again they revisited the discussion on the likely targets to be selected by Banerjee. The conclusions they drew were the same as earlier.

Conrad Dexter thought of his wife and three children back at home in Houston.

"When the bombs go off, will we be safe on board these ships?" he asked.

It was the first time he'd given thought to his own safety.

"We should be safe at sea," replied Admiral Stone, "but there may be an outside chance of danger for ships close to the target zones."

Dexter nodded taking another sip of his whiskey. The two Admirals had considered the risk to the Fifth Fleet when they first heard their instructions to stay in the Gulf. After they had consulted with Washington, both Admirals had agreed that the likely targets were large civilian centres vital to the oil economy. As a result of their discussions, Admiral John Stone pushed the ships into the safer waters away from oil cities along the coast.

If the final destination of the missiles was inland, like Riyadh in Saudi, then Admiral Stone assured Dexter that they should be safe.

"It just depends how the wind carries the fall out," said Admiral Downey.

Over the course of the day, they had taken numerous reports from the US Meteorological Office and other weather satellite stations. In the end they had based their final coordinates on the location least likely to be affected by the wind.

Conrad Dexter looked up at the clock again; the final countdown had begun.

"Well gentlemen," he said raising his glass above his head.

His eyes were brimming with tears as he put down the photograph of his youngest daughter.

"Here's to missile failure!"

Smiling, the Officers raised their glasses with him.

Thursday, 21ˢᵗ October 2008
The Pentagon, Washington

If Banerjee held good to his threat, then the missiles were scheduled to launch at half past eleven in the morning on East Coast time. It was eleven o'clock now, and the fully manned Operations Centre was silent as the rows of intelligence officers sat at their computer stations focusing on the job to be done.

In front of them was the screen with its magnified image of the Middle East. Those officers who had finished their last minute checks watched the screen in anticipation. They remembered the flashing lights and the noise that accompanied Banerjee's first bombardment of Pakistan.

It had been a long night and most personnel on duty had been at their stations since the previous evening. Desperately, they had made attempt after attempt, to locate the hidden missile launchers.

Standing on the bridge of the Operations Centre were General Magnus Graham, Director Conway, Colonel Schwartz and General Karpurov. They too had been there all night, clinging to the last chance they had for finding the warheads. Their last vestige of hope disappeared when darkness set across the Gulf making any further surveillance impossible.

During the night they had been joined by Doctor Ramsey, Head of the US Space Defence Program at the request of General Graham. The General had been adamant that if it came down to it they would have at least one final option with Project Sabre. During the day Doctor Ramsey had finalized the procedures for transferring control of Project Sabre from Montgomery up to the CIA Headquarters.

The Operations Centre had also been connected with flat screen monitor's linking them directly to the White House. The President was kept informed of each and every development as it occurred.

President Whiting prayed silently for the success of the agents. Every other avenue led to catastrophe. _'Sure'_, he thought, _'they could blast India to kingdom come afterwards,'_ but that was not the responsible way to reply. _'How could they take retribution on the millions of innocent Indians who played no part in the pantomime acted out by this madman?'_

Banerjee was a ruthless, cold-blooded murderer prepared to press the button destroying so many lives. No one doubted that he would go through with his threat. It was the act of a heartless soul. President Whiting was lost for words in describing the power-crazed mind of an individual capable of such universal devastation.

The ultimatum delivered by Banerjee had caused pandemonium in the populated regions of the Middle East. The word had spread like lightening across the Gulf causing widespread chaos. Everywhere the people panicked as they reacted to the possibility of a nuclear bomb landing on their city.

The airports were besieged but offered little chance of escape for the common people. There were no fuel reserves at the airports. Even for the Western Nations trying to evacuate their citizens it was impossible. Any commercial plane landing at the airports was attacked by the swarming masses, desperate to flee before it was too late.

There were a lucky few who managed to force their way onto departing flights, but for most, the journey out to sea or the drive into the interior offered the best chance of escape. Gathering whatever belongings they could, families fled their houses and travelled to the ports, trying to secure a passage out to sea.

Chaos was high on the list of Banerjee's objectives. By remaining steadfastly silent on the cities to be targeted, he guaranteed that he would cause widespread panic across the entire Gulf region.

The roads out of all major towns and cities were choked with angry crowds fighting to put enough distance between themselves and the possible targeted site of Banerjee's nuclear missiles. Their anxiety was borne out of the primal need for survival and the protection of their loved ones. They had all watched the catalogue of death unfold in the aftermath of the detonations at Lahore and Islamabad and needed no further prompting on the potential incoming wave of destruction.

Along the roadside, thousands of people without transport lined the highways leading out of towns. There were hardly any vehicles on the roads as the petrol stations had long since run dry. At the outset of the oil crisis, the ruling Arab families had impounded any petrol reserves that were still available and distributed any surpluses beyond their own requirements to their family and personal friends. Occasionally a vehicle attempted to drive slowly through the throng of marching families, honking its horn. The importance of the passengers in the car or four-wheel drive vehicle no longer mattered to the crowd, and every now and then, the vehicle would be bombarded with stones and other debris that lay at the side of the road. Law and order had disappeared; it was now a question of survival for everyone and without exception it meant looking after yourself and your family first.

As the time approached when the missiles were to be launched, an eerie silence hung over the cities of the Middle

East. In the early evening darkness they had become ghost towns. The streetlights were switched on because automatic timers operated them but the roads were devoid of life except for the occasional stray dogs left behind. Some occasional noise remained, mainly glass breaking, as looters smashed their way into the shopping malls.

"We have fifteen minutes to go," said General Graham in a loud voice to everyone in the Operations Room. The screen at the front had a digital clock counting down the minutes and seconds.

'Christ this is it,' thought Director Conway staring at the screen in a trance. Karpurov stood behind him, he was talking in Russian updating his Premier in Moscow.

"Get an open link through to MI6," shouted Colonel Schwartz to one of his communication officers.

The President was sitting behind his desk in his office at the White House. He put down the telephone receiver and stared at the monitor that had been specially erected in one corner of the room. His wife Pam had been on the phone trying to give him strength for the events ahead.

The picture showed the Operations Centre. He could see the look of desperation on the face of his top aides as the time drew nearer.

For the second time, President Whiting prayed for the success of the undercover agents battling against the odds in Delhi. He looked up at the clock, fifteen minutes left. *'It's probably too late now,'* he thought.

Thursday, 21ˢᵗ October 2008
Government Building, Delhi

Luke pulled open a pocket on his combat trousers. He slid out two metal struts that he quickly assembled to form a miniature crossbow. Turning them perpendicular to each other, they clicked into place and he pulled the cord taut to cock the device. He listened intently for any signs of the guards as he placed a bolt on the ridge of the crossbow. Luke had to gain access as soon as possible, and his modern version of the crossbow could be fired without causing any unnecessary noise.

He glanced in both directions, checking the path was clear, and sprinted towards a bush that lay ten yards from the overhanging balcony to the Prime Minister's office. The bolt had a pointed end capable of piercing the building's stone façade, and taking aim he shot it into the brickwork above the window next to the balcony. The bolt was attached to a length of steel cable. It made a whipping sound, like the reel of a fishing rod, as the coil unwound, trailing upwards behind the bolt.

As he heard the small thud of the bolt hitting its target, he saw two of Ashraf Nawani's Special Forces walking around the patio at the far corner of the building. He stayed low behind the bush considering how to tackle the oncoming guards. He knew he couldn't wait for them to finish their inspection; the path they were following would lead them straight under the balcony.

Talking to each other, they shone their flashlights around the garden as they headed along the patio below the balcony. Their voices grew louder as they got closer. They had not heard the bolt, but they would soon come across the cable hanging down.

The Paradigm Shift

Without taking his eyes off them, he felt in a pocket down by his ankle and pulled out a second bolt. *'My timing has to be perfect,'* he thought as he reloaded the crossbow.

The guards reached the balcony, and one of them flashed their torchlight at the building during one of their random checks. He immediately highlighted the cable running towards the balcony. The guard only had time to make a small cry of recognition as he realized what the purpose of the cable was. In the same instant, the masonry bolt from Luke's crossbow smashed into his chest lifting him off the ground. His dead-weight body fell against the back of the second patrolman. The second guard, jolted by the sudden force, spun around in surprise.

Luke raced across the paving stones, as the guard lifted his head to raise the alarm. Before he had a chance, Luke wrapped the cable hanging down against the wall, around his throat, and jerked it tight. His face and eyes bulged as he tried in vain to get his fingers between the cable and his neck.

The wire cut deeper, and after a minute the gurgling stopped, and his stuttering body finally went limp. Luke released the wire and dragged the bodies below the undergrowth of the bushes. He was worried that the incident would have been picked up by a random sweep of the surveillance cameras. If he had good fortune on his side, then maybe by moving their bodies out of sight, it would give him a few extra seconds or minutes. He could not hear any unusual sounds, *'maybe I've been lucky,'* he thought.

He tugged the cable, testing to make sure it was secure and then threaded it through two small metal wheels that formed part of a pulley system. Holding the handle above his head, he pressed the button with his thumb, launching himself into the air. In seconds, hanging from the grip, the pulley device lifted him off the ground up the length of the cable towards the bolt. Reaching the level of the second floor, he stopped the device and swung down. He landed, crouching on the balcony in a kneeling position, careful not to make a sound. He was close now; he could see the occupants of the room through the double windows. Checking his watch, there were five minutes left.

Half a mile across town, Kirin leant down by the engine and touched the two protruding wires together.

She had been busy while Luke was gaining access to the Prime Minister's residence. At the back of the showroom, she had broken in through the service centre and switched off the main lights. Passers-by could no longer see the vehicles on display through the large window frontage. With the only light being provided from the street outside, Kirin made her way towards a Suzuki trail bike at the front of the showroom. Taking the bike off its stand, she rolled it out through the doors connecting the showroom to the service centre.

As the wires touched she twisted the throttle and the bike roared into life. She jumped on the saddle and rode the bike through the garage that was full of cars in various states of disrepair. Before starting the bike, she had rolled up the shutter which led to her means of escape from the backyard.

Earlier she had taken a plank of wood that had been lying around the yard and propped it up against a pile of bricks. The result was a ramp; albeit a very narrow version, pointing towards the top of the wall she had just clambered over.

On the other side was a big drop to street level. Before taking on the jump, she wanted to get a feel for the responsiveness of the bike and she sped down the yard, spinning the bike to a halt.

Kirin returned to a point in the yard that offered the longest run up to the ramp. Looking up at the ramp one last time, she revved the engine and accelerated at full speed. Although it was a trail bike, it had a 250cc engine and it really demanded a longer stretch to build up to top speed. She compensated by driving around in an arc before giving the bike maximum throttle.

Kirin hit the ramp, racing up the narrow track, and launched into the air. She sailed over the wall as the bike's engine screamed with exertion. Holding on tightly to the handlebars and leaning back, she landed on a car's roof. Kirin had aimed the ramp towards a parked car that would break her fall.

The windows of the car shattered as the bike bounced up again before reaching the main street. Skidding in the darkness, she brought the bike under control. Ignoring the open mouths, and looks of astonishment coming from the traffic and on the sidewalk, she revved the engine, and sped off in the direction of the Government offices.

Thursday, 21st October 2008
Prime Minister's Office, Government Building, Delhi

Banerjee stood looking up at the ornamental clock, set in ivory, on the wall of his office.

"This is truly a great moment in our country's history," he said with his back to Balan.

"No one can stop us now, our dream of making India the most powerful nation in the world is about to become true."

Balan smiled at his leader's words as he began to imagine the future. The day would come when he would make the Americans pay for the life of his son, starting with President Whiting.

"General Gupta is waiting for our signal," Balan replied. As quickly as his thoughts of victory had arisen he pushed them into the back of his mind and reverted to the serious task at hand. He was keen to get the job done.

"Patience, patience my friend, we are nearly there."

The clock showed them entering the last few minutes. Banerjee continued to stand in the same position with his back to Balan. His face pointed upwards, with his eyes closed as if he was in a hypnotic trance. Two more minutes passed as he stood there, reflecting in silence.

"I think you can get General Gupta now," he said calmly.

Balan watched as Banerjee spun around and glared at him. The apparition that faced him shook him to the core. This was not the respected leader he had become accustomed to every day. Something more possessed him.

His eyes burned with evil as he flashed the maniacal look of someone bordering on the insane. Even his most trusted lieutenant, Balan, questioned whether he was in league with the devil when he encountered such an expression.

Regaining his composure, he quickly pressed the buttons on the satellite phone and heard General Gupta speaking to him at the other end. He sensed his voice was trembling. _'Don't let us down now General,'_ he thought as Banerjee continued to stare at him.

"I have him on line, shall I give him the comm. – " but that was all Balan could get out.

Luke kicked the double doors to the balcony. They swung open smashing against the inside wall with the force. He took two steps in side with his gun raised.

Balan and Banerjee swung around to face him. Balan's face registered total shock, as he stood paralyzed holding the satellite phone.

Luke's gun was fitted with a silencer. Holding it with both hands, he swung his arms in an arc so that he had Banerjee's head in his sights.

For a second, he stood rigid, looking into the eyes of the devil.

Banerjee's voice was completely calm as he spoke to Luke, "you can't kill me you know I'm – "

Luke fired the gun. The bullet killed Banerjee instantly. Blood splattered across the wall and the ivory clock, as it ripped through his skull.

"Fire! Fire!" Balan screamed into the phone before Luke could turn the gun on him.

It was the last words Balan said, as the next bullet pierced his right temple.

Luke ran towards Balan's fallen body and picked up the phone.

"Stop that instruction!" he screamed in to the mouthpiece. "Stop! Do not fire! Do you hear me?"

General Gupta's voice filled with terror, quivered at the other end of the phone.

" What? Who's that? Its too late, where's Balan?" he shouted back in desperation.

"This is the British Government, both Balan and your leader Banerjee are dead, do not fire those missiles! Repeat do not fire those missiles!"

Luke heard the shouting at the end of the phone and the sound of thunder as one of the missiles left the mobile launcher in the background.

"It's too late – its too late – one has gone," General Gupta yelled amidst the chaos going on around him. The damage he had just unleashed on the world flashed in front of him.

"Where are you?" Luke screamed, cursing himself for not shooting Balan first.

The General had gone over the edge. As his mind clouded with the thoughts of Banerjee and Balan being dead, he wailed the coordinates of their position, as if it was an act that could redeem him from the terrible tragedy he had caused. Luke made one attempt to get him to stand down the other missile before his attention was diverted to the noise building up outside the room.

The door to the Prime Minister's office burst open and Luke fired at the first new arrivals as he put the satellite phone in a trouser pocket. He checked his watch; he didn't have much time if he was to make it out alive. Racing over to where the two guards had just crumpled to the floor, he pushed the door shut and pressed the latch locking it.

It gave him a few more seconds; the door would soon give way with any serious effort to get in. Luke saw the handle turning as he reached in an inside pocket of his jacket and pulled out an explosive device, similar to that which he had used in the Delhi slum. He slapped the silver detonator to the door and primed the timer for ten seconds.

Turning, he ran back across the room and out onto the balcony. Peering over the edge, he expected to see more of Banerjee's bodyguard waiting for him below. However the way was clear, *'the noise must have only alerted the guards inside,'* he thought. Clambering over the stone balcony, he leapt onto the lawn and rolled behind a bush.

Using the satellite phone he had taken from Balan, he quickly dialled the emergency code which would connect him to MI6. Nawani's secret police would be listening to his call but that did not matter now.

"Commander Tremett," he heard almost immediately through the receiver.

At the same moment the explosion took place above him in Banerjee's office.

"Mark, both Banerjee and Balan are dead, the remaining missile is at Jiwar on these coordinates," he repeated the information General Gupta had given him.

"Ok, I've got that," shouted Tremett but the line went dead. He heard the blast in the background and could only imagine the danger that faced Luke at that point of time. *'I hope to God he can escape,'* he thought before dialling another number to give Sir Thomas the news.

Luke threw the phone into a nearby hedge. Moments earlier, he had heard the shouting and hollering from the guards as they tried to break in to the Prime Minister's office before the explosive detonated. Alarm bells started ringing, and Luke was showered by some of the flying glass and debris blown over the balcony by the force of the blast.

In the aftermath of the explosion, keeping low, Luke set off towards the perimeter of the grounds. At that moment, he did not realize he had been seen.

Ashraf Nawani walked through the smoke onto the balcony, looking over the edge, he saw Luke diving through the shadows towards the gate.

Thursday, 21ˢᵗ October 2008
Operations Centre, The Pentagon, Washington

"We have one missile airborne," shouted the Intelligence Officer looking at the console in front of him.

They all looked up at the screen and saw the flashing light as it started its journey from the Western tip of Pakistan.

"I want to know its destination now," shouted Colonel Schwartz.

"Ok General, that's it, we have one last resort," said Mike Conway.

He looked at General Graham, his face was drained of emotion but he became more invigorated at the thought of using Project Sabre. Director Conway approached the monitor to speak directly to the President. In the background, he could hear Dr Ramsey and the General barking orders to initiate control of Sabre.

"Mr. President, we have one missile in the air, no explanation as to why its only one but we need your authority to go ahead with Sabre?"

"Go ahead, Mike, and let's pray it works!" the President replied immediately.

General Graham, along with everyone in the Operations Centre, watched the screen as they observed the giant satellite taking the shape of a weapon in space. As Doctor Ramsey had just pointed out, their chances were considerably enhanced by the fact that they only needed to concentrate on tracking one missile.

"It would appear the destination is Riyadh, Sir," shouted the target operator, sitting in front of the bridge where General

Graham was giving orders. It was her job to try and program Project Sabre to home in on the missile's flight path.

"How long until it reaches its destination?" Schwartz shouted.

Every second counted now. The Colonel looked at the screen and saw that the flashing light was over the Arabian Sea heading towards the heart of Saudi Arabia.

"In-bound missile will take fifteen more minutes to reach its target," another operator shouted from the console to his right.

'What has happened to the second missile?' Thought Director Conway.

"I have a lock on the target," shouted the female program officer staring at the flashing coordinates on her console. The day before, she had been imported from the Defence Program in Montgomery as part of Dr. Ramsey's inner circle. He stood leaning over her shoulder checking the information as it came through on her screen.

"Right, we have to hold the lock for three minutes" Dr. Ramsey said turning to address his audience on the bridge.

Director Conway, Colonel Schwartz, General Graham and General Karpurov stood and watched the new digital display that appeared on the screen counting down from three minutes.

"Where's the second missile?" General Karpurov said, leaning over and speaking quietly to Director Conway.

In the Oval Office, Jim Allen joined the President. They watched the proceedings unfold on the special monitor link with the Operations Centre.

"What will happen to the missile if Project Sabre is successful?" asked the President.

"The nuclear warhead on board the missile will not arm itself until it enters the last five minutes of its journey to its target," replied Allen. "If the missile can be detected and shot down before this point of no return then it will descend to earth without risk. No impact of the 'nuclear jolt' hitting the missile or the subsequent collision as the warhead hits the ground will cause the plutonium to fuse and trigger an explosion….the question is can they knock it down in time?"

The Operations Centre which had been full of noise at the launch of the warhead, now watched in silence as the seconds counted down. Two clocks were shown on the screen, the timer on the left showed twelve minutes until impact in Riyadh. On the right, the timer showed the remaining fifteen seconds needed to be covered by the most sophisticated tracking system in the world.

'Jesus Christ let this work,' thought Schwartz as the clock approached zero. On the screen via another satellite link up they could see the protruding transmitter of Project Sabre as it swung into position. The clock counted down from ten.

"Firing on zero," shouted the Program Officer in front of Doctor Ramsey. In the bank of controls and dials in front of her was a circular, black panel. Lifting it up, she revealed the switch that would command Project Sabre to fire the nuclear jolt.

Another Intelligence Officer counted down the seconds, "Five, four, three, two, one…"

Dr. Ramsey flipped the red switch and they all observed the flash of lightening from the antenna of the satellite. The whole Operation Centre watched and waited for the outcome.

The Program Officer broke the silence.

"We have a miss, I repeat we have a miss…."

The overwhelming sense of despair was tremendous as the stunned faces turned around to look at each other.

On the screen, they saw the missile's trajectory lit up as it continued on its course. It was over the Arabian Sea now and edging closer to the interior of Saudi Arabia, and the capital Riyadh.

"Do it again," shouted General Graham above the noise. He was a dogged character, and his voice was so loud that people turned around sharply to see the source of the outburst.

"Do we have time?" he yelled, and the Program Operator nodded.

"Well, do it again!" he shouted, his face lined with determination.

The clock on the left showed nine minutes until impact. There could be no further attempts if this wasn't successful. The warhead would be primed and the detonation would be irreversible.

"We have a lock on," the Program Operator called for the second time.

In the warm breeze of the Gulf, Admirals Stone and Downey were joined by Conrad Dexter outside the bridge of the US Missouri. Their mood was solemn. They knew that only one missile was airborne and had seen the initial attempt by Sabre end in failure.

The clap of thunder and the flash of electric tentacles had lit up the heavens around them.

Along the decks below them, the naval seamen lined the bow of the boat and stood in clusters on the carrier's flight deck waiting to see what happened next.

"I have Sir Thomas on the line Sir," the Communication's Officer handed the headset over to Director Conway standing on the bridge. He quickly clipped it in place over his ear and pulled the microphone round to his mouth.

"Go ahead Sir Thomas,"

Despite their failure, his face lit up as he heard the news from MI6. *'Jesus I don't believe it,'* he thought as the smile spread across his face.

The rest of the Officers on the bridge looked at him curiously. *'Riyadh was on the point of extinction, an event which could lead to global catastrophe, what could be such good news at this time?'*

Director Conway quickly thanked Sir Thomas and pulled off the headset. In view of his fellow Officers, he walked briskly up to the monitor link connecting him to the President.

The President sat behind his desk. The build-up of hope in Project Sabre followed by its abject failure had been hard to watch. He saw Director Conway's face appear on the screen.

"Mr. President, I can confirm that Banerjee is dead, Codename Amber has been a success!" Director Conway spoke directly into the camera.

In the stunned silence that followed, the President finally looked up and nodded, there were tears of relief in his eyes.

Director Conway heard the overjoyed cries behind him as he gave the President the news.

There was no remorse for the dead Banerjee in the Operations Centre.

"You bastard!" exclaimed Colonel Schwartz banging his fist down hard on the top of the control panel in front of him.

"Just hit that missile," said the President, and the temporary reprise from the news of Banerjee's assassination was over. The flashing light on the screen ahead of them showed the warhead on its final run to Riyadh.

The timer on the screen showed the global tracking system with twenty seconds to go until connection was established and the fire button could be used again.

'This time…it's got to be this time,' Doctor Ramsey spoke quietly to himself. Only the Program Officer he was assisting with the controls heard him.

The same Operator as before called out the countdown. Everyone, including the President through his monitor, stared at the magnified screen in front of them.

The screen showed the satellite revolving in space ready to dispense Project Sabre, the live camera pictures were superimposed over the map of the Middle East.

Again, the Operations Room listened in silence to the Officers voice as the countdown was called,…."Four, three, two, one…"

Dr. Ramsey flicked the switch for the second time and they watched the incredible display of power, as the harnessed energy was unleashed towards Earth. The flash of lightening streaked away from the satellite for a second time.

On the bridge of the US Missouri, they heard the sound of thunder again and saw the electric fork in the skies. In the same instant came the deafening explosion. The sound and light ripped through the skies and heavens above them.

The nuclear jolt had hit the warhead with seconds to spare before the device could arm itself in its final approach to Riyadh. On the deck of the carrier, the darkness turned to daylight as the sailors pressed their palms hard against their ears to protect themselves from the deafening crackle.

"We have a direct hit, I repeat a direct…" she barely got the words out in the eruption that followed. The flashing light tracking the warhead on the screen stopped.

The united and spontaneous outbreak of jubilation drowned out the girl's voice. The Operations Room was alive with celebrations as the relief took over. The tension was lifted through the smiles and the cheering.

A few tears rolled down Conway's face, choked with emotion, he watched the scenes around the room. Karpurov returned Colonel Schwartz's embrace as everyone got to their feet clapping their hands.

General Graham beaming from ear to ear walked up to Dr. Ramsey and clapped him on the back.

"I knew you could do it," he said, and he held out his hand.

The Doctor took his grip and they stood smiling at each other, shaking hands, in the midst of the raucous celebrations going on around them.

On the deck of the US Missouri the sailors on the flight deck were cheering wildly. Admiral Stone had kept them informed and they realized immediately what had happened.

Director Conway rubbed his chin with his hand as he tried to regain his composure. He walked towards the monitor to speak to President Whiting.

They looked at each other for a moment, at times like this there was no need for words.

The President looked exhausted but the relief was evident as he smiled broadly at Director Conway.

"Thank God, Mike," he said hoarsely.

Thursday, 21ˢᵗ October 2008
Prime Minister's Office, Government Building, Delhi

Ashraf Nawani pulled out the pistol from his belt as he saw the figure escaping through the darkness. Climbing over the ledge he jumped the twenty feet to the ground and began following in Luke's footsteps.

Seconds earlier, Nawani had been giving the orders to push open the Prime Minister's office door when the explosion had gone off. His face and uniform were splattered with blood from the dismembered bodies that had recoiled onto him.

Nawani served Banerjee with an unquestioning loyalty. Although he was often subjected to regular outbursts of humiliating abuse, his devotion remained undiminished. The urgency to break in and save his leader raged through his body. His heightened state of emotion brought added strength as he pushed the bodies littering the doorway and ran into the smoke filled room.

Almost immediately, he found the body of Banerjee lying on the ground with his eyes wide opens, the frozen look of hate still on his face. It was the look he had given Luke when he turned to face him.

The anger in him seethed as he gripped Banerjee's hand. Kneeling down, he lowered his head in respect to his dead leader before getting to his feet. He looked towards the open balcony doors with just one thought on his mind; *revenge*.

As Nawani followed Luke, darting in-between the bushes and the shadows, he felt like a man possessed as the pent up rage cursed through his veins. Banerjee had believed in him and he needed to repay that faith, he would gladly have stepped in front of Luke's bullet, but it was too late for that.

The Paradigm Shift

Luke approached the gate and checked his watch again. *'Where is she? She should be here now,'* he thought, listening for the noise of an engine.

When they had formulated there escape plan it had been difficult to estimate the likely danger from the security guards at the gatehouse. As he peered from behind the bush, he could see them; several guards were running towards the building. The message that Banerjee had been shot was out, and the chains of command were disintegrating fast. Fortunately for Luke, in their disorganized state of alert they had left the security post un-armed.

Luke heard the roar of the Suzuki and decided it was time to make his move. He sprinted down the passage alongside the gatehouse and out into the street. Just as Luke appeared at the exit, Kirin screeched to a halt in the middle of the road. Pushing his gun into his waistband, he ran across the road and climbed on the back.

Behind him, Ashraf Nawani darted down the passage and appeared in the street just as Kirin was about to twist the throt-tle. Luke clung to her waist, and hearing the shout behind him he turned to see Nawani's snarling face. In his outstretched hands was a black revolver pointing directly at his chest. The bike began to accelerate but they were no more than fifteen yards away when the gun fired.

'Thank God he's missed,' thought Luke at the instant of the gunshot. He looked over his shoulder into the cold, smiling eyes of Nawani and felt the deadweight of Kirin's body as she slouched forward towards the handlebars.

"Kirin!' he yelled in horror as her head slumped forward. The purple blood oozed through her soaked shirt.

The bike tottered as he grabbed the handlebars just in time. He tried to cradle her body between his forearms whilst his feet plunged to the ground as he fought to regain control of the heavy trail bike. Her head fell forward motionless. Luke's face contorted with the strain and effort of clinging to her body. Desperately he tried but he couldn't hold her. The bike slid to the ground sideways and he fell holding her, trying to cushion her fall.

"Kirin!" he screamed again. Desperation filled his cry but there was no response. Her eyes remained closed and her body lay contorted and motionless on the ground. The blood continued to ooze from her open wound.

The anger flared up in Luke, they had been through too much together for it to end like this. *'Kirin you can't be dead!'* he cried to himself.

In his fury, he got to his feet jerking the bike from Kirin's legs. The concentrated rage which seethed through his body could only be satisfied with the thought of revenge. All he could picture was the 'cold, twisted face of Nawani' smiling as he aimed his revolver. The emotion dispelled all thoughts of personal safety.

He jumped on the bike and hit the ignition button. Twisting the throttle, the tyres screeched as he held the front brake whilst the back of the bike skidded around in a hundred and eighty degree turn. Looking up he saw that he was no more than fifty yards from the entrance to the Government Building. Nawani had walked out into the middle of the road alone. Luke revved the engine and raced back towards him.

The Head of India's Secret Service smiled calmly as he watched the returning bike. Slowly he raised his arm and pointed the gun directly towards Luke's head.

The Paradigm Shift

His first shots missed as Luke accelerated towards him. As he got closer Nawani had him perfectly in his sights. He took aim again and fired. He heard the metallic click of an empty gun chamber.

Instantly, the arrogant smile disappeared to be replaced by a stunned look of terror. He turned from the gun to the bike roaring towards him. There was no time to move, Luke skidded to a halt, took aim with his revolver, and sent one shot crashing through Nawani's temple. The bullet killed him instantly. The first guards on the scene watched his body fall backwards to the ground.

Luke did not stop but sped back in the direction of Kirin's body. The unthinkable had happened but he wasn't leaving her. The disorganized guards fired randomly at the fleeing bike as they rushed, shouting, towards Nawani's dead body.

Dismounting, he quickly straddled Kirin's lifeless body across the bike before remounting himself. He held her tightly while kicking the gears and roared off towards the end of the street. Luke knew he wouldn't be able to travel far but he had to get out of sight of the guards before they marshalled their pursuit.

Luke continued down the road bouncing through potholes as he dodged the guard's shots. Still clutching Kirin's limp body, he escaped around the corner and into the darkness. Two streets away Luke ditched the bike and began the first stages of an elaborate escape plan they had concocted together.

The murderous rule of Banerjee was over.

The First Week of November 2008
The President's Office, The White House

The President was wearing casual clothes, a pair of jeans and a chequered shirt unbuttoned at the neck. Although it had been another long night, he felt more relaxed thanks to his wife. The First Lady, Pam Whiting had insisted that he sleep in for a few days until he recouped some of his lost energy. That morning he had risen at nine, instead of the usual six o'clock. The rest had made him feel better, but it would take a lot longer before he was completely back to his old self.

For the past few weeks, the story of Banerjee's death and the success of Project Sabre monopolized every paper and all the TV stations. In all the four corners of the world, politicians and their people alike, started cautiously looking forward to the resumption of normality and the period of rebuilding ahead.

Project Sabre was praised and applauded by the experts as Dr. Ramsey became a celebrity and the centre of media attention. He appeared on numerous television programs explaining the defensive capabilities of Project Sabre, and what it meant for future world peace.

The Chinese Government had stood down almost immediately after the news of Banerjee's death had been released across the globe. Their silos closed and they ceased further hostilities with Taiwan.

The democratic world was not prepared to let the matter rest there. China was unceremoniously expelled from the Supreme Council of the United Nations and removed from all world political and economic forums. Without exception, sanctions were passed against China, as world leaders condemned

Prime Minister Ziang and his followers for their treacherous acts.

With the passing of time, the powerful business leaders of China also wisely withdrew their support for the leader and his deputy who were quietly asked to step down and make way for the new leadership. The business leaders driving the economy recognized that they would never be allowed back into world trade whilst Ziang remained. Despite their inherent arrogance, China needed the rest of the world. Even so, before they would be re-accepted, they would pay heavily for the damage they had caused. No longer would China be considered a major player, as the cost would deplete their economy and their foreign currency reserves for years to come.

The coordinates of the remaining warhead passed on by Luke had been confirmed minutes after the first missile was airborne. Whilst the Operation Centre dealt with Project Sabre, the information was passed on to Air Marshal Reiger. He immediately commanded a taskforce of US Marines to capture and extinguish the remaining threat from the last nuclear warhead. They took off in four, heavily armed helicopters heading for the Pakistani region of Jiwar.

When the Operations Centre had first lost track of the Indian warheads, Colonel Schwartz had speculated that the two missiles would be transported to two different locations. In the end, this turned out not to be the case, as the marines discovered when they landed.

When the helicopters put down, they found the dead body of General Gupta pinned to the mobile launcher that carried the second nuclear missile. He had been strapped to the vehicle by chains. His body was beaten badly where the soldiers under his command had tortured him before fleeing into the hills. Before disappearing without trace into the surrounding rocky mountains, they had formed an execution squad and shot him. They had their vengeance for the General making them play a part in Banerjee's murderous plan.

The team of experts who came with the marines threw off the camouflage net that was still covering the missile and set about deactivating the warhead. In under an hour they reported the success of the mission back to the USS Missouri, which in turn fed the news to Washington.

The missile that had been successfully struck down by the 'nuclear jolt' from Sabre had been hit whilst travelling at ten thousand feet in the air. The warhead casing together with a section of the carriage had plummeted to earth in Saudi Arabia, about eighty miles to the northeast of Riyadh. The wreckage landed in the open desert and the nose of the rocket containing the warhead had to be carefully dug out from the sand dunes before the team of experts could dismantle the threat. As one of the specialist team later filed in his report: the nuclear warhead's timing device showed that it would have been fully activated if another nine seconds had been allowed to pass.

With the nuclear threat removed, the gratitude of King Mohammed and the other ruling families was abundant. The President and the Leaders of the Alliance worked quickly to restore the fractured relationships. The King invited President Whiting to be his guest of honour at his palace in Riyadh. He cordially accepted the invitation as an opportunity to strengthen the ties of their respective countries.

However, never again would the Alliance and the US Administration underestimate the importance of controlling the world's supply of oil. For the time being, the Middle East oil fields remained under the temporary control of the Alliance as

The Paradigm Shift

the world's energy supplies were returned to normal. However, in the fullness of time they were returned to the stewardship of their rightful legal owners under a Cooperation Treaty that gave the Alliance the right to safeguard their interests.

In the days that followed the crisis, the Alliance's strategy to build up support for the opposition leader Yashwant Puri also paid dividends. He didn't return to India immediately, but promised to do so in the short term. This was a calculated political statement and his lobbyists in India banged the drum for his imminent return.

The Indian nation had been carried away by the words of Banerjee and did not know where to turn in the void that followed. Censorship had been strict under Nawani's old regime but the newly found freedom of the press lent its support to Yashwant Puri's credentials for office. As support mounted, they showed his acceptability to the Government's in the outside world.

With the support of the sheikhs and the Amir's in the Middle East, Puri carried out a tour of the main cities in the Middle East. He appealed for the restoration of peace and the return to friendly relations between the Indian expatriates and the indigenous Arabs. The ruling sheikhs joined Puri on the stage, and they held up their arms together as the people rejoiced at the breakthrough. The Arab families vowed never to take the efforts of the working class for granted again.

The Arab Governments stepped in to repeal some of the more punitive and Draconian laws on non-nationals. To bolster the spreading goodwill, employment laws and conditions were changed to reflect the move towards a more democratic and harmonious society.

At the end of Puri's two-week tour of the Gulf, the Indian nation was clamouring for his return and he landed amongst scenes of jubilation at Delhi airport. In a public address, he promised to restore India's international credibility. Apologizing to Pakistan and Bangladesh, he promised to restore their sovereignty and help them rebuild their countries.

Meanwhile, it was a sunny day for this time of year in Washington. The President sat reflecting on the unpleasant task ahead of him. His popularity had soared since the crisis had finally passed, and his second term in office was assured.

He recalled his conversation with Mike Conway when at one point he had seriously considered handing in his resignation. He smiled to himself as he remembered how his friend had convinced him to stay. '*I was right to listen to him,*' he thought.

His smile faded quickly as the difficult and pressing matter ahead of him returned to consume his thoughts. The news would still rock the American people but he felt secure that his own position was not in jeopardy.

'*Ok, lets get it over with,*' he thought and pressed the intercom. "Catherine, please come in, and invite the others as well."

A few minutes later, Director Mike Conway opened the door. Jim Allen, Secretary of State Henderson, Vice President Martins and his Chief of Staff, Catherine Dennison followed him into the President's Office.

Only Mike Conway knew the purpose of the meeting, the others believed the reason they were called in was to discuss routine matters of business. Conway had offered to carry out the meeting himself without the President being present, but Whiting had flatly refused the offer of assistance.

His four senior aides sat in the comfortable chairs surrounding the glass table in the centre of the room. The President, taking his time, got up and walked round to sit on the front lip of his desk.

He had taken care to avoid all their expressions when they entered. He didn't want to set an unnecessarily friendly tone which would be out of place for the bombshell he was about to drop.

The President had decided that it was time to unmask the traitor who had been secretly leaking information to General Vu in the China. He had discussed the unveiling of the culprit in detail with Director Conway. They had debated keeping the person in office until the end of President Whiting's first term, after which they could quietly take him out of politics without the people ever knowing the truth. This was unacceptable to the President's sensibilities. He wanted to do what was right and pushing the matter aside was not the correct way to deal with the situation.

"I'm afraid that I have the very gravest news concerning one of you," he began, and he saw the startled looks that shot back at him. This one line was enough to set their pulses racing.

"I have known you all for many years now, but I am afraid one of you has not been the person I thought I knew."

Apart from Director Conway, they looked at each other and then back at the President with a look of incredulity. All except one.

"Since I learnt of the news during the recent crisis, I have asked myself many times how could this have ever happened? What drives someone to do this?....I guess this is something I'll never fully know or understand."

The President hunched his shoulders. He looked down at his feet, he was deeply upset with the news he had to give. He felt lost for words. How could someone pass secrets to the

Chinese like this and get away with it for so long. It seemed even more incredulous that they could reach such high office.

Director Conway looked at Secretary of State Henderson, Vice President Martins, National Security Advisor Allen and the President's Chief of Staff, Catherine Dennison.

He watched them looking for signs that only the real mole would make.

"Do I have to go on?" the President said without looking up.

A silent pause lasting a few seconds followed. They looked at each other furtively before they gasped in amazement as one amongst them rose from their seat.

Vice President Martins stood up. In astonishment, the remaining three executives stared at him in stunned silence. His face was blank without any traces of emotion.

The President looked up and held his gaze before he watched his deputy turn and walk numbly towards the door. President Whiting had not known whether he would see any signs of remorse but there was no outward trace.

He watched his Vice President close the door. He remembered the moments of friendship and the intimate conversations they had shared during his election campaign. On the other side of the door four CIA Officers were waiting for him.

As the door closed behind Vice President Martins, the President waved to Mike Conway to explain the events that lead to him discovering the traitor's identity. The old, black and white picture was produced showing Vice President Martins as a teenage boy. Also in the photograph was his father who had been the Ambassador to China for over fifteen years.

The Paradigm Shift

Standing next to the young Vice President was another teenage boy. It was General Vu with his arm around his shoulder.

Director Conway had recognized the face although many others had not. He explained the elaborate relationship which had been built up between the two over the years; General Vu was the half brother of the American Vice President.

His father, Ambassador Martins had an affair with a local girl who became pregnant with his child. He managed to keep the fact from his wife for years by supporting the girl and his son in secret. When his wife died early at the age of twenty-nine there was no longer a reason to keep his two sons apart and, although he introduced them to each other, for the sake of his public standing, they lived apart.

Director Conway mapped out the path that both teenage boys took with the support of their father. His Chinese son rose quickly through the armed ranks and became a powerful figure in the Chinese Administration, befriending Ziang at an early age.

For his part, Vice President Martins grew up in the ways of the Chinese, learning their customs and cultures. In the beginning, it seemed very simple when he was asked to supply his half brother with information but in the end he became hooked by the power of his position.

As he rose through the political echelons, it was Chinese finance that built up his reputation and helped him gain crucial votes. Conway built up a picture of a man who they hitherto had not known existed. Behind his friendly and diligent façade was a mercenary that would go to any lengths to reach the full powers of presidential office. During the course of the CIA investigation which followed Director Conway's findings, they unearthed more Chinese informants working with the Vice President, albeit at lower levels of office.

As Director Conway finished the story, the President stood up and walked towards his window looking out over the White House lawns. He stood there for a moment with his hands clasped behind his back. Catherine Dennison cast a glance in Mike Conway's direction.

He saw her out of the corner of his eye and turned to look at her. For a few seconds they gazed at each other. She desperately wanted a friendly sign after their recent encounters.

Suddenly, his serious expression fell away and he smiled broadly. *'Their secret was intact,'* she thought, and smiled back at him.

Still looking out over the lawns and the Rose Garden next to the colonnade, the President broke the momentary silence.

"I would like to thank all of you personally," he said. "You have all performed beyond what could be expected and I'm proud to have you on my team."

In the end, the American people were subjected to a short and public trial as Vice President Larry Martins was tried for treason against the State. The high profile nature of the hearing ensured his public humiliation and the associated treachery of the Chinese was broadcast around the world. In response, the Chinese Government attempted to orchestrate a trade-off with political prisoners passing one way in exchange for Martins asylum back in Beijing. Throughout the one-month trial their diplomatic advances were snubbed.

The Department of Justice controlled the legal process, working closely with the President's Foreign Intelligence Advisory Board (PFIAB) and the Intelligence Oversight Board

(IOB), until the final day of the hearing when the unanimous verdict of guilty was reached.

Despite many campaigners outside the court petitioning for the death sentence, the disgraced Vice President was condemned to life imprisonment with no grounds or opportunity for parole.

As President Whiting's Administration had expected there was an enormous backlash against the Intelligence Agencies from the politicians and the public at large for allowing such an inherent threat against the nation to reach such high office. *'How could the NSA and the CIA have allowed the facts surrounding his questionable past to escape their attention?'*

The President turned away from the window. Through the valiant efforts of Mike Conway and his team they had managed to pull through.

"I must say, we and the American people owe a huge debt of gratitude to those agents…" the President stated seriously, looking in the direction of Director Conway while the others smiled and nodded their agreement.

"Codename Amber wasn't it Mike?" he asked.

"That's correct Sir."

"Well you make sure that she receives my heartfelt thanks and the gratitude of the United States for her bravery," he meant every word he said.

Mike Conway looked at the ground. The British Secret Service, MI6, had only recently heard what had happened to Codename Amber and he had not yet told the President.

Three months later....
Rajasthan, Northwest India.

Luke Weaver stood on the shore looking out over the calm waters of the lake. He had spoken with Commander Mark Tremett and Sir Thomas Boswell at length and agreed with them that his existence and whereabouts should continue to be unknown.

He had considered his options long and hard before agreeing to remain undercover until the next assignment came through. Luke was the best in the service and Sir Thomas Boswell knew it. The old master had used all his powers of persuasion in getting him to stay and was delighted that Luke had finally agreed.

Luke picked up a stone and threw it out into the lakes waters watching the ripples roll their way back to shore. This was the lake that Kirin wanted to see. This was the lake where her grandfather served as the Royal Treasurer to the Rajah. It was from these banks that he had been forced to flee after the British rogue stole the priceless 'Neelu necklace' with its faultless sapphire stone.

'*That's some story,*' he thought to himself as he flung a second stone further out into the lake.

In the distance, he could see the white walls of the magnificent palace rising from the middle of the lake.

It was an incredible feat of architecture, like no other palace in the modern world. He dropped the stones and put his hands on his hips looking out pensively across the waters.

He silently contemplated the events which had led to him standing there by the lake's pebbly shores.

Behind him the voice called: "well are you going in or not?"

The Paradigm Shift

He felt the swell of happiness as he turned around and saw Kirin walking gracefully towards him. Her arm was still tied up in a sling and her pretty face broke out into a broad smile. Since their fortunate escape, Luke had stayed by her side in hospital until she had recuperated from intensive care. The gunshot wound had passed through her neck and shoulder and she was lucky to be alive. Each day that passed had brought them closer together.

Finally, she was discharged and he was allowed to fulfil his promise.

'She doesn't know how happy she makes me feel,' he thought, as he watched her glide down the shore towards him.

When she got right up close she lifted her head with her laughing smile and he leaned down to kiss her on the lips.

"Are you going in or not?" she laughed at him and he smiled back.

"Not so tough now are we Luke Weaver?" she said poking fun at him.

"Alright, alright," he said and began pulling off his shirt and unbuckling his trouser belt.

"Do you realize how cold that water is?" he pretended to shiver.

She was devastatingly beautiful and since the assignment was over he had barely been able to keep his eyes from her. She pushed him towards the water, laughing. Her joy was infectious and they both smiled as he got ready for his invigorating task. In a moment's madness the night before when she had repeated her father's story, he had agreed to dive into the cold water and look for the 'Neelu necklace'.

"Are you sure that is what your father said?" he asked reluctantly, wading his way into the water carrying an underwater mask and a flashlight.

"Yes, positive – " she called, " – remember to look for the pole!"

Her grandfather had passed on the story to her father and so in turn he had passed it onto Kirin. She was not sure how serious to take it. *'The story must have changed down the years,'* she thought. She watched Luke, he had reached up to his waist and started to pull on the mask.

"If I don't find anything I'm throwing you in!" he called back over his shoulder.

In the story, her father had told her that the boat had sunk only twenty yards from the shoreline. He told her that his father had scrambled to the shore opposite three Juniper trees which stood alone in the shape of a triangle.

Luke and Kirin had gone looking for the trees. On their first walk along the shore they had found nothing that resembled such a shape but on the stroll back they came upon something that could be close. There were two Juniper trees standing side by side and when Luke started prodding the ground where a third could be, he came across a dead old stump.

Luke plunged in and swam out into the cold, clear water. When he was about twenty yards out he dived down into the depths holding his breath. He swam to the bottom shining the flashlight. Just as his lungs were about to burst with the effort, the flashlight hit a white piece of wood sticking up out of the mud and silt. *'Christ, surely that can't be it,'* he thought racing to the surface to recharge his lungs.

She saw him break the surface.

"Well?" she shouted.

"Maybe something!" he yelled back and took a few deep breaths before plunging back downwards.

He headed straight for the piece of wood only this time he could see it was sticking up from the side of a boat. Grabbing the side, he used it to propel himself forward along the main part of the deck.

Shining the torch from side to side, he saw something to make his heart race faster. Luke could see something shining in the beam on the floor of the cabin. His lungs already needed air as he twisted through a narrow gap and stretched out his hand reaching for the shiny object. The disturbed silt obscured his vision and his hand lumped around where he had seen the reflective glimmer. Suddenly he felt something hard and dragged it up to the torchlight.

'This is incredible; I don't believe it,' he thought as his lungs began to sting with the lack of oxygen. The 'Neelu necklace' simply came away from its resting-place in the mud. Luke held on to the jewels tightly as he forced his way back through the gap and up towards the surface.

His screaming lungs burst open for air as he hit the surface.

"You were down too long," Kirin shouted out at him. She was annoyed that he had made her worry unnecessarily.

He breathed deeply again, hiding his treasure below the water, and swimming back towards the shore.

"Yes, it's a good idea, you should come out now," she scolded, and went to pick up a towel for him.

He threw the torch and mask on to the grassy shore and caught the towel she flung at him.

"You know something Kirin?" he said drying his chest as he stepped out of the water.

"What?" she replied.

"I'd like to give you a surprise, now close your eyes," he instructed.

"I love surprises," she said closing her eyes and pointed her face upwards. She pouted her lips, pretending she was ready to receive his surprise.

"Now keep them shut," he said pulling out the necklace out from the towel. He leant over, putting his two hands behind her to close the necklace's clasp.

"Luke?..." She whispered feeling his touch against her skin.

"Keep them closed now," he repeated looking at his handiwork. The sapphire and diamond necklace was stunning.

"Ok, you can open them!"

Her hazel eyes opened wide in astonishment as she stared at the necklace hanging around her neck.

"I don't believe it...its beautiful," she gasped.

"Its yours then," Luke said laughing and they hugged each other for a moment.

"Luke, you remember I once wanted to tell you something when we decided to separate in Delhi?" Her voice took a more serious tone and she looked up at him, her eyes shining with joy.

"Yes, I remember," he said pulling her closer to him.

"Well, I'd like to try again!" she said smiling.

Author's note

The storyline, as well as all characters in this publication are fictitious and any resemblance to any real events or persons living or dead is purely coincidental.

I have really enjoyed writing this first book and would like to thank my mother Joan and my wife Carolyn for their encouragement, support and patience. Also my children Alexander, Henry, Issie, Max and Tilly and their cousins (Jamie, Will, Charlie, Harry, Hugh, Thomas and Katie) whose eagerness to hear my bedtime stories prompted me to write a book in the first place...

It is no coincidence that a lot of the book is centred on the Middle East where I first came to live in 1973. My family lives in one of the most exciting and dynamic places in the world - Dubai. We have many friends here and I would like to express my sincere appreciation to the visionary ruling Maktoum family who have made Dubai the great place it is today.

Researching the book was also very enjoyable and I would like to thank the following for their wholehearted support: Stefan Cassar, Piers Burton, Dennis Ciappara, Huw Arthur, Malcolm Glenn and Lt. Colonel Andy Charlton.

I hope you enjoy reading the book and that one day I can go on to publish my second...

Made in the USA